THE BOOK OF APEX:
VOLUME 1 OF APEX MAGAZINE

THE BOOK OF APEX:
VOLUME 1 OF APEX MAGAZINE

EDITED BY
JASON SIZEMORE

AN APEX PUBLICATIONS BOOK
LEXINGTON, KENTUCKY

The Book of Apex: Volume 1 of Apex Magazine

Cover Art "Machinery of the Stars" © by Vitaly S. Alexius
Cover design by Justin Stewart

Apex Publications, LLC
www.apexbookcompany.com

10 9 8 7 6 5 4 3 2 1

ISBN TPB: 978-0-9788676-9-0

For Deb Taber and Gill Ainsworth. Thank you for everything.

TABLE OF CONTENTS

TABLE OF CONTENTS

Post Apocalypse

James Walton Langolf

The letter came on Tuesday marked "Post Apocalypse."

It smelled like Aspen cologne and there was a smudge of barbeque sauce on one corner.

Sarah ripped it up and threw it in the trash.

The next one came on Friday, also marked "Post Apocalypse", no barbeque sauce. But this one had an ornate gold seal on the flap that said, "Today is the last day of the rest of your life."

Cheery.

Sarah ran it through the shredder by her desk along with the letter that said she might have already won twelve million dollars.

When Monday's letter came Sarah just sighed and tore off the end of the envelope.

There was nothing inside.

"Ha ha. Very funny."

Down the street, she heard the tinkling music of the ice cream truck. She stepped out onto the porch, and the mushroom cloud was on the horizon.

A sepia colored overlay, a movie played on a life size screen, the soundtrack coming through the fillings in her teeth. All around her people were running and screaming. There was the sound of gunfire in the distance. Her neighbors' house was burning and the ash that covered the lawn was thick enough for angels.

Huh. Well.

In her pocket the phone was ringing. She answered it with, "Nice touch."

"Like it?" Ian said. "I saw it and thought of you."

"It doesn't match my outfit."

"Sure it does. You're wearing the red dress I bought you. Nothing says nuclear sunset like Dolce & Gabbanna."

She was wearing ripped jeans and a Grateful Dead T-shirt.

"When is this? I thought I had another week."

She pulled the R-13 form from her back pocket. Purple, the standard color for willful self-destruction. It was smudged, but she was pretty sure it wasn't today's date.

"You do. I just thought you'd enjoy a little preview. Of course if this is too much for you, you could always come home."

"No, Ian. I couldn't."

She closed the phone and headed inside to pack for her next assignment. When she looked back over her shoulder, the ice cream van idled at the corner, children in an orderly row waited for orange push-ups and popsicles.

It looked like it might rain later.

They'd met at a hurricane party in the French Quarter just after the turn of the 21st century. Sarah was a graduate student collecting data on pre-versus post-disaster societies. Ian was shirtless, pouring mojitos too heavy on the mint.

The music was too loud. Guitars with strings made of razor wire, drums with an irregular rhythm, and a blue-black woman chanting low, in a language Sarah couldn't quite decipher. She understood the hunger though. The wanting and the need. She could taste it like the sugar and salt and lime on her own skin.

The August heat was heavy and damp. Sarah could feel the lightning inside.

She liked his slow drawl and his quick smile, his soft grey eyes and the way his callused hands made that whispering sound across her sweat-slick skin.

"You know," she said, slivers of ice clinking against the side of her drinking jar, a sprig of mint pressed to her lips. "I really shouldn't be telling you this, but that levee isn't going to hold."

"What? You mean the storm? Honey, a little bit of rain ain't going to hurt nothing."

Sarah ran the damp mint down the hollow of her throat, and Ian's eyes followed it.

"I'm not talking about just a little bit of rain."

He swallowed thickly and shook his head as if he was already underwater.

"You can't listen to a thing those old weathermen say. Fools wouldn't know a rain cloud from a strong fart."

She took a step closer to him. They were almost touching now, their bodies swaying slightly in time with the band.

"This time, they're right."

"That bad, you think?"

"Honey, I know it."

The muscles of his chest sang to her stroking fingertips.

Drowning would be such a waste.

"I can show you."

She breathed warm rum across his neck when she whispered in his ear. If he'd struck a match, they'd have both gone up in flames.

The next day Sarah woke up back in her own bed with a brand new rose tattoo on her ass and an unauthorized, undocumented time traveler tangled in her sheets.

Over breakfast she'd tried to explain and somehow Ian just… got it.

He nodded his head as he shoveled in his eggs. He asked questions, all of them thoughtful and intelligent. He wasn't freaked out.

That should have been her first clue.

"I want to go back," he said when she finished.

So once they'd filled out the paperwork (there was a mountain of it). They'd booked a trip for the days following the storm.

They'd stood together on a bridge overlooking his hometown, sleeping restless beneath the green water. Trees, cars, and the bloated corpses of dogs floated by when Ian first asked her the question, "If they'd known for sure that this would happen, you suppose they could have done something different?"

That initial question was like a stone dropped into a pond. Bigger questions, theories, disasters, rippled all around them, and it seemed like only Sarah could see the ugly, hulking shapes of things swimming just below the surface.

Ian had asked for and received a grant from the University. He was convinced that if he could foresee the end of the world he could forestall it.

Sarah thought he was a genius. All her life, time travel had been used for nothing but recreation or dry academic research. Together they set up the Apocalypse program intending to make a difference.

But then they didn't.

Month after month, year after year, time after time, the world just kept on ending. And they watched.

And watched.

And watched.

Sarah tried to calculate how many millions of people she'd seen die. She could barely make it to the john before she threw up.

Still they had no idea how their own timeline would end.

She'd tried to talk to Ian about her doubts and they'd had a fight that ended with a black eye for her, and him spitting a tooth out in his hand.

Sarah had taken the next ticket to the end of the world. She hadn't seen Ian since.

The shift change seemed rougher than usual.

Sarah was sitting at the breakfast table drinking a cup of coffee when the vortex opened practically at her feet without so much as a courtesy call. If her bag hadn't been there beside her, she'd have been forced to go on without it—all of her research with its carefully drawn charts and painstaking notes would have been lost.

The invisible walls of the time shift sealed tight around her, shrinking her skin and squeezing the air from her lungs. Her bones creaked with the pressure and the copper taste of blood and bile slicked her throat.

Sarah couldn't help feeling Ian had booked it that way on purpose to punish her.

When the vortex opened up again and Sarah was spit out, she could tell it wasn't the faded and lumpy linoleum of the kitchen underneath her bruised ass.

She opened her eyes.

She was lying on the beach who knew how many miles from the house. It shouldn't have even been possible, but there it was.

The water was a cool murky green. Low waves barely ruffled the surface but they still managed to pull at her left shoe. Her bag was already bobbing a few feet out.

"Goddamn it."

The sky was the same odd green as the water, dotted with ugly, yellowish clouds and, once again, it seemed to be on fire.

The letter was already there beside her on the sand, the envelope red as a wound, URGENT stamped infection black.

"Lovely."

Inside was the R-13 form. Powder blue indicating a Celestial Event.

What is the nature of The Event?

Blanks for the date, time and weather conditions.

Please state, in your own words, what you observed leading up to The Event.

Be SPECIFIC.

Remember details MATTER!!!

Behind the form was a small white card. In Ian's handwriting were the words, "Real time."

God, he could be such a dick.

The comet, or asteroid or whatever it was, streaked through the sky apparently aiming for a point somewhere between her eyes. The wind screamed in her ears. Her teeth vibrated in their sockets and her bones felt ready to shatter. It started to break apart and chunks of fiery rock rained down around her. She could smell her hair burning and see blisters rising on her hands.

The ocean was beginning to boil, and foul-smelling steam, like rancid fish, rose up around her. Sweat stung her eyes.

"Shit."

The vortex was closed.

She looked down at the envelope.

"Post Apocalypse." That joke just keeps getting funnier every time you tell it.

Asshole.

Sarah thought that if she had a pen she might just start filling out the form for the hell of it.

She would write, "huge motherfucking rock" in the space next to Nature of The Event.

August 29, 2113.

She looked down at her watch.

3:27 p.m.

Weather conditions?

Who gives a fuck?

In her own words she wrote, "THIS SUCKS!"

Is that specific enough?

The vortex opened beside her and Sarah stepped through.

The observation posts they used were more or less the same in each dimension. Sometimes the color of the walls or the stains on the shabby carpet varied, but not by much.

The house Sarah's vortex opened onto was positively opulent.

She tumbled into an overstuffed Italian leather sofa, creamy and soft as meringue. The floors were marble tiles laid in a beautiful, intricate pattern. Thick, chocolate-colored, velvet drapes covered a window the length of one whole wall.

The phone was ringing.

"Fuck you very much, Ian," she answered cheerily. "Nice fucking weather we're having, don't you think?"

"Sarah, honey, is something wrong?"

"I am tired of your little game, Ian."

She was grinding her teeth together so hard she could taste enamel dust on her tongue. Mixed with the bile in her throat, it made her feel lightheaded and a little buzzed.

"You're pathetic, shuffling through dimensions all these years and you've learned nothing except that eventually the earth always ends one way or another, and there's nothing you or anyone else can do about it."

"Are you finished?"

"Not even close. That was it. My last armageddon. I'm coming back, and I'm reporting you and your useless research to the University. You're finished. How's that for an apocalypse, you sorry piece of shit?"

"I was calling to apologize. My timing on the last shift change was a bit off. I didn't mean to cut it so close, but I won't say I'm not glad for the opportunity for such a close observance."

The last sentence was so oily she could almost hear it squeak. The lying bastard, he was enjoying every minute of her discomfort, savoring her rage and humiliation like a warm bath.

"We're so close honey. I swear to you. We get just a little bit closer and then you're gonna see it for yourself. I promise you, baby. It's gonna be wild."

"I meant it, Ian. I'm going to the University."

"You do whatever you feel you have to. Our work doesn't need defending."

He tossed that "our" out as casually as a blow dart, and she felt it prick her skin, draw a drop of blood.

"Just tell me when the event is scheduled to occur and when you'll have my ticket out."

"Don't worry about that, Sarah. You've got plenty of time. I arranged a sort of vacation for you. You've been a lot of help to me. I've treated you poorly, and I'm sorry."

"Whatever. Let me know when you're ready."

She closed the phone before he could speak again. Who knows? Some time or other they might have actually been in love.

Out of habit she turned on the TV and switched it to a news station. She couldn't remember how long it had been since she'd seen nothing but rapes and murders and robberies. No prophets, no alien overlords, no countdowns to doomsday. Here was a place where they really believed things would just go on forever. Sarah could get used to that.

She made a sandwich and poured herself a glass of wine. She was half dozing when the doorbell rang.

Crawling across the porch was a man in a blue uniform and a jaunty hat. His neck was swollen and his face had turned the shiny blue –black color of an overripe plum. Greenish pus oozed from his sores and his eyes were filled with blood. The man was choking, his mouth opening and closing trying to speak. Spit flecked his lips and misted up into Sarah's face. She touched the dampness with the tips of her fingers. Fever heat rolled off him like evil thoughts.

In his outstretched hand was a smooth cream colored envelope.

"Post Apocalypse."

She tore the end off the envelope and the yellow sheet fell on the ground at her feet.

The color of plague.

Oh no, Ian, you dirty son of a bitch. How could you?

The mailman pitched forward across the welcome mat, sputtered and died.

A breeze caught the paper, and it tumbled end over end down the walk into the street and out of sight.

THESE DAYS

KATHERINE SPARROW

April is pure rot.

Posters with body parts are wheat-pasted up and down our block. Radio stations are mid-theory about why women get the wild, men get the crack, and kids get the numb, when the signal just bleeds out into howls. No one works at the grocery store anymore, and you can take what you want, but all that is left is unlabeled canned goods.

Our band only leaves the house as a pack. We carry tin foil balls, tasers, and baseball bats. No one we see is normal. Only a couple of people show up to our gigs, and they throw bricks and bottles at us.

At the end of April we get evicted for the fourth time in three months. Our landlord, who is at least half with it, lets us know by nailing demolition signs to our front door. At least he doesn't blow it up while we're inside.

We stir-fry the last of our veggies, eat them with undercooked rice, and pour gasoline over the living-room floor. We torch it and leave.

Outside on the concrete we watch the house turn from wood into fire. Flame fingers dance up and down the walls of the living room. The windows crack and shatter. We take a step back.

"Where do we go now? Any ideas, Tom?" Zaki One asks.

"Nada," I say.

"At least we've got lots of options," Miranda says. She knuckle-rubs the shadows under her eyes. "At least there's nothing to be scared of."

We watch fire climb up the stairs of the house.

"Let's get out of here."

"Think it will be different anywhere else?" Zaki Two asks.

"It has to be. There has to be somewhere..." I pull down my sleeves and check to make sure they hide my arm-cuts. I do little ones to let out some of my pain. I never look at Zaki and Miranda too closely. I don't know what they have been doing to get through April. I don't want to know.

We have to hitch out of our neighborhood because the roads have been blocked off for days. National guardsmen with flat faces and big guns have locked it down. They pretend they don't have the crack but shoot people all the time for no reason.

A big rig stops for us a couple miles out from the bridge. If you can drive and are rich enough to own a car, they'll let you out. We walk toward the trucker's cab, but he opens up the empty cargo container in back instead.

His shirt has an old patch that reads "Bob."

"What do you call a man with no arms and no legs who swims in the ocean?" I ask, as I step into the container. The smell of rotten vegetables, trash, and rough-cut steel sours my mouth.

Bob throws the door shut and locks us in.

That's how we get out of the south side three hours before the riots start and five hours before the carpet-bombing. We learn about it from Zaki's radio, tuned to a station that has news some of the time.

We sit in the pitch black and eat our cans of food one by one, guessing what they are from the taste: peeled mandarin oranges, refried beans, and metallic tuna, maybe. After that we play music.

We were lucky to get out before the riots.

Rewind to five years ago and press play. Imagine any given day at any boring high school. I sat out behind the portables, smoking stale cigarettes stolen from my dad. Three kids walked toward me. I knew everyone at school, but I'd never seen them before. There was one cute girl and two smaller twins. A senior and two freshmen? The girl stopped a couple feet away from me and looked me up and down.

"We've been searching for you," she said. "I'm Miranda. This is Zaki. Zaki's twins, but just one, get it?"

Zaki One spat. Zaki Two glared at me.

I didn't get it. "Do you even go here? I'm Tom."

Miranda didn't answer. She started singing instead. She wailed.

The sound hit me like water flooding into the desert.

She sang and I believed.

Her voice drowned out my fogginess. I could breathe even though I hadn't noticed I'd been holding my breath. Zaki One started playing his flute. Zaki Two played the harp. Animals and desert flowers woke up from a hot, dry summer. Frogs slipped into the water and started swimming.

When they stopped, Zaki One said, "That's your song. We wrote it for you because we need a guitar player."

"I'm not musical," I said with regret. Piggybacked on my words was shock that I felt regret. That I felt anything.

"Come on." Miranda led us to the boarded up band room. We broke in. Teachers never left their classrooms, so it was easy. Miranda let me choose and the second I saw my dreadnought fender sitting all lonesome in a dusty corner, there was no other.

"Things are going to get a lot worse soon. We need a tight band. You with us?" Miranda asked.

"Sure. Why not?"

I started eating lunch with them, just like real friends.

I started practicing my guitar all the time. When I wasn't playing, I thought of chords and moved my fingers. I hummed constantly. I got blood blisters, then sores, and then half-inch calluses on my fingertips. It took me two months, and then I could play any sound I could think of.

"We'll need to start playing a lot of gigs. We'll need a band name," Miranda said.

"Well there are four—" Zaki glared at me, "—I mean three of us."

"I like dragons," Zaki One said. "They're fierce."

"I like carnies," Zaki Two said.

"Three Ring Dragon," Miranda said.

So that's who we are.

The cargo container grows hot and bounces us all over. Roads suck these days, and even if Bob is just headed to the north end, it takes us hours to get there. Days, maybe. Who knows? Everything lasts longer in the dark.

"There's an enclave I've heard of. Full of kids. They have a resistance 'zine," Zaki One says.

"Have you seen it?" Miranda asks.

"No."

Of course he hasn't. I scratch a scab running along my shoulder blade. I dig my nails into it. There's always that place people talk about—Eugene, Doswallops, Glacier—where it's better. Where the food is safe and no one's sick with any of the diseases. Yeah, right.

"We'll find it," Miranda says.

Even in the darkness, I can't conjure up belief in a safe place. I don't ask if Miranda and Zaki believe. I need them to have more faith than me.

The truck stops and Bob opens up the rig. He holds an axe in one hand. Rope lies draped over his shoulder.

"There's no more cargo. I have to sell you," he says. His voice is flat. His eyes are angry. He has the crack—maybe he isn't that far gone yet, but he is traveling on that road.

He raises his axe and steps up onto the rig. The axe catches the sun and reflects light into the cargo container. It blinds us for a moment.

Then the Three Ring Dragon smile at each other.

Did Bob think we couldn't see him coming from a hundred miles off? These days you always have to have a plan.

Zaki plucks his harp and plays his flute. Miranda lets sound grow in her throat. I drop notes around everything. I strum an E minor and a B flat.

Bob unfurls lengths of rope.

As we start to play Bob's song, I hope we'd get at least some of it right.

Where does music come from? Nowhere. It's something out of nothing. All we know about Bob is he looks old, tired, and like he used to have fun, but that was twenty-thousand miles and two decades gone.

So we make shit up. We play like there isn't property, or crack men, or hard times. Our song says there is just a nice guy named Bob having a hard time.

Miranda stretches upward like a cat and dances in front of his axe. She throws her body into her voice. She sings higher than an angel, lower than Tom Waits.

I play faster, strumming the strings and pressing the wood. Just for that moment, just for then, I don't have to feel scared and rotten. I feel gigantic.

Bob's song wanes to a trickle of notes. He tilts from side to side before Miranda and then falls onto the metal floor. He curls up baby-style.

We jump out of the rig and down onto a root-buckled street. Zaki One takes Bob's axe; Zaki Two takes his rope. The air smells different at this end of town. Not better: less slime mold and paint fumes, more rotting meat and burning tires.

Miranda turns around in a slow circle. "That way." She points. "Due north. That's where we'll find the enclave."

I want someone to know where we're going, so I don't question her as we start walking.

"It's the music that keeps us safe. We should have turned a long time ago," Miranda says.

"Or because we have each other," Zaki One says. "We have love."

"It's because we're still virgins and the magic unicorn light protects us," I say.

"I'm not a virgin." Zaki smiles at each other.

"It's because we're too wimpy to let go," I say. I want them to stop talking. It hurts to think about it.

"No. It hurts more to notice," Zaki Two says. "We're brave warriors."

Miranda nods and starts to say something else, but I interrupt her. I don't like thinking about being whole and trapped in the brokenness. It makes me itchy. "I'm working on a new song," I lie. Lying is the best way to start a song.

I make up something and teach them the chords. I mean to make it light and fun, but by the time we figure out the chorus, it's goth times ten.

"These days the grey bleeds into me like water. These days of praise and promise fall away."

Miranda walks beside me. I try not to notice she wears bruises underneath the collar of her shirt like a necklace. She rubs the bruises as we walk.

Rats run across the road from one overgrown lawn to another. The grass could be hiding things, I think, a moment before —

"Lock them in the basement!"

"Kill the music! Kill them! Hurt!"

Women run at us. They pour out of the houses. They leap up from the grass, carrying sewing needles and kitchen knives. They run on skinny legs encased in ragged pantyhose.

"Kill them! Bad!"

"The basement! The basement!"

Each of Zaki throws tin foil balls up into the air. Wilds love foil. Some women stop and watch the balls ascend and then fall down. When the balls hit the ground they fight for them. Some wilds keep coming though.

Miranda starts running. We follow her.

"Fuck this. Fuck this," Miranda says with every stride. I look back and a woman is right behind me. I smell her—unwashed and musky. Her mouth is open and her face is blank with an emptiness I could fall into, should fall into. It could be over. What's wrong with over?

"Tom!" Miranda yells.

I look forward and see the road coming to an end. A dead end sign looms to my right, and I laugh because isn't that the truth? I jump over the thigh-high metal median and then see Zaki and Miranda floating out in front of me. They fall into nothing. We've run off a cliff and it takes us a while to land. I like the way down but then—

Crunch.

Ow.

Everything pops with pain.

The women on the cliff top above us howl. They could climb down, but this looks to be the edge of their territory.

"Fuck wilds!" I yell up at them.

"The basement," one yells. "The basement!"

I spit blood on the ground and ask, "Are you guys okay?"

"Fine," Miranda says.

"Wonderful," Zaki One says.

"I heard a snap—a bone break. It wasn't mine," I say.

Miranda looks distant.

"Wasn't me," the Zakis say.

"A twig?" Miranda says.

"No. Bone."

"A branch?"

"Don't be a masochist. We can go to the library and check out books on bones. I can make you a cast or something."

"Tom," Miranda says.

"What?"

"Pain helps. Let it help," she says. "Don't worry."

"Fine. Whatever. But if I see bone I'm going to be pissed."

"Uh..." Zaki Two grins.

"Oh, ha ha ha," I say, and then laugh for real.

Everyone loves a boner joke. At least we do. It feels good to laugh and not think about pain and breaking apart. When we start walking, Miranda hunches over and both of Zaki limps.

Before I left home, things got bad.

My dad would come home from work with his briefcase full of half-rotten fruit and hunks of raw meat. He'd yell, "Honey, I'm home." He'd have a dead snake slung across his back and would dump everything onto the kitchen table and glare at me. My mom, wearing a perma-glazed stoner grin, would clap her hands in delight.

My mom threw wet laundry into my dresser. She let the kettle boil on the stove for so long that it melted. She went out shopping and wouldn't come back for days.

My little sister carried a walking stick everywhere she went. She randomly hit the floor with it. I tried to talk to her, but she would stare at me with the wizened, desert-strained eyes of a hermit and growl.

Every night my mom made us sit around the dinner table, say grace, and eat.

"Our holiest of high up fathers," she began, and then squinted and looked confused. "Our thanks to our joy and shit, it's all dog shit and starlight, and fuck you..."

On and on. No one else noticed.

Then Dad started yelling, "Amen, amen, amen," and then we dished out our raw snake steaks with canned beans poured on top.

I asked, "Can I be excused?"

"No. Fuck you," Mom said.

"We've been sitting here three hours."

"No. Asshole. Shit-spawn."

The night before I left for good, I strummed in my room, working on a tune that didn't yet know what it wanted to be. My sister came in, hobbling behind her stick.

"Tom," she said.

I smiled. It had been a while since she'd known my name.

"Tom, it's ending, isn't it? We're all going on a long trip, aren't we?"

I didn't know what to say. Every generation thinks it's going to be the last. Everyone in history is always waiting for everything to end, but then it never does. Right?

My sister looked like she wanted to cry, but didn't remember how. She curled up like a dog at the foot of my bed and slept. The next day I packed a duffle bag and went to school.

Miranda and Zaki took me to their apartment. It was easy to make rent. Whenever our landlady showed up, we just gave her flowers, postage stamps, tin foil balls, or whatever.

"Almost there now," Miranda says. She turns and gives me a look. A come-hither look?

Maybe.

I walk closer to her. I could hold her hand. I could put an arm around her, that wouldn't be weird, right? Is that what she wants, or would it ruin everything?

The sound of breaking glass cuts into the moment—if we were even having one. The band draws closer together and follows the sound to a row of junked-up cars tilted onto their sides. People peek out at us in between the hoods and trunks.

"Looks good. Looks paranoid," Zaki One says.

"Paranoid's still afraid. Paranoid's good," Miranda whispers.

"Paranoid is awesome. What could be bad about paranoia?" I say. "Can we come in?" I yell. "We're kids from the south side."

They poke rifles toward us. Zaki Two takes a step forward, a sick grin on his face, like let's get this over with.

"We'll play for you." Zaki One holds up a flute. He runs up to stand beside his brother.

"We're the Three Ring Dragon," Miranda adds.

They grunt, lower the guns, and push aside a Geo Metro to let us in.

"Welcome," a girl says. She smiles and for a second there's someone home, but then she blinks and goes away inside of herself.

We walk up a little hill and the first thing I notice is kids milling about in a grassy field. They look skinny and tired. Beyond the grass sits a sprawling old hospital next to a smokestack with something silvery balanced on top of it.

When the kids see us, they get up and shamble toward us. The band holds hands. Zaki Two has something sharp embedded in his hand. I look down and see a piece of wire jammed into the flesh between his thumb and pointer finger. I have two thoughts: that's disgusting, and that's a really good idea.

The kids come closer. Hundreds of them. They smell nasty and look broken—but who doesn't look bad these days? They seem excited, almost agitated, to see us.

"They're a band," one kid says.

"All our batteries are dead," another adds.

"Everything downloaded is gone. We miss it," a boy says.

The kids nod and all lose interest in us.

"We miss a lot of things too," Miranda says. "It's been hard, but we'll be okay now?"

"We're keeping safe," a girl mutters. "Safe as a time bomb. What?"

A boy scratches at an infected cow brand burned into his forearm. The pain wakes him up a little. "Will you play? We need you to play."

"We'll play."

Pain helps. Music helps. Coffee helps. Whole wheat bread, the sound of bells, and cranberry juice helps. So do dogs and cats.

Beer doesn't. TV doesn't. Magazines and most books don't. Talking helps, but it's getting hard to talk and not scream.

Someone graffitied pictures of wolves along the concrete walls of the hospital. Graffiti helps, especially if it takes a while to figure out the lettering.

"Maybe the wolves are the problem," I say. A couple years back they'd bitten a lot of people.

"Nah, they're extinct," Zaki One says.

"Like us," Miranda whispers. She presses her hand against her collarbone and winces.

"What's that silver thing up on the smokestack?" I ask to change the subject.

We walk to it and see a big metal dog cage lying perched on top of it. A girl in pink and white sits up there. I can just make out her pout from the ground.

Someone has done a half-ass job of mortaring spiraled stairs up the smokestack. I climb them with Miranda. Zaki stands watch below with folded arms. The stairs hold and we make it all the way up.

The caged girl is pretty in a high-school popular kind of way. "I know you," I say. "How do I know you?"

Miranda hums a melody, and the girl sits up and smiles. Her cage creaks and shifts. The bottom of her dress is soot stained from the tendrils of smoke that rise from the smoldering biohazards beneath.

"You know my song." She turns her head from side to side, and it is like looking at an advertisement for something I don't want to buy.

Miranda sings, "Baby I long for you. I want you. Ooh. Aah."

The girl echoes the words. Where Miranda's voice hits every note with an easy precision, the girl's throaty voice grinds sex into everything.

I know who she is: the tweeny crooner, perfume huckster, pop princess of an empire long gone.

Let her rot, I think as she rises to her knees. The dog kennel is too low to let her stand. I see that she's had to stay very still to keep it from tottering off the smoke stack.

"They've stopped feeding me. They've forgotten about me, even though they launched this huge fucked-up mission to rescue me," she says. "They got jobs at the hotel I was staying in, and after my show they smuggled me out in the service elevator with all this talk about seizing the means of entertainment production and liberating the iconic goddess. It was cool for a while. They liked to listen to me sing, but then they stuck me up here and forgot." She coughs and spits blackened phlegm down into the hole of the smokestack below.

"You sound... normal," I say.

The princess nods. "I'm immune or something. I've been writing my own songs up here. I never got to do that before. You have to get me out."

The clasped lock lies outside of her reach.

"We have a band. Three Ring Dragon," Miranda says, as she undoes the lock. "We could use a backup singer."

The girl rises and looks Miranda up and down. I can see her thinking—too chubby, too dark, too plain—but then the princess slouches forward. "I was never that good at singing anyway," she says.

"We know." Miranda smiles.

As the princess steps out, she kicks her cage. It falls over the other side of the smokestack, and we hear it clang onto the ground.

"Not cool!" Zaki One yells up.

"You almost hit me," Zaki Two adds.

"Sorry," the princess says airily. She leads the way down. Her legs wobble, but she stays upright.

"You're still the princess," I whisper to Miranda.

"I'd rather be the revolting peasant," she whispers back. We make it down to the ground and none of the kids minds that we liberated their princess from her tower.

No one notices.

Looking for a place to practice, we enter the cold halls of the hospital and take the stairs up to the roof. A docked helicopter sits like a forlorn spider, and we can see the city from every direction. We see the blast-marks and smoke from our old neighborhood. When we start practicing, we face away from it.

The princess makes us more powerful. She adds in sound where there'd only been silence before. She gets us, and maybe soon, if everything goes well, we'll become the Four Ring Dragons.

We play and look down on the kids on the hill. They move like puppets whose master keeps forgetting about them. I can't look too long without a numbness floating up in me.

We write a song about them. Not a song to start with, but one to end with. We've never written a song for so many people before. Maybe with the princess it will work.

At dusk we walk down the cement stairs and out onto the overgrown field. Kids lie motionless on the grass. Others light a pile of dried brush and throw slabs of grey meat onto the flames.

"Think it's safe to eat?" Miranda asks.

"No. It probably comes from around here," Zaki One says.

"Going to eat it anyway," Zaki Two says. "No choice. We never get a choice."

"Let's play first," I say. "Let's play hungry. It'll give us an edge." Something in the air feels different tonight. The fire reminds me of summer camp, sing-a-longs, and marshmallows.

I tune my guitar and play like Jimi, then Page, and then Johnson. Just to show off a little. Then I start to play like me. Like everything I know and everything that's happened comes into my music.

"Been standing so long," Miranda croons, and then repeats it.

The princess echoes, "So long, so long," on the backbeat. Zaki's flute and harp come in under and over my guitar.

"Been standing so long I forgot how to sit. How to leave. How to fly." It's one of the first songs we ever wrote together. We rock it. Even the princess doesn't miss a note.

Like mosquitoes at dusk, kids draw near and surround us. They stand too close. The princess swirls around and forces them to back off. We reach the end of our first song, and I see a few kids crying.

Pain is good.

Our next song cuts deeper. It's stripped down and harsh. We wrote it a couple of years ago; back when we were playing to sold-out shows and kids remembered how to thrash. Miranda screams and I break a guitar string trying to match her. Around us kids sway like it is a love song.

Feel, I think as I play. Remember. Wake up. We can still make something in this world. The anger in the song thrums out between my fingers like artery blood from a deep wound.

We play another song, and another. It feels like every kid left in the entire city gathers around us. I see someone smile. I see a couple of people dance together. I focus on the music and what we are saying with every word and chord.

Survive this. Wake up. Wake up.

We are playing better than we ever have. I feel reality changing around us, just a little. Then it comes time for us to sing their song—the one we wrote today. My hand cramps. I feel thirsty and a little dizzy, but none of that matters. I let the music use me.

Their song is big, brash, and violent. It starts hard and it keeps on going. We play it like the numb doesn't exist. We play it to break them apart. As I play, I imagine we could start something here. We could grow food and keep everything bad out. We could have parties, make clothes, and maybe one day make babies. We could become a tribe.

"Nobody remembers who you are. Everyone remembers what you want to be," Miranda wails, twice as loud as any of our instruments.

I see them changing just like I did, like we'd been trying to make people change from the beginning. Even if it wakes them up to an awful world, I want them here. I want them with me.

The song hits the guitar solo and I start rocking. The princess takes a step forward and away from the band. I think she is going to swirl around again, but instead she starts singing.

"To the roof, to the roof," she yells. I look at Miranda and Zaki One. They shrug. I play louder to drown her out. Miranda starts ululating, but it's too late.

The princess bolts toward the hospital and, like lemmings, the kids follow in her wake.

Miranda sings louder, but there are only a couple dozen kids left. They're numb and stare at us dumbly.

I play the wrong chord. Miranda forgets the lyrics, and Zaki Two isn't playing his harp at all.

We hear yells from the roof. Zaki One plays a fierce flute melody that should have, maybe, been able to reach them up there. I play with him. Miranda too. We aren't playing a song anymore; we're just making noise.

I see a flash of long golden princess hair. She stands on the edge of the roof, and then throws herself over. She flies like a bird, like a triumph, and I ache to be up there with her. Only my guitar keeps me on the ground.

Rivers of kids follow behind. Dark shapes drop off the roof. Down and down, and I would have thought they would hit silently, but they don't. They scream. Their bodies thump and crunch.

One scream is louder than the others. It's nearby. Zaki One screams and flails and throws his flute down.

I pull my gaze away from the flying, falling, dying kids and see that it's only Zaki One screaming. Zaki Two is gone. My head whips back to the kids falling, and I think I see Zaki Two, but I'm not sure. Miranda moans and kneels beside Zaki One. I go to them, to my real tribe, and wonder how we are going to survive this.

Zaki One scratches his cheeks deep enough to make scars. Miranda tears off her shirt, and I see the rough edge of her collarbone jutting out. I hold them both. I push up my sleeves to show them that I hurt, too. Behind us, the kids keep falling.

After they blew up our neighborhood—after the rig and the axe, the deranged housewives, and the suicide party, we hop a train heading south. We talk about reaching avocado and salsa land, but our voices are brittle and fragile. It's better not to talk at all. The train veers east and north, and it gets a lot colder.

We watch each other and hold each other when one of us wants to jump off. The train moves faster and faster every hour. We see soldiers marching through wheat fields toward small towns. We see mountain lions running alongside the train. I tell a story about never getting off and riding until we become the wind. Or I tell a story about riding until we get so far north, up to the ice caps, that people can't get sick because the air is too clean. Maybe there is a place like that left. Maybe.

In the Seams

Andrew C. Porter

There isn't much time. If I am going to tell this story, I'm going to tell it now. It's late, I know, but the dogs are spooked and that means it's on the way. The skin on my face is peeling. The backs of my hands are raw meat. If I hadn't found Annie's old tape recorder, then I wouldn't have been able to document the facts. I can press record. I can pull a trigger. I'm going to tell the whole story because I know that when they find what's left of me, or what isn't, they're going to ask questions, and I don't want them... you, whoever you are, to think this was a murder. This was a feeding. You'd better just put down the cause of death as "mauled by animal." You'll probably have another name for it soon.

This all started out in the fourth district a year ago when we got bogged down in the war with Iraq. Gas prices jumped a dollar fifty and as any coal man in Kentucky would tell you, expensive Arab oil meant it was time to clean off the dozers. Sixty dollars a ton, that was what did it. Who in western Kentucky had ever heard of that? Those East Kentucky mines got that, sure, but they pulled it out of mountains. That wasn't cheap. Here we just peeled back the top soil and there it was: money.

After the price went up, every old coal baron got into his equipment barn and started calling back the miners he'd laid off in '79. Course, most of them were dead or enjoying black lung settlements so they sent their kids. That's how I came into this. I was on a road crew running a backhoe when Snodgrass called.

"Phe'ps," he said, shortening Phelps like every Butler County septuagenarian does, "your daddy worked for me. Now I got a golden opportunity for you. What's Scott paying you to run that hoe?"

"Pretty good, Mr. Snodgrass." I didn't want to ruin any offer with the truth.

"Would you come work for me for twenty-two an hour?"

"Can I get overtime?"

He laughed at me. "Boy, you're gonna be begging me for a Sunday morning off. We'll get going at Aberdeen Grocery at four-thirty tomorrow morning."

We talked for awhile about the old days, my father, his purchase of the Lindsey land back when everyone thought coal was dead. I was almost off the phone when he asked if I knew a good dozer operator. Two more seconds and I would have been off the phone. Two more seconds and I might not be sitting on my porch with a loaded shotgun and a tape recorder. I'm not saying that all this wouldn't have still come down eventually had I not recommended Zan. It was in the seam after all, and somebody would have run across it before too long, but maybe, just maybe, if I had gotten off that phone, I wouldn't be the one waiting to die.

Zan had come back from Iraq six months before. He'd joined the army after high school, encouraged by his recruiter and the possibilities opened up by his unusually high ASVAB scores. His daddy was a dozer operator and so was his older brother. The army would get him out of that terrible inevitability. That was what the recruiter had said. Two months after signing up, Zan was in Felujah, running a dozer in the grand task of pushing down neighborhoods deemed "lost to the insurgency." It turned out he was genetically predisposed to being a top notch dozer operator.

I found Zan that very night, lying in his underwear on his blue couch in the den of his pink trailer, smoking pot.

"Come in!" he hollered when I knocked, not bothering to find out who it was.

"Zan, it's me, Andy," I called out as a precaution.

"I know, I could hear Annie's car from a mile away. What's new? You want to hit this?" He extended the three-foot red plastic bong toward me.

"No, I'm fine. I got you a job." He pulled a long, gurgling lung-full of smoke as I talked, then held it in, his upper body poised awkwardly upright by the tension of maintaining his expanded chest cavity. Curling fingers of blue-white smoke trailed out of his nostrils and the corners of his mouth, drifting in the stale dead air of the living room and into the cone of light emanating from the television. It was the History Channel showing a documentary called *The Battle for Felujah.*

"They drug test?" I told him they didn't, and he agreed to meet up with us at four-thirty in the morning.

He was on time. Everyone was; the money Snodgrass had promised was too good. I left the house at four; the stars were bright and cold, as I warmed up the truck and my breath fogged heavily in the pre-dawn November air. Aberdeen grocery was a ten minute drive from the house, but I planned on getting a sausage biscuit down while I was there and buying a bologna sandwich for lunch. Aberdeen grocery would slice off the bologna as thick as three slices at other places, and they steadfastly used real mayonnaise. I came into the grocery and immediately found the crew. Surrounded by the haze of a dozen cigarettes, twelve men sat around the picnic table that occupied the middle of the fishing tackle room. I sat down beside a bleary eyed Zan and ordered a coffee while we waited for Snodgrass to arrive. It was a good crew. I knew three of them well. The rest I knew fairly well. I had played ball with Curtis Ward; he would be a mechanic. Owen Kelley and B.J. Smith would be on equipment. Eric Ingram and his brother, Jay, would be running the trucks. We were all about the same age. Only Johnny Lindsey had experience from the days before the '79 bust and, as Johnny was a mute, he wouldn't be telling any stories. He would be another mechanic.

Our small talk ran in short rounds, punctuated by yawns as the low, wet gurgle of the minnow tank aerators lulled us all to sleep. Occasionally, one of the group would fall into light slumber only to be jolted awake as the table shifted on the ancient and uneven planks of the floor, sending coffee spilling everywhere. Then Snodgrass arrived and we were caravanning north on Highway 70 to the wide open ridge-top fields of the county's fourth district. Zan rode with me in the old Chevy truck I had resurrected from my yard the summer before. Its front wheels had been scavenged from a smaller truck, causing it to ride at a pitched-forward angle that made your butt want to slide off the cracked vinyl bench seat.

"I can't believe I'm doing this shit again." Zan said, as we whipped along the dark, cold, ridge road.

"What's that?" I asked.

"Dozer work. I mean, Christ-sake, dude. I wasn't meant for this. I can do so much. Remember all those ferns and fossil fish your dad used to get from the shale? You know I learned the name and age of every single species of those things. I was only eight! I should be a scientist or something."

"Yeah," I replied. "You remember that trip to the Kentucky Museum in the sixth grade? That tour guide was showing off those worm fossils and you told him they belonged to some other species and he tried to say you were wrong, but when we went back in the seventh grade they had changed all the tags on them to what you had said."

"They were called nautoloids. Yeah, I remember." We rode along in silence, then Zan continued, more subdued, "When I was in Iraq, we had this job where we were looking for hiding places in some rock outcrops. While I was running some equipment I uncovered some caves. At the end of the day I got down off the dozer and all of a sudden all these towel heads who lived nearby came running up to me screaming and waving their arms and shit. The infantry guys who were with us almost popped 'em right then and there. One of them spoke some English and managed to convince the guards to come and get me. Turns out they wanted me to cover the cave back up. They said they wouldn't sleep until the cave was closed. I was shit tired, but they were practically in tears. Kept saying the *Djinni* will come out."

"The gin?"

"No, *Djinni*, genies. Like with the lamps."

"I thought those were good luck. Three wishes and all that."

He was quiet for awhile, staring off to a bright star rising on the horizon, "No, that's just Disney shit. Over there the *Djinni* are terrible things. They're like spirits of hate made from the elements. Some of them are just like pranksters, the *Djinni* from the sky. They steal your goats, knock over your piss pot while you sleep. The ones from underground—" He chuckled. "Well those are the bad ones. They're imprisoned underground by the gods, or by God I guess now, and they get loose and it's all your asses. They come down from the sky and eat the skin off whole herds, not one goat, the whole herd. They carry village girls out into the middle of a field and tear their arms and legs off, then when people come to help them they tear off their limbs until the whole village is a big pile of limbless bodies."

"Well, I know what I would do with three wishes," I offered lamely. Zan didn't reply.

Two semis waited at the site. The drivers had already unloaded the two dozers and two end-loaders, and Snodgrass had signed for them. After a brief consultation with a surveyor who showed up in a shiny new Dodge truck, Snodgrass gave us our orders.

I was put on one of the end-loaders, a heavy dirt shovel that had seen better days, and dispatched to the middle of the bowl-shaped expanse that made up the Lindsey mine. Zan followed me on the E-6, a mammoth dozer, and Eric brought up the tail in a dump truck. The other crews were dispatched at the back of the five-hundred-acre mine.

We went straight to it. Zan peeled back the topsoil and I scooped it up and put it in the dump. When the truck was full the spoil was packed off to a pile for later use in reclamation. Zan and I worked well together. I could anticipate his moves, his strategy, and before noon we had two trucks packing off our spoil. Zan was good. There were no wasted moves. He seemed able to predict the material under the brown sage grass of the field. He knew rocks were there before he hit them, and when a clean run of clay was found he pushed it hard. We worked like that for the rest of the day, and the day after that, and the day after that. After a week of prep, we got into the black.

The seam was not deep. We cut through a layer of clay, then shale, and that was it. The run of coal was around two feet thick and looked good. The crew on top of the ridge had been pulling coal for two days so we were both anxious to get it out of the ground, and get it out we did. We had a smaller crew, thinner seam, and older equipment but, by the second day, Zan and I had already matched the others ton for ton.

When we kicked off at dark we busted on the other crews. "How two dozers and two loaders on a four foot seam can't keep up with me and Zan can only mean one thing!" I yelled at the ridge crew.

"What does it mean?" Zan called out from the truck bed, shot gunning a beer as he did.

"Pussyitis!" I cried to a reply of 'fuck-yous' and the high-pitched throat squeals of mute Johnny's damaged laughter.

That's how it went. For a week, a month, all the way to spring we cut and busted the ground. Hundreds of tons became thousands, tens of thousands. The Lindsey mine was rich, unusually rich, and now so was Mr. Snodgrass. We all got raises. Zan and me both got up to forty dollars an hour, and I knew we were the highest paid. Zan moved into a house not far from mine on Green River. I got a new truck. Zan got a motorcycle. Annie started talking about us having kids. That's how it goes when times are good. Slow changes. Nothing good happens fast. It may seem good, but it's really just difference playing tricks on you. Abrupt things are hateful to life. I could not appreciate that until recently, so when Zan and me were on my porch drinking beer and half watching the grill on a warm March Sunday and he suggested that we try a new strategy at work, I didn't have the sense to say no.

"That seam we've been chasing, it's been the same thickness since we started," Zan said.

"Yeah it has. Nice and regular. No hide and seek."

"Well I think we're missing something. We been peeling that thing north to south from day one. It's time we take a sharp turn to the west."

"Boss won't like that. Anyway, he has test drills all over that mine and they don't show shit where you're talking about," I said, taking a pull from my beer.

"Boss don't know what I know." He leaned over to me, speaking in a low, conspiratorial voice, "Due west from the strip we're mining is a seam thirty feet thick."

"Now how do you figure that?" How indeed.

Strike is the angle a layer of strata takes in its journey through the crust. Most layers of strata pitch at a shallow angle that, not counting faults, crustal deformities, or such contortions as kimberlite pipes, run from the place the strata hits the surface to the point where they meet the gluey depths of hell thousands of feet underground. It's the little deformities that make the money, and as Zan explained it, just to the west of where our equipment was working six days a week, was a vast pit of coal, deep as hell and thick.

Monday morning we ran the idea by Snodgrass. I did most of the talking, selling Snodgrass on the strike of the seam and fossil unconformities while Zan backed me up on the finer points of geology. I finished off our argument with the "gut feeling" approach. Snodgrass, eyes narrowed, looked at the two of us without speaking. I liked to think he saw a streak of the old wildcatter he used to see in himself. It was the kind of thinking that drove his generation to make dynamite out of fertilizer and blast away at hills while hiding under pickup trucks.

"We'll see," was all he said, but while Zan and I worked nearby, he and Johnny did a test bore to the depth Zan had suggested. Thirty feet was an understatement.

It was deep, it was thick, and it was perfect. We had to go and rent a longer bore bit to find out how thick it really was. The coal was high sulphur, as was all west Kentucky coal, but also high BTU. In fact, this coal was so high in heat output that the Paradise power plant bought every ton we could produce on spec. We got new equipment. Me and Zan got bonuses. We thought things could only get better. That's rapid change for you.

By the end of March the Lindsey mine looked like a crater on the moon, as we bore into the giant orb of coal that hid at the bottom. Long, hastily constructed, earthen ramps spider-webbed the grey shale walls where endless streams of dump trucks carried overburden to the rim that now made up the horizon line in all directions. On the lip of the pit a whole army of yellow earth moving equipment waited, looking like dinosaurs posed into a strange tableau. Snodgrass had not revealed the true dimensions of the seam to anyone, and asked us to keep quiet as he signed over our bonuses. "I don't want to get a bunch of Frankfort busybodies down here. Regulators ran me out the first time around. Longer we can pull this out of the ground without anybody getting too interested the better."

Nobody came to see it. Nobody came to study it, and we just kept on digging.

The spring thaw held off until April, then came a kind of half-assed spring that doesn't clean the winter out of your pipes and leaves you feeling stung until August. It was the first chill week of April that we found the bones. I was on the loader trying to dump a shovel load into the dump truck. I knew Zan had kicked the dozer engine off because the endless, bone jarring vibration that surrounded me shifted pitch, causing a tickling in my inner ear and nostrils. I dumped the load and locked the break, turning to see what had happened. I thought it would be a split hydraulic hose, maybe empty of diesel. Instead I saw Zan crouched down in front of the dozer pouring out his soft drink and wiping the liquid around with a blue grease rag. I radioed the driver of the dump truck to hold on, and climbed down from the end-loader to go and see what was going on. As I got close I saw what had stopped him.

In a long arc, running at a shallow radius across the entire layer of coal we had just exposed were hundreds of fossils. Not ferns, nor small lung fish that miners saw with regularity, but giant four-legged monstrosities, eight- and ten-feet long. Their legs were short, a foot long or so. The rear legs had elongated toes and on many of the skeletons I could discern the faint trace of webbing between them. The front legs had shorter, more rotund feet that were tipped in tiny sharp nails. The tail was also short with large protrusions on the individual vertebrae. The heads were shark-like, torpedo shaped with rows of jagged, needle -like teeth turned back at an angle.

"What the hell are these?" I asked Zan.

"I have no clue. I have never seen anything like this. Not in here, not in the upper carboniferous."

"Are fossils usually laid out in circles?" I asked.

"No." He looked at the arc of bones that disappeared into the cut and his eyes continued to move around the crater of the mine. "This circle goes around the entire seam. I bet there are more of them further in too."

"We should stop and call up to Western. I bet they'll send a scientist down. You'll be famous."

He turned to me. His face serious and pale. "No I won't. When some guy uncovers a bone in his backyard the history books don't give him credit. They give credit to the scientist who first identified the bone. They say 'so and so' discovered 'such and such' after some bumpkin found it. I'll be known as 'the coal miner,' that's all." He crouched back over the skeletons. "No, I'm going to do this. There ain't no reason to call Western. We'll work the higher seam for awhile then after work I'll come back here and dig some of these out. Promise you won't tell nobody."

I promised. Now that I think back on it, that is when my life really ended.

We worked the higher seams during the day. The ultra rich coal coming out by the hundred-ton load to go to the Paradise furnace. In the evening, after everyone knocked off, Zan would go to the lower seam and excavate bones.

"It's a perfect circle of remains," he told me one evening while having a beer on my porch, "Every skeleton is facing the same direction too. They are all pointing to the middle of the coal deposit. It's like nothing anybody's ever seen. It's like thousands of animals came to this one place and died, one on top of the other. I don't know what kind of animals they were. I can't find any examples of anything like them online."

As the days wore on, Zan began to look worse and worse. I noticed that the lower excavation was also growing. One night I swung down by the mine and saw the lights of Zan's dozer in the pit as he cut further into the seam. It was one in the morning.

"You're going to get your ass fired." I said the next day.

"No way." he replied, "I discovered the damn seam. Snodgrass wouldn't do shit to me. Ten minutes stripping pays for the diesel I use. Anyway, I've discovered something you should see."

After work I went with him to the excavation site and what I beheld took my breath away. Zan had indeed gone further in toward the middle of the crater. The track he had cut was now only about one-hundred feet from the center. The bones were there too. It was apparent that they were arranged, not in a circle around the crater, but in a disk, a complete disk of fossils that covered the entire seam at that level. They did not seem to occur beneath that disk nor above it, and every single skeleton was oriented toward the center. The only change in the bones was the bones themselves. The skeletons closest to the middle looked nothing like the ones that had been uncovered at the perimeter.

"Look at the head!" Zan exclaimed, as he dusted off a particularly large specimen nearly twelve feet long. This head wasn't a torpedo, but was anvil shaped. Its jaws extended two feet to each side and were filled with regular, three-inch-long teeth. "And look at the feet," he said, pointing to the back feet. The webs were gone. The toes on the rear appendages now had three joints and looked nimble and dangerous, tipped with wicked claws. "If I walk back to the edge of the fossil bed I can see the feet change. Thirty feet back the last of the webbing disappears. The jaws start extending to the anvil shape you see here at about fifty feet back. These are the same animals we found at the edge. It's like they are evolving right in front of our eyes!" He seemed manic, jittery. If I hadn't known better I would have thought he had taken up a meth habit.

"Listen, Zan, I'm worried about you," I said, crouching down beside him. "You're doing all right. Maybe you should take a few days off. Say you got the flu or something. I can keep this safe."

He turned toward me, his face frantic and contorted with fear. "No! No, no, no! I am getting close to something here. Something big. It's in the middle. Something is in the middle. Something big. I'm going to find it. I'm going to get out of this shit-hole once and for all! So either help me or leave me alone!"

What was I supposed to do? I helped him. That night I came back to the mine and found him on the dozer, gingerly pealing away at the fossil shelf, working toward the center. When I got out of the truck and went to fire up the loader, he waved to me, nothing more. As the night wore on we worked the layer of overburden, pulling out the priceless tons of coal and pushing them aside as if they were so much shale. About four hours into the dig Zan climbed down from the dozer and began to dig with a shovel, uncovering the fossils that lay not forty feet from the middle of the pit. He waved to me and I came down, leaving the loader running.

"Look at this." He called out over the competing roar of the diesel engines, his breath coming out in great, ghostly torrents of steam in the chill air. He pushed aside the black, crumbling coal with a booted food to reveal the latest skull.

I have to confess that at first I didn't recognize what it was I was looking at. I didn't see a skull, or even a thing produced by a natural process. There was too much order to it to be a thing of random creation, but there was nothing in the form that suggested a linear or sensible derivation from understandable life. I can say, however, that the first thing I recognized, were teeth. Hundreds of them, of all sizes, jutting out at obscene angles from what must once have been four distinct shelves of a mouth. They interlocked and ground into one another in a manner that must have insured a life of constant gnashing and pain. The only consistency in the mass was that every tooth was uniformly sharp and terrible. It would seem the evil god that had spawned this abomination could not find a design more awful than the predator's tooth, and so made it more dreadful by forcing it to hurt the predator as much as the prey.

"What the hell is that thing?" I was shaking as I spoke and it was not from the cold.

"Those are holes for the eyes." He sounded like a child discovering the mechanics of some simple device for the first time: this is how a bicycle works; this is how a skateboard rolls; this is how an animal fits fifteen eyeballs into its head.

He jumped up from the wretched thing and climbed back onto the dozer, roaring up the engine. I was glued to my spot, beholding the bones in the dead lights of the dozer's halogens. Zan called down to me, "Come on, we're going to see what these things were looking at. He plowed the dozer toward the center of the crater, unconcerned for the fossil bed he had gone to such great lengths to protect until then. The tracks of the giant Cat twisted and shattered the skeletons as Zan charged hard into the remaining overburden. I stumbled over to the loader, dreading the act with every halting step. I know I could not have stopped him even if I'd wanted to.

Zan charged into the remaining feet of cover. Black dust boils rose in the lights, and cracks rang out as the coal seam splintered in the petroleum-powered onslaught. Then I heard the ear shattering ping of steel breaking. The dozer's engine went dead and I watched Zan leap from the cab and run around the front of the machine. I killed the loader and climbed down, not sure if I wanted to know what had happened. As I came around the dozer I found Zan looking down at the base of the dozer's blade. Two of the inch-thick steel teeth that lined the bottom of the blade were cleanly broken off, rent back under the blade by the terrible pressure of the Cat's unrelenting drive.

"What the hell did that?" I asked. We might be able to hide the fact that we're using up fuel, but two teeth busted on a new dozer was going to be trouble. "Shit. We're going to have to weld those on before Monday or it's going to be our ass. What did you hit?"

Zan dusted off the black ground the teeth had apparently struck. He spat and, using his shirt sleeve, rubbed the spit on the patch of ground. It quickly took on a reflective, even luminous quality like black glass.

"What is it?" I asked.

"It looks like obsidian, but that would never have broken steel teeth." He dusted around the broken steel and withdrew a six-inch-long shard of the glassy material, sharp and dagger-like. "I'm going to see what I can figure out about this stuff."

We decided to knock off. It was four in the morning and even though we weren't working on Sundays anymore, I knew my wife would skin me for staying out so late. It was freezing outside and Zan was on his motorcycle so I offered him a ride. We loaded the bike into the back of the truck and set off down the road.

We pulled out of the mine's gravel access road and out onto the deserted Highway 70. "What do you think all that shit is?" I asked, trying to keep fear out of my voice as best I could.

Zan's voice was calm, reserved in a way it had not been for days. "Do you know much about the Pennsylvanian age?"

"It's full of coal. I know that. Bowling Green is Mississippian, at Hadley Hill you climb up into Pennsylvanian."

"Yeah, well back during the Pennsylvanian age all this was a great big swamp. I mean really big. The Appalachians were bigger than the Himalayas, and all the moisture got trapped on this side making one giant swamp at the edge of a hot shallow sea. All that shit died and sank and became coal, all the trees and ferns and fishes. But something happened then. Nobody knows why, but everything died. Every fish and fern and tree. All of it. Scientist think it was a meteor."

"Oh, yeah. Off the coast of Mexico. Killed all the dinosaurs. I saw it on the Discovery Channel. That show about the T. rex."

"No. That was millions of years later. That was a meteor, and it killed like, sixty percent of the world's species. The extinction that I'm talking about was bigger, and they're not certain that it was a meteor at all. There is no evidence it was, and this extinction took out over ninety percent of the species. The dinosaurs first appeared a few million years later. Plants started bearing seeds, shit started running on two legs. Everything that survived the extinction got a lot meaner and they got meaner really fast. It was like all of a sudden a whole bunch of pressure was put on every living thing. The ones that survived did so because they could run, or hide, or have lots of babies."

"What are you saying?" I asked.

"What if it wasn't a meteor, or volcanoes changing the climate that made everything die? What if it was some new species, or old species that changed real fast and had the edge all of the sudden? Not in a million years where everything could get used to it, but in just a few thousand years, or even a few hundred. What if something was changing the animals that came near it, like a virus, or some sort of mutation? What if all those bones were the generations of some new super-predator that got, I don't know, changed, and then started killing off all the other species that were just too weak to compete?"

I didn't have an answer. I dropped Zan off at his house, then drove home, an uncomfortable pit of anxiety in my gut.

That night I dreamt of swamps, great reeking swamps floating on miles of hot, rotting filth. I dreamt that deep, deep down the rottenness beat like a heart, slowly rising up until it bubbled onto the surface, a vast black pool of vile contamination. I heard the screams of the tiny, unfortunate amphibians as the black pool engulfed them. And I heard them change. I heard it. It was the sound of bones breaking, of skin splitting. It was the noise of an incomprehensible power, ancient even in infancy, a remnant sound from the bridging of the gulf between a dead universe and bloody, fecund life.

I was roused from sleep by the gasp of my wife. I didn't need to open my eyes to know something was very wrong. In fact, I couldn't open my eyes. Pain came on quickly and did not stop.

"What the hell is wrong with me?" I cried.

"Your face is... is... it's cooked!"

I knew what she meant. It was the pain of twelve hours in the sun, of scalding water poured on the arm. From my neck to my forehead the skin was tight and throbbing. Every time I tried to speak I felt it crack, sending jolts of misery into the core of my brain.

The ER doctor questioned me for an hour. He all but accused me of botching a batch of meth. When I continued to deny any drug activity he threw up his hands. "Well, have you been exposed to any radioactive material?" No, no of course not.

I had to have my wife dial the phone and hold it to my ear. My hands were wrapped in gauze. My face was covered in a mask of thick, white cream. I could smell the blisters festering on my skin. The phone rang until the answering machine picked up. "This is Zan, leave a message or don't."

"Hang it up." I told her. She was convinced I was cooking meth with Zan, and no amount of pleading would convince her to give me a ride to his house. With no other option left, I called the sheriff's office. Two hours later a white police car pulled up into my drive.

"We didn't find Zan. Something got his dog though. Poor thing got tore to pieces. His house was trashed, but it didn't seem like anything was missing. Just a bunch of food everywhere and the tub was full of black water." Even through my half closed eyes I could see that the deputy was suspicious. I looked every bit like a victim of mishandled anhydrous ammonia, and it must have seemed like I was trying to use the police in some sort of backfired drug burn. "You mind if I have a look around?"

"Go ahead," I muttered through split lips, hearing the skin around my mouth crackle with the words. He poked around the yard and shed for several minutes then returned.

"Well, if he ain't turned up by this time tomorrow his family can file a report." He was halfway out the door when he stopped and turned back to me, "You sure you and him ain't been into nothing?"

I didn't bother replying.

It rained hard that night and into the next day, and the day after that. Snodgrass called to see how I was and to tell me that the walls of the coal pit had collapsed in the rain and work would be halted in the bottom seams until they could get the water and mud out. Zan's father filed a report. Zan stayed missing.

By the end of the week the bandages were removed and my face no longer caused people to look away. Now they only winced. I got the call at around noon.

Mr. Snodgrass sounded tired, shaky as he said hello. "How you doin' boy?"

"Fine, Mr. Snodgrass. I'm a whole lot better."

"Good, that's real good. I got some bad news for you. Seems Owen and B.J. had an accident. Well, they um, they're dead. Ain't no mincing words here. I ain't got any operators worth a damn and Monday we are going to be hitting the seam hard. I know Zan was your friend, but the kid's gone AWOL and I need all the help I can get. What are the odds of getting you onsite Monday morning? You ain't got to operate, just keep an eye on the new ones, make sure they ain't screwing around."

I didn't know what to say. I had known Owen and B.J. half my life and on top of everything else, it was just too much. "Mr. Snodgrass, I'm going to need more time than this."

"How's Wednesday then?" he replied, not taking my meaning.

"I'll call you next week and we'll figure something out." A thought occurred to me then, and I asked the question, "You're not planning on digging out the crater are you?"

"That's where we are going to be digging. I hired a dirt crew to come in and they've already got it cleaned out. It was a big mud hole when they started, and now it's dry. Just a big oily pool at the bottom, but we'll get that drained out Monday, I guess."

"Did you notice anything weird down there when they were cleaning it out?"

"Well, that's odd. B.J. found a frog he'd run over with the track hoe. Thing was big around as a dinner plate and had five eyes. Damnest thing I ever saw." He paused, then added, "how did you know that?"

I gave no reason and got off the phone. It was a five-minute drive to the county impound lot where the truck B.J. and Owen had been killed in was being kept. The big red Ford diesel was still on the back of a long flat bed hauler, chained down to the deck. It was obvious that the truck had rolled several times. The cab was crushed down to the level of the dash and the whole body appeared twisted. That those two had wrecked didn't surprise me; hardly a day ended that they hadn't consumed a case of beer apiece before heading home from the job. What was unaccountable was that both doors were missing, and along the crushed holes where they should have been hanging were deep gouges in the red body that left jagged rents in the metal. I turned to leave, noticing off in the distance, thirty miles or so to the west, a vast black cloud drifting up from the ground. Paradise. The old coal plant had its environmental scrubbers off. They never ran them unless the EPA was going to do a fly through, and the smoke was as dark as the coal they burned, our coal, full of heat, full of something else. I thought about all the millions of tiny particles of the bones and black glass that must be rising up in that midnight plume, drifting up and up to rain steadily back down across the earth.

I raced home and started looking up numbers. Curtis Ward, no answer. Jay and Eric Ingram, answering machine. I called what cell phones I had numbers for, but nobody picked up. Finally I even called

Johnny Lindsey, why the mute had a phone had always been a point of humor for all of us at the mine, but as he answered with his back throat squeal. I was glad of the fact.

"Johnny, listen. It's Tom Phelps. Listen to me now. I think something's wrong with Zan. I think, well, it doesn't matter. You get yourself out of the house and come over to my place. Bring a gun with you and you don't stop."

He started to make the affirmative squeal, then, halfway through, cut off. I heard a loud banging in the background, like someone beating a door down. Johnny made a low, suspicious moan.

"Johnny, Johnny! Don't answer it! Get your gun." I screamed into the receiver. In answer I heard the sliding clunk of a shotgun pump. There was another sound then as Johnny's door must have exploded, followed by a shotgun blast.

I have to ask you if you've ever heard a mute scream. I think it was worse than normal screams. Maybe they save 'em up for really important moments. The noise that came from Johnny's throat was like nothing I had ever heard, primal and utterly free of restraint. It rose and rose, higher in pitch and volume, then, suddenly, seemed to fill with gurgling liquid. Then all was silent. I listened, not daring to breathe. Seconds stretched out unbearably and I strained to hear. A slippery sound finally came across the line, a sound like wet rubber being pushed across metal. The phone popped and a voice came over it. "Hiiiiiii Tommmmy." It was a whisper made through wet leaves, "Caaann Iiii cooomme ooooverrrr?" I dropped the phone, then scrambled to pick it back up.

"Zan! Zan, is that you?" But there was no one there.

Mr. Snodgrass didn't answer the phone when I called. Everyone that had worked the Lindsey seam was away from their phones and their cell phones. So were their families. I sat on the couch staring at my burned hands. Every bit of exposed skin I had was cooked by the black substance and I had been around it for less than half an hour. Zan probably experimented with the shard for hours. Did he notice what was happening? Did he feel himself changing? I wondered what would happen if he'd tried to taste the thing? He had been desperate to keep our find a secret. How much more did that matter after he'd realized what was occurring to him? Did he take the shard and flee into the woods? Bury himself in the cold dead ground like some grub, shedding skin and hair, coming out changed into something new, something mean and repellant?

I had to get Annie out of the house. She refused to go to her parents until I gave her a good reason. I know she thought I was hiding something, drugs probably. In a last desperate bid to get her out of the house, I slapped her. Whoever finds this tape, make sure she knows I didn't mean it. I just wanted her to be safe for as long as possible. I know that nobody will be safe for long. Whoever you are, don't let the Lindsey mine open back up. I hope to God that the coal price drops. As long as it's running high, some fool will try and open up that godforsaken pit.

I can hear him. He's on the roof. I know what feet sound like on our roof. The neighbors kid cleans my gutters and I know the sound of feet. That's not what I'm hearing. I'm not hearing feet. I can't tell you if I am hearing limbs. The bugs and frogs have gone quiet. Even the mosquitoes have stopped buzzing in my ears. I hear its breath, like a hot-air balloon inflating.

THE NATURE OF BLOOD

GEORGE MANN

I fell in love with a red-head on the bus.

Her eyes were sparkling windows of blue, glassy and serene. Her hair was a shock of amber that fell in waves about her shoulders. Sometimes she wore it tied back in a taut ponytail. When I think of her, I see a pair of skinny trousers, cut short, in black and white pinstripe, and an old cream jumper wrapped around her body, pulled up underneath her chin. It was winter. Our breaths made steaming clouds in the night air; fogged up the windows on the inside of the old Leyland bus. We watched each other with cautious eyes.

Her name was Isabella.

She spent her time making blood. Later, she would talk to me about the nature of blood; show me her little laboratory that smelled of formaldehyde. She would hunch for hours over her enormous electronic microscope, rearranging plasma, synthesizing the fluid of life. She would smile to herself at little triumphs; rub the back of her aching neck with her left hand. I never quite grasped the complexities of those hours, the nuances that made the blood of one person so different from that of another. Still, now, I have difficulty understanding the allure, the reasons she did what she did. Looking back, with the benefit of hindsight, I think she saw it as a failure on my part, this lack of comprehension, and it undermined our relationship from the very start. But at the time we were full of hope and optimism, and all things were new. If I showed my ignorance she would simply smile at me knowingly, and then kiss me brightly on the forehead, her lips leaving a cool, damp impression on my skin.

When I first saw her she was poring over the pages of a scientific journal, her lips carefully following the words of some difficult passage, silently committing them to memory. The bus shelter curved in a protective arc over her head, its dirty plastic barrier holding off the snowflakes of yet another miserable English night. They tumbled gently around me, catching every now and then on my cuff or sleeve, only to wink silently out of existence like tiny stars.

I smiled.

She didn't even notice me.

I took my place under the shelter and willed the bus to come around the corner.

Beside me, an ancient, careworn woman was standing hunched over the figure of an elderly man, lecturing him on the benefits of having turned up the sleeves of her cardigan.

"I just cut them off about here," she said, indicating with her finger, "and then turned them up to here. I did one the same for little Violet, you know."

"They just come down to me knuckles, these do, these sleeves." He looked up at her plaintively.

"Just pop round one afternoon Tom, I'll do anything, me." A pause. "I'm up at the cemetery tomorrow mind, about twelve o'clock. Shan't stay long, be home for quarter-to."

"Aye. I'll be at the bookie's, meself." He looked up at me and winked.

I turned away quickly, embarrassed. Two eyes peered up from the pages of the journal, momentarily lost, as if the sudden segue-way between theory and reality had left her disorientated, out-of-sorts. She looked over. I held her gaze. She smiled. I smiled back. The bus came around the corner.

It skidded to a stop about three feet from the shelter, causing a wave of dirty water to slop up onto the curb. The doors slid open with a pneumatic hiss. We clambered on board. Noisily, the driver gunned the engine and we headed off into the night, surrounded by the odd, uncomfortable bustle of disparate strangers trying to make their way home.

The next day I was surprised to find her take a seat beside me. I shuffled up to make room and pulled my headphones away from my ears, unsure of her intentions. I glanced over. She was smiling at me expectantly, wanting to talk.

"What are you listening to?" Her voice was soft and sugary, perfect.

"The Throwing Muses."

"I love their *University* album."

"Really?"

"Yeah, I've got it at home somewhere. Haven't listened to it in years though. Too busy with, well…" She indicated her reading.

I smiled. "I know that feeling." I rubbed my hand over my chin, the rough, unshaven bristles like sandpaper against my palm.

"Sometimes it just feels like the whole world is conspiring against you, and you only wish you could step back for a moment to take a breath."

I stared at her for what seemed like an age. "Do you fancy a drink?"

The pub was cozy and out of the way. Snowflakes spattered on the windowpanes, rolling across the wet glass like tiny beads. An open fire flickered in the grate, casting dark shadows across the faces of the other patrons, exposing their sinister sides to anyone who cared to look. Couples whispered to one another in hushed tones. I spilt her drink.

"I'm so sorry. I'll just get you another."

"No, please, let me."

"No, really."

We laughed at our awkwardness. I bought the drink.

Later, when I thought she wouldn't notice, I watched her breathing, the little bird-like fluttering in her chest as she formed her words, the gentle pursing of her lips as she exhaled. I was exhilarated. She caught me watching and smiled at me inquisitively. I looked away, embarrassed. Her blue eyes flashed with amusement.

It wasn't long before we found ourselves back at my place.

I never got past putting the kettle on. We tugged at each other's clothes, awkward and still unfamiliar. She wrestled me to the ground amongst a pile of magazines and old wrappers, planting kisses over my face and hands. I followed the contours of her delicate body with my fingertips, enjoying the curve of her hips, cupping her small, round breasts in my palms. Her skin was warm and soft and smooth.

Quietly, gently, her lower lip clasped tightly between her teeth, she reached down and pulled me inside her.

In the morning I woke to find she had gone. A little yellow Post-it note was stuck to the alarm clock, flapping gently in the draught from the half-open window. Light filtered through in hazy streams, picking out the dust motes that swirled and danced in the air all around me. I reached over and tugged at the message. It came away in my hand.

Tomorrow night, 56 Westbrook Ave, 8pm
Isabella xxx

I smiled to myself and clambered out of bed. I could hardly wait.

Fifty-six Westbrook Avenue was a crumbling old Victorian townhouse; enormous, with large red steps leading up to the front door and a little iron railing that ran parallel to the road. Inside the front yard, huge leaves flapped like elephant's ears in the cold breeze and moss poked up inquisitively through the cracks between the paving slabs. A lamp glowed dimly from behind the curtains in the downstairs living room. I rapped the knocker briskly and drew my coat up around my neck to fight off the chill.

After a few moments the door creaked open and Isabella was smiling at me from within. The sight of her face filled me with a sudden sense of well-being and relief.

"Hi."

"Hi."

I handed her my coat and struggled to find something to say as she hung it over the banister. A tall grandfather clock ticked ominously in the corner. "Nice place. How was your day? Isn't it cold tonight?" I mumbled incoherently.

Isabella laughed, and, stepping closer, touched her finger against my lips. I relented. Her face gleamed in the low light of the hallway. I took that face in my hands and kissed it. Twice.

Afterwards, she clasped my hand tightly between her own and led the way to the dining room. Candles spluttered, arranged in a random fashion upon the large table. The flickering shadows they cast on the walls and ceiling reminded me of tiny butterflies darting to and fro, dancing in myriad patterns and shapes.

She handed me two glasses and smiled.

I cut my hand opening the bottle of wine.

"Bugger!"

"Oh, I am sorry, have you...?" She never finished her sentence, but took my proffered hand and held it still for a moment. Tiny beads of red blood swelled to the surface of my fingertip before trickling down across the back of my knuckles in little tributaries. I shifted slightly to stop them from dripping. Isabella had a strange look in her eyes. I wondered for a moment if she was exasperated with my constant clumsiness around her.

"Stay there for one second." She dashed out of the room. The blood felt warm and sticky against my skin.

"Here you go." I heard her voice from around the doorway before I saw her hurry back into the room. She held out a swab of cotton wool and I took it gratefully, dabbing at my sticky hand. She kissed me sympathetically on the cheek.

After I had finished she took the cotton wool and showed me to the bathroom. The old stairs creaked and heaved as I presented them with my weight. I rinsed my hands and found a plaster in the mirrored cabinet that hung on the wall above the sink. I rubbed some of the cold water over my face, judging my reflection in the mirror. I felt like a buffoon.

Isabella's towels were flung haphazardly over a chrome rail that ran along one wall; they were soft and pink and smelled of her. Cursing myself for being so clumsy, I dabbed myself dry and found my way back down to the dining room.

Later that night, as we lay together in bed, warmed by the soft glow of candles and each other, she stroked my hand as if to apologize for the violation of the broken glass. I held my breath and listened to the sound of cars passing beneath her window, to her gentle exhalations as she quietly fell asleep. Just then, at that point, the future seemed so welcoming; a bright, exhilarating place filled with opportunity and promise.

The next week I borrowed my brother's car—an old, blue Ford Fiesta with patches of powdery rust over each of the wheel arches—and drove us up to Whitby. We stopped on the way by a quiet patch of moorland and bought an ice cream from the back of a makeshift stall. The old man behind the hatch had smiled at us warmly, and Isabella, trying to catch each tiny tributary of melted vanilla as it ran down the side of her cone, managed to end up with smears of it all over her chin. She drew herself up to me and laughed, trying in vain to keep a straight face. As I wiped her clean with the edge of my thumb, her eyes shone, and I think I'd never felt so happy. Her fingers trailed in mine as we made our way back to the car, the man on the ice-cream stall watching us, amusement flashing in his eyes.

We arrived in Whitby just after noon; I swung the Fiesta into a car park immediately outside the town centre and we walked in along the water's edge. We ate fish and chips on the docks, sitting on little benches and huddled against the spray, and watched the fisherman unloading their hauls in large crates full of ice and silvery scales. Isabella pointed to the Abbey high on the cliff top, sticking out against the horizon like a jagged, broken tooth. It seemed ominous to me, a brooding ruin facing out toward the sea, warding away all unwanted visitors.

After lunch she dragged me into a little bookshop next door to an amusement arcade.

"Come on. I have to get a souvenir!"

I sighed theatrically but was disarmed by her childlike glee.

Isabella bought a copy of *Dracula*; the elderly woman behind the counter looked expectant and tired, as if worn down by the constant repetition of her day. She perked up for a moment when I asked her for a copy of *Titus Groan*, but then sighed and shook her head.

"We're not that type of bookshop, honey."

Isabella hurried me out of the door, her book rustling in its brown paper bag.

"Now for the beach!"

We made our way down to the seafront for a walk. It was quiet with just a handful of children playing amongst the rock pools, searching for crabs or other monsters left behind by the retreating sea. Isabella kicked her shoes off to run in the sand and I watched her dance, the breeze coming in off the water to whip her hair up around her face. I couldn't stop myself from smiling. I couldn't believe my own luck.

The drive home took three hours and Isabella fell asleep in the passenger seat.

It started to rain and the windscreen wipers on the old Fiesta creaked and moaned like a metronome as we made our way along empty roads, the twilight and the misty rain leaving me with the impression that we were driving through our own private universe, a pocket world of our own devising.

When we finally pulled up outside her house, I shook her gently awake. She unbuckled her seatbelt and sleepily nuzzled my shoulder. Her hair smelled of vanilla.

"Is it still raining?"

"No, it stopped about half an hour ago."

"I've had a lovely day. Thank you." She planted a kiss on my cheek.

"Go on, go and get yourself some sleep. Call me."

She clambered out of the passenger seat, her bag slung easily over one shoulder, and made her way up the little red steps at the front of her house. She stood and waved from her front door as I pulled away, the car radio blaring an old, fuzzy version of The Who's "My Generation."

The following weeks passed by in a heady frenzy of conversation, laughter and sex. Basking in each other's company, we spent all our free time together. We took trips to visit old country houses, shared secret laughter in the solemnity of a portrait gallery, ate greasy pizzas at her favorite fast food restaurant, had rough sex up against a tree in her childhood park. We strolled the streets together long after midnight, watching the patrons stumbling out of the clubs, vibrantly alive in the neon glow of the city. We took a slow walk by the riverside, our fingers and hearts entwined, the rain thrumming down all around us, hiding us behind its thin veil, secreting us away from the outside world. Our orbits changed; we circled each other like gravity wouldn't let us come apart. I had time for nothing else in my life.

It was during those days that I often found her working, hunched over her microscope in the little laboratory at the back of her house, or else receiving samples through the post, tiny vials of red blood that she would set to work on immediately, decoding their new enigma, solving their puzzle as if it meant she were saving the world. She threw herself into her work as though it somehow redeemed her, made her whole. For my part, I was due to start lecturing again at the nearby college and so, after nearly a month of living in each other's pockets, it was with a heavy heart that I retired to my flat on the other side of town to begin preparatory work for the course. I found it difficult to concentrate on Shakespeare, though, when every word reminded me of Isabella, every passing car made me think of those long hours spent lying beside her in her bed, every song on the radio somehow relevant to how I felt. She was a siren, and I was the sailor caught up in her spell.

Three days later I received a call.

"Can you come round?"

"What, now? I thought you were working?"

"I'm finished. Look, I have a present for you." She sounded nervous, full of energy.

I laughed. "In that case I'll be round in twenty minutes."

In truth, it was nearer to an hour. The bus was late, and I shivered underneath the shelter, my only company a squat, grey pigeon that fluttered about the street pecking at abandoned cigarette ends.

When the bus finally arrived it was empty. I took a seat toward the front, pushing myself up against the window. Dirty rainwater lined the rubber seals around the window frame where the edges had perished. I shifted to avoid getting wet. Moments later, a man hopped up onto the platform with two small boys in tow. I watched them push and pull at each other's clothes as their father dropped his change into the ticket machine.

"Won't be a tick, I've got the change in here somewhere." He fished around in the pocket of his jeans and then fed some more money into the machine. One of the boys pushed the other onto the floor. The man pretended not to notice. He hesitated for a moment, and then the ticket machine emitted a stream of gaudy paper.

"Come on, get up off the floor! We've got to go and find a seat."

I closed my eyes and tried to pretend I was asleep.

The boys hurtled up the stairs faster than their father could keep up; I could hear their feet pounding on the upper deck, the sound of it creaking underneath their weight. And then: "Pack that in! Now stop that!"

The bus rolled slowly away from the pavement, the driver gunning the engine to try to stir some life from the ancient machine.

A few minutes later, we pulled up by a stop a couple of doors down the street from Isabella's house. As I clambered down from the bus and gave my thanks to the driver, I caught sight of Isabella peering out from behind the curtains of her living room window. I smiled and waved. She pressed her hand against the glass in brief acknowledgment, then disappeared from view. I made my way quickly along the road, passing the dreary façades of old houses which seemed to loom out at me like tired, care-worn faces. My breath steamed in front of my face in the cold. I had the feeling it was going to rain again.

Moments later, I tried the handle of Isabella's front door and found it was already open. I stepped inside and drew myself into the warmth, rubbing my hands together to restart my circulation.

The house seemed quiet. "Hello?"

"I'm in the back, come on through."

I slipped out of my overcoat and dropped it over the arm of the rickety old chair that served as Isabella's telephone seat, then made my way through to the rear of the house, passing through the dining room on my way to the kitchen. There was a lingering odor, like scented-candles that had long since burned themselves out to leave a cloying, opium-like quality to the air.

Isabella was standing in the kitchen doorway, her lab coat draped around her shoulders, her hair tied back severely from her face. She looked up as I came into the room and smiled at me coyly. I moved to step forward and embrace her. Laughing, she turned about deftly on her heel and disappeared through the side door into the other room.

Her voice trailed behind her. "I've been working in the lab. Come on in."

"I thought you had a present for me?"

"I do!"

"Well what..."

"Patience..."

I stepped into the laboratory, my nose bristling at the stench of formaldehyde and bleach. Isabella had her back to me, fiddling with something in a refrigeration unit on the back wall. I admit I'd found it odd that someone so clearly talented, with such a demanding specialization, would work from home, but times continued to change and, with technology developing as it was, she'd been able to set up an entire cottage industry here in the northeast of England. Her little laboratory was an extension to her house, a small side room off the kitchen with gleaming clinical surfaces and banks of daunting computer equipment, their screens flickering in the stark glare of the overhead lights.

I fidgeted uncomfortably and glanced out of the window. Two tiny birds danced around each other on the lawn, fighting over a worm they had managed to extract from the flowerbed. I glanced back at Isabella.

"Isabella, can't you just explain...?"

"In a minute!"

I waited.

A few moments later she turned around to face me, smiling like she was about to reveal a secret, and ceremoniously placed a package on the table before me. I looked into her eyes, seeing myself reflected in their glassy surface, noticed how her lips were slightly parted, how the soft skin around her eyes seemed so smooth, so even, so perfect. I looked down at my present, already full of trepidation over what it might be.

It was a large plastic sachet filled with a dark red, gelatinous substance. Condensation beaded on its surface like rainwater on tarpaulin. Isabella rubbed her hands together nervously. I pulled a face.

"There."

"This is it?"

"Your present, yes."

"But what...?" I didn't know what to say, what it was supposed to represent.

"A pint of your blood."

"*My blood!*" I started, and then stuttered something incoherent. Isabella was smiling expectantly. I must have seemed confused. She pulled out a chair from behind one of her workbenches and guided me to sit down. I looked up at her, speechless.

"Remember when you cut yourself? Well, you know what it is that I do."

I shook my head. "Yes... but why?"

"It's not just a replica of your blood. It's been adapted, tinkered with... improved, I suppose. I've bonded the platelets with tiny nanomachines. They ride on the red blood cells, hitching a piggyback through your system. When the adrenaline in your bloodstream reaches a certain level they become active, triggering the pleasure receptors in your brain to generate a natural high. It's particularly effective during sex. Packets of this stuff fetch thousands of pounds on the black market. Yours even more so. O-Negative is fairly rare." She looked at me pointedly. "All we need to do is give you a small transfusion..."

I glanced back from Isabella's smiling face to the package on the table, then back again, incredulous. I felt violated, disgusted. Abruptly, I pushed myself up from the table, sending the chair skidding across the floor, and struggled past Isabella into the kitchen. The stench of the laboratory was beginning to make my head spin. I heard Isabella returning the chair to its rightful position by the door. I felt like I couldn't breathe, like I needed to get some air. I couldn't understand what she'd done.

It was only then, as I stood in the kitchen rubbing my face in my hands, that I realized I'd brought the sachet of blood along with me. It felt cold and damp against the warmth of my palm, the plasma inside it sloshing around like putrefying jelly. My stomach heaved. My mind went blank. Isabella was calling my name from the doorway. Something inside me snapped.

I reached out for one of the kitchen knives from the block upon the windowsill and pressed its serrated edge against the bag of blood in my fist. At first the plastic gave a little under the pressure, but then it burst with an expressive pop and showered the worktop with little red droplets, a patter of crimson rain. The smell of iron replaced the odor of bleach, and I almost retched as I drained the fluid away down the kitchen sink, watched it swirl and gurgle as it was swallowed by the hungry maw of the drain. Isabella stood expressionless throughout.

Now, when I look back on those moments with the clarity of hindsight, I can't help thinking that a small part of me was also washed away down that hole in the sink, that this one simple act has come to define me, to set out who I am. It is as if, by committing this transgression, this spurious rejection of my own bodily fluid, I displayed my frailties to the world and embarked on a course from which there would be no return, stumbling down one route without properly considering another.

I had turned to Isabella, angry, emotional and unsure of myself, the hairs on the back of my arms matted with speckles of my own blood. I didn't know what to say, or how to give voice to my feelings of violation. I didn't know how to tell her I still loved her, still wanted and needed her, still clamored to hold her and tell her everything was going to be okay. I simply stared at her, my hands covered in blood.

She hung her head, refusing to look up, as if she couldn't bear to meet my eyes. As if she were judging me, like I'd let her down in some way. As if everything was my fault, that I'd failed some obscure test she'd prepared for me. As if something had broken between us that could never be repaired.

She uttered only one further word, which seemed to stick in her throat as she spoke it: "Go."

It was terrifyingly firm and hollow.

I could do or say nothing more. I left.

It took me a further two days to pick up the telephone.

"Hi. Isabella? It's me." I offered hesitantly to the receiver. I could hear her breathing softly in the background and thought of her as she had been when we had lain together in bed, listening quietly to the cars rolling by in the street below.

"Isabella? Hello?"

I was met with only the bubbling sound of static as she returned her handset to the cradle.

A week later, as I lay half asleep on the sofa, a bottle of cheap Italian wine drained and empty by my feet, I thought I heard the sound of someone rapping on my door. I hesitated, and by the time I made my way along the hall and pulled drunkenly at the latch, they had gone. A gust of frigid air swirled in and hit me like a wall; I felt dizzy and inebriated and returned myself to my makeshift bed.

The next morning I convinced myself it had been her. I resolved to lay my hands on the Fiesta and drive round that afternoon, to apologize for my reaction and explain that I had misunderstood her intentions; that I had failed to appreciate the implied intimacy and trust in her gesture. I still felt uncomfortable, violated, even, but felt also that I'd come to an understanding of Isabella and her emotional needs. Blood was her livelihood, her *life*. By rejecting her gift of blood I was, in essence, rejecting *her*, rejecting everything she stood for. By the same token, if I could only make her see why *I* had reacted the way I did…. I played the scenario over and over again in my mind's eye, saw her reaction in a thousand different ways. In some of my fantasies she embraced me earnestly as soon as I stepped through the door, having been through a similar revelatory process, the whole sorry affair helping us to achieve an even greater level of intimacy than before. In others she would look at me awkwardly, chewing her bottom lip and taking her time to come round as I offered her platitudes, before the curl of her lips would betray her true feelings and she would jump to her feet, laughing brightly, clasping my hand and dragging me off to the bedroom where transfusions were unnecessary and the exchange of bodily fluid came in forms less macabre and indecipherable. At the time I had no idea which — if any — of these myriad scenarios would come to pass yet, regardless, I knew I had to find out.

I took a shower, and then afterwards sat for nearly half an hour on the edge of the bath, drying in the cool draught from the open window. I cut myself shaving, and laughed at the sheer irony as blood spattered stark against the white porcelain of the sink. It seemed almost obscene that something as vital as blood could run so freely, so easily, and that at the same time was so easy to re-engineer, to tinker with, to reconstruct.

I put the thought out of mind as I attempted to gather myself in preparation for the afternoon's encounter.

It was with a knot tied firmly in the pit of my stomach that I drew the car up to the curb alongside Isabella's house later that afternoon. In my mind I ran through the events as I had planned them, and appraised myself in the rearview mirror. I felt tired and anxious. I had no idea how she was going to react.

I sat there for a while, willing myself to get out of the car and walk slowly up the path toward her house, to mount the little red steps and rap confidently on the door. There was no sign of her at any of the windows. I waited.

Finally, I got out of the car, slamming the door shut behind me. I could have been any pre-pubescent schoolboy or condemned man; my heart was hammering wildly in my chest and my palms were clammy with sweat. I knew it was foolish to feel so nervous, but in confronting

Isabella I also knew that I was bringing the situation to a head. Whilst the words were left unspoken there was still a chance that everything could be redeemed; once she opened the door there was no turning back, and all the answers would be revealed.

I brushed myself down and made my way slowly up the steps to the door. I cleared my throat and then rapped the knocker. Standing back, running my fingers nervously through my hair, I took deep breaths and shuffled my feet on the top step.

There was no reply.

I waited for a moment longer, and then tried again. A minute passed like an hour. I peered through the curtains into the living room. It was empty, the TV switched off, a plate of half-eaten food on the floor by the sofa. It looked like the debris of a microwaved lasagna. A magazine lay open on the windowsill. I could just make out the headline at the top of the article, printed on cheap paper in large, lurid fonts: "One Hundred Ways to Impress Your Man!" I shook my head, feeling a brief pang of remorse.

When I was sure that nobody was going to answer, I decided to try the handle. To my surprise, it turned in my hand. The door creaked open with an expectant sigh. I peered into the hallway. There was no sign of Isabella.

"Hello?"

No response.

"Isabella? It's me. Can I come in?"

The silence was eerie, like an absence of something familiar punctuated only by the measured ticking of her old grandfather clock, monotonously counting away the seconds, crawling steadily toward the future. I wondered if she'd gone out and accidentally forgotten to lock the door. Feeling awkward and uninvited, I slipped inside, clicking the door shut behind me.

"Isabella? Are you home?"

Nothing.

Unsure what else to do, I decided to see if she was working in the lab at the back of the house where she may not have heard me come in. I made my way down the hall, through the dining room and into the kitchen. There was a smell of over-ripe fruit and burnt toast. I felt a sharp stab of guilt at the sight of the kitchen sink, this time full of dirty pots and pans, as if I were a criminal returning to the scene of his crime. I called her name again, just to be sure. This time I heard a sound of movement from within the laboratory. My heart lurched.

"Isabella?"

The door between the two rooms cracked open a few inches and suddenly she was peering out at me from around the edge of the frame.

"Oh."

I stepped closer. She opened the door a little wider.

She looked disheveled, in disarray. Her hair was unkempt and her clothes were crumpled as if she'd been wearing them for a number of days. There was a disturbing, almost forlorn look in her eyes and her face was drawn and pale, pasty, even. She looked tired, unraveled, as if she were starting to come apart at the seams. I had to fight the urge to suddenly gather her up in my arms and hold her, to try to save her from the world, from herself. Behind her, the laboratory was a riot of noise: the sound of a pump, gurgling with fluid; a printer spewing out a data file; a radio insistently hammering out an unfamiliar dance tune. I understood why she hadn't heard me calling her name from down the hall.

I tried to get her attention, but she seemed distracted, keen to get back to the lab, or to get away from me.

"How have you been?"

She shrugged. "Okay." Her eyes flicked back and forth nervously as though it made her uncomfortable to look me in the eye.

"Look, can we go somewhere to talk?"

Her reply was drowned out by the insistent droning of the pump from the other room. I pushed on the door, trying to see over her shoulder. I raised my voice above the clamor. "What *are* you doing in there...?"

Isabella shuffled awkwardly, blocking my view. "No. Not now." Her voice was firm. I realized she was responding to the first of my questions. "You need to go."

I wasn't sure what to do, what to say. I reached out to put a hand on her shoulder, to try to reassure her that I only wanted to make things right between us, but she winced and twisted away from me as if the simple act of me touching her was enough to cause her pain. Her elbow struck the door as she shifted around and it bounced open, banging loudly as it clattered against the wall. I caught a view of the inside of the lab. A naked male corpse was lying prone on a trolley in the centre of the room, wired up to a host of elaborate medical machinery. Cables snaked from the man's chest in a web-work of plumbing and bags of unidentifiable fluid hung on intravenous drips from a metal framework over the bed. It looked like a scene from a cheap horror movie; the workshop of a latter-day Frankenstein, a crazed scientist in the process of creating a monster. I pushed past Isabella, forcing my way into the room. Electric light gave everything a clean, clinical sheen. The radio continued to hiss with the pounding of drums and static.

"What the hell?"

The pump was thumping noisily as it sucked blood from the body, feeding it through long coils of piping. I could see it sloshing into a large glass bottle by the foot of the trolley red and dark and syrupy.

I wheeled on Isabella, confused and a little scared. "Where did you get a human corpse?"

She stared at me, a stern, emotionless expression on her face. "It's not a *corpse*."

I looked again. The body, although emaciated, was still breathing, its chest rising and falling to a slow, soft rhythm, in time with the labored wheezing of the apparatus that was slowly alleviating it of its lifeblood.

She shifted closer. Her voice was gentle in my ear. Her breath felt warm against my cheek. "Look closer." And more quietly — "It's you."

I gazed down in abstract horror at the man lying on the trolley before me. It was true. He had my face.

For a moment everything seemed to stop. The noise was gone; replaced only by the roar of blood rushing through my ears. I stared down at the body before me in grim fascination. His eyes were closed, his face unshaven and covered in a burr of fine black bristles. He had the same long, equine nose and the same square chin that faced me in the mirror every morning. Yet he was thin, painfully so. His cheeks were hollow and drawn and his ribcage was clearly visible through his translucent, papery skin. His lips were dry and cracked. It was clear he was both severely undernourished and dehydrated. His blood was flowing freely through the fat tubing, sloshing into the glass demijohn with every beat of his weak heart, assisted by the pump that was inexorably drawing him closer to his death. I wanted to feel sick but, instead, I felt simply numb. He wasn't me, *couldn't be me*, but he was a *part* of me, somehow.

I turned to Isabella, unable to speak. She could see the question in my eyes. She took a moment to fiddle with the volume on the radio, then turned to me and began to explain.

"Accelerated cloning." She shrugged, her face still an emotionless mask, unreadable. She hesitated and I thought for a moment that she wasn't going to continue. I think she was as numb as I was, shocked by the confrontation, the need to relive everything all at once. Then: "I grew him when I thought you weren't coming back." A pause. "I wanted to be close to you. I *needed* to be close to you." It sounded like she was pleading for forgiveness. I couldn't believe her, couldn't understand how she could do this, how she could go to these incredible lengths. I shook my head.

"Then why this?" I waved at the jar of blood on the floor and the tubing coming out of the man's—out of *my*—chest. My voice was a hoarse whisper. "Why?"

"It didn't work. He's got no mind. He's not you. He's just a body, a bag of blood and bones. I didn't know what to do." I realized now that she was weeping, tears running in sparkling tributaries down her cheeks, splashing her clothes. "And then it hit me. O-Negative blood. Anyone can take a transfusion of O-Negative blood. If I drained him I could sell it on, make a fortune. I'd already seeded him with nanomachines, the moment he was fully formed. All I had to do was bag it up..." She sobbed, coughing back on the tears. I think my face must have betrayed my horror, my judgment. "*What else could I do!*" She broke down, collapsing to her knees, her face in her hands.

I looked back at the body on the table before me. "It was never me, Isabella. It never could have been." And then I did the only thing I could. I couldn't let it live like this. I grabbed for an implement from a nearby tray—a sharp, surgical scalpel—and thrust it deep into his throat. It was soft and offered little resistance. The body shuddered and began to spasm, but his eyes remained closed and no sound escaped his lips. I pulled the scalpel out and thrust again, channeling all my anger, my frustration, my fear into those blows.

"*No!*"

I heard Isabella scream behind me and turned, realizing too late that she was rushing me from across the room. She fell against me hard, sending us both sprawling to the floor. I jarred my elbow sharply on the trolley and cracked my head against the tiles.

For a moment, the world turned upside down. I lay there, dazed, the pressure of Isabella on top of me like a dead weight. My head was spinning with pain. I tried to speak, but the weight of her on my chest made it difficult to breathe. Gasping, I pulled my arms free, then pushed her to one side, before rolling over and scrabbling up onto my knees.

"Isabella? Are you okay?"

She was still, unconscious. Her hair had spilled out across the floor and her face looked slack and peaceful, all the tension, the concern, the confusion drained out of her. I blinked, trying to get my bearings. One of the medical monitors was screaming, a howling alarm to warn us that the man on the trolley had arrested, his heart failing, the remaining blood draining out through the gaping hole in his throat. I turned to Isabella; shook her gently to rouse her. She remained still. Confused, I looked her up and down. Then I saw it: the scalpel sticking out of her chest, surrounded by a growing Mandelbrot of blood. It was stark and red against the clean white of her lab coat. The knife had struck her straight through the heart, like a stake, so forceful in the fall that it had buried itself almost halfway along its shaft. I fumbled, unsure whether to pull it out or not. My mind went completely blank. I became aware of a terrible, animal keening sound and, for a moment, thought the clone on the trolley was still alive before I realized that the sound was coming from me.

I gathered Isabella up in my arms, rocking her from side to side, telling her everything was going to be okay. Only, in truth, I knew that was not the case. She was already dead, and, in more ways than one, so was I.

There was no panic, no call to the police. For some time I sat with Isabella, the world in tattered shreds around me, the red ruin of the laboratory and the spilt blood a mockery of everything her life had been. I couldn't forgive her for what she'd done to me, her strange, exotic form of vampirism. She had taken the very essence of what I was and toyed with it, made it something alien, turned it into something it was never intended to be. But all the same, I never wanted *this*. I smoothed her hair back from her face, closed her eyelids with my fingertips.

After a while, sitting there in stunned silence, the sounds of the medical equipment still loud and insistent around me, my remorse began to give way to a strange kind of shocked relief. There was a sense of peace, of closure. It was over. At least, this way, I had my answer.

In a haze, still numb from the shock, I took the corpse from the trolley, disconnecting the myriad pipes and wires, and laid it beside her on the laboratory floor. Then, after cleaning myself up as best I could, I fled the house, leaving the two of them together, peaceful, as if sleeping. I hoped they were happy in their dreams.

Outside, night had fallen and the world existed only in the impassionate glow of the streetlamps. I made my way back to the car. Behind me, the house was silent, still.

I dropped my jacket onto the passenger seat, running a hand over my face. I clambered into the driver's seat. My heart was pounding in my chest. I looked back at the house, thinking of her there, in the lab, her eyes tired and glazed, her smile fixed and unmoving. It was as if there had been only one inevitable outcome of our dark and passionate affair, only one possible resolution, and there had been nothing I could have done to stop it. Now, finally, it was over.

I knew the police wouldn't come looking for me; as far as their forensic tests would show, I was dead, lying on the floor beside my lover, murdered in bizarre circumstances, in a strange laboratory at the back of an old house. The clone and I had changed places, adopted each other's roles. Now, like him, I was new to the world. A world without Isabella. Somehow I had to find my place in it, had to start again. I had no idea where to even begin.

I turned over the car engine and crawled slowly away from the curb. I could hear Isabella's voice, echoing around in my thoughts:

"Sometimes it just feels like the whole world is conspiring against you, and you only wish you could step back for a moment to take a breath."

A moment later, I flashed the car headlamps at a pedestrian making his lonely way home, and moved off into the anonymity of the night.

SCENTING THE DARK

MARY ROBINETTE KOWAL

Lifting the stopper from the vial to his nose, Penn inhaled slowly. Against the neutral backdrop of his ship's cleanroom, he picked out aromas of quince, elderberry, and bright Martian soil that hinted of blood, with undercurrents of cinnamon and Zeta Epsilon's fragrantly sweet longgrass. He sighed, blowing the scents out again. The perfume was still out of balance.

The boarding chime rang, letting him know that Madison had returned. The round tones resonated off the glass labware and sent vibrations across his scalp as it slowly, slowly faded. God, it was gorgeous—picking up the temple bell when they were on Mosholu had been one of his better choices. He'd eventually get the whole ship converted to real things instead of all the virtual hoo-ha it came with. Well, maybe not the whole ship; the skip drive had to exist in quantum state, but by God, the controls at least were made out of real ebony and brass.

The intercom buzzed and Madison's honeyed voice came over the wires, "Hey there, Mr. Man. Got a surprise for you."

"A musk lion?"

"Maybe. Maybe not. Come on out."

"I anticipate the pleasure of your discovery." He slid his left hand forward until he found the wire stand that held his work trials. His fingers followed the trail of braided metal up to the smooth glass vial. He slipped the stopper into it with practiced ease.

With one hand touching the stainless steel work bench, Penn paced the distance to the cleanroom's door. Opening it brought a chaotic swirl of scents containing the dark mineral oils that lubricated the doors, and the green plants grown to filter the air, and dog and... something else. Something new. Penn lifted his head, scenting in anticipation. Madison, that tease... she must have found a musk lion.

The boarding chime rang again. Maybe more than one. Good.

"Cody?" He held his left hand down while the tick-tick-tick of claws hurried to his side. Cody thrust her damp nose into Penn's hand, and licked once with her warm tongue before sliding forward into working position.

Penn fondled his dog's silky ears, as she slipped past to bring the harness under his hand. The leather handle was warm where it had lain against Cody's back.

"Airlock."

Without hesitation, Cody led him down the hall, her shaggy tail beating against the back of Penn's legs. Truth be told, even if his blindness were repairable, he would be hard pressed to give up his dog. She was a real lady. Not like a machine or electrodes in his brain. Loyal and true. Hell's bells. The fool dog was so excited to be working that Penn didn't even have the heart to let on that he knew the ship well enough to find his way to the airlock without help.

The new scent was so rich. Pungent with sexual intensity and spices that only flirted with the familiar. Penn quickened his pace; his clients would pay top dollar for a perfume with this. "Smell that, Cody? That's why parfumiers like Lenox will never rise to the sublime. Synthetics. Feh. Any Joe with a copier can make a fake." That's why he did expeditions to new worlds before they were opened for colonization. Hitting the market with a unique ingredient guaranteed that he maintained the top position in his field.

Around the corner, something heavy scraped against the metal deck of the ship. Penn had wanted oak floors, but had to concede that they would not survive the heavy traffic through the boarding area. The thing, probably a cage, held something that squealed with a high rough voice. "Sounds like Madison had a successful expedition, eh, Cody?"

She whined in response.

The new aroma was definitely coming from the boarding area. It was mixed with the more familiar smells of Cody and the salty tang of Madison, but even with those distractions, the spicy musk begged him to breathe deeper and absorb the aroma into his pores.

As they neared the boarding area, Cody hesitated.

The boarding chime rang a third time and with it came a dry hissing, like sand blown across the steel floor. Cody flinched again. Then stopped.

"It's all right, lady."

She whined.

"Cody, forward!" He fumbled, searching for her head with his free hand. Cody trembled and shifted. What had gotten into her? He smoothed the fur on her ruff. "C'mon, lady. You're on duty."

The air in the corridor shifted and brought a smell like blood and offal. Sweat suddenly beaded under his arms and ran down his ribcage. "Madison?"

Somewhere in front of him, the musk lion squealed once as if in answer to his call. Penn gripped Cody's harness tighter. "Find Madison."

For a moment, Cody did not move. Penn's mouth dried; if she refused to work.... She huffed—not quite a bark—and stepped forward. Hugging the wall, Cody led him down the corridor to the boarding area.

The cage rattled and an animal raged in a high chattering voice. From the cage came the heavy spice of alien musk. Despite its intrigue, Penn found himself holding his breath.

Cody whined as they crossed the threshold into the airlock but did not falter. The altar bell chimed their departure.

On the ramp outside, warmth bathed Penn telling him that the sun was out. The dissonance of what passed for birdsong on this planet had stilled. Wind hissed in his ears, walling him in with white noise. At the end of the ramp, Cody led him across a spongy, uneven surface. The wind pushed him as if it were a bully on the playground, teasing the blind kid.

Cody did not take him far from the ship—only nine paces—before she came to a dead halt. "Madison?" The wind tossed his aide's name aside.

Under his grip, Cody hunkered into a crouch. Stiff and beginning to shake, Penn knelt with her, reaching out with his free hand. The ground was soft with thick short fronds like a living shag carpet—the moss Madison had described when they'd first landed. He slid his hand forward until it met cloth.

Startled, he pulled back for a moment before reaching forward again. Quickly now, he recognized Madison's arm and slid down it to grip her hand. Warm and sticky with what must be blood, it lay unresponsive in his grasp. "Hang in there. I'm here."

Penn toggled his communicator to call for emergency services. Flat tones confirmed his request, but he was so far out from a settled world it might be weeks before his call was answered.

But his ship was only nine paces away. He could find his way without holding onto Cody, so enabling him to carry Madison.

It wasn't that far.

Penn inhaled to steady his nerve and almost choked as the wind shifted to blow from his front. Something rank and wet with blood and urine lay along the wind's path. Penn squeezed Madison's hand again. "We'll take care of you."

He let go of Cody's harness.

Using Madison's arm as a guide, he slid his hand up to her shoulder. Raw wet meat filled the top of her sleeve, then nothing. Penn jerked his hands away.

He fell back on his rump, retching. Something warm and moist touched his face. Penn screamed and slapped out, slamming into familiar fur. Cody yelped.

"Oh God. Cody, I'm sorry. Sweet lady, I'm sorry, I'm sorry." He reached for her, sobbing with relief when she came to him. Penn folded his arms around her and buried his face in her soft coat. Clinging to her, he rocked back and forth.

Madison's hand had still been warm, which meant it hadn't been removed long ago, which meant she might be alive and needing him. His mind shied away from the likelihood that Madison had already bled to death. It hadn't been more than five minutes since the boarding chime had rung and — "Bloody hell."

He was on an open plain. Even if Madison hadn't described the place when they landed, the strong breeze and unfiltered sunlight should have told him.

Whatever had killed her was probably still in line of sight. Penn grabbed for Cody's harness. They had to get inside.

Halfway to his feet, Penn stopped. What if the thing hadn't spotted him because he was kneeling? He listened, trying to hear anything past the sound of his own heart and the wind. It carried nothing but scent: moist, verdant moss; the heavy under notes of loam and stone; when the wind shifted and flicked to come from in front of him, it brought the harsh sharp smell of urine mixed with blood.

The thing would be there.

Or perhaps not. Cody had not shied away. Maybe Madison lay ahead and Penn was about to abandon her.

He rubbed his thumb over the leather grip on Cody's harness. He would trust his dog. If she hesitated, even a little, they would go back to the ship.

"Cody, forward," he whispered, still half-crouched. His good dog led him smoothly ahead. Through her harness he felt no hesitation.

He sniffed, searching for where the scent was strongest. "Left," he whispered.

What could have done this? Not a musk lion—despite the ruff that gave them their name, they were no bigger than a capuchin monkey. The survey reports had said that there weren't any larger predators on this planet.

They had gone eleven paces when Cody slowed, then stopped. No matter in which direction the wind blew, the hard ammonia smell of urine stayed in Penn's nostrils. He crouched again, braced this time for what his hands might find.

He patted across the soft moss until he touched cloth, coarse twill, Madison's trousers. Her leg beneath was warm. Penn followed the line of her thigh up. The material was soaked. Blood? His hands followed the topography of her body, sinking into valleys of savagery. Gashes carved out of her hip. When his hand touched the broken end of a rib, it moved.

A shallow gasp.

"Praise the saints. Hold on, Madison." Penn pulled his shirt off and wrapped it around her. The wind moved over his bare torso like dozens of tiny cold fingers.

He tied the sleeves around her chest and slid both hands under her. He fixed the location of the ship in his mind. All he had to do was retrace his steps.

Eleven paces, then turn slightly and take nine more. He could do this.

Penn pushed to his feet. Clutching Madison to his chest, he turned to his right. That was far enough. Wasn't it?

He slid his foot forward over the spongy ground. One. Setting his weight, he stepped again. Two. Wait. He had been crouching when he came this way, so his stride had been shorter. He wanted Cody's grip in his hand. She would take him back to the ship. Penn licked his lips. It was a decent-sized ship and he hadn't gone that far. Worst case scenario, he'd run into the side of it and have to follow it around to the ramp.

The spreading dampness in the shirt wrapped around Madison reminded him that there were other far worse scenarios. He had to take the shortest path back the ship.

Cody pressed against his left leg and Penn staggered a half-step to the right. He cursed and tried to correct for the misstep, but Cody was in his way. Fool dog was so used to working position that she wouldn't—

No. Fool man couldn't realize that she was herding him. His throat tightened. He would have cried if he'd owned a working set of tear ducts. "Good dog."

Her tail beat against the back of his leg.

"Take me home, Cody."

With her warm body pressed against his leg, Penn felt his way over the uneven ground. His arms burned under the strain of holding Madison. She had not made a sound and only that single gasped breath had told him that she was still alive.

His ankle twisted under him and Penn went down. His hip caught against Cody. As his knees jarred against the ground, Penn lost his grip on Madison. Pitching forward, one hand slammed into the moss, the other against Madison's leg.

She did not make a sound.

Holding his breath, Penn laid his head on her chest. Praying for a heartbeat he stayed bent over her, counting senselessly in his head as if the numbers might help. She lay under his ear without stirring. At one hundred and twenty-seven Penn sat up.

He pressed his hands against his face, digging his fingernails into his forehead. Madison was dead and he had no idea what had killed her. But, by God, he would have it found and shot. And as for the survey team that had somehow managed to miss a giant predator, every credit in his account would go to suing them to penury.

Cody put a paw on his knee and whined. Penn dropped his hands to reach for his dog. He gathered her to him, burying his fingers in her warm fur. She licked his face.

"Thanks, lady." Fondling her ears, Penn said, "Let's get back to the ship."

Gritting his teeth, he picked Madison up again. His right ankle sent a stab of pain up his leg, but he'd be damned if he was going to leave Madison's body out here for the thing. Cody took her place by his side and herded him back to the ship.

Every step jammed an ice pick into his ankle, but Penn Would Not Leave Madison. When his foot hit the bottom of the ramp, he almost fell again but caught himself with his good leg.

The ramp had never seemed so steep. At any moment Penn expected the thing to come charging out of nowhere and clamp its jaws around him. Or mandibles. Or whatever it had. Someone would pay for this.

The floor flattened out as Penn entered the airlock, and then he crossed the threshold into the ship. The altar bell chimed as if it were a prayer for Madison's soul. He had brought the stink of blood and shit into the boarding area with him, almost obliterating the scent of the musk lions. At least they had stopped yipping so he could hear the cleansing chime.

Without asking, his mind replayed the boarding chimes. Once: Madison had come in to set down the cage. Twice: She had gone back outside. Thrice.... She had never come back inside.

Cold sweat suddenly coated his bare torso. Penn swallowed. "Cody, go to my lab."

The scent of dead skunk, vomit and blood swept down the corridor from the bridge. With it, a sound like sand blowing across steel.

By his side, Cody growled.

They'd have to pass that corridor to get to his lab. No time. "Cody. Outside!"

She pressed harder against his side. Penn kicked her, desperate for her to flee. "Outside!"

The hissing came faster. Penn turned back the way he had come. Two steps and he tripped over Cody. He and Madison landed in a spatter of oily fur scented with sweet musk. The hissing became the sound of a thousand nails scraping across a blackboard.

Penn rolled over, pulling Madison's body on top of him. He screamed wordlessly. Moist, hot and rank with death, the thing's breath blasted him.

Madison's body was yanked out of his grasp. Cody snarled then barreled past him.

"Cody! No." Flailing, searching for anything he could use as a weapon, Penn got to his feet.

Everything in the boarding area was permanently bolted down. Except—

The fire extinguisher. Where was that?

Snarling and a roar like a steam train came from behind him. He had to get Cody away from that thing. Penn slid his hand across the wall to the right of the door until he found the cylinder bolted to the wall. Panting, he yanked the extinguisher free of its holder and fumbled for the nozzle.

Thumps sounded against the corridor's sides and Cody barked and snarled.

Staggering forward, Penn shoved the nozzle against the thing and squeezed, blasting it with freezing CO2. The cold air billowed around his hands. With a cry like a bandsaw, the thing jerked back.

"Cody! Let's go. Go!"

The blast of cold air stopped as the canister emptied. Penn swung the extinguisher wildly, praying that he wouldn't hit his dog.

With a thud, it connected with something. Cody was still growling, so Penn hit the thing again. Bashing it with one hand, he waved the other, searching for Cody where her growling was loudest. He touched a tuft of bristles so sharp they stung. Penn jerked his hand away.

"C'mon, lady. Leave it!" He had to get her away. Again he reached and his fingers sank into a wet, viscous mass. The creature screamed in rage and yanked back.

Then, soft familiar fur. He didn't know what part of Cody he'd grabbed. "On duty! On duty!"

He hauled backwards, falling as she suddenly moved to his side. Pushing back, he slid toward the boarding door and slammed into the wall.

"No!" He'd gotten turned around. Which way was the door? Cody would know. "Outside! Cody, outside."

The extinguisher shuddered in his hand and twisted away. Half crawling, he followed his dog.

His right calf went hot with pain. A flash of anguish painted his brain and a detached part thought, This must be what 'white' means.

Yelling, Penn kicked with his free leg. He struck something unyielding. He kicked again.

The thing loosened its grip on his leg. Penn jerked free, feeling his flesh rend on the thing's teeth. Falling, he felt the airlock threshold under his knees. The altar bell chimed as he crossed. Penn let go of Cody's harness to push himself up.

Cody barked. Her voice was hard and savage.

Penn slapped the door sensor. An eternity passed before it hissed shut. With a dull thud, it impacted on the thing. And then the damn safety made the door slide open. Cody's claws scraped the floor as she lunged toward the opening.

"Cody, stay!"

Penn threw himself on her and tried to get between Cody and the door. He slapped again at the control. She squirmed to get past him, snapping at the thing. "No! Fool dog!" He scrabbled to grab her by the scruff and threw her away from the door.

Teeth scraped his shoulder as he turned with the throw. Penn spun, shoving with both arms against a surface that was covered in bone and bristle.

Behind him, Cody yelped as she struck the far side of the airlock's wall. With strength he didn't know he had, Penn yelled, "On duty. Stay! STAY!"

The inner door of the airlock hissed shut, sealing off the smell of corpses, musk lion and the salty tang of Madison.

Penn swayed for a moment, expecting the thing to still be in front of him. He heard nothing but the wind from outside. He reached for the airlock door and slid his hand down the unyielding surface.

"My God." With a trembling hand, Penn wiped the sweat and blood from his face. "Cody. Cody, we're safe."

Penn steadied himself against the wall and sank to a crouch. "Come here you wonderful dog."

He waited for the tick, tick, tick of her claws to come to him. The wind dried the sweat on his back, chilling him. "Cody?"

He swallowed, remembering the yelp she had made when she'd hit the wall. "Cody, come here lady." Penn crawled forward, patting the floor with his hand.

Her claws ticked on the steel, moving away from him.

"Cody? Where you going?" Penn held his hand out, beckoning her.

She backed away again, leather harness creaking. Maybe she wanted him to get out of the airlock. Penn pushed to his feet and stepped forward, reaching for her harness.

Cody ran.

Outside, her claws scraped against the boarding ramp as she almost slid down it. Careening forward, Penn chased her. He didn't know what was behind them but, if it was enough to scare Cody, he would be dead if he stayed.

At the bottom of the ramp, he fell, knees mashing through the moss to the rocks beneath. The wind filled his hearing and he strained for some hint of Cody. To his right, a faint creak of leather skipped through the space in the breeze. Penn got to his feet and staggered toward it. He cursed every time his weight came down on his right foot. It threatened to fold under him.

"Cody?"

She huffed, not a bark, but a warning. She was more to his left. He followed the sound, sniffing.

"What's the matter, lady?" He inhaled deeply, trying to catch a whiff of where she was. The stench of the thing burned his nostrils. His bowels contracted as slow understanding seeped down. She was afraid of him. He smelled like the thing and he had hit her. Kicked her even. No wonder she wouldn't come. He'd told her to stay away from him.

The ground gave way. His ankle exploded with fresh pain and Penn pitched forward. The land rolled him over, carrying him down a shallow slope. He stopped on his back. For a moment, the wind did not fill his ears with its rush.

Beyond the shelter of the small hollow, Penn heard a hissing like a thousand fingers scraping across steel. Another one. Why had he thought that there would only be one on the planet? His heart kicked wildly at his ribs. He had to get back to the airlock. He could hide in there until help came.

Except—the fall. He'd gotten turned around. He didn't know where the ship was.

Penn sat up carefully, and the hissing disappeared into the rush of wind. The thing could be anywhere.

Sinking back down so he could hear again, Penn shivered. The hissing was louder. Penn sniffed the air, searching for the scent of dog. He whispered, "Cody? On duty. On duty..."

THE LIMB KNITTER

STEVEN FRANCIS MURPHY

With a spade in one hand and a burlap sack in the other, the Limb Knitter dug for trench tubers in the Beaten Zone as the early morning rain gave way to a foggy Western dawn. Down on her belly in the mud between the Invaders to her South and Forces Velaysia to her North, she found the pickings pretty slim. She gave up poking at the mud for a moment and looked toward her lines.

Spring filled the lower elevations on the southern face of the Canarus Ranges, sowing the valleys and slopes behind the trenches in emerald foliage. From the gates of the mountain redoubts of Forces Velaysia, the Limb Knitter caught sight of the Brigades Invalid, on the march with their machines to stiffen the mere flesh and bone Frontists of the Brigades Defender along the Southern Front. Mixed in amid the rusty, black bipeds were the Invalid Harvesters, their bodies whitewashed to prevent friendly fire and their backs burdened with empty harvest drums.

No more trench tubers for a while, the Knitter told herself. Her two stomachs rumbled in agreement. She was sick of digging for the tasteless, decayed bits anyway.

The Knitter could see all of this through the morning fog, but her true prey, Frontist Delauchen Severis was only human. Shivering under his poncho, he could see no further than the insectile, maggot-blown corpses of crucified Invaders on the reserve slope of the trenches.

You look miserable, Delauchen, the Limb Knitter thought.

He was jittery too. The Limb Knitter's prey jumped every time he heard her spade bite into the soil.

She watched him collect his weapon and begin the long crawl out of the Beaten Zone toward the forward trenches of the Southern Front. The Knitter put her spade away, still hungry, and crawled behind him, slow and steady.

Only when he was safe in the flooded trenches did he remove his rusty brain bucket and scratch madly at his greasy, matted hair. The Limb Knitter eased up to the trench with envy deep in her chest. She could just hear their conversation.

"Morning, grouch," his conflict spouse, Thalia Vetraslev said. She gave him a peck on the lips. "See anything out there?"

"No," he said, avoiding her eyes, as was his nature. "Not a damned thing. Just thought I heard some Knitters digging about."

"I'll get chow," the Knitter heard Thalia say.

Delauchen started to snore while still on his feet.

Thalia thumped him in the shoulder. "Hey, did you hear me, Delauchen? I'm going for chow."

He jerked awake, "Yes, sorry. I think I need sleep more than food."

"You'll want your tea," she said. "I know how you are."

It must be nice to have someone, the Knitter thought. She watched Thalia head eastward to join a line of male and female Frontists headed for the bombproof kitchens. Thalia was big-boned and had wide hips which formed her short, pear-shaped frame. When the Frontist waved back at Delauchen, it was possible to see the vanilla-scented ointment that covered the albino patches of skin on the right side of her face.

The Knitter's Mark.

Delauchen waved back to Thalia and plopped himself down on a pinewood ammo box. Her peers avoided her and others with the same albino patches as if they might catch something. It was just a lack of melanin that caused the discoloration. The Master Knitter still hadn't solved that problem. But it didn't matter if they stayed away from the likes of her.

Thing is, Knitter's Mark or not, Delauchen didn't let anyone get too close to him either.

When he was sure she was out of sight, Delauchen reached for a tar canvas satchel and pulled out a worn spiral pad of rice paper. He settled into his spot, kicking loose a few rocks, which rolled down into a brackish shell hole.

Draw something beautiful, the Knitter thought, sliding forward a bit closer.

Here is why the Knitter waited all night: she enjoyed this part the most, the mornings when Delauchen would draw something. Maybe he would sketch a collection of empty ration canisters or barring that, he might do his dirty left hand again. Sometimes, as a joke, he liked to hold his thumb out and sketch that. And every so often, on good mornings when both were in high spirits, Thalia would let Delauchen sketch her face in the hopes that perhaps she could finally catch those evasive brown eyes of his.

The Limb Knitter eased up closer still, almost to the point where the top of her slouch hat was visible. But Delauchen didn't pick up a charcoal stick or turn to a smooth, crème sheet of nude paper. Instead, he turned to an old sketch and stared at it.

No, she thought. *Draw something. You don't have much time.* The rank, randy scent of the Invaders grew in the hours before an attack. It was enough to make the Knitter gag. Humans were spared due to their own limited senses, perhaps for the better, or maybe for the worse.

The Knitter moved closer, shifting loose a few bits of dirt and rock.

Charcoal rubbings and lines gave the woman in the sketch a pudgy nose. Dark curls brushed against her bare shoulders, pulled back to show off her ears. Sharp dimples flanked her close-lipped smile. Her eyebrows were feather-fine yet overemphasized above a pair of flat, almond-shaped eyes.

One look at those imperfect eyes was all it took for the sobs to come in shoulder racking bursts. If the other Frontists noticed his pain, they left him be, busied with the tasks of getting on in the trenches for another day.

The Knitter brought out a gold plated oval locket and opened it. Inside, Delauchen looked back at her from the small heliotype image. He appeared startled, frightened, but it was the only time he had ever made eye contact with her, through the heliotype maker.

The Knitter sighed. *You never change, Delauchen.*

The soil beneath her heavy frame shifted and dumped the Limb Knitter down into the puddle next to Delauchen's boot.

Whoever threw something into the shell hole managed to do so in such a way that it splattered urine-fouled water all over Delauchen. A white haze fell over him when he saw his sketch of Yvette Mobori, preserved for two years since her death, was soaked with mud and feces. He threw the pad down and stood up, looking for the jackass that had thrown the rock into the puddle.

"Who did it this time?" The telltale smirk always gave someone away, or at least a cluster of Frontists, but there were only pale, fearful faces instead. Delauchen's peers skittered, cowered and backed away, staring at something behind him.

Maybe I've finally beaten enough sense into them, he thought.

Water sloshed around in the shell hole behind Delauchen. He turned to see.

An overcoat patched in places with tar canvas and burlap rose from the muck, first to its knees, then one leg at a time, until it stood at a full two meters. It bent over to retrieve its slouch hat, floating on the surface, and replaced it upon its burlap-bag-covered head. Through two ragged holes, its yellow eyes watched Delauchen Severis with great care.

"Look at this!" Delauchen pointed at his ruined pad and forgot that he was supposed to be afraid of the Limb Knitter. "Do you know what you've done?"

The Limb Knitter held its jointed, ceramic hands out, palms up, cowering ever so slightly.

He retrieved the pad, stepped forward and held it up. When he did, he noticed a tarnished, gold-plated oval locket around the Knitter's neck. It was still open and in it, he saw a heliotype of himself staring back.

Delauchen knew who it belonged to and she was supposed to be dead.

He pointed at the locket. "Where did you get that, you freak?"

The Knitter took another step back. It stumbled on something in the hole, almost falling back into the muck. Its robe quivered and rippled along the torso, which made the patched fabric flap back and forth.

He thrust the sketchpad at the Knitter. "You recognize her, don't you? Where is she?"

The Knitter's shoulders heaved and shook. It made a high pitched scraping sound akin to nails being dragged down a slate board in a lecture hall. Other Frontists scrambled into their bomb-proofs, not sure what would come next when the Knitter fell to its knees, wringing its hands. The ceramic fingers tinkled like a china tea set, the scraping sound grew louder and began to warble.

"Take a good look!" He threw his pad at the Knitter. It landed on the ground at the edge of the puddle. "Why don't you answer me? Where is she?"

"Step back from that thing!" Out of breath, Thalia took Delauchen by the shoulders and made eye contact with him. "Look at me. No, at me, Delauchen. Sit down over there and take a deep breath. Okay?"

He nodded numbly, his anger spent, and did as he was told.

Thalia murmured words to the effect that the Limb Knitter had best leave and rejoined Delauchen on her own ammo crate. A whining sound in the background made it hard to hear her. She dropped the ruined sketch pad at Delauchen's muddy brogans and sighed.

"I'm not sure," she said, "but I think you made it cry."

Microturbines heralded the arrival of a pair of Invalid machines, their two-meter tall bodies slid down into the trenches, bringing one of the crucified Invader's corpses down with them. Thalia and Delauchen watched the machines watch them before they turned and made their way down the trench to the West. Silver buzz saws on the whitewashed machine caught the sunlight with a flash before they rounded a turn in the trench and moved out of sight.

Delauchen pulled Thalia's hand, her Knitter hand, to his lips and kissed the albino skin. She squeezed back, but her right wasn't as strong as her left. He tried to look into Thalia's eyes. It was hard, not because one was red and the other was blue. It was hard to open himself up, to get his head up and look at her, really look at her.

Once the whining turbines faded away, he let go of her hand.

Thalia kicked Delauchen's foot. "Two years we've been together and you still keep things from me."

"Sorry," Delauchen said. He put the pad aside, out of Thalia's sight. He hoped the sun would dry out the pages enough for him to salvage something.

"Why? I've got a fairly thick skin. I think I can face her."

"She's dead, Thalia." He shrugged. Now that he had seen the locket, he wasn't quite so sure. He remembered buying that locket at a sutler wagon for Yvette on their first visit to Kalentine Orchards on the northern slopes three years ago.

"I know that," Thalia said.

"Then why worry about it?"

Thalia fixed him with a stare. "Because you still love her."

He nudged a bit of mud next to his brogans; the heel was coming loose again. It was not an accusation, he realized, looking at his brogans. It was a fact.

"Can't you say that about your last battle spouse?" Delauchen asked. "Don't you get angry that the Knitters didn't save him? It would be far better than ending up in one of those machines."

She took him by the chin and held him up. "The Knitter saved me, Delauchen, not him. He was an ass anyway. Besides, one good thing came of it."

"What?" he asked, still looking away.

"I met you." She let go of him. "Is that a bad thing?"

"We're going to get hit soon," he said, trying to change the subject.

"Oh, come on. You don't believe that crap, do you?" Thalia twisted the bottom of each ration can to start the heating process. "Imminent doom foreshadowed by the presence of a Knitter at Dawn and all that? Plenty of times I've seen them and nothing has happened."

Delauchen kept his mouth shut. It wouldn't do any good to say anything else. He could feel it happening in him. That moment when you had to shut yourself off and go cold to the world because someone was too close, too important.

He took a minute to consider Thalia, snapping a heliotype into his mind. Where the long-dead-and-gone Yvette Mobori had been olive in skin tone, Thalia Vetraslev was pale and red freckled. His lost lover had thick auburn curls where Thalia had short blonde hair, cropped close.

She smiled at him.

Smiles didn't really mean anything; Delauchen had seen too many fake ones over the years. And when they started to mean something, as Thalia's smile did at this instant, that was when he started to shove them away.

She's too close, he realized. He didn't want to hurt her like he had Yvette.

"You know, the Brigades Invalid might have—"

"Don't," Delauchen said. "Just, don't. Okay?" He shook his head.

The Knitter's locket bothered him.

She probably threw it away after we broke up and the Knitter found it, he decided.

Thalia looked away, unaware of what traipsed through Delauchen's mind. She popped the top on a can of tea and handed it to her partner. "Here. Drink. You're depressing me."

He reached for the steaming can of tea and in so doing, made himself try, just one more time, to look her in the eye. She watched him watching her, breathing deeply, looking down into her when their eyes finally met. He held himself there in her mismatched red-blue eyes, the fear and panic pulling at his guts.

Don't push her away, he told himself. *Don't quit just yet.*

She blushed. "You're such a grump. You're lucky I love you, you know that?"

He nodded, hot can of tea in hand. He brought it up to his lips.

There was a flash of light.

"COVER!" someone shouted. "TAKE COV—!"

Lightning seared his eyes as a hot thunderclap slapped them down into the mud. He struggled to pump air back into his lungs, as he slid down into the shell hole. Rats streamed past him, but one stopped to nibble at something, a bit of rag, muscle and fresh bone.

Delauchen could see Thalia sprawled out not far from him, face down in the dirt. He tried to crawl toward her, but he couldn't move.

There was another burst of light and something busted him in the face.

The darkness took him.

Delauchen opened his eyes to a grey murk. Someone was screaming loud enough to pierce the remnant ringing in his ears. A high-pitched mechanical whine obscured their screams until metal bit into flesh and the whine dropped into a low moaning grind. It drove the screams into the inhuman range.

Buzz saws, Delauchen realized. *Invalid Harvesters.*

He blinked and turned his head. He could smell a metallic tang mingled with the stench of putrid rotten flesh close to his body. Sharp, burning jabs of pain pushed from his fingertips to his biceps in both arms before degrading into a duller incarnation that radiated through his shoulders and pushed deep into his neck before burrowing into his skull. Someone kneaded the flesh around his biceps as if it were bread dough.

He coughed and tried to clear his dry throat. He was thirsty.

"Hello?" he croaked.

"Do you require a Limb Knitter or do you wish to be inducted into the Brigades Invalid?" a toneless voice asked.

He coughed again. "What?"

"Knitter or Harvester." The voice was insistent.

"Why... why can't I see?"

"Frontist, your wounds are treatable but I need a decision. Do you want a Knitter or not?"

"Limb Knitter? But..." This was going too fast. "Wait, what about Thalia?"

"Frontist, I can't spend any more time on you. Either accept the Knitter or I'll send for a Harvester."

Thalia would chose a Knitter, Delauchen told himself. She had done it once already.

"I'll get a Harvester, Frontist."

"No, no, a Knitter," Delauchen shouted. "I'll take the Limb Knitter."

He couldn't hear a response in the growing scream of micro-turbines and metal-shod feet stomping closer. The Invalid Harvester was coming. He'd be chopped up and dumped into one of those drums, then hauled off to wherever it was that you went to become an Invalid Warrior. A two-meter cybernetic zombie, the living electric death.

"I said I'll take the Knitter!"

The screaming turbines and footsteps faded away along with the buzz saws and screams. He heard a door slam shut muffling the sounds completely, leaving him with only the ringing in his ears. Delauchen thought he could hear heavy fabric falling to the floor but he wasn't certain.

"I'm here, Delauchen," a voice said. He could hear a rapid, frantic clicking sound. Something hairy took him into its arms. The stench of rotten flesh was overpowering. "I have always been here."

Small points of cool, hard rods touched his ribs, wrapping themselves down and around to embrace his torso. Delauchen felt the rods tumbling him around; rolling him as hot, sticky glue-like string plopped onto his ankles. The substance began to wind itself around his shins, working up around his legs, pulling them tightly together. It sweated a blood-warm fluid that filled the dead spaces around his legs as the substance increased in speed, winding up to his torso. When it reached his lower ribs, the substance pulled itself taut. The fluid advanced behind the material, which caused Delauchen to break out into a cold, clammy sweat.

The rolling came to a stop.

Two of the coils, or rods, Delauchen wasn't sure, touched his arms. They rubbed themselves back and forth, tugging at his skin.

Something bit him.

"Breathe, Delauchen," the Knitter shouted over his screams. "Breathe."

He strained at the bindings in a futile attempt to inflate his lungs. "I can't."

He felt the Limb Knitter's hands grasp his head. Strands of filament oozed from its fingers, creeping their way across his skull. They pressed, shoved and rutted themselves into his ears, under his eyelids and down his nose. Delauchen tried to speak but found himself gagging on the advancing filaments that crawled through his sinuses and invaded his throat. The sharp-toothed coils in his stumps continued to rut, suck, pull and push into him.

"I'll breathe for both of us," it said, and kissed him full on the mouth. He felt himself pulled upright inside a powerful pair of legs locked behind the small of his back. The thing mounted him when the mouth pulled away, causing him to vomit. A warm, wet cloth cleaned the bile from his face.

"There will be a sharp pain, and then it will pass," it said.

He heard a crack at the base of his skull, followed by something grinding against bone, penetrating deep into his brain.

The darkness came for Delauchen again.

Silver tones and dark shade permeated the Kalentine Orchards, not far from the Canarus Redoubt's Northern Gate. Delauchen didn't recall the walk on this visit, but he had been here before with Yvette. Their last weekend together had been during the Fall Harvest and they'd spent it camping out in the open and making love under the star-splashed skies.

His presence at the Orchards made him feel like an ass and it re-minded him of why he hadn't brought Thalia here, even though he was close to doing the same thing to her. Yvette had never suspected he was going to end it after that weekend.

Where is Thalia? He wouldn't have come alone. It was too depressing.

Now in the springtime there were abundant blossoms on the oldest apple tree that swayed in the afternoon breeze. Two patched, careworn field blankets were spread out around the trunk of the tree, its bark rubbed bare from campers over the decades. Someone had sliced smoked cheddar, apples and some sausage on two tin mess plates. He remembered the galvanized bucket in his hands, heavy with iced-down bottles of hard cider. The sutler wagon down the trail sold them from the Orchard presses to a Frontist for a modest discount.

He set the bucket down and took a slice of cheddar from the near-est tin plate. When he stood up Delauchen noticed a hapless Velaysian apple mite caught on a spider web. The spider moved swiftly, immobi-lizing the mite with a bite and winding it up for supper later.

I don't remember planning this trip. Delauchen figured it must have been the cider, too much of it during the trip up, which might explain the sludge in his head. He slid the slice of cheddar into his mouth and sucked on it thoughtfully. Yvette and Delauchen had gorged them-selves on hard-to-get delicacies when they were here last time. The smoky, creamy texture pulled up a painfully sharp and clear memory of the first of the final kisses he shared with Yvette.

He swallowed the bit of cheese. *You're a coward, Delauchen. You know that?*

"Beautiful, aren't they? The blossoms that is," a woman said from behind, her voice young, fruity, melodic in tone. Familiar. "I'm glad we're here to see them together."

He froze.

Fingertips traced their way around Delauchen's shoulder, sending chills down his spine. He held his breath as the woman's hand circled around until she was face to face. Her auburn curls spilled down over her shoulders, lush and thick. Sharp dimples flanked her close mouthed smile.

Yvette? Delauchen started to breathe again, but didn't trust himself to speak.

"I've found you." Her smile brightened. "Took you long enough to get the cider."

She drew Delauchen into her embrace. He found himself hugging her in return, his right hand located her shoulder blade, his left still holding the bucket. She nuzzled against his chest as his hand started to descend the solid, firm curve of her back. A hint of lavender in her curls caught his attention while his hands came to a wandering stop around her hips.

Fits like a glove, Delauchen thought, drawing her closer still.

"I've missed you," he said.

Yvette drew back from him and took a long look. He tried to meet her eyes but his own gaze darted off to rest on sandals. Her toenails were painted with gold.

"Oh, I made you something. Sit down and fetch me a cider while I find it," she said, turning to her Forces Velaysia issue canvas knapsack.

"Sure," Delauchen said, and did as he was told. On all fours, Yvette rooted around in her knapsack. His eyes wandered to her butt and he found himself fascinated with the fact that he could stare at her rear end all day but not look her in the eye. Thalia's was wider, bigger, softer, not the hard leanness of Yvette. He always had to bend at the knees to hug or kiss Thalia. She never really felt right in a physical sense.

He felt shallow and crass, embarrassed and repulsed at his thoughts.

Yvette handed him the paper-wrapped parcel from her knapsack. She plopped down next to him, blew an errant curl from her face and took the offered bottle of cider.

"Here it is," she said, her face in full blush. "Knitted it myself."

Delauchen squeezed the package, hefted it, then shook it. It was soft, light and noiseless.

"Open it, silly."

He pulled at the twine to unwrap the paper. There was a bundle of knitted red yarn, folded nicely and neatly inside.

Delauchen smiled, turning the sweater back and forth to get a good look. "You made this?

"That's what I said. Try it on."

He rubbed his fingertips back and forth on the fabric. It wasn't wool or cotton. It was sheer, warm, and he could swear it was throbbing.

A nervous chuckle got away from him. "Not exactly sweater weather."

"Oh, humor me, babe."

"Okay."

He pulled the warm, sheer material over his head and shoved his arms out through the sleeves. The cuffs ended in the middle of Delauchen's forearms. Waves of scalding hot pain washed back and forth across his hands and arms, sucking and pulling at his finger tips. He couldn't move his arms at all. It hurt that badly.

"Oh, dear," Yvette said.

"Burns," Delauchen said.

"I know. Get your arms up," Yvette said, reaching for him. "No, no, Delauchen, up over your head. You can be such a child, sometimes. Come on, I've got you."

The pain passed once the sweater came off. He sat there, numb for a moment before cracking open a cider for himself and taking a long pull.

"I got you something else." Yvette reached over and pulled a new rice paper sketchpad out of her knapsack along with some charcoals. "Why don't you sketch something for me?"

"Like what?"

"Oh, something beautiful. There is plenty here to work with."

He took the offered pad, opened it and ran his hands across the blank, creamy smooth sheets of paper.

"But…" he swallowed and tried to settle his feelings. "I didn't bring you anything."

She looked up from her pile of knitting tools and yarn.

"Delauchen, you're so dense sometimes. Just seeing you is good enough. Okay?"

He nodded. "Okay."

A couple of bottles of cider later, Delauchen noticed the fading light of the Eastern Sunset casting long shadows through the Orchard. He sat back against the apple tree, stretched the kinks out and considered his sketch in progress.

Like his previous efforts, many of Yvette's best features were crafted with loving care, curls, dimples, smile and so forth. He used to spend hours in the trenches sketching her, usually on the day when it was her turn to clean the weapons. She always seemed angry, distant for some reason he could never quite fathom.

He started to work on her eyes.

This afternoon it had been different. Yvette knitted away on the sweater, a faint smile that grew when she'd catch him snatching glances at her. She didn't seem angry now, and he couldn't remember her ever knitting before.

"You've been awfully quiet," he said.

She looked up, "I'm just enjoying the moment."

"It's nice this evening," he said. He used his charcoal to draw a faint orb into the space where her left eye would go. "Clear skies. Warm."

"Dry." Yvette chuckled. "I like the fact that it is dry here."

He nodded in agreement. "Dry is definitely good. I've seen enough mud to last me a lifetime."

Happy as he was, he still couldn't sort it out. Either Yvette was dead or she wasn't. And where was Thalia? How had Yvette found them and managed to get furlough at the same time? He felt like he had been handed an algebra problem. If only he'd done better, he'd have been in the Brigades Artillery instead of another stupid Frontist in the trenches.

"It was cold the morning we went over the top," Yvette said, her focus back on her knitting. "The blizzard, you couldn't see your hand before your face."

"I remember," he said. The ill-fated Winter Offensive had happened a couple of months after they'd separated. Yvette had been moved to another part of their brigade and Delauchen was alone when the storm blew down out of the Northern Reaches. Suprema Strategic Velaysia felt it would mask their attack from the orbiting Invader, enabling them to take the entrenched enemy, supposedly hibernating, by surprise.

Not one of their better plans, he thought.

"My feet hurt so much from the cold, I wanted to cry," he said.

"Some guys were pissing on their feet to warm them up," Yvette said. "Only made it worse. A lot of them were inducted into the Brigades Invalid. Frost bite. I think some of them did it on purpose. I think I might have done it if I could."

She fell silent and continued to knit.

"How...." He was afraid to spoil it, the moment. "How, rather, what happened? You didn't come back."

"You noticed?" Her knitting needles continued to clickety-click away with their one-two-one-two beat.

"Of course I noticed," he snapped, angry more with himself than anything.

"But that is why you ended it, isn't it? Afraid to let anyone get to close." She met his eyes. "As if you are the only one that has suffered."

Damn it, keep your head up, Delauchen, he chided himself. Yvette wasn't his mother. She wouldn't smack him for looking at her.

"I never said that," Delauchen replied. That much was true.

"You didn't have to." She returned to her knitting. "I'm not stupid."

"But you're alive. Why didn't you find me? Did you end up in another Brigade?"

She shook her head slowly.

"When I saw the Knitter with your locket this morning..." the answer kept slipping back into his muddy mind "...I knew you were still alive."

Yvette nodded; her knitting needles continued clicking along.

"I figured you threw the locket away," he said. "I wouldn't blame you if you did."

"I didn't throw it away."

Delauchen was confused. "But... the Knitter had it. I saw it."

Yvette reached under her blouse and produced a locket, the same heliotype locket he had given her years ago. The same locket the Knitter had worn. "Delauchen, listen very carefully."

He looked up.

"I—Still—Have—It," she said. "Do you understand?"

He shook his head. "No, Yvette, I don't. Nothing makes any sense."

The only way it would make sense is if Yvette Mobori and the Knitter he'd seen that morning were the same person.

And that just wasn't possible.

"May I see it?" She nodded at his sketchpad. "You seem more interested in your sketch than me anyway."

"What?" He looked down, embarrassed with himself. "Yeah, sure."

Yvette set her knitting aside and took the offered sketchpad. She was silent for a long time, her fingers tracing the charcoal features of her face on the pad. Delauchen imagined he could hear the skin of her fingertips sighing across the paper.

A tear fell onto the pad. She sniffed and looked up, her shoulders rising and falling with each tortured breath.

She sniffed a second time. "I've done it again."

The realization started to sink in. Delauchen waited for her to stop crying before opening his mouth.

"We're not at Kalentine Orchards, are we?" he asked, easing the tear-stained sketch pad out of her hands.

"Depends on your perspective and philosophy about such things, but physically there right now?" she shook her head, her curls swaying back and forth across her face. "No, Delauchen. We're not at Kalentine. In fact, we're not too far away from the Southern Front, in physical terms."

"So, you're the Limb Knitter?" he asked, feeling incredibly stupid. He still didn't want to buy it. "Two meters tall and smells like a month-old corpse? Forgive me, Yvette, but you don't look like any Knitter I've ever seen. You certainly don't smell like it."

"She," Yvette corrected, "is not an it and she is sitting here in front of you. What is the last thing you remember?"

"Thalia and I were talking about..." He shook his head. "She said something about me making the Knitter cry."

"Do you remember getting hit?" Yvette asked. "I do because I was there. It was a downward fragmentation air burst. You lost both arms, had shrapnel in most of your body. You also took a pretty good chunk of dirt in the face which busted your retinas. Those are going to be the hardest to fix."

"A nightmare," Delauchen said. "I think it was a nightmare."

"About?"

"Something bit me, wound me up in some sticky goo." He looked at the spider, now consuming her apple mite on the web. "Spiders. I think it was about spiders."

She held up the sweater, exasperated or disappointed, Delauchen wasn't sure. "Here, may as well try it on now."

Delauchen wasn't quite so sure after the last painful attempt. He looked it over. "Is this going to hurt?"

"Not if I got the sleeves right," Yvette said. "Arms are pretty tricky, especially the hands. Your brain remembers how long they were, even if they aren't there any more."

He took hold of the sheer, warm red sweater, rubbing it between his fingers.

"What happens if this fits?" he asked.

This time Yvette looked away.

"Well?"

She picked at a bit of cheese, avoiding him. "You'll go back to the Front."

"And what about you?"

She shrugged. "What does it matter?"

"Do you have someone?"

"Are you kidding me?" she asked.

She never liked being alone, he remembered. "It must be difficult."

"It hurts, plain and simple, Delauchen. Try on the sweater, will you."

"What if I stay?"

She looked up, "What about Thalia? You going to abandon her for me, are you?"

Shit, he thought, angry with himself for forgetting about Thalia. "Is she okay?"

"Try it on and I'll tell you."

Delauchen took a deep breath, clenched his teeth and pulled the sweater on. His hands eased through the sleeves. He paused to gather his courage at the edge of the cuffs before he shoved his fingers through.

He stretched and flexed. A perfect fit. Yvette looked satisfied with herself.

"Well?" he asked.

Yvette looked off down the road of apple trees. "I saw a Harvester come for her."

What the hell am I going to do now? "A Harvester? Why didn't you save her?"

"Because you were there, asshole! You were bleeding to death. I had to kick the rats off of you and drag your ass out of one superbitch of an artillery barrage," Yvette said. "What else was I supposed to do?

For some reason I can't fathom, I still love you."

"So, the Brigades Invalid have her," he said.

"Did another two years in the trenches make you deaf? Yes, probably. Damn, you are so bloody dense," she said, exasperated with him. "You never change."

"How will I ever get back to her?"

Yvette grabbed Delauchen, pulled him to her and kissed him hard. He fought it for a moment but she turned out to be surprisingly strong, more so than he remembered. Delauchen found he didn't really want to pull away in any case.

When they finally parted, he felt his knees buckle.

"I'll finish up now," she said quietly, wiping her mouth with the back of her hand. "You won't remember a thing."

"Yvette, don't."

"It'll be better this way. You can find someone else," she said, disappointment etched on her face.

She's not my mother, he told himself. *She won't hurt me.*

"Yvette." Delauchen steadied himself, took a deep breath and met her gaze. Yvette's wet and heavy eyes grabbed hold and wouldn't let go. He held himself there with the woman who had come back for him. She shook her head and looked away when the moment lasted longer than she had anticipated.

"I love you," he said. "Is there a way?"

The horizon was dark now with the first of three moons climbing into the sky. Her face was carved out of reality with soft blue light. She faced him.

"Yes, there is."

After a moment of pondering, he made up his mind. "Anything. Whatever it takes."

Yvette let out her breath and nodded. "All right."

Yvette disentangled herself from Delauchen's egg and laid him down in the warm mud near her chamber. She took her time covering the egg, slathering the mud around the brown, leathery surface before easing him down into the bubbling depths. Once she was done, she stood under a warm stream of mineral water and cleaned the aftermath from her heavily modified form. Only then did she dress and go for something to eat.

In the next chamber, the buzz saws had come to a stop. Mud and blood splattered, the lone Invalid Harvester rinsed its blades free of chunked flesh and muscle, chipped bone and clotted blood. It was silent except for the sound of running water ringing off the silver blades to dribble on the stone floor. Six black drums, harvest pods, each with the molting snake sigil of the Brigades Invalid, filled the corner of the chamber. Four more drums, those of Invalid Inductees, were already strapped to its back.

Yvette nodded to the silent cyborg.

"There should be enough scrap to hold you and your Initiate for the next couple of days," the Harvester said, its voice a mash of metallic echoes and vibrations. "The current engagement continues unabated, thus, there will be more tomorrow."

"And the one I mentioned? Were you able to induct her?"

The Harvester reached into a drum and pulled an albino-skinned right arm from the collection of limbs and flesh. The trunk, brain, and vitals were in the Inductee drums on its back. New guts for the Brigades Invalid. The Knitter never got those, not that she wanted them.

"Sometimes it is best to take them with minor wounds, but she did not have any at all," the Harvester said. It gave the limb to Yvette for her inspection. "No matter. She will be of more use to us."

With a snap, a finger came off and Yvette chewed on it thoughtfully.

"Does this arrangement meet your satisfaction?" the Harvester asked.

She spat the finger bones out, noting the odd aftertaste that Knitter crafted meat had in contrast to regular human meat. She had long since gotten over her issues with how the Limb Knitters fed themselves.

"Yes," Yvette said, satisfied that her lonely days were at an end. "I believe it does."

I Know an Old Lady

Nathan Rosen

I know an old lady who misused a teleportation chamber to merge her genetic structure with that of a fly. Perhaps she thought the compound eyes were desirable. Her true motives can never be known, as the replacement of her mouth with a proboscis rendered her completely incapable of speech. The total extent of the damage done is indeterminable. Her demise may occur soon.

I know an old lady who misused a teleportation chamber to merge her genetic structure with that of a spider. She is now capable of casting a fibrous web from her abdomen. She spends most of her time in a corner by the ceiling, waiting for prey. It is, frankly, amazing that she still survives, especially considering the previous damage done by the fly incident. Her demise may occur soon.

I know an old lady who misused a teleportation chamber to merge her genetic structure with that of a bird. Two of her limbs have become feathered wings. Despite already being part spider and part fly, she still survives. Such a thing is unheard of in the history of teleportation science. Her demise may occur soon.

I know an old lady who misused a teleportation chamber to merge her genetic structure with that of a cat. She now possesses fur and retractable claws. Her ears swivel to pick up even the slightest sound. Nobody can comprehend why she is still alive, yet she survives as a being in roughly equal proportions: cat, bird, spider, fly and human. Her demise will surely occur soon.

I know an old lady who misused a teleportation chamber to merge her genetic structure with that of a dog. Her sense of smell must be unparalleled. She appears to be happy, if the wagging of her tail is any indication. Dog, cat, bird, spider and fly. We're starting to take bets on how far this can go. Her demise will surely occur soon.

I know an old lady who misused a teleportation chamber to merge her genetic structure with that of a goat. She has horns now. This is getting ridiculous. Goat, dog, cat, bird, spider, fly! Her demise will surely occur soon.

I know an old lady who misused a teleportation chamber to merge her genetic structure with that of a horse.

She's dead, of course.

BLAKENJEL

LAVIE TIDHAR

1. A Stenchtown Tale

Blakenjel bilong mi is black like unlit coal. His open wings are like smokers' lungs. His skin is taut and fine like expensive vellum that was blackened in flames. There are many blakenjels, but only one bilong mi. I follow him in the darkness.

"Smell this!"

"Sniff my hair!"

"Taste my breath; it's fresh; it's fresh!"

"Remember ice cream? Oranges? Soap? Authentically guaranteed, the smell like you remember!"

But there is not much call for that.

"Sniff my armpits! Real human sweat!"

"Toes! Toes! Inhale the smell!"

And further down the road of Stenchtown, away from the fake smells of oranges and soap, where the great unwashed line the road and put the merchandise on display. At the far end, one white boy almost naked but for a thong. Angelic-looking, almost hairless, fine blond hairs that lie like newborn wheat along the pale contours of his body.

The sniffer comes close to the boy. He wears a dark coat, too hot for this city, this place. His eyes are hooded. The boy smiles. "Smell my crotch?" he offers. The sniffer looks and doesn't speak. The boy shifts in place and tries again. "Armpits? Hair?" the usual routine. The sniffer doesn't speak, and the boy's smile suddenly grows wider. "Sniff my ass?" he whispers, and there is something unspeakably lewd about the way he stands. "Stick your nose deep inside my asshole, let the nostrils touch the brown ring?"

The sniffer twitches in place, and the boy smiles like a predator. "I just had a shit half-an-hour ago," he confides. "Not wiped, either. Soon as I saw you I could tell you were a connoisseur."

The sniffer comes closer. His voice is like rusted blades being scraped. "How much?" he says.

"Thirty."

"Ten..."

"Twenty-five and you can stick your tongue in there, too."

"Fifteen—" The sniffer doesn't quite finish the sentiment. His body twitches and his face, which was sheathed in the darkness of the street, becomes visible. The boy steps back, but there is only the wall behind him. He says, softly, "Shit," and for once it isn't sales-talk.

It's fear.

The sniffer smiles. His face is a horrid, writhing mass of unquiet flesh. His eyes are large and round and inhuman, clear and strangely innocent in that ravaged face. He has no nose, but two slits for nostrils gape out of the moving, worm-like scars. "Smell... good..." the sniffer says. His mouth is a jagged line filled with small sharp teeth like a predator-fish.

"I... I don't do f... fear," the boy says. "Go somewhere else!" But of course he knows it is too late, that he made a bad mistake, and you are not allowed mistakes in this place, this time. The boy whispers, "Open Sore."

The sniffer raises his arm. His hand extends and grabs the boy's throat with ease. His nails are claws, long and black and foul. The boy chokes. The smell of shit fills the air, free, and the sniffer's mouth opens in what may be a smile. A red worm-like tongue protrudes and search-es the air.

"P... please," the boy says, but quietly. "Don't."

The other hand reaches for the boy's crotch. Pulls aside the narrow thong. The boy quivers but remains silent. Perhaps he thinks that this is how it ends—with fear alone, and not with death. But of course that is only delusion. The swamp-thing will kill him when it is done. And so the boy does the only thing he can think of, and in his fear he prays, and so he says, almost inaudibly:

"Blakenjel. Blakenjel bilong mi."

In the darkness something moves and halts. Fine leathery wings beat once and are still. The blakenjel listens. It is hard to tell what he does next. I cannot see in the darkness, only guess. There are no distances in the darkness.

The sniffer's face comes close to the boy's. The naked nostrils open and close like air-vents. The red-worm tongue quests along the boy's skin. The sniffer shudders. So—although for a very different reason—does the boy.

Suddenly the sniffer's head is jerked back. His eyes stare at the boy, a few inches away, eyes clear and blue, the way the sky once was. Slowly, there is a strange, soft, *sucking* sound.

The sniffer's left eye disappears inside its socket. There is a wet-red tunnel through his skull. The eye is like a false opening at its end. The eye moves away like a locomotive through his brain. The sniffer tries to scream, perhaps, but the only sound coming from his mouth is the sound of loose nails falling. His hand lets go of the boy's crotch. The boy feels wetness running down his legs. The sniffer's other eye disappears with a quiet *plop*. An eyeless thing stares at the boy, no longer seeing. Then the sniffer falls to his knees.

Behind him there is only darkness. The boy shakes but manages to bow his head. There is a price to pay, there always is, but every time it's different.

In the darkness I can suddenly *smell* him, my blakenjel. He has acquired smell. His smell is not pleasant, although it can be intoxicating. It is the smell of fear. My blakenjel flies through the darkness, and I follow his scent.

2. The Grisly Growths of Gristown

There is a scentless boy whose name is Dak who, having lost his path like all the other scentless boys and girls, now works in a Gristown hotel.

Stenchtown lies in a row of crumbling brick houses on top of the hill. Down from it is the sea, black and toxic, where the fishermer hunt by the light of poisoned algae. Away from it, the great mountains rise where, so it is said, the blakenjels go to lay their great obsidian eggs, as hard as diamonds. Between town and hill lies the vast corrupt forest. Things live there: they call them Open Sores. To the west are the swamps where the Open Sores collect like poisoned water dripping down a drain: do not go there. To the east lie other towns, other lost suburbs, the squalid dwelling places of the human-born: Gaslight and Tooth-bridge, Cancer Ward and Golgotha, Smokers Hill—and then there is Gristown.

The boy, Dak, having lost his trade, took gainful employment in Gristown.

Gristown! The things that live in Gristown, it is said, were human once. Dak does not believe it. A race of alien deep-sea life-forms, others say. Who rose from the depths and took to the land when the great darkness came. Dak does not believe that either. They are slumbering gods, others say, but quietly. It is humanity's duty to ensure they do not awake. And some say they are mutated nano-goo, which is the same as saying gobbledygook.

Those who smell human dare not go to Gristown. The Grisly Growths are always hungry. The scent of meat drives them mad with lust. To feed them, the fishermer provide a steady stream of ocean-spawn, and the scentless boys and girls feed them to the pits, and the 0wnerz grow rich while the cycle of economics is maintained. For the Growths can pay.

Dak works in Pit-Stop Namba Six. He has no name in Gristown. Here he is nambafaef. The others, all more senior, are nambafo, namba-tri, nambatu and nambawan. They speak the pidgin of this place, this time. Nambawan is shift-boss. She is a girl, with light-black skin, and deep blue eyes, and gold ear-rings. Outside her name is Naet.

Dak follows Naet on the perimeter of the pit. The Growths pulse below, great masses of organic grief, hungry cancers, shapeless. Dak is tugging a cart. On it are heaped the dead corpses of sea-creatures, poison and evil-smelling, things with fins and things with tentacles and things with eyes like bunches of grapes hanging upside down.

"Sakem," Naet says, and nambafaef obediently chucks the chunks of rotting meat into the pit. As he comes too close to the edge he totters and almost falls.

"Lukaot," nambawan says. "Ples is gris."

Then she sniggers. Dak smiles. It's an old Gristown joke and has never been particularly funny. "You ever lose anyone down here?" he asks.

"About once a month."

He stares down at the pulsing mass beneath. Pseudopodia rise from the shifting masses and stare up mournfully. The meat Dak threw ebbs on top of the green-brown mass. Then the feeding begins.

The Growths *absorb* their food. Dak watches as the slimy masses begin to glow and the rotten poisoned meat is sucked inside them, losing colour, losing *definition* as it disintegrates into the blobs. Today is a good day. Feeding from above. But on bad days, Dak and the rest are sent down, *into* the pits, and they have to clean the blobs, massage them, soothe them. They should be in no danger, they are told. Scentless, they are of no interest to the Growths. So they say, but Dak doesn't believe it, and neither do the others. There have been... accidents. Too many of the workers in the pits are missing fingers, hands, patches of skin. Some have lost eyebrows, teeth. They say you don't quit working the pits: you merely lose your definition slowly, ebb away, until one day you are simply not there any more.

"What are you doing tonight?" Dak asks, and Naet grins and says, "Why, what do you have in mind, nambafaef?"

Dak blushes. Naet has that effect on him. He says, "Would you like to—" and Naet says, "Sure, why not."

"Oraet," Dak says. "Oraet." For a moment they grin at each other. The Growths pulse below.

I follow the blakenjel through the darkness as I always do. He has long lost his human scent. While he still had it, I had the sense, in the middle of the dark, that he had met another. Perhaps the human smell attracted him. I got the sense of leathery bodies meeting, of wings rubbing against wings. But perhaps I merely imagined it. I cannot see in the dark. When it was over I could no longer smell my blakenjel, but I could still follow him. There is no Darktown. The darkness is not a city; it is a living thing.

"How did you lose your scent?" Naet asks Dak that night as they lie in his bed in Gaslight. Dak shares a crumbling old house with plug-in twins: they were once separate but they bored holes through each other and threaded one another's flesh together, knitting them into one. They can still disengage, although he has never seen them do it. Their names are Amp and Fuse. Apart from them there is a fishermer's son, living in exile in the flooded basement, and a bird-like thing that hangs upside-down from the ceiling and can speak pidgin, but rarely does. "I dig your pad," Naet says.

"Thanks," Dak says. Then, "How did you lose *your* scent?"

She flashes white teeth in the dark. "Yu no save toktok bilong it, huh?" she says. "Oraet. It no problem." Then she says, "Nothing complicated. I was born without it."

"Oh."

She laughs, and they make love again, with only the bird-thing watching from the ceiling. In the darkness, as they fall asleep together, Dak thinks he can hear Naet saying, softly, "I love you."

The next day is cleaning day and so the crew goes down to the pit, nambawan first, the others following. They walk amidst the pulsing moving Grisly Growths, rubbing them, whispering to them.

"I love you," nambafo whispers to the green-grey goo. "Mi lovem yu. Mi lovem yu longtaem."

"You," nambatu whispers to the Growths. "Just you." He bends over one blob, his trousers down, his erection rubbing against the pulsating meat. His penis is translucent. "You. Just you. You. You. You."

Nambawan touches the Growths delicately with only the tips of her fingers. She runs them across their changing skins. "Mother," she says. "Mother. Mother." Her fingers leave a strange trail of luminescence on the Growths' skin. "Mother. Mother. Mother."

Dak goes slower than the rest. It's a strange feeling being amidst the Growths. There is a strange sense of calm down there. Almost of euphoria. He taps a gentle rhythm on the Grisly Growths' flesh, and the body underneath seems to shiver with satisfaction. Dak is lost in the rhythm. He comes closer to the blobs, and closer still. He doesn't even hear when nambawan breaks from her own trance and shouts to him. By the time she reaches him he had already disappeared into the Growth.

Somewhere I think there is a meeting of blakenjels. I meet another human in the dark. An enjelvaljer. Another like me. "Blakenjel bilong mi," he says. "Blakenjel bilong mi," I say.

For one dangerous moment we hover on the edge of light. The darkness recedes around us. We can't feel our blakenjels.

"Mine was in Smokers' Hill last night," the other says. "A woman on the street prayed to be released of cancer. He healed her. He took her cancers away from her. All of them."

"What happened?" I ask.

"When they were gone there was nothing left of her but a bleached-white skeleton," he says. "So pretty..."

"Mine was in Stenchtown—" I say, but then I hear the beat of blackened wings and hurry back into the darkness, and the other is lost behind me. I follow my blakenjel through the corridors of night.

3. The Corridors of Night

"Dak? Dak, can you hear me? Dak!"

But he can't. When he wakes up it is dark. It feels like being in a coffin. He can't move, he can't breathe. Cold slimy tendrils brush against his skin. Somewhere in the distance, was that sound?

"Dak!"

Nothing. The silence presses on him. And in the dark, and in the silence, the tendrils caress him. And something comes.

Not sound. Not vision. But something. It communicates with him, a rhythm against his motionless body. He is a drum. He is a tamtam. If the rhythm had words it might have said something like:

> The savages beat tamtam drums
> The ocean echoes with their sound
> The waves gang up against the reef—
> This night, they say, you'll come to grief.

> The moon beats like a great ill heart
> And silver light falls down like dust
> The waves are choked, the trees are still—
> This night, they say, is ill, is ill.

Remain inside, and shut the door
Pretend that all is as before
And when the tamtam drums do beat—
Into your cold dark bed retreat, retreat.

Dak screams without sound. *Let me be!* The rhythm is of laughter. The rhythm shows him things. Machines, their blueprints. An abandoned altar in a cave that lies below the tide-line. Star charts. Insectoid silver-black creatures darting through an electric storm. And he learns something: this is how the Growths pay. This is what the Ownerz get. The rhythm laughs harder. *You have just been paid with knowledge,* it seems to say.

Paid for what?

The rhythm grows excited. Hard. It beats on his skin in thousands of shards. Dak sees something black like unlit coal. Something black like the corridors of night.

Blakenjel, the rhythm says. *Blakenjel! Blakenjel!*

No, Dak wants to say. There is always a price to pay.

The tentacles withdraw. He is left alone, unmoving, cold. The dark and the silence grow like fungus, and inside his head he screams.

The tentacles return. A tap-tap-tap, gentle and slow. They seem to be saying—so?

Dak would pray. He would do anything. But suddenly, although he is frozen, something from the outside penetrates, someone calling, and Dak cries, *No!*

Naet calls a blakenjel. Dak screams, and feels the triumph of the rhythm against his skin.

In the darkness he wails. Cold tentacles drag slime against his cheeks.

Blakenjel bilong mi stops in the dark. In the dark I feel him ponder. His wings rustle and I feel the slow movement of his head. It is as if he were tasting the air. I hurry after him, groping blindly.

In the darkness of his coffin Dak can move. The walls of his coffin are mucous. They ooze. They are dissolving. What do the Growths want with blakenjels? His head pulls out of the mass. He is new-born. He tastes the air and sees the blakenjel.

The darkness seems to emanate from within the Grisly Growth. Has time passed? Have the blakenjel and the Growths somehow communicated? He doesn't know. He sees the darkness rise from the Growths and he cowers, but it isn't for him that it comes.

It is for Naet.

The blakenjel kisses her. There is the sense of leathery wings flapping in an unseen wind. Then Dak is out of the Growths and on the ground. His clothes have been dissolved. The flesh of his arms is translucent. He stares up at Naet, and he wants to cry, he wants to scream, he wants to be a baby again. Naet looks at him without expression. She shakes her head, a confused gesture. Why did she call the blakenjel? Never mind. She doesn't seem to have lost anything, and it is time to get back to work. She turns to address the new boy.

"Nambafaef," she says. "Go bak bilong wok, hariap."

Dak, helpless, says, "Naet..."

"Nambafaef," she repeats. "Go back to work, quickly."

The blakenjel is gone. The Growths pulsate lazily like oversized brains. And Dak stands up and, without words, walks away.

There is always a price to pay.

My blakenjel is different as he stalks through the corridors of night. He is burdened with a terrible thing. My blakenjel loves. In the darkness I hear sounds. My blakenjel sings. It is a horrid sound. There are cries and howls in the dark. My blakenjel stalks through the darkness, never stopping. What is he looking for? Maybe, I think, he wants to find another blakenjel with this thing, this love.

But perhaps the love he has acquired is of the unrequited kind.

4. Ownerz

That night Dak sleeps with the bird-thing who lives in the ceiling. The sex is short, savage and unsatisfying. The bird-thing keeps speaking Pidgin throughout it. "Mi fakem yu. Mi fakem yu. Faken as. Yu kan. Mi fakem yu." Its vocabulary is not large. That night, when the bird-thing falls asleep, Dak cries. Then he makes a decision. He will follow the blakenjel. He will summon him back. He will fight him. He will plead with him. He will get Naet's love back.

When he falls asleep at last, his sleep is restless. Perhaps it is only the ground-tremors that shake the house at night, the after-thought of seismic forces out at sea. But he is used to them, just as he is used to the occasional short, sharp screams outside that end in sudden silence, or to the hiss and splatter of the steam engines as they go about their tracks, the coal-beasts running and belching and the metal bob-sledges go grind and go bump. There is something else, something new out there, and it filters into his sleep until it wakes him, but by then it is, of course, too late.

There are four shadows standing by his bed like bed-posts and the bird-thing is a smear of red wetness on the ceiling. Goodbye, avian friend. And I never even knew your name. The four shadows move forward and a light comes on, emanating from them, green and sickly, and Dak sees they are hafmek, and he thinks, *Oh, shit*. Instinct tells him to keep quiet. There is little point in pleading or gabbing. The hafmek move with the whirring of motors. Their legs are wrought-metal tree trunks with delicate designs etched into the metal, whorls and vortices. Their bodies are patchwork armour, their heads the only vaguely human thing about them, although they bear more similarity to the swamp mutants than they do to people like Dak. Their eyes are hidden—*How trite!* Dak thinks even as he is frozen in his bed—by mirrorshades. The four hafmek pick him up—delicately, as they would something terribly light yet valuable—and carry him outside. There is a near full-moon that night and it gives the buildings of Gaslight an insubstantial appearance, and the air is humid and there is a smell of rotting vegetation, as if the jungle were that night encroaching into the town. Dak notices all that as the hafmek carry him into a giant steamroller and then climb inside themselves. The vehicle is like a moving house. There is something faintly organic about the walls. It rolls away from Gaslight, and strange beams of radiance erupt from its underbelly as if it is moving forward on light. It is some tek Dak had not seen before, although that, he readily admits to himself, isn't saying much.

They go over Tooth-bridge, cut across Cancer Ward, avoid Golgotha and pass into Gristown and beyond, moving away from the sea. The dark mountains tower above them.

Dak says, "Where are we going?" He is not expecting an answer.

One of the hafmek turns its head fractionally. It is hard to tell what lies behind the mirrors of its eyes. It says, "Open Sore."

Dak stares out of the window of the steamroller. They are away from the suburbs. They are going into the jungle. They are going beyond Man Place. Further inland than he has ever been, or wants to be. Open Sore. Shit shit shit.

He says, "Why?"

This time the hafmek don't bother with an answer.

The steamroller rolls across a land of enormous, unhealthy growth. The moon lights up gnarled trees, branches looped and shaped like giant spiders' webs, flower-heads as large as skulls, as pale, that follow their movement on long sinuous stalks that are like blind, malevolent snakes.

They come to a halt. There is a clearing in the forest, and in the clearing a house. It is a shocking thing to see in the midst of this place. It has a red tiled roof and light shines in the windows, and outside there is a small garden and a vegetable patch. There is a scarecrow positioned between two rows of plants. The hatch of the steamroller opens. The hafmek step out and Dak follows them. It is a place from a picture-book. A place that should no longer exist.

They walk up to the house through the vegetable patch. Dak brushes past the scarecrow and the moonlight falls down and the scarecrow's hand falls onto Dak's shoulder and holds him, and the scarecrow screams. Dak fights for release. The scarecrow looks like a mockery of a human body, moulded in some dark-green, pliable gunk. Its features run as it fights Dak. Its eyes are smeared across its face. Its mouth melts as it screams. Dak screams too. The hafmek watch impassively.

At last someone says, "Enough." The scarecrow freezes. Dak tears away. His palms are covered in green slime, like foul-smelling resin. The speaking voice is cool and calm and pleasant. "Please," the voice says. "Come in."

Dak looks up. The man standing in the doorway is of medium height and has brown hair and a mild, pleasant face. He extends his hand toward Dak. "Hey, man. Great to see you. Come in." A little dazed, Dak shakes his hand. "Dak, right?"

Dak nods. Dak follows the man into the house. Dak is scared shit-less. The house is warm and well-lit and pleasant. There are two couches and a desk and a desk-lamp and a sturdy wooden cabinet and a low table and two chairs made of the same honey-coloured wood as the cabinet. "Hey, sit down, man. Make yourself comfortable." The man closes the door. The hafmek stay outside.

Dak sits down on one couch. The man takes the one opposite. "So glad to meet you, Dak. Pit Stop Namba Six, right?"

Dak nods. "And before that, Stenchtown?" The man gets up and walks over to Dak. He bends over the boy. His face comes close to Dak's. The man trails his nose along Dak's cheekbones, down to his neck. Dak can feel the man's soft breath on his skin.

"Remarkable," the man says. He stands up and returns to his couch. "Can I get you anything? Tea? Coffee? A beer? Are you hungry?"

Dak shakes his head. The man smiles. "Oraet, Dak," he says, switching to Pidgin. The smile melts away. "Yu-mi gat wan problem. Yu gat wan samting bilong mi."

What? Dak says, "I took nothing—" And the man shakes his head. "You gat savvy bilong mi," he says. "Let's not yu-mi plaeplae, Dak. The knowledge you have is mine. I'm an 0wner. The 0wner of Pit Stop Namba Six, as it happens. So what you have in your possession—" he shrugs "—belongs to me. It's a fair trade, don't you think? They feed us knowledge. We feed them poisoned fish and clean them and keep them alive. I think that's more than fair. I think that's fucking *generous*."

Dak says, "I—"

The man says, "Are you an 0wner, Dak?"

Dak says, "I—"

The man says, "No. You're not. Are we agreed on that?"

Dak nods.

The man smiles. "Oraet," he says. "So we have a problem. So what do we do?"

Dak shakes his head. The man's smile grows larger. "I could kill you," he says. "I could torture you to see if you remember any more stuff the Growths may have divulged to you. Even their scraps have value. You know what this is? This is an information-scarcity environment we live in, Dak. Information is *God*, Dak. How to build certain machines. How to manufacture certain pills. How to do things you didn't even know you wanted to do until you found out you could do them.

You following me?"

Dak shakes his head, then nods. The man says, "I won't kill you, Dak. Why should I? I'm not a bad guy. I'm into knowledge for its own sake. Do you know what I am, Dak?"

Dak nods. He knows. He wishes very hard to be away.

He says, "You're Open Sore."

Blakenjel bilong mi stalks through the darkness like an avenging angel. He is not calm. He goes and he comes. In the early hours of the morning someone calls for him, a skull-head from Golgotha, coming down hard from Plateau. He begs for the power of the drug to be taken away from him. My blakenjel complies. As he leaves, I hear the screams of the skull-head. The drug can no longer affect him. But the wild craving remains, and it could never now be satisfied.

My blakenjel stalks away. He cannot stand still. I feel the passing of other blakenjels in the dark. It is a dance of blakenjels. I think they are speaking, and I wonder what they say.

"Open Sore," the man says with amusement. "Yes, well. That's what they call us, isn't it?" He stands up and stretches. "Etymologically interesting. But what we are—what 0wnerz are all about, Dak—is open *source*. Do you know what open source is, Dak?"

Dak knows. It's in the jungle all around them. It's in the scarecrow frozen in undeath outside. It's in the swamp-things. Open Sore. He wishes the man would stop calling him by his name. It is making him very nervous.

"Open source," the man says. "Information wants to be free. Not free to everyone, of course—that would be madness—but free to the people who *matter*, Dak. People who make a *difference*. We work to save the world. We're the fucking *heroes*, Dak!"

The man is no longer smiling. He is pacing around the room. There is the slightest sound of whizzing motors and Dak realises the man has mek inside him. Mek and the blakenjels know what else. The man says, "Why did the Growths want you to summon a blakenjel?"

And now, Dak realises, they are coming to it. The reason he is not, at this precise moment, a smear of blood on a ceiling in Gaslight.

He says, "I don't know."

The man backhands him. The impact throws Dak across the room. He groans, and thinks, with a savagery that surprises him, *You fucking freak.*

The man stands above him, looking down. "Stand up," he says quietly. Dak gets up.

Suddenly the light dims and changes. Around the man others appear: men, and women. They seem to materialise out of the air itself, a blakenwaet rainbow forming around him. Some of them are hafmek. Some of them have growths coming out—one woman has tentacles emerging from her nostrils as if a shell-creature lived inside her skull. The man who was speaking to Dak begins to change then. His features run, just as the scarecrow's did; he seems to melt in place. His skin turns a darker shade, and wings unfurl from his shoulder blades and open with a snap. The 0wnerz look at Dak. They are chanting.

"We are the open source," they say, "We are the 0wnerz. We protect you, we employ you, we give you life. We are open source."

Other things crawl and slither into the room. Jungle-things. Wild things. Open Sore things. There is a swamp-man with a lizard's tongue hissing out of the gap that is his mouth. There is an armoured crocodile with human eyes and grafted metal blades for the ridge on its back. They form a perfect circle around Dak. Their chanting rises in pitch and intensity. "We are Open Source. We defend you. We *save* you. We are the 0wnerz and we 0wn you!"

And Dak, terrified, prays to his blakenjel.

And only then does he see the triumph in the 0wnerz' eyes.

5. Blakenjel

For the length of a heartbeat, nothing happens. The 0wnerz close on Dak. Then the room is plunged into darkness.

Blakenjel bilong mi. blakenjel bilong mi. The words are swallowed in the velvety darkness. The words are cushioned by the absence of light. Blakenjel bilong mi. Blakenjel bilong mi.

Somewhere in the last hours my blakenjel acquired a voice. A singer from the opera-pits of Cancer Ward, begging to be released. He left her voiceless, and for once, in peace.

In the darkness he croons. In the darkness he sings. In the darkness he whispers words of love and of grief. I trot behind him. I am always there.

My blakenjel stops. My blakenjel snaps open his wings. My blakenjel turns, and I follow him.

The darkness expands across the room. Outside a howl sounds, of something feral moving around the perimeter of the house, and it is echoed inside by the 0wnerz. Something wet flops to the ground and someone screams, and the scream is cut short.

In the inky blackness Dak imagines he can hear voices.

Why should I let you live?

"Grab him!"

Laughter. A warm thick wetness sprays Dak's face. There is another scream.

"Wait!"

An amused, expectant silence.

"What *are* you?"

Is that all you wanted to know?

"Yes!"

We are blakenjel. We suffer you to stay. We protect you. We are your shepherds.

"I don't understand."

This is our place. Enough.

The sound of a body falling to the ground. The smell is suffocating.

"Wait!"

Silence.

"What do the Growths want with you? Why did they summon you?"

They do not belong here. Like you, small human. We let them in like we let you in. But now they want to leave. The dark is no place for the quick.

The human voice, the 0wner's whose house this is, is excited. "Leave? Go where? How did they come here? How did people come here?"

The blakenjel says, *There is always a price.*

There are no more sounds. Dak blinks. His eyes are wet. The house is quiet. There is no life inside. The darkness compresses around him. Light coagulates at its edges, tracing, like an artist's brush, the outlines of the carnage, corpses like chalk-figures sprawled on the floor, the light picking out small details, a smeared eyeball there, a puddle of green goo *there*, a surprised expression in a dead crocodile's curiously human eyes, and there—

There is a man standing in a corner of the room, where the walls and ceiling meet in a pyramid of shades. The man is small and bald and white and his skin is flabby and hangs loosely from his frame. The man looks at Dak hungrily. He has nervous eyes and he blinks a lot.

The darkness coalescences before Dak. He bows his head.

His blakenjel is there.

Blakenjel bilong mi. Blakenjel bilong mi! I hate him. I hate to share him. I hate to follow him. I want to be free of him. I look at the boy and know that my blakenjel loves him. He does not love me. He came to me as he always comes when he is called. And he granted my wish, as I knew he would. He let me follow him. In my case, the wish and the price paid were the same.

The boy bows his head to my blakenjel. And my blakenjel embraces him.

The blakenjel feels like old leather and metal wires. The blakenjel has no smell. The blakenjel doesn't speak. But the way he touches Dak is familiar: it is the way Naet once touched him.

The blakenjel caresses him.

Then something happens. The blakenjel pulls away. The sudden light nearly blinds Dak, but then his eyes adjust, and he can see.

All around him, the bodies on the floor, like darkness, coalesce. They re-form. They reassemble in hideous forms. They manufacture pseudopodia, eyeballs and naked mouths hanging on grisly stalks, and they speak as they ooze closer. "We are the source. We are *open* source. We are the 0wnerz—" and a familiar voice, the first 0wner, Dak thinks, shouts, "Grab him!"

The blakenjel turns and whirls. The re-formed 0wnerz ooze light. Dak wants to run, but there is nowhere to go. "Grab him!"

But it isn't to him that they go.

The mutilated corpses assemble into crawling, grabbing things, and they approach the corner of the room where a small bald white man with loose skin is standing kneading his hands. "Enjelvaljer!" the cry goes. "Grab him! Take the vulture!"

In the centre of the room there is inhuman laughter. The blakenjel comes to Dak. He wraps his form around him, and light and sound fade. *Come be with me,* the blakenjel says, *and be my love, and we shall all the darkness prove.*

Behind them Dak imagines he can hear a faint scream, but he can't be sure. He follows the blakenjel into the corridors of night.

6. Codicil

You measure out the days in sunsets
And months in moons
And dread the darkness.

Dak follows his blakenjel and he loves, which is a rare thing. He follows him through the corridors of night.

Once they return to Open Sore. They emerge from the darkness in a clearing and Dak sees the things that call themselves the source, and they are hideous yet still alive. They are tenacious. But the blakenjel pays them no attention. In the centre of the clearing is a shrunken wasted man, with skin grey-white and ill, and he is hanging upside-down from a gnarled and twisted tree. The man's thin lips move silently in prayer. It seems that he is saying, over and over, *Blakenjel bilong mi. Blakenjel bilong mi.*

Dak looks at the Ownerz. They clamour and they try to speak, they ask questions—they beseech. But the blakenjel pays them no heed.

He kills the hanging man with one sweep of his great sharp wings, and Dak follows him back through the darkness. There is always a price to pay.

And once, Dak follows his blakenjel to the high mountains that rise away from the towns, beyond Open Sore, where the air is clean and cold and it is quiet; and Dak's blakenjel lays a great obsidian egg in the fine-grained black sand.

Behold: Skowt!

Jason Heller

My eyes are dinosaur eggs. My tongue cracks like lightning. I been there, done that, drunk it, fucked it, lived it. I am the hole in the roof where the brains leak in. I eat jerks like you for breakfast. Behold: me! Behold: Skowt!

I slink through the street with my dick in my fist and fireworks up my ass. It's Friday night on the Protein Delta, and the cold cuts are queuing up for inspection. Can't sleep on this shit, son. When you're an old ho of fourteen like Skowt, you gotta work it.

And work it I do.

The sun comes up, blue on chrome, pushing away the moon and its huge blinking billboard hawking vaccines and tooth creams. Could use some of those myself. My gums taste like rust. I had this one jerk around four a.m., into blood. Fucking pervert, all of seventeen. Give me a tired old jerk any day. I'll pop him like a balloon and send him on his way, twenty bills and a teaspoon lighter.

My head screams for naptime, but I know I can't. Naps cost paysa—paysa for a room, paysa you'll get rolled for, paysa you're not out making.

Plus, I got a mission to complete. It started the day I was born. It ends the day I die.

I have to tell the world about Skowt.

My old name is Oso, but you'd better call me Skowt now, bitches. If you need a reminder, I'll burn it on your ass. Or you can just check for my tag. You won't have to look hard. My paint's everywhere. I'm nationwide, coast to coast. Or at least I'm working on it.

I take last night's paysa and head east of the Delta, across the crap swamp and blacktop frizzy with waist-high weeds. I make it to Wowoyo Market before noon. I stop by the Datra's and make arrangements for later. Then it's time to stock up on the regular supplies: krosi, plague shots, and chem-drops to purify my piss for drinking water.

Oh, yeah, and paints. Gotta have my paints.

You'll never know what it's like to shake them cans of paint and feel the ball bearings clang around like planets. I rip my tag across brick walls and bed sheets drying on the line. "Behold: Skowt!" Then again. And again. Andagainandagainandagain. "BEHOLD: SKOWT!" My tag is bright like a peacock, crazy like a spider web. Honed by centuries of sharpening it against the skulls of dumbfucks. No cop ever caught me. I suck and spray, suck and spray, and they don't get the time of day.

"Fo waka, Skowt!" It's Erl.

"Fo waka, Erl."

Erl is all right.

"You tagging today?"

"The fuck you think?"

"I dunno, man, I thought you might be down for a dunk in the canal."

I laugh my ass off right in Erl's fat face. "The canal? Are you real? You'll catch more crud in that canal than you will in some old jerk's olo."

Erl sniffs. I forgot to take it easy on him. He's pretty big for eleven, but still, he's just a baby.

"Hey, Erl! It's good, it's good. We'll hit up that canal. But let's go tag some first, huh? You with me?"

Erl's face lights up. "I'm with you, Skowt."

I'll be straight: It was no accident I ran into Erl. I knew where he was gonna be, when he was gonna be there. Erl's predictable. Not like me. You never know which way my dick is gonna be coming at you. Ha!

Mostly I tag alone. That's kind of the whole point. It's just me, my paints, and an empty space crying out to get filled. Sometimes the vids in Wowoyo show old stories, ones about fucking for love. Fucking for love! I don't get it. But I bet it feels like tagging.

Today, though, I need Erl. I need a sidekick, a pack mule. A lookout.

Some big shit, you understand, is about to go down.

You'd think hustling on the Delta, busting ass, dodging cops and pimps would be plenty of ambition for a young businessman like myself. But I got something no one else around here does: the tonton of a cheetah. I came into this world with no one. None of that mama and papa crap, as far as I can scope. I had a little brada once, Imi, but he didn't last on the Delta too long.

That's when I knew I had to make it. Not just make it: fucking *triumph*.

Babies like Erl, they're good kids. Strong kids. But they don't have *vision*. That's where Skowt comes in.

It squats there like a castle in the dark. See, I'm smart. I can read. I seen books and lifted handhelds. Castles used to look just like this: big and blank and beautiful.

Oh, the fucking tagging I'd give this place. I can see it now: "Behold: Skowt!" Each letter as tough and sharp and tall as me. But I got bigger jerks to fry.

This particular castle has razor wire instead of a moat and some skinny old fuck in a blue suit for a knight. Me and Erl sit scoping it out in the bushes, eating crispy roach and using the red-specs I got when I went back to the Datra earlier. That woman can rig anything, fix anything, for the right price.

I blew a whole roll of paysa at the Datra's today. She finally finished building my virus. It took her months and cost me plenty, lots of overtime on both our parts.

Her disc I put in my pocket along with a couple other vital pieces of hardware. The rest of the shit I loaded up into Erl's rucksack like he was a burro. Poor Erl. Then we headed out from the Market for the castle, where we now crouch like hyenas with nothing to laugh about.

Leaping from the leaves, we time everything just right. We use the old stopwatch and the metal-cutter we got from the Datra's junk pile. It's not like it's that hard to break in anyway. No one has the paysa to do shit right anymore. Not even the kings of the cocksucking castle.

We're through the moat, past the knight. Then another one of the Datra's toys—a scrambler—gets us in the door. Dressed in black and humping shadows, I want to roar at the sky.

I'm a fucking dragon. I feel like a fucking dragon.

"Skowt. Skowt, I'm scared." Erl's been quiet so far. I should've figured he'd get spooked. "They won't even bother giving us to a judge if they catch us. A couple of Delta rats. They'll just torch us."

"Erl. Too late. We're in. We're in!" I have a hard time keeping my voice down. "The moment is at hand. We're dicking the moon in the earhole, Erl. We're skull-fucking that bitch!"

Erl starts to whimper. I drag him into the maze of dark hallways, scrambler in one hand, the Datra's map burned into my brain.

Deeper we go.

Finally, the door.

I stand there for a second, and for that second I feel little Oso inside me. I hear him. I hear him whining in the alleys, licking garbage, slurping out of puddles. Puking. Snot all over. A jerk takes him, hard, and soon he figures out he can trade one end of himself for the other.

It's not easy. What is? But none of that matters anymore. Oso is Skowt now, and Skowt is an ice-hard bastard of the street. Skowt *is* the street. Stone. A Protein dragon. Long, black, scrawny. Scales made out of footprints and burnt rubber. I spit fire, and my fire fucks all.

With a final blast of juice from the scrambler, I blow the door open.

Fuck! I'm blind.

It's a room of crystal. Cables dangle from the ceiling like cave rock. Vids blink like lizards' eyes. Smoke and greasy steam pours out of everywhere. Erl runs back down the hall like a fat tapir, but I don't care. I made it. And I have a mission.

My eyes get used to the sparkles, and I head for the first terminal. I pull out my handheld, a gift from some old jerk who fell asleep on top of me and never woke up. I've run through the Datra's instructions a hundred times, but it's different when it's real. Trickier. I slip the disc, Datra's virus, into the handheld and hook the handheld up to the terminal.

The terminal starts sucking it down.

I move from terminal to terminal, plugging and tapping, plugging and tapping. The keys are little gems, cut-glass barnacles. It's a mess of light and color in there. The Datra used to know someone who programmed here, and she told me all about it: The system's a total scavenge job, held together with jizz and paperclips. Steaming pistons spin the disc drives. Oil sizzles. It's hard to breathe. And it's fucking hot, hot as the blacktop in summertime.

Even worse, I figure, I've only got a couple minutes. I was stupid to bring Erl. I just figured out where he's running.

An echo rings down the hallway outside. That fat little shit is faster that I thought.

"Down here! You'll tell them, right, mister? You'll tell them that I told you?"

I keep tapping away like crazy at the last terminal. Erl sticks his head in the doorway. The skinny old guard in the blue suit is right behind him.

It's funny the shit the Delta will make you do. Sometimes you hurt yourself so other people can't. Sometimes you just hurt them first. I don't blame Erl. I know he's just a kid, a baby. He shouldn't be out there queuing up every night, nothing to anyone but a slab of cold cut. Some kids ain't made for that. Erl ain't. Imi wasn't.

I am.

I take the old guard's bullet in the armpit just as a last rush of juice gushes from my handheld and into the terminal. Steam jets out of it, scalding me. I slump to the floor.

The guard's head turns into a puff of red mist as I pull a one-shooter out of my back pocket and fire it at his eyes.

I yell at Erl. Stuff comes up in my puke. My lungs make a sucking noise, like this: *foko foko, foko foko*. Erl is crying, a dry cry, and he starts to pull me out of the hissing machinery.

"No!" I yell. "Leave me here!" Erl won't listen, which is good, 'cause I don't know what I'm saying. I catch one last look at the control room's vids, but it's all steam. Steamsteamsteam.

When I wake up I'm outside in the bushes, flat on my back. Alarms are going off. Erl is blubbering and saying sorry. The cool night air is pouring in through my ribs.

I look up.

The moon is orange, swirly, like a drop of blood in a glass of water.

Huge. A hole punched into the night.

In the middle of that hole is the billboard. But there aren't any commercials for vaccines projected on it tonight. No ads for tooth creams in letters a hundred miles high and visible from the deepest alleys of the Delta, from all the other alleys of all the other Deltas, from sea to shitty sea.

Instead it's a tag. Bright like a peacock, crazy like a spider web.

I grip Erl. "It's okay," I say. "Take me to the Datra," I say.

Like I told you already: I'm a thunderbolt in heat, a fucking rocket manned by a panther astronaut. *Ancient.* My mission started the day I was born, and it ends the day I die. But Skowt ain't nowhere close to being dead yet. All the world knows is my name, my tag, hanging there in the night sky like a black eye all purple and yellow on the ugly blue face of the moon.

That's a lot. But it's just a start. Skowt's still got plenty to learn you bitches. *Plenty.*

Behold, motherfuckers. Behold.

SHADED STREAMS RUN CLEAREST

GEOFFREY W. COLE

Your wife will keep cheating on you, at least until the world ends," Calais said. The young husband seemed resigned to his fate. Calais led him to the door, and flipped the sign to 'Closed'.

Calais ordered a pizza from the Italian place at the other end of the mall while he shut down the temponeural coils of the amplification array. The machine powered off, but he remained in the un-amplified future that always hummed at the edge of his perception. So many intertwining streams. There was a chance the cheated husband would leave his wife, a chance she would reform her ways, but these days no one had any impetus to change, not when every licensed precog saw the same mushroom-clouded future.

A knock on the door drew Calais out of the trance. The pizza boy? It would be a first if he were early. Calais unlocked the door.

"If you're closed, I can come back tomorrow," the Independent Senator said. She hid behind oversized sunglasses, a copper wig, and a Seattle Aquarium T-shirt.

"Of course not," Calais said. "Please take a seat."

He switched the amplification array back on.

"I've never used your profession's services before," she said.

"Then you're unique. A wise politician. Most are foolish enough to keep precogs on their payroll. The process is simple. Ask what you'd like to know, and I'll trace the flow for probable answers."

She placed her sunglasses on the desk between them. "The Presidential candidates have both asked for my endorsement. I've heard the rumours on the street, what your colleagues see coming. I try not to believe them, but in that I might also be unique. I want to know what our country will look like under both candidates."

Calais sighed. He didn't need the array for this, but the Senator would require more than just his word. He dove into that part of his mind that never stopped muttering, the intertwining streams that led to the future.

"Nothing is fixed," he said. "But some futures are more likely than others. The election is a close thing and could go either way, but it doesn't really matter."

On the screens, images drawn from his mind were distilled to a meaningful sequence. He turned the screens so the Senator could see them.

"If the Democrats win, war will arrive seven months after the President is sworn in." On the screens, ships and airplanes loaded with troops steam for distant borders. America and her allies engage in a pitched battle in the ruins of an ancient city. Then a blinding flash. "The bombs fall, overseas first, on our soil hours later."

"And the Republicans?"

"Little better," he said. "The war will start later, a year and a half after the election. The bombs another year after that, though in some streams they'll arrive a few months earlier."

"There must be some futures where we avoid this madness," she said.

That dark place beyond the bombs was not a place Calais strayed often. Only a few silver threads of possibility flowed past the nuclear winter, and those were less likely than the Mariners winning the World Series. Then, as he watched, a new stream trickled into the future, a stream he'd never seen before, but it was overwhelmed by the tsunami of war and destruction following behind it.

"Those futures are rarer than a wise politician," Calais said. He stood. "This foretelling is on the house, Senator. I can't charge you for such bad news."

She remained seated.

"What if I run against the other candidates?" she said.

The silver trickle thickened into a creek. A new future, born here in his mini-mall office. Calais sat and followed the flow, tweaked the amplification array, and turned the screens to the Senator.

"You could win," he said. "The chances are slim, but not insurmountable."

The stream widened as if swollen by a flash flood. Images filled the screens: the Senator at a music festival, the stage filled with musicians singing her praise; an abandoned air force base, the runway packed with supporters; the Senator, no longer Senator, in front of the White House, answering questions for the press.

"What about the war?" she said.

He turned the screens back to face him.

The creek was a river now, and the war and the mushroom clouds washed ahead of the clear current of hope. "There are eddies, forks, where the war and the megadeaths find us but, for the most part, the stream runs clear. You can prevent the war."

Then he found it. A flash at first: the Senator, now President, in an interview at her lake home, then a small explosion and the home disappears. But assassinations were in every President's future. Then Calais found another: she's shot, as she throws the first pitch at a Mariners game. And another: her motorcade is destroyed by explosive-filled laundry trucks.

"What is it? What do you see?"

Calais kept the screens turned to him. The College of Professional Precognitives prohibited showing a client their own death, but the Senator would learn of it from someone else if not from him. She offered the only hope he'd foreseen in years. Would he dam that hope by showing her? It wasn't for him to decide. He turned the screens that showed her probable deaths.

"Do I survive anywhere?"

"Nothing is fixed."

"But some futures are more likely than others," she said. "I see why wise politicians don't use your services."

She unfolded the glasses and put them back on. She walked to the door. The stream they'd set flowing, although beset on all sides by darkness and war, still rushed toward a future unmarred by nuclear winter.

"What's your name?" she said.

"Calais. After the town in which I was conceived."

"Can I count on your vote, Calais?"

He waited for the pizza to arrive after she left, but he knew he wouldn't be able to eat. Something else filled his belly, part awe, part dread, and neither left room for hunger.

Plebiscite AV3X

Jason Fischer

1. Cast your primary party-preferred vote for the next President of the United Australasian Republic:

      A) Sharon Nicholson, National Party, Australia

      B) Kade Suharto, Muhammadiyah, Indonesia

      C) Gavin Pollard, Labour Party, New Zealand

      D) Ghera Wanganeen, Indigenous Forum, Australia

2. Do you support the proposed amendment to the Lunar Settlement Act?

      A) Yes

      B) No

      C) Amendment to be re-read in the Senate

3. What is your most frequent online purchase?

      A) Medicine

      B) Weapons

      C) Sex/Cybersex

      D) Regulated Criminal Services

4. Do you support the joint invasion of Antarctica?

      A) Declaration of War by UAR

      B) Cessation of Hostilities

      C) Await final reports from U.N. Xenotech Inspectors

Civic duties giving you a burning thirst?
Enjoy Cannie,
the drink of Olympic athletes!

5. How do you find the defendant in State vs Becker?
    A) Guilty—Death
    B) Guilty—Custodial sentence (please specify):
    C) Not Guilty
    D) Mistrial
    E) Trial by combat

6. What is your preferred datacom?
    A) Telstra
    B) GapComm
    C) Jakarta Kreatif
    D) None of the above (Neo-Luddites Only)

7. How happy are you? (please indicate %):

8. Who do you want to vote out of "Starvation Cage!"
    A) Jerry the plumber
    B) Brenda the model
    C) Bradley and Trevor, the platonic life-mates
    D) Hank the sensitive trucker

Depressed? Can't carry on?
Why not call Euthentikit
and we'll take care of everything

9. How much money should be allocated to Education this financial year?
    A) $UAR 5 billion
    B) $UAR 7.5 billion
    C) $UAR 1.3 billion (user-pays model)

10. Should aid be continued to the Pederast colony on Titan?
      A) Yes
      B) No— Bring the sex offenders back to Earth for custodial re-
          settlement.
      C) No – Grant the Pederast colony unconditional autonomy
      D) No – Detonate the embedded warhead

11. Do you support Defence-UAR's proposal to cleanse all Class 5 sub-
    urbs? (lower socio-economic, high crime, high fertility)
      A) Yes (complete destruction of life)
      B) No (continue aid and relief work)
      C) Yes —Senator Walker's proposed selective cull

12. Nominate a suspicious character, as defined by the Good Neigh-
    bours Act. (Note: a failure to complete this section will result in
    your automatic nomination, under the above Act)

Submit this week's Plebiscite *here*. Your Will be Done!

A Splash of Color

William T. Vandemark

The average human body holds six liters of blood.

I should have known Travis would need more. He always needed more.

Twenty years old, Anna arrived at his studio unannounced, chin upraised, eyes of cornflower blue. Assorted piercings bellied her innocence, as did the holographic tattoo in the small of her back. Each registered as she stepped through the doorway. The studio's security system provided audio to my cochlear implants; chips in my contacts cast readouts to my retinas. As I processed the data, the scan hiccupped. Her tat, a Celtic knot, had discharged a fractal trap, jacking security into a worthless whorl of minutiae. I bit my tongue and forced a re-task. Then, despite indications that this girl had plated her wares, I directed security to run an iris tickle.

Protocol warnings tinted my vision amber. *Anna Chenko, daughter of Alexander Chenko.*

Shit. I reset with a hard blink, my eyes watering from the effort. T-minus one hour till one mother of a migraine would lay me out.

Travis turned to his canvas. He loaded up a painting knife and spread a daub of ultramarine along an arc.

Don't be an ass, I thought. Acknowledge her at least. His implants had received the same info as mine. Instead, he made her wait, setting the ground rules.

Anna folded her arms and surveyed the studio. Her gaze swept over the furnishings, which amounted to a few folding chairs, a stainless steel table, and an old church pew, where rags, jars of pigments, and crumpled tubes of oil paints lay strewn. Then she turned her attention to Travis's floor-to-ceiling canvases, which canted against the brick walls. The works included abstracts painted with handmade pigments, cellular mosaics tiled with scales from butterfly wings, and etched aerogels, the scrim lines lit by plasma. All resided in varying states of completion.

My work was on display in the raftered ceiling, five meters above, where a magnetic bore hung from a spaghetti of conduits, ductwork, and cables. Brow raised, Anna took it in. She glanced at me and nodded once, in what I took to be tacit acknowledgment of my role here.

"We weren't expecting visitors," I said. I knocked over a canister of brushes, as I stood to greet her.

"My father would like Mr. Bonsanti to paint a portrait of my family. A surprise for my mother on their anniversary."

Travis stabbed his canvas and turned. The painting knife dangled from the rent. "I don't take commissions," he said.

Anna's eyes widened, but she spoke with a measured calm. "You answer as if I made a request. Access your data snatch. I gave you a two -second deep search."

"We don't snatch," I said. "That'd be illegal." By the time I'd finished my denial, her dossier was back in my brainpan or, more precisely, in a wedge of qRAM splined to my occipital lobe. As I initiated a wet-sync, Travis jigged the juice and left me a sludge of public records. Not a day went by when I didn't regret giving him access to Ops.

"Six million," Travis said. "Euro." The price was exorbitant; he was trying to send her packing.

"Done." She pointed at me, her fingernail tipped in iridium. "You the piggy?"

Bitch. I wiped my hand on my pants and held out my palm. She drew her fingernail along my lifeline and zipped the terms, payment, and assurances into a New Delhi bitfold.

"It's going to be a pleasure working with you," she said. Then she glanced at my pants and smiled. "I see you feel the same way."

Goddamn. A bio-script, woven into the transfer, had burrowed past my security and was giving me a hard-on. Cute. Real cute. Everyone was setting ground rules but me.

"Combs and hairbrushes," I said. "Get them to us within a week.

One from each member of the family. Label them, and don't mix them up. Underwear works too. Dirty of course."

"You want mine now?" she asked.

She was not being helpful. I turned for a modicum of privacy, reached into my pants, and made adjustments.

Bio-scripted worms aside, something about her piqued my curiosity. Clearly, she wasn't just some nouveau riche walk-in looking to snag a Bonsanti for the guesthouse. Perhaps it was her air of assurance. Perhaps her damned fine glam-tech. Still, I couldn't pinpoint my interest. She was cute in an off-the-shelf kind of way, but not close to the body-modded beauties Travis employed for nudes. I made eye contact with a sensor across the room and scratched my nose.

Ops ran a syn-pheromone check. *Nominal.*

"Mr. Bonsanti, your studio boy has nice manners. Not a single attempt at body mapping. But he likes to sniff me."

"Don't get your panties in a bunch," I said. I fished a vial from my satchel, snapped plastic, and slid out a swab. I took her by the chin. "Open up, Sunshine." Angling her mouth, I worked the swab around the inside of her cheek, resisting the urge to flick her uvula.

Head shaved, coiled filaments drooping from his scalp like silver dreadlocks, Travis finished a figure study. He was at the end of a ten-minute creativity boost, transcranial magnetism manipulating his brain activity.

He had rendered an abstract of Anna. The piece captured her form, spirit, and yes, with a smudge of red, arcing from her mons pubis to the negative space of the canvas, he'd captured the tension of her presence. I'd exhaled a short, sharp breath the first time I saw the work.

Travis stared at his canvas, repeatedly pressing his thumb against the tip of his painting knife.

I shifted into conductor mode and mimed his stim settings to OFF, shutting down the magnetic bore in the ceiling. Then, eyes closed, I examined a skein of his neural activity. Hotspots were already cooling, blue regions warming. When I opened my eyes, Travis was still thumbing his knife.

"Looking to shiv someone?" I asked.

"I bet she'd donate to the cause."

"Excuse me?"

"She'd give up some of her eggs. You can run the harvest. Want a little peek-a-boo time?" His brain's inhibition center, such as it was, had yet to re-fire after the brainstorm session. In that moment, even if he had been stone drunk, he could not have been more obnoxious.

"Not funny, Travis. Not for one second. She's a Chenko. As in the Chenko Oligarchy. Tell me you understand."

"She's cute. She's hanging around here. Do the math."

The math. Right. The last time Travis did the math, he'd harvested human eggs from donors, scrambled them for tempera, and painted a Christmas mural. Sure, sales and prices quintupled overnight, but my sleep retrograded proportionately as death threats poured in.

"You can mag her," Travis said. He bobbed his head, filaments rasping. "Take her to joy-ville. Give her a taste. She'll book a return trip."

"What are you, a pimp or a painter?"

"Binder and pigment, baby. When the mix is right, it's all in the application. Hell, I bet I can get her to jump your gourd."

"That's enough. I'm not kidding." Sometimes I wondered if prolonged doses of magnetism hadn't cooked his grey matter. "Just stop," I said. "I bet our windows are already lased, pane vibrations read as we speak."

A month after returning with DNA samples, Anna sat across from me, prepping burnt umber for her family's portrait. With mortar and pestle, she mashed kidney organelles cultured from her brother. The smell, earthy and pungent, mingled with the fragrance she wore.

I gestured an inquiry.

Lilac water, Ops responded.

"You could have just asked," Anna said without looking up. I bit my lip and watched her work.

When she'd first returned, she'd offered Travis a sizable sum for painting lessons. He told her that money meant nothing to either party—at which point I suggested he access last month's invoices. Instead, he agreed to an exchange and set her to work under my tutelage. "You two work out the details," he'd said with a slap to my back.

Now, as she leaned into the mortar, her grip tight on the pestle, I watched the subtle dance of her clavicle and the shifting hollow of her throat.

"Who's your favorite artist?" she asked, breaking my reverie. She looked up; I looked away.

"Leonardo," I said.

"Da Vinci?"

I nodded. "Yeah. No contest."

"He means me," Travis called from across the studio, where he had stretched an epidermal canvas, the skin cultured from Anna's cheek swab. With a sweep of his arm, he plastered progenitor cells across the scaffolded skin and directed Ops to flash them with UV. After another pass, he tossed his trowel into a bucket and joined us.

Anna withdrew a pipette from a beaker and dribbled some lactic acid into her mixture. "How about Jackson Pollock?"

Travis made a dismissive snort. "Dripping paint across a canvas takes as much skill as pissing your name in the snow."

"Depends on the pisser," I said.

Anna nodded. "And the name."

Travis moved behind her. He leaned in, his head next to hers as if inspecting her work. I closed my eyes for a quick settings check. He had been off mag-stim for a good thirty minutes. His neural cloud looked fine.

"I splined a documentary," Anna said. "In it, Pollock said that a good painter paints what he is."

Travis grasped Anna's hand, his fingers overlapping hers. He worked the pestle through her. "A good painter paints desire," he said. "Nothing more, nothing less." He let go of her hand and ran his fingers through her hair.

"Hey, watch it." She swatted his hand away.

"Artists need muses," Travis said. "What do you say, would you like to amuse me?" He leaned over and whispered into her ear.

With a quick turn, she slapped his face. "Make your own pigment, *mudak.*" She stood, tossed the pestle onto the table, and headed for the door.

Travis followed her. "My mistake, my mistake."

"Just let her go," I said.

"But she's earned a lesson." He caught Anna as she opened the door. He stepped past and shouldered it closed.

"Get out of my way," she said.

Travis locked the deadbolt. "Or what, you'll call Daddy?"

She swung at him, a roundhouse that glanced off his shoulder. Travis laughed, but Anna silenced him with a kick to his shin and an uppercut to his stomach. He bent with a grunt.

"Are we done?" she asked.

Travis, still bent, bowed more deeply. He gestured at the door with a flourish. "Your carriage awaits."

Anna glanced at me, and I shrugged a helpless apology. Then, as she turned to leave, Travis stepped behind her, reached out, and yanked her backwards by the shirt collar. Fabric tore and buttons popped off. They skittered across the floor like broken teeth.

Anna cried out. "Let me go this instant," she said. "Or you're dead. Do you hear me?"

"Ah, violence," Travis said. "The Chenko *oeuvre*." He dragged her to the center of the studio.

She screamed, a strangled cry of frustration, and clutched at her blouse. "I'm not joking."

"No, I don't suppose you are." Travis pulled a painting knife from his back pocket and set it to her throat. "Neither am I."

I stood in disbelief. "Travis, what the hell? Take it easy."

"Take it easy? It doesn't get any easier than this." He shifted the knife to Anna's cheek and angled it back and forth, flashing light across her eye. "Tell me, does Daddy collect Picassos? A nose for an ear might look nice. How about a tongue for an eye?"

"Stop," Anna said.

"But I've just begun." He slipped his free hand through the buttonless gap in her shirt and moved it across her stomach, his thumb along her lower rib. Then, as he swept his hand up her side, fingers to her armpit, the fabric separated.

"Goddamnit, Travis," I said.

Anna trembled and closed her eyes.

I closed mine too and brought up an interface. I gesture-flicked through stim settings as fast as I could, searching for a way to circumvent safety protocols on the magnetic bore. I rifled past programs that could induce kinesthesia, lucid dreaming, and out-of-body experiences, but found nothing that would paralyze Travis in one electromagnetic shot. Instead I settled on targeting his brain's sleep centers.

I opened my eyes and pointed at him, my hand miming a pistol.

Ops read the gesture, and the bore in the ceiling swung around, its housing whirring like a Gatling gun. "Let her go," I said. "Or so help me, I'll drop you in a narcoleptic second."

Travis stepped to Anna's side, placing her between the bore and himself. Although the armature tracked his movements, I hesitated. Anna wore no filaments to translate the radiation, but Ops had never run a clean scan. I'd no idea what implants she carried.

"Let her go," I said.

Travis pulled his hand from Anna's shirt and waggled his fingers, glossed with her sweat. "I have what I need," he said, "Dial it down, and fire up the chromatograph."

"What are you on about?" His demeanor had changed, but I had no idea why. It was as if the assault had been a joke, and he'd just delivered the punch line.

He grinned and blew across his fingers. "Fear and anger added to the palette."

Then it hit me. He wanted her scent for the portrait. "You've got to be kidding," I said. "All this for her pheromones?"

"Nice and ripe."

"The progenitor cells—that's why you infused the canvas?"

"We differentiate them—"

"—Into apocrine sweat glands," I said, finishing his thought.

"Exactly. By the time I'm done, that portrait will glisten under a pheromone varnish." He kissed Anna on the head and tossed his knife onto the table.

The color drained from Anna's face. "Wait," she said. "This was just an act? Some twisted game to scare me?"

"Don't be ridiculous," Travis said. "Think of it as a defining moment. When people stand in front of the portrait, when they behold your family's gleaming smiles and sparkling eyes, they'll whisper, 'How wonderful.' Then, with each passing moment, palpable dread will grow. After a few minutes, people will wish to flee. But I ask you, what person would dare turn his back on the Chenko Family?" Travis laughed, his eyes bright with glee.

"You're sick," Anna said.

Travis winked. "So endeth the lesson."

Anna began to shake. "I've got to get out of here."

I took her by the shoulders. "Take a deep breath," I said, trying to settle things down. "He wasn't going to hurt you. Everything's fine."

She shook her head. "Everything's not fine."

"Look, I know he could have done things differently—"

"You don't get it. I'm tripwired."

A cold weight settled in my stomach. *Tripwired*: she carried a distress beacon. Nodes tracked adrenaline and half a dozen other neurotransmitters. If biometrics reached designated levels, an emergency call tied to GPS alerted police or private security firms. I'd looked into getting one for Travis after the tempera incident. "Did it fire?" I asked.

"I don't know."

"Can you reset?"

"Look, it doesn't matter. My father will tear this place apart. He'll tear you apart. He won't stop until he finds out what happened. You've got to disappear."

"Someone's on a short leash," Travis said.

Anna threw her hands up. "Forget it. Forget the portrait, forget the money, forget I was ever here. What a mistake I've made. What a waste of—"

A high-pitched whine pierced the air; pain shot through my teeth. A moment later, the entrance door groaned, metal on metal. It bulged inwards, a fizz of paint flecks popping from the casement.

"Oh, God," Anna said.

With a thump, the room pressure changed.

Anna dropped to the ground. "Get down," she said.

Before I could move, the door snapped back and crashed into the hallway. Immediately, four men, dressed in suits and ties, burst through the roil of dust and debris. They could have been executives arriving for a meeting. Instead, they carried laser-sighted pistols with blood-red beams that crisscrossed the air. The laser lines stopped, two on Travis, two on me.

"Wait!" Anna said. She scrambled to her feet and ran at the men, cutting across the beams.

The lead man holstered his weapon and stepped to meet her. He snatched her by the wrist and, with a quick pivot, picked her up like a child.

"Put me down," Anna said. "Put me down this instant." She kicked and screamed as he carried her from view, her words tumbling into curses. From the hall, came one last cry, "Don't hurt them. Please, please, don't hurt them."

The average human body holds about six liters of blood.

Travis needed more. He always needed more.

Upside-down, cables tied about his ankles, Travis hung like a side of beef in a slaughterhouse. Beneath him lay a canvas I'd unfurled at gun-point. With ruthless efficiency, Chenko's men had jacked Ops, flayed the data banks, and stripped my qRAM. Then they'd flooded Travis's creativity centers, dampened his pain transmitters, and opened the veins in his wrists with the same painting knife he'd set to Anna's throat.

Now, Travis's movements alternated between composed and frantic, as the men took turns swinging him over the canvas. Part of him seemed to know what was happening, but part was unconcerned, immersed in the experience. Every few minutes he'd strain to reach his bonds with blood-slicked hands. But eventually, he'd fall back and sway with exhaustion, as threads of blood fell from his fingertips.

By the second canvas, Travis began to paint. Whether it came from the loss of blood, the magnetism flicking his neurons, or a realization that this was to be his last work, I'd no idea. But rapidly, he achieved surety. Looping and gliding to an inner music, he directed his symphony of blood–his drips, lines, and spatters. With a drifting beauty that iterated, never repeated, Travis painted his life away.

Midway into the third canvas, one of Travis's languished moments exploded into a spray of rapture. He hurled collected fistfuls of blood. With it, I reached my limit. The horror pierced my numbness. "No more," I said.

In unison, the men turned from Travis and raised their pistols. Lasers placed a solitary red dot on my breastbone.

I took a deep breath. "Just end it," I managed. Motes glittered in the beams.

In response, my cochlear implants burst with static. Breathing replaced it, each breath punctuated with a short wheeze. "My daughter is quite unhappy with me," a voice said.

Alexander Chenko.

Whether he waited in the hallway or a continent away, I'd no idea. His words came through a tightcast directed at my implants.

He sighed. "She fails to apprehend that a man in my position cannot afford to leave certain insults unanswered." He paused. "Ah well, such is the idealism of youth, *da*?"

"Anna—she's all right?"

"That you have a tongue with which to ask provides the answer." His voice boomed, omni-directional. Godlike, it filled my head.

"Tell her I'm sorry," I said.

"And you expect this to provide sufficient recompense?"

"No. Not really. I just want her to know."

Silence fell and my vision darkened; Chenko was making sure I knew who was in control. In the muffled darkness, I felt as if I were trapped in a coffin awaiting the thump of burial dirt. Such was the moment of his judgment.

Then static ate the silence. My vision returned with a burning flash.

"Consider her intervention as the sole reason you will not join your associate in collaboration."

Without a word, Chenko's men turned from me. I was free to go.

Filled with a hollowness that has only deepened with time, I watched Travis's blood pressure plummet. My vision blurred with a cascade of Op warnings and my ears rang with a klaxon, echoes of which awaken me yet, in the deep of night, to sheets soaked with sweat.

Suddenly, the data ceased; the alarms snapped silent. Chenko, of all people, was sparing me the final details.

All but one.

In the quiet, I realized Travis still had time to assess his work. His spatters had become random; his lines, thin and lifeless; his flow, stagnant. His final painting amounted to little more than a Jackson Pollock knock-off.

I wanted to say something, to offer comfort, to ask forgiveness.

Words wouldn't come.

Turned out, none were needed.

With one last gesture, blood dripping from his fingertip, Travis signed his canvas.

Organ Nell

Jennifer Pelland

Nell Gabrielli: They tell me I've saved nearly two hundred people's lives already, and helped almost five hundred more. (Pauses.) That's important. That's real important.

Richard Forrest, Medical Ethicist: Ms. Gabrielli is a prisoner of the medical system, plain and simple. What's been done to her is a travesty. And the fact that she was convinced to consent to it only makes it worse.

Dr. Sylvia Burbage, New England Medical College: Nell is a miracle. All our team did was take the genetic bounty that nature provided her and find a way to make it benefit others. I understand that people find this disturbing, but how could we let this gift of hers go to waste? Now that would have been irresponsible.

Father Raymond Cleary, St. Cecilia's Church, Lowell: I'm generally wary of medical professionals declaring things to be miracles. That's the church's job. But in the case of Nell Gabrielli, I find it hard to argue. And like most miracles, it comes at a high cost for the grantor.

Nell Gabrielli: When was the last time I left the hospital? (Looks out window.) Maybe six years?

Dr. Neil Steffensen, Minneapolis School of Medicine: Any doctor who accepts a transplant from Nell Gabrielli is playing Russian roulette with his patient. We have no idea what's going to happen to these people down the line.

Mick Coombs, Transplant Recipient: I've gotten two years of life that I wouldn't have had without this replacement kidney. They wouldn't even put me on the regular transplant list because I was so old. I don't care if I start sprouting horns or turn green tomorrow—I would never have lived to see my first great-grandchild without this kidney.

Megan Ferretti, Medical Reporter for NBS: It all began at Lowell Memorial Hospital, a public hospital twenty-five miles north of Boston. Lowell Memorial serves predominantly low-income patients, many of whom get free or low-cost insurance coverage from the state. The hospital was suffering a staffing crisis, and its president started asking his friends in the local medical community for help. One of the doctors who answered the call was Dr. Sylvia Burbage, a professor and researcher at New England Medical College, who started volunteering her services on weekends. One of her first patients was Nell Gabrielli, an unemployed twenty-six-year-old woman.

Dr. Burbage: Nell came to me presenting with a small fleshy sac, growing from the surface of her stomach. Her chart indicated that she'd been treated all her life for benign, mature teratomas. Teratomas are tumors that mimic other body tissues, most commonly teeth or hair, but sometimes more complex organs as well. Now, it was unusual enough that she produced so many of them, but to make her case even more unusual, the teratomas didn't grow inside her body, but on the surface. I decided to perform a biopsy and an ultrasound before excising it, just to be safe, and was astounded by the results. Her body had grown a tiny, functioning kidney. So I asked her to please come back with me to New England Medical for further tests. My research team was already working on genetic regulation of organ formation, so it wasn't hard for us to adjust our focus from growing new organs in mice to working with Nell.

Nell Gabrielli: I just wanted the thing removed. I was so sick of growing those stupid skin bags all over my body. Especially the ones with teeth in them. If I had to hear one more guy ask if I had teeth in my hoohah... (Trails off.) I guess I was hoping Dr. Burbage could cure me.

Richard Forrest: Oh, they could completely cure Ms. Gabrielli. But they've convinced this poor woman that her life's purpose is saving other people. I hope she some day realizes that her own life is just as worth saving.

Dr. Burbage: We were able to accelerate the organ's growth by essentially performing chemotherapy on it, which seems contradictory, but teratomas don't behave like a typical tumor. The results were amazing. Within a month, we had an adult-sized kidney that could be removed through a simple outpatient procedure. Better yet, with Nell being blood-type O negative, we had a kidney that could be transplanted into a wide range of recipients.

Megan Ferretti, NBS: As news leaked out about Nell's abilities, colleagues of Dr. Burbage dubbed her "Organ Nell."

Random on-the-street interviewee #1: I'm glad she exists, but man, would I hate to be her. Her body's freaky. Freak-show freaky.

Dr. Burbage: Of course, we then had to deal with changing the way Nell's major histocompatibility antigens were expressed so we could help minimize the possibility of rejection among potential recipients. That took some time and experimentation, but Nell was amazingly good-spirited about it.

Nell Gabrielli: I hadn't had the money to pay the rent in months, so I was about to be evicted. No one wants to hire someone who's in the hospital every month or two to get stuff removed. And the lumps freaked people out. It was nice to have a roof over my head, even if it was a hospital roof.

Dr. Steffensen: I can't even begin to list all the rules of medical ethics that Dr. Burbage and her team have broken. You don't experiment like that on a human being without first spending years working out computer models, then more years experimenting on mice, then primates, before moving up to experimenting on actual sick people. Ms. Gabrielli was a healthy human being with an unfortunate and unusual predilection toward sprouting benign but disfiguring teratomas before Dr. Burbage and her team got their hands on her.

Ted Ousterhout, AIDS Action Committee, Massachusetts: A person can live decades with HIV nowadays, but if they suffer organ failure, even if it's completely unrelated to their HIV status, that's it. Lights out. End of show. Our clients' only options used to be to accept organs from high-risk donors. Now, we've got Nell.

Megan Ferretti, NBS: The organs and tissues grown by Nell's body are only being transplanted into patients who otherwise wouldn't be considered for the surgery. This has prompted many people on the official transplant lists to question why they're being left to die while those who have been deemed medically unfit for new organs get new leases on life. It's also led others to wonder if Nell's doctors are preying on the desperate to further their research.

Dr. Steffensen: There is no guarantee that these transplanted organs won't start sprouting teratomas of their own. True, none have yet, but we've hardly had enough time to observe how these organs will behave in the long run. Plus, if they do, I'd say there'll be zero chance that they'll be nice, easy-to-remove surface teratomas like Ms. Gabrielli's. Now, I ask you, do you think it sounds like a good idea to put a transplant recipient—especially one who was sick enough that they couldn't get on the official transplant list—through additional major surgery?

Richard Forrest: As you know, it's illegal to pay money for an organ, so Ms. Gabrielli isn't getting any compensation for what she's going through. New England Medical provides free room and board, but that's it. She doesn't even earn a salary. That's just one of the many tricks they're pulling to keep the government from shutting them down. So if Ms. Gabrielli decided to walk out the door tomorrow, she'd be destitute.

Nell Gabrielli: Oh, the staff here are really nice. Dr. Burbage buys me things. (Holds up computer gaming system.) This plays movies and music too. And some of the people I grow organs for buy me gifts. The people from the AIDS group make sure I always have flowers. They tried buying me books, but I don't really read, so they get me movies instead, which I play on this. (Scratches lump on neck and winces.) Forgot about this one. I'm not supposed to poke it. It's an eyeball, so it's real sensitive. I wish they wouldn't grow stuff on my neck. I make them take stuff off of my face before it can turn into anything, but they won't take stuff off of my neck.

Dr. Burbage: Never in our wildest dreams did we think we'd be able to develop her abilities to safely produce so many functional organs all at the same time. We really got lucky with that. I won't bore you with the medical details, but needless to say, we're thrilled. We just wish we could predict what her body was about to grow, or even direct it, but it doesn't matter. There's always at least fifty people waiting who can use whatever her body chooses to produce.

Dr. Steffensen: We're all waiting for the details on that particular development, but New England Medical isn't sharing them. Frankly, many of us in the medical community are skeptical about this one. Not that Ms. Gabrielli's body has this ability. There's no denying that. What we're skeptical about is the means they used to encourage her body to produce organs so fruitfully. If they're not talking, then that means they've got something to hide.

Random on-the-street interviewee #2: I think I'd rather die than put a part of that woman into my body. Aren't teratomas tumors? Why would I want to get a tumor transplant?

Vandana Vidyarthi: Nell gave me a new pair of corneas, so I went to the hospital to thank her when I was healthy again. I... I don't think I'll ever forget her. (Puts shaky hand over mouth.) My god, what it must be like to look like that. She's a saint for doing it. I don't think I could live that way.

Nell Gabrielli: What else am I growing? Um, right now, I've got the eyeball. It's my first eye. I've grown eye parts before, but never a full eye. Uh, there's a couple of kidneys on my back, some liver bits, a bunch of teeth, a thyroid, a little tiny lung that they don't think they'll be able to use, and a heart. The, um, ventricles, they say they look kinda messed-up. But they say they can put little mechanical ventricles in it and make it work.

Dr. Burbage: We're very excited about the possibilities for hearts and lungs. Obviously, we won't be able to leave them to grow to their full size on Nell. That would be too much of a strain on her body. Our plan is to remove them once they're well-formed, but still small, and then attempt to complete their growth in the lab.

Dr. Steffensen: I find it interesting that they draw the line at letting hearts and lungs grow to full size on Ms. Gabrielli's body. How is it not a strain on one's system to have a dozen maturing organs of other types growing from one's skin?

Unidentified Transplant Recipient, presented in silhouette, voice altered: My body had rejected two liver transplants already, and my doctor told me that he couldn't get me on the list for a third. Then we heard about Nell, and I have to admit, I was afraid. I wasn't sure I wanted a piece of her inside of me. What if it made me become just like her? But in the end, I accepted it. It's been difficult, though. I can't stop thinking about what might happen if it... I... (Fist goes up to mouth.) I've started drinking again.

Megan Ferretti, NBS: The issue of how best to manage the national transplant list has become a political hot potato, and not surprisingly, there's been no official word from Washington on the Nell Gabrielli situation. During this mid-term election cycle, no one wants to risk alienating potential voters on either side of the issue. The Commonwealth of Massachusetts assures us that they are monitoring the situation, but refused to have an official connected to the case comment on-camera.

Nell Gabrielli: Oh yeah, someone from the state checks in on me every month to make sure I'm still okay with volunteering. I'm still the only person who can do this, right? So I gotta keep doing it. If I don't, people will die, right? It'd be nice if they found someone else who could do it, though. Then maybe I wouldn't have to grow so much all at once.

Father Cleary: I pray to God every day to give Ms. Gabrielli strength. And I pray to God every day that He not give any other person the same gift. What a heavy burden it must be. God chooses our trials for us, and there are times that I wish He wouldn't impose such difficult ones on such innocent people.

Richard Forrest: There are plenty of people out there who like to say, "Look, it's not like the woman was doing anything important before this happened. At least her life has meaning now." They may be right, but I'd still challenge them to imagine themselves in her shoes. Perhaps we should see this as an indictment of the society that left Ms. Gabrielli with so few options in life that she was willing to become a one-woman organ farm. Ask yourself: could you see the president's son in Ms. Gabrielli's place? He's not doing anything important with his life either. Well, unless you think becoming the poster boy for DUI is important work.

Dr. Steffensen: How convenient was it for them to find this ability in a lower-class, unemployed, undereducated woman with no children and no strong family ties. I wonder how many other people have this ability and are having it kept quiet by their family doctors? I certainly wouldn't let any of my family be used this way.

Dr. Burbage: Of course, our goal is to find a way to isolate the specific genes in Nell's body that cause her to produce these tissues and organs.

Megan Ferretti, NBS: There is real fear in the medical community that, if these genes are isolated, gene therapy could be created to turn other people into organ farms. Hospitals might pressure families of coma patients to allow them to use their bodies this way in exchange for lowering the cost of their hospitalization. And, of course, there are whispers of nightmare scenarios, such as the homeless being given this treatment in exchange for room and board, or prisoners in countries with poor human rights records being forced to grow organs against their will.

Dr. Burbage: No, of course we're not interested in asking anyone else to volunteer to grow organs and tissues. It's wonderful that Nell is so willing, but we'd never deliberately do this to another human being. What we're instead hoping to do is to find a way to use her genes to grow organs in a laboratory setting. Unfortunately, that day is still at least a decade away, if not more.

Dr. Steffensen: They'll never make this work in the lab. They're just saying that to string their patient along. If they have their way, she'll be there for the rest of her life.

Nell Gabrielli: If this all stopped tomorrow, what would I do? (Stares into space without answering.)

Jarel Padovano: They say she's started growing hearts. I've been waiting for one for years, but they keep passing me by. They say it's because other people are sicker than me, but I know it's because of all the time I spent in prison. I know it. If I can just get a new heart, I'll make a clean start of it. Just you watch. That woman is my only hope.

Dr. Burbage: I'm so grateful to Nell. We all are. She's a living miracle, and I am so honored to have been able to help her give this gift of hers to the world.

Nell Gabrielli: It's... it's tough. Yeah. Every day, I wish it had happened to someone else and not me. (Sighs and prods lump under her shirt.) But it did. And it's important. So I guess it's good that I'm here. Isn't it?

A Night at the Empire

Joy Marchand

Between nightmares about mail sorters that reeked of brimstone, Len dreamed of his workstation at the Salem post office. In his dream, the computer had become part of his thigh, and the proximity of its motherboard to his groin had given him erectile dysfunction and prostate cancer.

It wasn't hard to guess what that was about.

Len walked to work in a snowstorm, feeling older, balder, and lonelier than ever. He couldn't work up the energy to hate Lizzie for leaving, so he hated her cyber-age Don Juan instead—the high-speed internet connection, the Teflon chin implants, the LoveMatch.com tagline:

Net-savvy Senior Seeks Virtual Goddess With Webcam.

The hate boiled his brain. He dreamed stop-motion silent films, mailroom mayhem made dramatic with the wailing of oboes, the tinkling of a player piano.

As always, Len felt his mood lift as he passed the Empire Theater. He yearned for an evening in its dusty black and white paradise, sitting among like-minded strangers in the fluttering darkness, undeniably alone and yet buoyed by anonymous trembles of laughter, gratified by gasps of fright and moans of sympathy. He craned his neck at the brick theater front, but the marquee still read C-O-M-I-N-G S-O-O-N, so he trudged on, the wind whipping away his body heat. No one went to the movies any more; they stayed home and flipped cable channels, cruised chat rooms where they lost themselves in anonymous venom.

The poor bastards. The browsing dead.

People lined the steps of the post office, shielding their bundles from the blowing snow. A disturbed rumbling centered on a woman in a green chenille scarf, who was fighting to keep her fluttering newspaper open against a flurry. "Third one this week already," she announced to the huddled masses. "Dead from heart failure, and his TV gone. They say someone's waiting for people to die, then stealing their televisions and laptops and cellular phones." She snatched Len's arm as he passed. "You think they could let us in early? Page five says they found someone frozen to death on Washington Street."

Len disengaged his arm from the woman's grip and slipped past the bulb-nosed Irishman guarding the door. As usual, Len said, "Hey, Sully, why don't we let 'em in," and, as usual, Sully glared at Len around his cell phone and mouthed, "Shut the fuck up," and it was settled, although not to Len's satisfaction.

The computerized workstation felt like the visitor's window of a federal prison. Len's neighboring inmate, Keith The Mouth-Breather, had a habit of sharing little gems of philanthropy as he polished his view screen. "Any one of dose people out there could be the TV thief. Ya think of that?" Keith slapped a box of sanitary wipes beside his register, his fingers wet and pink inside latex gloves. When he got no response from Len beyond a look of disgust, Keith wriggled a gloved finger into his ear to touch a forbidden cell phone ear bud. Keith wore the ear piece constantly, and stroked a handheld e-mail whatsit on every smoke break as if it were the girlfriend he'd never have. When asked what he found so interesting coming in over the wireless, Keith just gave a look that said the answer was fucking obvious.

Len wondered if Lizzie still lived that way, shielded from reality behind a curtain of constant input. He wondered if she still had sex with her geriatric lover in antiseptic keystrokes. He wondered if she'd strayed because he hadn't given her enough of whatever it was she had needed. Whatever it was that Keith got out of his e-mail device.

Goddamned mystifying, that's what it was.

Sully let the customers in, and Len chewed over the Lizzie dilemma in the mind-numbing void of metering mail and dispensing stamps until right before noon, when the bastardly computerized workstation went toes-up. Red-faced, Sully shoved a Polaroid at Len. "Old fuck wants a passport photo. Make sure he can pay."

An old man had come to the counter, his face an aggravated pucker between a navy beret and the prodigious coils of a scarf. "I can pay for the photograph." The accent was French, the hot breath like compost in summer. Tucked under the man's arm was a squishy garbage bag that burped a miasma of stale beer even less pleasant than the stink of its owner's tooth decay. "These pig never think I can pay, but I can pay."

Len watched a foul wad of greenbacks unfurl in the cup of the old man's withered palm. Keith's lips drew back in a feral grin of disgust, and Len resisted the urge to kick him under the counter. He hefted the camera. "You need a proof of citizenship to get a passport, sir, but a photo is just eight bucks."

"The photo, *oui*, the photo." The old man tottered to the photo backdrop where he dropped his trash bag and clutched a leather case close to his heart. When he offered a toothless grin like the yawn of an ancient turtle, Len couldn't help but smile back. So few people smiled any more; it was like finding ten bucks in the street.

"I'll put the picture in a reinforced envelope for you," he said, "if you're mailing it overseas."

The old man bellied up to the counter, his expression wary. "You are kind," he said, "not like these *cochons dégoûtants*." He set a worn leather case on the counter. "I have motion pictures camera. You shoot some footage of me, *oui*? For my family." A starving man hoping for a crust, the old man put a deeply lined hand on Len's wrist. "I need this very much. You like cameras, *non*?"

"I think most machines suck your humanity out through your eyeballs." Len gently disengaged his arm. "But this old camera isn't hurting anybody. It's almost like watching a magic trick. The image develops so slowly—like it's waiting for you to want to see yourself bad enough before it gives you the goods."

The look on the old man's face had changed in the course of the conversation, his twisted cockle of wrinkles relaxing, until his true face lay revealed, pink and moist and somehow youthful. He pressed a twig -like finger to his old leather case and spoke as softly as an addict sharing a tidbit of coveted dream stuff. "Never doubt, *monsieur*. Some machine, she help you see good."

They'd come together over the counter in sympathy, Len and the old man, but Keith slammed the box of sanitary wipes on the counter between them and they sprang apart. Keith smoothed his hair as Napoleon might have done had he worn a thinning mullet. "Time for *mon frère* to move along."

Before Len could say anything, the old man snatched up his garbage bag, shouldered the camera case and stormed out into the snow blanketing Washington Street. With the plastic bag banging into his knees, the old man hobbled through traffic, unmindful of the piss trail of beer he was leaving in the snow. His grip on the camera was far less casual; he cradled it as if he were afraid the passing cars would tear it from him. Once across the street, he glanced furtively around, and then vanished into the entrance of the Empire Theater. The precarious marquee had been updated: SUSPIRIA! KILL, BABY, KILL!! DEVIL'S NITEMARE!!!

Wistful, Len smashed the box of wipes into Keith's concave chest and yanked the miniature cell phone out of his ear with an audible plop. "Would it have killed you to be nice to the poor bastard? Christ, Keith. He's just a lonely old man."

Keith snatched at his cell phone like a toddler deprived of its lollipop, and Sully gave a merciless bark of laughter. From that point on he filtered the undesirables into Len's line. Len had his stapler stolen by a bag lady in a pink rain slicker, and had to call Sully over to remove a nut job who insisted Len speak into the empty battery compartment of a micro-cassette recorder. While Len worked, he glanced periodically at the sign across the street: *Welcome to the Empire.*

At the end of the day, Len returned the miniature phone to Keith but, still simmering about Lizzie, he swiped the zero key of Keith's register and dropped it into his pocket. Although the small act of sabotage had been inspired by that morning's report of the TV burglar, it wasn't the first time Len had done such a thing. Lizzie had spent hours making love to her cell phone and laptop, talking to Mr. Chin. Len had expressed his rage by stealing batteries, and staging elaborate laundry accidents, but Lizzie had laughed him off and taken the opportunity to upgrade. She said home electronics brought people together, but the funny thing was, with every thingamabob she plugged in, Lizzie became a little less friendly, a little less social, until one day she packed up her devices and vanished.

Tormented by Lizzie-memories, Len stood in the snow outside the Empire Theater, breathing in billows. Under a cupped hand, nose pressed to the glass door, he scanned the lobby, expecting to see ticket takers, concession workers—at the least, a man in a tie guarding the velvet ropes. There was no one attending the candy counter, and the leaves of the plastic rhododendrons hung heavy with the dust of years.

Len slipped the photo folder from his pocket, dislodging a molar-shaped object that landed soundlessly in the snow. When he bent to retrieve it, the silence of Washington Street howled down the back of his neck. Len plucked Keith's zero key from the drift, and the folder with the old man's photo slipped from his pocket into the snow.

"Not a bad picture." The old man was standing in the lobby door as if he'd been watching Len for some time, all turtle-grin and compost breath. "Nice angle hides my flobby chin. You will take footage of me with the motion pictures camera? The others say *non*, but I say, *this man, he is one of us*."

Len wasn't sure he wanted to be included in whatever group would embrace a man who smelled of beer and urine, although guilt gnawed at him for thinking such a thing when he'd been so hard on Keith for his disrespect. He looked past the old man to the abandoned popcorn counter. "I just wanted to make sure you got your picture, but now I'm thinking I might be in the mood for a movie. Is the theater open? It looks—" *Ancient*, he wanted to say. *Bald. Shabby. Empty.*

The old man waved Len in. "The Empire, she is lonely for company in the digital age. Come pay your respects, *oui?*"

Holding his knit cap, Len stepped in. The moist, cavernous warmth was such a shock that the luminescent statue guarding the threshold to the house came as no surprise. It was a goddess of Mount Olympus, but it was also his favorite movie queens of days long past: Jane Fonda confronting the evil Durand Durand, Erika Blanc, stepping doe-like through a Carpathian village square. A wall of shattered television screens behind the statue reflected her glory from a hundred angles. For one confused moment, Len wondered where all of the televisions had come from, and then the hair on the back of his arms stood on end. The televisions of the dead; the old man was the murderous TV burglar.

"Hey now." Len backed toward the lobby door.

The old man arranged the photo folder at the statue's bare feet, unconcerned. He propped up a fallen candle, patted a limp bouquet of daisies into shape. "Terpsichore. These things roll in on their own. They are drawn to her. There is no thief."

A woman burst from the theater doors swinging a frying pan. "Jean Tom, Mr. Sergei brought the popcorn!" She stopped the pan mid-swing. "Well, I'll be whipped. It's Mr. Len."

The old man, Jean Tom, gripped Len's arm. "Come in, oui? The others will be happy to see you."

"Hey, no," Len said. "I'm not a grave robber. No matter how much I hate my job." He pulled his gloves from his pocket, and out tumbled the zero key of Keith's workstation.

The woman brought a smooth, pale hand to her mouth to cover a smile. She shook the foil frying pan, making un-popped kernels rattle. "Popcorn and a film? We have a full house tonight."

It wasn't right, and it certainly wasn't nice, but the idea of two old psychotics robbing the dead of their TVs inspired the spastic belly-butterflies of incipient hysteria. Len plucked up the zero key and, using a trick he hadn't done in years, made it dance over his knuckles. "Popcorn and a film would be swell."

The audience had lost its collective mind. Snapping at one another with bedraggled scarves, stamping across puddles of snow with scuffed galoshes mended with duct tape, they danced through the aisles of red velvet seats—dozens of shabby villains, all touching one another and laughing. The Empire rose over them in decaying splendor, moth-eaten velvet, peeling gilt wallpaper and leering cherubs. The silver screen was ripped at the edges, but still good in the middle.

The woman in the pink slicker popped the corn over a camp stove, which gave a flame when she turned a crank. A tall girl in charcoal eyeliner cranked on a gramophone, which spat baroque melodies from a porcelain disk. The man with the micro-cassette recorder cranked away at a tiny handle in its side, interviewing an ancient silver poodle while a middle-aged man in Ben Franklin spectacles knelt in the aisle, winding up a toy robot.

Len wiped his eyes. Red candles burned in the empty light bulb sockets, runnels of wax trailing down the flaky wallpaper, and the smoke burned. "This is... what? A homeless shelter?"

Jean Tom grunted, and shifted the leather camera bag slung over his shoulder. "The Empire is a shelter, Mr. Len." The old man peeled off his beret, his hair salt and pepper waves spilling on the loops of his scarf. He grimaced as a woman in her seventies pattered by in a red flannel nightgown, blowing bubbles. "She is our refuge, the Empire, but not the kind you mean."

"Angels!" said the woman in the slicker. "It's Mr. Len."

The people scrambled from the stage like puppies. A dozen-or-so leaped across the theater seats to congregate—wriggling—in the aisle. The pink rain-slicker woman shooed them from the gas burner, protecting the huge foil mushroom of freshly popped corn. The seat jumpers were a motley bunch, dressed in bits of business attire, message t-shirts, and taffeta skirts, and they crept forward to touch Len, beaming at him with ageless smiles.

Angels of the movie theater. Kindred spirits.

That they were illegal squatters was a certainty. From the moment he'd stepped into the theater, he'd known it wasn't right for them to be there capering in the candlelight like children. Despite his minor vandalism of Keith's computer workstation, Len was nothing if not law-abiding, and just being in the abandoned theater was enough to turn amusement into dread, especially when Jean Tom opened the leather case and Len had a look at the black machine lying inside. "Hey, Jean Tom, look. I know what I said about the Polaroid and all that, but I pretty much hate anything that needs batteries." *Home electronics took Lizzie away. They steal your soul,* is what he wanted to say. But he couldn't ever say such a crazy thing. Not even in a madhouse.

Jean Tom brought out the camera. It was the size of a tin lunchbox with a lens at one end and a hand-crank, like the wire crank of a jack-in-the-box, on the side. "Touch her, Mr. Len." Jean Tom put the camera in Len's hands. "If you don't love her, you give her back to me, and together we will watch the films on the marquee. We will have a triple feature!"

Len glanced at the crowd, aware of how closely they watched him. It was inexplicably important to them all, that he do this thing for Jean Tom. Unlike Lizzie's laptop and Keith's cellular phone, this machine really had brought people together.

As he took the camera and turned it in his hands, Len felt something inside the machine shift. The camera was heavier than he had expected, yet strangely buoyant and, as he held it before him, assiduously avoiding the perplexing crank, he felt a rush of joy for the smell of buttered popcorn. Ecstatic, the cinephiles pressed around him, reaching to touch the camera and Len laughed with them. If sharing a smile was like finding ten bucks on the street, this pre-movie bonding was like a shopping spree at Fort Knox. This was the kind of audience that made even the worst B-list movie into a religious experience.

Hallelujah and amen, brothers and sisters.

Len lifted the camera like an acolyte hefting a holy relic, aware of the absurdity, too amused not to pander to the crowd. A siren wailed out on Washington Street, a warning from another world, distant and meaningless. "Time to roll film," he said.

There was a flurry of excitement as the chair jumpers and the stage dancers bumped and pushed their way to the stage under the screen. They sat in mobs, some on each other's laps, cross-legged, passing the popcorn hand to hand. Jean Tom directed Len to set the camera on the tripod, and helped focus its eye on the ancient movie screen. Jean Tom turned the crank, and a flashing leader appeared.

The odd camera, it seemed, was also a projector.

Well, why the hell not?

Conscious of his bald spot and ever-increasing paunch, Len sat beside the rain-slicker woman, with his hands on his knees like a little boy. The perfume she wore struck him deeply, the same heavy musk that Lizzie had favored. In the hazy light, the rain slicker woman looked so much like his ex-wife that Len felt his heart open like a flower. It was incredible that he hadn't noticed the resemblance immediately.

With Jean Tom cranking the camera, the leader ran out, and the film started. On the screen, a woman with a micro-cassette recorder climbed into a silver coupe. With the device pressed against her wet, crimson mouth, she whipped the Jaguar through a crosswalk and ran over a man in a tweed coat walking a standard poodle. The man's head hit the street with a sickening bounce and blood spilled from his cracked skull in a shockingly crimson torrent to pool around the poodle's feet.

"Mr. Sergei," said Jean Tom. "Poor Mr. Sergei. Victim of the Digital Age."

In the audience, Mr. Sergei shook the recorder next to his cheek, spun the tiny handle to play something back that sounded like the thready tune of a music box. The poodle licked his ear and cocked its ear at the melody.

Len watched the crowd, unsure of what he'd just seen. The clip was like a driver's education film from the 80s, meant to convince teenage drivers to wear their seatbelts. The audience members closest to Mr. Sergei reached out in benediction and touched his head.

Another leader—4, 3, 2, 1—and the man with the Franklin glasses appeared on the screen, lying in an operating theater while a beam of light sliced into his pulsating brain. A wall-eyed scrub nurse grabbed for her shrieking pager, the surgeon twitched and sent an errant beam of light across a swatch of healthy pink tissue, causing the patient's feet to curl up like shrimp sizzling in a pan. "Mr. Dwayne," said Jean Tom. "Poor Mr. Dwayne. Victim of the Digital Age." The audience members whispered the chorus, in rounds like "Row, Row, Row Your Boat."

Victim of the Digital Age. Victim of the Digital Age.

Pushing away from the audience, Mr. Dwayne rolled onto his side and cranked the gear in his toy robot, sending it spinning and jerking across the stage. He wiped a string of drool from his mouth and used it to write D-W-A-N-E on the stage floor.

The last clip blew frost over Len's heart. On the movie screen, the pink rain-slicker woman sat in a motel room with a laptop, searching through photos of naked female bodies, bound and spattered with blood. The bathroom door opened and out came a smiling, wrinkled Don Juan in a velvet bathrobe. Don Juan saw that the rain-slicker woman had discovered his secret stash of pictures, and his pleasant expression never flickered. He took a syringe from the pocket of his robe, and stuck it into his lover's neck, and watched her mouth go slack and drooling.

Jean Tom was saying something about the rain-slicker woman and the Digital Age, but Len's legs kicked out reflexively, and he backpedaled into the audience, which sighed and swayed around him like kelp in an ocean current. When presented with the pan of popcorn, Len blinked. He took another handful, unmindful of the dirty hands also dipping into the communal resource. "Great special effects," he mumbled, wide-eyed. "Great crowd."

The pink-rain-slicker woman stroked his knee, her eyes like gleaming green jewels in the light of the film. "It's a comfort to see them all together here, all the angels." She gave Len a searching look, and then blushed. "You can stay with us, if you like. The rules are really quite simple."

"Um." Len wiped away butter on the hem of his trousers and took her hand, feeling like a teenager on his first date. Surrounded by a gang of lunatics, knuckling smoky tears from his eyes, he'd never felt such a sense of belonging. It all seemed unreal, but still he sensed that they feared the things he feared, and loved the things he loved. He warmed the woman's hand as they watched the short subjects unfold, and his thoughts went to Lizzie. "I lost my wife," he said, struggling with the images unfolding on the screen. Victims of the Digital Age. "And it feels so good to be here with you. You know how it is out there."

"Yes. We all feel that way. The Empire herself feels that way. Look at all of her empty seats, lonely for the company of those who once worshipped her. People watch the classics on TV as if their tiny screens and squeaking speakers could do justice to stories meant for the silver screen."

The emergency exit doors next to the stage rattled on their hinges until the mascara girl jogged down, hit the crash bar and stepped back to let an unaccompanied television set bump its way in. It thudded through the door and thumped its lonesome way up the carpeted steps, trailing its cord like a disconsolate tail. When the television set reached the top of the steps, it crashed through the swinging doors and rolled into the lobby to sit with its vagrant brothers at the feet of Terpsichore.

Len looked at the pink-rain-slicker woman, at her face so caring and lovely. His eyes burned and he coughed. "Are you a film director? Are you filming a movie right now?"

With a tender expression, she took the camera from Jean Tom and blew across the lens. "Jean Tom's ready for his take, Len."

Jean Tom stood on the stage, nodding at the lounging crowd, winding and unwinding his dirty scarf until he'd knotted it into an ascot with shabby chic. "Crank it up, *oui*? Roll film."

There was no viewfinder, so Len framed the shot the best he could over the topline of the camera and turned the crank in the counterclockwise direction the pink-rain-slicker woman was indicating with a whirling finger. He expected friction, the sensation of gear teeth meshing and the sound of film rolling, but the motion was smooth and soundless, like drawing a paddle through oil. He cranked and cranked, and Jean Tom spoke.

"It was a crazy Irishman who said it the best. 'We are the music makers, and we are the dreamers of dreams.' It should have been a Frenchman who said this—" Jean Tom moved his age rounded shoulders in an expressive, Gallic shrug "—but the Empire makes me forgive the theft." With a naked glance to the woman in the pink rain slicker Jean Tom swept off his knit cap, moistened his wrinkled mouth and began to sing.

It was the voice of a wounded man, a broken echo of what once must have been something fulsome and wondrous. The chair-jumpers embraced one another, sniffling, and the girl with the charcoal eyeliner took a stub of oil pastel from her coat pocket and drew a remarkable V twined in power cords, like the leading letter in an illuminated manuscript, but her grip was crippled, and the pastel crumbled. She bit her lip until it bled.

As Jean Tom sang, the lines around his eyes faded. His grey hair grew darker and richer in luster. The crowd was agitated, ageless faces suffused with a frenzied light. They waited as he moaned and choked through the tune, and when at last, the final note faded, they leapt to their feet and swept him up onto their shoulders. They paraded him around the shadowy, candlelit house in a victory lap, chanting.

Victim of the Digital Age, Welcome to the Empire.

The rain-slicker woman touched Len's hand. "Welcome."

Len turned to look at her and wasn't surprised to see that her skin had become smooth, opalescent as a girl's. She touched a hand to her hair, which rippled over her shoulders like cream-colored silk. She slipped free of the pink plastic rain slicker and, standing naked, lifted ivory arms to the ceiling. "Behold, Terpsichore."

Len looked at her, and saw the scream queens of the silver screen, the doe-eyed Erika Blanc, the luscious Cinzia Monreale, the brooding Soleded Miranda. She was all of them, and she was Lizzie too, but also entirely herself. Technicolor crept up the shabby stage curtains behind her, washing the carpets, polishing the brass balcony railings and the leering faces of the cherubs. "Thank you, oh thank you, angels!" She clasped her hands. "And congratulations to Jean Tom."

The new Jean Tom, no longer turtle-faced, no longer reeking of disappointment and age, danced up the aisle and out the lobby doors. He appeared in the high window of the projector booth, and light washed across the silver screen.

The motley angels settled into their velvet seats, sending an assortment of bottles and crinkling cellophane packages down the rows. Without hesitation, flushed with the magic of it all, Len took a handful of Red Vines and a deep swig of some horrible bathtub gin that set his feet drumming on the theater floor.

Terpsichore, she of the golden hair and the pinup breasts tucked herself under the curve of Len's arm, and showed him how to bite his red licorice into a straw for a more serious drink of gin. "*Stolen by Mr. Sergei, my rascal angel,*" she whispered. "Isn't this wonderful?"

Something fluttered, terribly, in Len's stomach, and it was clear to him now, what Lizzie had been browsing for, what he had not given her. It was this feeling, a feeling of being embraced and understood. "Oh yes," he said. "Wonderful."

They watched the triple feature, Argento's *Suspiria*, Mario Bava's *Kill, Baby Kill*, Bismee's *Devil's Nightmare*. A flock of angels at play watched demons at work. The gin went to work on Len's heart, easing his sorrows, obliterating his worry, focusing the totality of his happiness on the sweet progress of the scream queens—their hands over their mouths, eyes shocked, yet subtly complicit. Terpsichore's hand on his leg was sweetly erotic, but Len found himself sinking into the velvet seat as if drowning, his arms and legs so heavy, so slow. He heard a spate of laughter, felt the sweet camaraderie of horror fans taking in a midnight showing of a cult classic—and as he rested his head against the red velvet chair, he felt the lips of Empire on his forehead, and thought, *I belong here. I'm an angel, oh yes.*

He understood, finally, what Lizzie had been searching for.

Len woke in a drift of snow outside the Empire Theater. Startled by the rising wail of a passing ambulance, Len fumbled something cold and heavy to his shrunken chest. A slimy residue of gin and Red Vines had glued his lips together. His clothing agleam with frost, he had a movie-marathon headache, a backache, and a profound sense of loss. Loss of warmth, loss of love. As the ambulance screamed by, the EMTs didn't turn to consider him, although he sat trembling and in serious danger of hypothermia.

Between the end credits of the last film and him awakening in the snowdrift, Len had dreamed of love for a hundred years. In his dream, it wasn't Terpsichore who sat with her hand on his leg, but his wife—Lizzie, as she had dressed in college, with her earth shoes, and her marijuana cigarettes—back before she had permanently jammed the cell phone into her ear so she could chat with her lover while her hands spidered across a keyboard missing the zero key.

He blinked at his wrinkled, liver-spotted hands, then up at the marquee. DATE WITH AN ANGEL! ANGEL SANCTUARY! RUN, ANGEL, RUN! With a cry, Len hurled himself against the doors, pounding with palsied, ancient fists. How had he become so old so fast? "Terpsichore!"

He expected no answer, and he got none. Across the street, a small crowd was gathering at the post office. Keith, glued to his palm device, stood just inside the glass doors, ignoring an old woman's plea to get in. She waved a newspaper, shouted, and pounded on the glass.

Watching her from deep in the snow drift in the lee of the Empire, Len wondered if Jean Tom, and Mr. Sergei, and Lizzie had sat there in this same drift of snow, watching the morning post office drama unfold, wondering how to re-enter the Empire.

Had they, too, waited in the cold on Washington Street, like angels yearning for Heaven?

STARTER HOUSE

JASON PALMER

Dale looked up through the ribbed Lucite dome of Asteroid Cintas II, his eyes lit from within by thoughts of a bright future. "I never imagined," he said, "I'd own a purebred house."

Pam locked her eyes on his. "I knew you would. I knew we would. This makes it all worth it."

They kissed.

A forklift driver smiled at them as he passed, trundling a giant spool of wire through corridors of stacked feedbags. He disappeared into the high dark bay of the feedlot.

Dale and Pam shivered with excitement when a giant discomfited *humph* came from the bay. They smiled into each other's eyes. "Do you think they're working on ours?" she said.

Dale waited a loaded moment to answer, slowly, "I think so. I think so."

Someone said, "Y'all got that male?"

A salesman.

"Yes," said Dale, cradling Pam's waist. "We want a little independence."

The salesman came around a stack of grain bags. "Can't say I blame you. People buy females, they know the payoff for breeding is good, but some don't realize it's a long road. These ain't chickens." He stuck out his hand. "I'm Stu Armstrong."

They shook. Armstrong tipped his hat at Pam, and then another massive *humph* beyond the lighted part of the warehouse made him look up. "Uh-oh," he said, grinning, "I think they've started on your boy."

They all looked at each other in suspense.

Armstrong said, "What say we go and watch them wire him up?"

Pam clapped her hands in excitement, and they crossed the warehouse to stand in the entrance to the vast dim bay. Beyond the boundary of the bonecrete floor and overhead lights, the soaring dome gave perspective to the universe.

There was a vast hiss from pressurization and a thickening of the hair smell of B vitamins.

Dale and Pam held hands while a gantry with bubble tires entered from the vacuum plains outside. Upon it stood something pink, bipedal, and male, forty feet tall. A humanoid, mongoloid mountain that looked one quarter armadillo.

Armstrong waved to some of the workmen, signaling *Customer here!* and a few waved back.

The giant standing on the gantry didn't move except to chew, rolling cud lazily in its mouth. It had a hayseed sort of look except for the bulging forehead. The workmen used long gaff hooks to bring it baying down into a painful crouch, then held the hooks firmly until it adjusted. It began chewing again, although its big human eyes looked wild.

Dale and Pam watched in fascination. Armstrong observed them. "Yep," he said, "purebred, perfect health, and one hundred percent aye -daptated. One big atmosphere suit for the family."

The slow workmen barked at one another, throwing loops of wire over the creature and catching them on the other side. A steel cable went over the back of the neck, keeping it bowed down. Tight loops bound the ankles to the thighs and the arms to the wrists like chicken wings, and it made Dale vaguely hungry. He glanced at Pam wondering if she shared the thought, but her face was that of a little girl filled with wonder and happiness.

The creature's stomach was brought between its knees, the chin to rest on the stomach. A faux Georgian porch was hung on a steel band over the eyes and secured with a giant padlock at the back of the head.

"Is it all done?" asked Pam.

"Oh, no ma'am," said Armstrong. "We still have to gouge and cauter and clean. I just thought you might like to see this part. I imagine, if it was my first house, I'd want to see everything having to do with it, top to bottom, except the gouging. All the moaning and baying and the mess, kind of turns people off. That's why we're full service. 'We Do The Dirty Work', that's our motto."

"We'll remember you, Mr. Armstrong," said Pam, her hand over Dale's heart, "the man who sold us our first house."

–Two Months Later–

Dale left work and piloted his cruiser across the Valley of the Shadow with two fingers on the stick. His breath turned to ferns of ice on the front glass, and he listened to the treads popping icy pebbles along the floor of the impact crater. The coolers burped to life, as the temperature topped 220 Fahrenheit in the sun that peeked into the valley.

Then he was home.

Home puffed and sweated in the heat.

Dale bounced across a short patch of asteroidal plane and then stepped through the wet membrane of the belly door. Setting down his helmet, he stood a moment in the entryway. The white and red Christmas tree lights in the living room soothed him.

Pam called from another room, "Honey?"

He sighed. "Yes?"

"The house was very shifty. Just a minute ago. Will you do something?"

Relieved. "Oh, okay." This he could handle. He set the helmet on a peg near the door and shuffled down the hall to an unadorned closet. Opening the door, he turned on a naked fluorescent light by pulling a chain, and picked up his worn cricket bat.

He crunched his fingers against the electrical tape on the handle.

Dale closed the door and rolled his shoulders, then took a first cursory whack at the loose, hanging scrotum that took up most of the closet. The yielding bulk was flaccid, and the exertion felt good. He hit it again, much harder, and an angry rumble ran through the walls.

Dale liked the reality of the closet. It disclosed the grit of the iron spars and utility pipes that structured the house's sore flesh into the familiar residential geometries. A man's realm.

He stripped off his atmosphere suit a bit at a time, working his hits in. A sleeve, whack! The other sleeve, smush! He finally emerged with the top half of the suit hanging from his waist and his T-shirt all sweated up, having banged away at the house's balls until the angry shudders turned to pleading and placating ones.

He found Pam crouching over little Tommy in his bath. "What," he asked, "got it worked up?"

"Guess."

"Tommy, were you sticking pins in the walls again?"

Tommy grinned and clapped his hands together in a puff of bath bubbles, and Dale forgot why he'd been upset.

"How are we doing?" Dale asked Pam that night, as she scanned their accounts. He lay behind her in bed, stroking her hair; in a moment she'd become annoyed by his absent-minded fascination with her.

"Okay. But the repair expenses have been pretty bad, lately. It's a lot more expensive now that we need a catheter man instead of a plumber, and a doctor instead of a carpenter."

"Even though we skipped the anesthesia?"

"Yes."

"And did you ask that antibiotics wholesaler about lobotomy?"

"He doesn't recommend it. He says people who lobotomize wind up with random fits and all kinds of craziness."

He stopped tracing the curve of her spine. "It is a willful house," he said, and his eyes became flat and shining.

She half turned toward him as she took out an earring. "Did you hear it trying to sniff around the Ybarri's place next door?"

"But the Ybarri's–"

"What if our house is gay?"

He laughed and pulled her across him, tickling her so she kicked and wiggled. "A gay house!"

–Four months later–

"I'm beginning to wonder," said Pam through the com in her atmosphere suit, "what we're going to do."

They looked out across Divine Redeemer's Landing, really just a few rows of houses squatting side by side on a plain with views of the nebula. It was a yellowish nebula, not one of the depressing blue ones. They held hands and the bubbles of their helmets touched.

"I know," Dale said.

"The feed is the worst. It gets more expensive every week."

He spread his hands. "It's a buyer's market, right now. Things will bounce back after the war."

"I hope so. Then maybe we can get a nice greenhouse, instead. I could get tired of all that meat."

Dale's head snapped toward her. He hated the way she always thought one step beyond what they could possibly accomplish, but he fought his anger. They couldn't afford another row, no matter how nice it was making up. Things felt... thin.

He changed the subject. "How has it been lately, the house?"

"How do you think? Trying to walk around, fidgeting all day. The plaster's cracked in Tommy's room again. If it gets an arm or a leg free, we'll be kicked out of the neighborhood."

"I'll take care of it."

"It doesn't do much good anymore, Dale. Especially with you wailing away in there any time you get stressed."

Her tone was withering. He watched her, his answer to the cold distances of the galaxy. The spectral light made her look suddenly chiseled and independent and even hawklike.

Dale suddenly perceived how little they knew each other, and he glimpsed a stark white fear.

–Six months of war later–

Pam kept shaking her head whenever he looked at her. He opened all the kitchen drawers until he found the filleting knife.

"Don't do it," she said. "We'll lose twenty percent of the house's value. What if the war is over tomorrow?"

"What if it isn't? We have to see if we can stomach it."

He took the knife into the hall closet. The walls shook and shivered as he carved out a good-sized steak, and he gritted his teeth against the irregular splurts of blood. Finished, he jabbed a big hypo of clotting factor into the twitching wall and left it hanging there.

When he came out, Pam and Tommy were holding onto the arms of their chairs, making him smile.

Dale slabbed the meat onto a gas-fired grill and rubbed his hands over the little blue flame, feeling a bit touched in the head. The savor of sizzling meat brought Tommy into the kitchen, wide-eyed and in his underwear. "Is that part of our house?" he said. There was a troubled, philosophical bent to the boy's question.

"Not anymore, buddy."

They had only candles to light their table, and above their fickle light Pam's face looked thin and ashen. A jagged fault line ran up the plaster wall behind her to the ceiling, where it continued horizontally to the dead chandelier. Its shadow jumped sides as the candle flames swayed in a draft. Dale stared out the window as they said grace, looking toward the Consortium for some sign of life in that seemingly bright but war-torn cluster.

"What have you heard on the post?" asked Pam, chewing and slurring her words.

He just shook his head.

Tommy, excited, said, "Are we going to be the last people left in the whole universe?"

Dale stopped chewing.

The silence was complete except for the clank of Tommy's fork. Only the boy remained dignified and confident, and after a moment Pam began imitating him—literally copying him—in an exhausted way that Dale found repulsive and threatening.

–Later–

Dale peeled the plaster away from the skinwalls all over the house and piled the furniture in the middle of the rooms. "We cut off what we need," he said, "and hold out as long as we can."

Pam held up a large plunger full of blue fluid. "We only have 1200 cc's of Worm Begone left."

"All right. Then we stop the daily doses and shock the system when things start getting ugly."

"And there's no chance," said Pam, "the others will find food on—"

"Citris? Oh, they've got grain on Citris. And the first thing those people will do is fire their rockets at any refugees they see. They're trying to hold out, same as us."

Pam sagged. "We can't reach Civix or the Inners?"

"Not directly." He leaned close to her and whispered, "The war's spread. We're safe here—" he led her by the arm to a membranous window. "—but you see that?"

"The Folk Rocks?" Pinpoints of yellow and pink light ringed by invisibly small, arable planets.

His nostrils flared. "Now? It's a tomb."

She nodded in defeat. When he kissed the side of her nose, it was cold.

Tommy clambered over the pile of furniture at the center of the room, looking the miniature philosopher, never smiling.

Dale couldn't stop his nostrils flaring. He slapped the angry red endothelium of the house's bare interior. "Now, who's hungry?"

"Dale?"

"Yes?"

"What do we feed the house?"

They fed the house bushels of the thumblike white worms that hung wriggling out of the infected walls like earthworms in a fresh grave. Pam added chaff and vitamin B to make them taste more like grain, but Dale still had to clamp the house's nose shut with a ratchet cable to make it swallow. They waited a month, then shot it full of Worm Be-gone, and the worms went away for a while.

"They're gone," Pam marveled.

He was still as she hugged him. During the last month they'd worked elbow to elbow together as they'd never done before, remaking their life into something that could survive the war. The previous night Dale had sat across from his wife at their empty table and told her that he'd never loved her this way before, not even when they were first married. They'd slept packed together limb in limb like blind baby mice, sheltered and guarded in each other.

He told her the truth: "No. They'll be back, and it will be worse than before."

When she sat down and began to cry just as suddenly as she'd been over-joyed, he sat at her feet in a pool of the limpid pus that slicked the floor.

He'd have to mop again soon; if he let it dry, it'd crust over like egg yoke.

The house grew thinner.

On a short, hot night in the asteroidal summer, Pam whispered, "What was that?"

For a long time, he'd sensed her lying awake, but finally they both must have slipped off. He flicked a thumb-sized worm off the edge of the bed. "What was what?"

"That."

"What?"

A rustling sound as the house slithered.

"That!"

He sat up, listening, and the house canted and nearly tipped him over. Tommy screamed, and Dale brought him into their room to sleep between them with the worms and ooze. He found it terrible listening to Tommy's moans, to watch his sleeping, emotionless face while the slitherings and the leanings carried on throughout the night.

At some point Pam said, "What is it?" but fell into exhausted sleep before Dale could tell her he didn't know.

Tommy actually pitched a fit the next morning. "Daddy don't go outside Daddy don't go!" He seemed to gargle his tears, and Dale didn't like the broken way his face looked. The Spacewalk classes had helped before the war, but now he'd begun regressing and closing off.

"I'll be back, buddy, I just need to see what's making that noise." He put on his helmet and slipped through the passive membrane, outside.

He gaped.

Next door on the Ybarri's side was nothing but a giant set of footprints that walked off into the silty asteroidal distance, taking the baby steps that the housemasters' special shackles permitted. On the other side was a collapsed wreck, giant bones showing through the papery skin like the masts of a stove-in sailing ship.

Dale bounced around to the back, looking up and down the bruised and lacerated hulk of his wretched, willful house. He hated it, hated its giant, stupid butt crack and scabby elbows, the tufted hair that grew along its spine.

Then he saw it. The right wrist, folded down against the forearm, glistened with red and black blood. The bone showed against the gouging wire. The arm twitched back and forth as he watched, sawing itself with the wire. The house had become so thin that the arm nearly fitted through, and soon it might get free like a double-jointed person slipping out of a straight jacket. Dale could sense the pain and the ambition.

He'd bought the mouth brace with the quarter-ton spring for this very reason when he'd thought of the house's teeth.

He didn't tell Pam about the arm. Instead, Dale shut himself in the closet and unleashed a storm of violence. He leaned against the sweating, swaying testicles digging his fingers into them when his strength ran out.

Dale used the exposed bones like railings to avoid slipping in the slick rivers of pus. He placed the filleting knife against a raw red strip of meat, expecting the house to twist dryly away from him again, but it didn't move.

Was it asleep?

Too weak?

It never occurred to him that the house might simply be distracted.

Then it tipped to the left rather ponderously, deep and slow.

Dale froze.

In the kitchen, Pam started screaming.

Dale threw down the knife and bolted down the stairs. He saw Pam with her rump backed against the edge of the dining room table, cradling Tommy in her arms and screaming, seemingly at him. He tried to run to her and tripped.

Over something.

He hit the floor hard but uninjured. He looked to his left and thought he saw a giant snake, something like a huge red boa constrictor, moving toward his family. His eyes flew wide open and a cold revulsion made him scurry back.

Dale gained his feet and saw it just as the wrist flexed and the palm spun and opened. The long fingers flapped in anticipation, and Pam's scream turned to a ripping, horrible sound. Her eyes looked about to pop out, and a ragged girl-child rose to replace the woman in her face, sunken-eyed and savage.

The long arm had come in through the belly door membrane. Dale stomped on it, crushing down with his heel, once, twice, six times. The arm retreated a little but more in surprise than pain, then plunged toward his family again.

Pam screamed his name, Tommy screamed Daddy, and it was like a nightmare. The complete lonesomeness of his responsibility seemed to press on Dale's head like a vice. For a moment his mind slid into a helpless swirl of stars and screams.

Then he jumped over the arm and grabbed the cattle prod. The arm leapt when stung, flying into the ceiling and bringing a rain of plaster. He hit it again and had to duck as it swept sideways sending light fixtures and pictures to the floor. Pam scurried beneath the table with Tommy and held a chair in front of her like a hysterical lion tamer.

The house howled and leaned forward, cracking more plaster, trying to get its arm through the door up to the shoulder. Blood dripped everywhere. Dale shocked it half a dozen times, then stabbed the prod right into the flesh like a spear.

The arm ripped out of the house like a length of anchor chain.

"Pam."

She sat on the edge of Tommy's bed, upstairs, staring straight ahead.

"Pam."

He snapped his fingers in front of her face.

"Please talk to me."

He looked over his shoulder. Something was moving over the exterior of the house. It whispered along the skin like a vampire bat, then pressed against the house's back like a face in a cake. Knuckles. Pam's face tightened and so did her grip on Tommy, who sucked his thumb on her lap. Mother and son had become one, but not Dale; he seemed to dance all around them.

"It can't get to us up here. It can't come up the stairs. Not *all* the way up."

Pam's ragged new girl-face was ghostly in the dim bedroom. The candles and portable lights had run out weeks before.

Finally her eyes fixed on his. "They're all dead, Dale. No one's coming."

He sat and stroked Tommy's forehead with one finger, sensing the furious youthful rationalizing going on in there.

They lay in darkness on Tommy's bed, listening to the thick sound of worms dropping from the ceiling like ripe fruit, listening to them writhe beneath the acrid mist that clung to the floor, giving a graveyard effect.

They could make all the worm mush they wanted now but couldn't feed the house: there could be no more going outside with the arm free.

Dale considered a run in a hub ship, and maybe they could find a friendly rock not too far away. But they'd probably wind up starving just the same, only adrift and in mindless horror.

Dale gave up on sleep and went to check the barrier blocking the front door. The boards with nails pounded through them hadn't been disturbed. Nevertheless, he looked over his shoulder as he baked pies out of diseased matter and connective tissue, smoking them in battered tins to cover a taste too vile even for real hunger.

He brought their breakfast upstairs, hoping Pam didn't notice how he had to duck into the room.

The house was getting smaller.

He set a big reeking pie on a bed tray where Pam and Tommy sat with their legs under the blanket, and that was when the house blasted through the barrier over the front door, sending boards clattering all over the living room. It howled with rage as the nails bit into its knuckles.

"No!" Pam snarled.

The house swayed drunkenly left and forward, plaster dust rained, and there was a sound like a German shepherd rampaging up the stairs.

In a corner of the doorway, Dale saw the tip of a big red finger. He gaped at it. The house tilted further over, and as the shrunken room canted, most of the hand came into view.

It wrapped around the doorframe and ripped off a chunk of the wall. The fingers scuttled on the floor.

Dale pried Pam's fingers from his shoulders. He went stonily to the corner of the room and picked up the twenty-pound sledgehammer he'd set against the nightstand. He raised it over his shoulder and smashed in the last knuckle of the longest finger.

He heard Tommy crying, distantly.

The hand flopped around like a giant bird and then whipped away down the stairs.

While foraging, he sometimes passed the unmarked closet where the house's blackly gangrenous testicles hung, hearing the faint creak of the metal ring that kept them locked in there, softly pendulating. Soon they would simply lie on the floor, a symbol of his lost control.

They moved Tommy's bed to the corner of the room to keep the maximum distance from the pattering fingers when they came in the night.

After keeping a long silence, Tommy said, "Why does the house hate us?"

"It doesn't hate us, buddy. It's just hungry, like us."

Tommy's eyes widened in expanding horror as he interpreted this, and Dale cursed himself. He stroked his son's hair until he fell asleep, Pam curled in his other arm and the sledgehammer handle laid across them.

"What's that sound?" asked Pam in the darkness.

"What time is it?"

"What's that? Listen."

A woody scraping noise like fingernails on a coffin lid.

Dale was grateful for the darkness as he frowned. "It's nothing," he said.

"Dale," she said, her voice rising in hysterical crescendo, "The bed is moving across the floor!"

It was. Just a few millimeters at a time as the house shrank and the walls compacted. The bed was edging toward the doorway.

But what amazed him was the way Pam had sprung up on all fours, covering not only his son but himself as well.

Dale's lines of tape retreated in concentric rings, day by day, until they reached the foot of the bed. But he didn't get angry or panicked.

He'd had a realization.

It was the house that mattered first and foremost. Its skin was all that held in their precious scrap of atmosphere, and it must be protected like one of them.

He was impressed by the flat hate he encountered in Pam's eyes as he shared this revelation.

Alone, he baked more worm pies and tried throwing them out the front door, through the membrane, but they only grew into a pile on the doorstep. Starved though it was, the incensed house preferred to hunt his family.

It blew great hollow farts all night, and its bloated, gassy belly seemed to be the only thing that kept it from reaching them. The arm that reached inside grew thinner and harder until it was all rage and bone.

They woke up one morning with the comforter and bedspread gone, along with the footboard. They huddled in the corner, where the ceiling was now too low to sit up straight.

Dale had a sense of being in a creature's body as he ventured out for food now, could trace the T lines of the torso and the sprocketed shoulders. He could hear a racing heartbeat through the thin walls in the stair. By the bedside, he now kept an electric saw.

When she did not experience one of her bursts of protectiveness, Pam seemed shell-shocked; the repetitive horror of hungry snatching fingers left her looking like a gawping, saucer-eyed rabbit, scratching against the sheets with rabbit feet as she tried to back away.

During an afternoon raid, although they had lain in a shivering bunch in the corner, Dale had felt the reaching fingers brush the hairs on his leg.

That night he woke to Tommy screaming right in his ear.

The title bout had come.

Dale flew to a crouch on the bed and felt a great shifting beside him in the darkness. He grabbed the nearest human limb and out of blind instinct pulled it toward the far corner of the bed, away from the threat.

To maximize his friction against the bed, Dale lay flat as he pulled. He found the slick-wood-feeling finger of the house that had curled around his son's leg and with both hands began to pry it off.

He'd forgotten that the footboard was gone and tried to brace his feet against it, and a great wrench from the house brought him and Tommy flopping to the floor, their legs sticking out into the hall.

The savage girl-Pam, the rabbit-Pam, rushed forward and threw herself across Tommy, bracing her hands on the walls. The fingers grabbed her ankle, and she lunged grunting back toward the bed.

Dale moved numbly toward the electric saw.

Pam had grabbed a leg of the bed and was being dragged with it back into the hall.

Kneeling, Dale brought the electric saw whining to life over his head. The house's arm pulsed against his thighs. His eyes grew and shrank with uncertainty.

"Dale!" Pam screamed. Tommy, his thumb in his mouth, walked white-faced toward him like a child zombie.

He could bring down the saw and end this nightmare, but a new one would begin.

With no way to stop the blood, the house would almost certainly die.

Yet if he didn't do it, the probing arm could now reach them everywhere.

He also couldn't sledge the fingers without shattering Pam's leg. She would probably get an infection in the worm-ridden house and die.

That left option number three.

He stole a moment to watch his family, imagined them calm and loving, and stored the picture away.

Then he knelt beside the entangling fingers like a doctor. He calmly pried off one finger —it took all his strength—and replaced it around his own ankle, where it took hold with insane strength.

He pried off another, smaller finger and did the same thing.

After three fingers, he heard Pam grunt and drop to the floor. She'd been racked between the tug of the house and her grip on the bed, wedged in the doorway. "Oh!" she cried, revolted, and sacked Tommy to the floor.

Dale began sliding across the landing on his bottom. He took hold of the doorframe as he passed it, knowing it would do no good. The fingers of the house seemed to know whom they grasped.

Pam turned to him with Tommy's face clamped against her breast, and Dale tried to smile. Her eyes went wide.

He studied her with a stunning clarity of vision as the big hot palm pressed against his back and two fingers clamped over his shoulders like a safety restraint. He watched her expression change from shock to horror to soul-wrenching loss as he floated backwards above the stairs, Tommy dripping into the crook of her arm, her small breasts hanging over him.

The boy only briefly turned, the stoicism of his ruined childhood and his mother's care already in his face.

Dale's hands were wrenched from the doorframe with an unstoppable ease. He supposed he screamed, and maybe it was long and loud, as the great arm lifted him through the air, but a sequestered part of his mind watched passively. The stairs and carpet passed beneath his dangling legs.

Then Pam was chasing him, her eyes so wild they looked slanted and cartoonish in her face. They grew with nearness until the back of his head collided with the transom, leaving him lolling.

The last thing he saw before the vacuum snuffed out his consciousness entirely was like a single slanted frame out of an ancient movie reel.

He saw the house's face. The crazed, bloodshot eyes, slanted downward with fury and hunger, the nose still belted down on one side with his ratchet cable, and finally the jaw, hanging and dislocated where the quarter ton spring had slid out of true and shot the joint apart. The swollen gums and missing teeth, the black gullet.

Dale barely heard the roar, not of hunger, but of outrage and ultimate triumph.

He had once lain beside Pam on a soft evening before making love. For a moment they had breathed into each other's mouths, quaking little breaths. As he entered the squishing cave of the house's mouth, it was her breath he smelled. Once his flesh mingled with the house's, and Pam put her knife to the walls, it would be her devouring him. He was quite aware of that.

On the Shadow Side of the Beast

Ruth Nestvold

Timo and I live on the shadow side of the Beast. It's a good place to live, because there are many hidden corners where the Hunters won't see you. Besides, the Beast protects us.

An older girl, Karla, explained to me once that in the times Before, the Beast was a statue of a woman and four horses. They called her Quadriga and she was on top of the Brandenburger Tor—the ruined columns where Timo and I have made our home.

I asked her what a horse was.

"It was a big animal people would ride, with hooves and a mane," she said, getting that dreamy look that comes over the faces of the older ones when they think about Before.

I looked more closely at the Beast, seeing now the bent figure of a woman with wings twisted with the hooves and heads of the creatures called horses.

"Are there still horses?" I asked.

Karla shrugged. "There never were many in Berlin. The only time I ever saw them was in a parade."

"What's a parade?" I asked.

She shook her head. "You wouldn't understand."

Perhaps I wouldn't, but I try, and I Remember things. Almost everything since the Destruction. I'm not sure when I started Remembering, or when I realized that not everyone did. I wasn't that old when the world died, but I know more than a lot of the older kids. I don't remember Before much, but when the others tell me things, I remember it all.

Now Karla is one of the things I have to remember. I will keep her memories too, for me and for Timo.

Timo and I have scavenged enough bricks and wood to make ourselves several rooms among the ruins of Quadriga at the end of Unter den Linden. It's cold in the winter; the wind whips through the shelter we've built between the columns, tearing at our clothes and hair. But out here it's not as easy for the Hunters to trap you as in tumbled down halls and rooms.

We didn't always live here. We used to live not far away in the remaining wing of a big building with Karla and a couple dozen other kids, a building she said was once a university—like a school, but a place for adults to learn. I had never been to school, but Karla had, Before. I asked her everything, and she taught me how to survive. But I have always been better at hiding.

I wish she had been better at hiding too.

It was summer, so we had berries and roots and vegetables to eat along with the pigeons and squirrels we caught and cooked. Since we didn't have to scavenge as much, we had more time to play. That day we were playing school in a room where one wall was missing; Andrea with the six fingers, Ingo with the sleeping head on his left shoulder, Fatima with the glowing feet, and maybe half a dozen others besides me and Timo.

Karla marched in front of us, teaching us a song in words we didn't understand. She said it was a language people all over the world used to speak. "Now you try. If any of you ever leave here, it would be good to know English."

I didn't see how any of us could ever leave or where to go if we tried since, as far as we knew, the whole world was like Berlin now. But we all liked Karla and we sang along.

"Three blind mice,
"Three blind mice
"See how they run,
"See how they run!"

It struck me that she was turning into an adult, and I wondered if we would still be able to trust her then. Some adults are not Hunters, like Frau Decker, the old lady who told me about the war that killed the world. But you never know; it's best to stay away from adults.

Karla would be one of the different ones, I was sure. I couldn't imagine having to hide from her.

"They all ran after
"The farmer's wife
"She cut off their tails
"With a carving knife
"Did you ever see
"Such a sight in your life
"As three blind mice?"

We were having too much fun and making too much noise, and we didn't hear anyone coming. Karla was writing the English words we didn't understand on the wall with a charcoaled piece of wood, so none of us was facing in the direction of the missing wall.

Mistake.

Karla turned to explain the words she had just written down — and screamed.

The rest of us turned to find a pack of Hunters, white like Karla and Timo, not brown like me. A wall of mean adults in place of the wall that had once been there. The only escape was through the single door next to where Timo was sitting cross-legged on the floor.

I grabbed Timo's hand and pulled him up, yanking open the door and running down the hall. The rest of the kids streamed out with us.

The faster kids were already far down the hall; Timo and I would have to hide. Timo was really big and strong for his age, but he was slow. I hadn't seen any dogs with this group of Hunters, so we just might have a chance. I dashed through an empty doorway and up a flight of stairs, my hand still clamped tightly around his. The stairs came out on emptiness, and we made our way carefully through the rubble to what was left of some walls. Once behind them, we sank down to the floor.

Below us, I heard screaming.

Karla.

Timo clapped his hands over his ears, and tears began to seep out of his eyes. Bad things always hurt him so much more than anyone else. It's one of the reasons I have to protect him.

I motioned to him to stay put, and he nodded. I crawled over to the edge of the building where there was still a fragment of wall and peered over, trying to see what was going on.

Six of the Hunters were standing around laughing, four men and two women, but I couldn't see Karla, only hear her, screaming and pleading. The Hunters were all looking at the ground, not up, so I leaned a little farther out.

Karla was underneath a seventh Hunter, pounding on his shoulders while he pounded her. The high whine she was making hurt my ears.

And then she saw me, and for a moment it stopped, somewhere between a hiccough and a shriek.

The Hunter stopped pounding, got up, and a second unzipped his trousers and took his place between Karla's bloody thighs. Karla's eyes were pleading with me, a message I didn't want to understand. When Timo and I did that, what the Hunters were doing with her, it didn't make me cry, it made me happy.

And then she screamed again.

I couldn't take it. I lugged the biggest piece of wall I could find to the edge, right above the man on top of Karla.

I pushed.

There was a high pitched scream, male this time, and then silence.

Without peering over again to see what had happened, I grabbed Timo's hand and ran through the ruins for the next stairwell.

"Frau Decker, Karla is dead, I killed her!"

Timo followed me into the old woman's apartment, crying more than I was, loud jerking sobs that only made it worse.

Frau Decker sat on what was left of the sofa in what was left of the apartment on Jägerstrasse. I once asked her why she stayed in a place with no roof, and she just said where was she to go, an old woman like her when all her family was dead?

"You can find a house with a roof at least," I had said.

She shook her head. "This is my home. My children grew up here. It is all I have, even if I must sleep in the hall."

But Frau Decker would not be able to comfort us this time or ever again. When I came around the front of her sofa, she was gazing out at the ruins of Berlin with empty eye sockets. I had no one to learn from anymore.

How was I to keep Remembering—and keep Timo safe?

The only one who could help me now was the Beast.

I became more careful and more afraid, as we all did. I once asked Frau Decker why so many adults were Hunters, but she didn't know either. She said that they were the hopeless, which didn't make much sense to me, since it wasn't any different from the rest of us. It seemed to me that the Hunters killed for fun, which meant that if we stayed out of their way, maybe they would kill one another. We children began to report to each other when we found bodies—it told us where adults were hunting, the places to avoid.

We couldn't stay hidden all the time, though, since we had to eat. One late summer day, Timo and I were tending our garden near the Reichstag when we heard a loud whirring in the sky, like thousands of wings beating the air at once.

We hid among the trees at the edge of the field and watched as a huge metallic bird with wings as fast as a dragonfly's landed straight down in front of the ruined building. The wind it created flattened the long grass in all directions.

Slowly the whirring wings stopped and several figures jumped down from the flying metal thing. They looked like people, but their heads were funny round things resembling the eyes of an insect.

This was something I did not Remember.

"Yasmina, should we run?"

"Shhh. They might hear us." As big as he was, Timo was always scared. I should have been too, but I couldn't tear my eyes away from the strange people and their machine.

One of them waved something shiny in the air and then reached up—and took off its head.

Timo gasped, and I clapped my hand over his mouth. "Look, Timo, they're normal adults!" I whispered.

After the first one had taken the bubble off, the rest did as well. There were only six of them—if they were Hunters, it was the smallest group I had ever seen.

And every single one of them was darker skinned than the darkest Hunter I had ever seen.

Timo took my hand off his mouth. "They're almost black," he said, remembering to whisper this time. "A lot darker than you, Yasmina."

I nodded.

Another one began waving something shiny in the air as well. It stopped, the piece of metal pointed straight at us.

The strange, dark people began walking in our direction.

"Run!"

Timo didn't need any more encouragement. We dashed out of our hiding place. "Not back to the Beast!" I yelled. "We don't want them to know where we live!"

We pounded through the grass for the ruins of the Reichstag.

"Wait, we want to help!" one of the strangers called out in German. The words sounded strangely different. "We are from Africa, a place not destroyed in the wars!"

The voice was that of a male adult, but I couldn't be sure if I had understood what he said. The words were all off in a way I had never heard. Sometimes Hunters spoke Turkish, words that brought back scraps of a life little more than a dream, my life Before. When those Hunters spoke German, the words sounded different too—but not as broken as that of the dark strangers trying to run us down.

We hid among the ruins of the Reichstag until nightfall, and then crept back to our home beneath the Beast.

I dreamt of Africa, a name I had heard once for a place far away. Africa and wars and dark skinned people with their heads in round bubbles.

That night, we were startled awake by shots and screams.

Timo and I held each other until the night was quiet again and then drifted back to sleep.

When the sunlight crept through the cracks between planks and concrete and woke us, we crawled out and looked around in every direction. The sun shone, warm and strong on our faces, and there was no movement except for the squirrels and no sound except for the birds.

I wished there were not so many empty spaces, but we made our way to the field in front of the Reichstag without meeting either Hunters or Strangers. The huge flying thing sat there, a burned-out shell, and all was quiet. Some of the tomato and bean plants in our vegetable garden were trampled. There were bodies strewn around the flyer, Strangers and Hunters both.

But more Hunters than Strangers. And the Hunters were mutilated in ways I had never seen before, or at least not before I had started to Remember.

Timo was whimpering, and I put my arms around his waist. "Shhh. We must try to find some of the other children so that we can bury them."

And then another voice called to us in the strange German I had heard the day before. "Is there someone there?"

I froze for a moment. But no one here could harm us, and I followed it, Timo following me.

One of the Strangers still lived, barely. Bearded — a man.

I knelt next to him, and he gripped my hand. "Please," he said in the same odd German as the one who had chased us.

"When more of our kind come, you must trust them."

"No."

"Yes."

"Why?"

Timo knelt next to me and took my other hand.

The Stranger did not answer my question. Instead he gave me a message. "Tell them, the ones who come after, tell them to save the children."

He was an adult, but he was dying. He couldn't hurt us. I took the head of the dark man in my lap and I began to sing.

"Three blind mice,
"Three blind mice,
"See how they run."

Perhaps it was the right thing to do. The Stranger looked at me with wide eyes and smiled.

I continued to sing. When he died, he was still smiling.

Most of the kids who used to live in the university before Karla died were still somewhere along Unter den Linden, scattered in twos and threes, in places where it wouldn't be as easy for the Hunters to find.

Timo and I went from hiding place to hiding place, telling them what had happened, so we could bury the dead before they started to stink and rot in the summer sun. Many of us had garden plots on the edges of the field next to the Reichstag, and no one wanted decaying bodies there.

Even though there were over thirty of us, it took us several days to bury them all. Not all of us were as big and strong as Timo, and our shovels were old and worn. We scavenged for new things when the old broke, but we couldn't always find exactly what we needed.

We were pushing the last of the bodies into shallow graves when Andrea cried out a warning. "Look! From the river!"

Over two dozen Hunters, and they had knives rather than just shovels.

"Scatter!" I yelled. "Run for the trees and the ruins!"

Everyone ran, most heading either for the nearest stand of trees or the Reichstag.

I couldn't run as fast as I wanted; I had to keep an eye on Timo.

And then he tripped.

"Timo!" I felt as if my scream scraped the hard blue of the sky.

The Hunters were too close, but I couldn't leave him there, I couldn't. I dashed back and pulled Timo up, supporting and running and dragging and doing anything that would get us out of danger. Luckily, many of the Hunters had stopped at the flying machine and were climbing in and throwing things out to their companions—more interested in scavenging than in us.

We reached the trees. I pushed Timo down beneath some bushes and knelt next to him.

"Don't make a sound," I whispered.

We could hear a Hunter nearby trampling the bushes and branches and underbrush, but he didn't notice us.

Timo and I stayed there long after everything was quiet again, and the birds had resumed chattering and chirping above. When I felt safe, I whispered to Timo that we could go.

He moaned and pushed himself up on both hands. "Yasmina, I don't know if I can walk."

I managed to support and drag and coax Timo back to our home beneath the Beast, but even now, with days and days of rest, he still cannot walk on his own.

The Beast protects us, but she cannot help me in this. When she comes to me at night, she folds her wings behind her and shakes her head sadly. *I know nothing of medicines, Yasmina.*

I turn away.

I am growing desperate.

I have checked on the others living on Unter den Linden to see if anyone knows what we can do about Timo's ankle. All of them are back in their hiding places except Kyrill and Verona, but none of them knows what to do for someone with a leg that will no longer support weight. I do not have the right memories to do what is necessary.

And now Timo's foot is growing huge and turning colors both bright and dull that scare me.

I am scavenging for medicines in apothecaries on Dorotheenstrasse when I hear the strange whirring noise again.

Strangers?

I throw boxes and bottles into my bag. My treasures bouncing against my hip, I run between the ruins in the direction of the Reichstag.

When I reach the corner of the building, I see for the second time one of the bird like machines setting down on the field, flattening the grass beneath it.

This time, the Strangers who jump down into the tall grass are not wearing the round bubbles on their heads, but they too have glistening skin so dark it is almost black.

As I watch, they walk around the abandoned flying machine, inspecting the debris on the ground, the broken pieces the Hunters left behind.

Then one of them, a woman I think, notices the recent graves. She cries out and drops to her knees. Even at this distance, I can see that tears are running down her face.

The rest run over to the graves we dug. One of the dark people is counting, shaking his head. Another draws the woman back to her feet and puts his arms around her. A third notices the gardens we have planted near where I am hiding and begins walking in my direction.

The man who died with his head in my lap told me to trust them, told me to tell them to save the children.

I cannot. Trust does not come easily.

I run back through the ruins, keeping to the shadows as much as I can. When I get back to our home on the shadow side of the Beast, Timo's skin is hot to the touch.

"Yasmina, everything hurts now, not just my foot."

I dump the medicines I found on the ground and start pawing through them, but the tears starting in my eyes are blinding me.

This is too hard. Even though I Remember, I still do not know enough to read all these strange words and find whatever will cure my friend.

I cover my face with my hands and turn away. Life would be no life without Timo.

"Yasmina? What is it?"

Squaring my shoulders, I look at him again, smiling. But he sees the shape of my eyes. "Don't cry, Yasmina," Timo says, stroking my hair. "You will take care of everything. You always do."

But I cannot.

Tell them to save the children.

I kiss Timo on the forehead.

A medication that describes itself as relieving pain and reducing fever calms Timo and puts him to sleep.

I lean my back against the stone wall of our shelter and watch Timo's even breathing, the slight smile on his lips as he sleeps. Despite how peaceful he looks, I worry. Timo seems to be better now, but I do not know if I have helped him or just made him unaware of his injuries for a time.

I am still afraid when I leave our sanctuary where Quadriga guards us. Darting between ruins and trees, I run in the direction I do not want to go, toward the field in front of the Reichstag. Perhaps, if I am lucky, the

Strangers will already be gone.

Perhaps, if I am lucky, they will still be there.

There, just past the second flying machine, they stand next to the graves we dug, gazing silently at the freshly turned earth, their hands crossed in front of their bodies, their heads bent. There is something about the way they are standing, quiet and intent, that makes me slow down as I approach. By the time they notice me, I am walking.

The woman closest to me pulls something I know must be a weapon by the way she is holding it. "Stop!"

I do as she says. We all stare at each other for a moment, silent, not knowing what to do.

I indicate the grave they are standing next to. "He said to tell you to save the children."

"Who did?" a man behind the woman with the weapon asks.

"The one who was still alive after the Hunters came."

"Baleka," the man says. "We heard it on the transmission."

"Hunters?" the woman repeats, her voice still laced with suspicion.

I nod. "The ones we hide from."

The black people speak among themselves in the strange language, their voices rising. I understand none of it. But when I sang the English song to the man who died, it made him smile.

I start to sing.

"Three blind mice,
"Three blind mice,
"See how they run,
"See how they run!"

The Strangers have stopped arguing and are staring at me. "You sang that after the battle," says the first man who spoke, in our language now. "We heard it through the radio."

"What is a radio?"

A reluctant smile flits across the woman's features. "You are the one who sang to him?"

I nod again. "I think he liked it. That was after he told me to trust you."

The woman finally lowers her weapon. "And said to save the children."

I begin to cry. "Yes, please. My friend Timo, he was injured the last time the Hunters attacked. He is as big as an adult now, but—can you save him?"

The Strangers look at each other, and without me seeing it, a decision is made. "We will try," a man who has not yet spoken says. "Where is your friend?"

Lightness fills my chest. I dash over and take the man's gloved hand, pulling him forward. "He is in the shadow of the Beast."

The man smiles and shrugs and allows me to pull him.

"Will you take us to Africa?" I ask.

Cai and Her Ten Thousand Husbands

Gord Sellar

Smoke in the air, a satchel full of squirming crystalline brains trapped in bloody skulls near my bare feet. I am *cai* once again. I kick the earth and turn my face north.

"*The calling springtime...*" I manage to sing, before I double over in agony.

We all expected the same things: husbands of our own to argue with, to walk beside in twilight, to make love to. Pretty babies to grow inside us, to unfurl into themselves and play at our feet.

It's different for us Hakka, my mother said. *Study hard*, she begged.

I did. Mornings, I hunched in rice paddies in sweltering heat. Afternoons passed in the library until sundown. Nights, my itchy eyes stared at a computer screen. Often, I woke to my wristlet's alarm with my head on a desk, and went straight to morning rice-field duty.

We girls knew something of the outside world from online newsfeeds and rice-field gossip. We followed the war in the border states and imagined dashing hi-tech Genghis Khans riding in from the Mongol Republic wastelands, or handsome Japanese and Euro CEO princes waving victory flags from the backs of robotic tanks, rescuing us from the onslaught.

Late one night my wristlet woke me. I fled the library, out into the courtyard, breathless and terrified, for stars still crowded the sky.

The other girls were already on the dormitory roof, screaming, "Fire, fire!" I scrambled up, and from the roof I could see it, too, off in the valley—a slim fringe of glowing orange light.

"That's the city burning," an older girl said. "Soldiers will be coming here soon."

Hours later, after sunrise, they did.

Not Japanese CEOs or Mongol princes. Just rough-faced footmen marching in tight, straight lines. They reminded me of green carrot-tops poking up along garden rows. They looked dignified, almost honorable, in their patchy green camouflage uniforms, and many wore earpieces or carried little computers on their belts. Many carried backpacks big enough to fit a girl into.

They spoke into machines that translated their dialect into ours. "We have liberated the city and come to liberate you, too," the machines boomed. "The whole province is now under our control."

We asked, "Whose control?"

"We cannot understand you," they answered, "Now come with us." They led us to a convoy of trucks waiting nearby. "Get in the trucks."

Our teachers stood there, watching silently. One older girl waiting beside me began weeping. "We're going to die," she kept saying. Another girl argued with her, told her to be quiet. But the older girl couldn't stop saying it.

"Why didn't they take our teachers too? Why only us?" another asked.

"Maybe there was a special truck for them?" the older girl snapped.

But none of us believed that.

After hours of thumping and rattling down brutal roads, of sleepless sobbing and prayers, the truck stopped. Soldiers threw open the back and their machines translated their command: "Get out."

"Where are we? What's happening?" We asked these questions, but the men ignored us, didn't even use their machines to say, "We can't understand you."

They led us into a filthy old complex. Inside were tiny rooms, each with a stained mat on the floor. One by one, we were tossed into the cells, alone, to wait.

I'd always envied pretty girls and wished I were like them. The other girls at the dormitory had said, sneering: "You've got a mother's face. A mama-face." I'd always hated it.

But when they threw open the door, looked me over, and muttered in their language, I was hopeful, thankful for my ugly face. I could hear the girls' shrieking through the walls, and the men. For once I was grateful for my mama-face.

I thought it would keep them away for a while, at least.

It didn't. It wasn't my face that interested them.

Memory, for me, is all fragments. Just tiny moments.

It's not what they've done to my brain—I think I've always been like that. I remember only brief, vivid things. The bite of sugared ginger-root with jasmine tea. The feeling of a fresh, hard persimmon in my palm. My mother's voice at night, singing about the returning cranes of springtime.

I cannot remember her face.

But I remember a dozen hands holding my body down, slapping my cheek as one soldier pushed his thing into me, then another, another. I remember that tearing feeling, as if I were about to break into two pieces. And filthiness. The slick of blood and sweat on my skin, and wanting to close my tired legs. Their voices howling strange, foreign words I'd heard before but couldn't understand, and the smell of their bodies, thumping against me, them breathing their reek in my face.

And always, that searing pain inside me. My ageless heart thumps against my ribs when memories of that night return to me. Sweat floods my skin, I quiver and curdle inside.

I'm not there anymore, in that filthy cell, bleeding onto that stained mat. But it's worse, remembering, than it was at the time, I sometimes think. I am still here, still haunted by them, but they are all long dead.

Peng-zu law dictates that all wives—we are called *cai*—are their husbands' communal property. Thus, the ritual: every so often all the brides of the *peng-zu* are shuttled off to a new complex. This pattern rules our lives, as seasons once did.

I have crossed snowy wastes, lived deep within brutally scorching deserts, slept in gardens of mottled bamboo, and poured out tea in mountain palaces so lofty I could gaze down upon cloud tops. Each stay has ended the same way: with a forced march.

How long ago was the first one? A dozen years? Hundreds?

For a long time I didn't know. What they did to me... I can't feel time's flow anymore. A blessing, maybe.

On every march since the first, I have walked freely. It was only during the first time that soldiers came, chained us with bands of iron at our necks and ankles, and shouted orders through their machines, waved guns at us. The pills they forced down our throats that first time made us bleed between the legs, from inside.

Only the first time. I never thought to run away after that. The chains were never needed again. The chains were in my mind.

Every march ends in the same way. We reach a wall with a door in the middle. It opens, and all the soldiers left behind flee as if from devils or ghosts.

The *peng-zu* are neither, but they *are* terrifying. They emerge, angelic, to lead us, the *cai*, to their bedchambers. So beautiful, every one of them unearthly, pure as fire. Living among them is like being locked in a prison full of sweetly smiling buddhas, each with a nest of demonic snakes coiled under his robes, each waiting for a chance to pounce.

Such exquisite rooms: silk cushions, scarlet bridal robes, golden hair-combs, looking glasses and jewels and unimaginable banquets. The ancient emperors look like beggars and filthy peasants beside the *peng-zu*.

An ancient *cai* with a very young girl's body, perhaps thirteen, taught me the most ancient tea ceremonies.

"If you do this right, they will love you and give you immortality," she said. "Make them come so hard they hit the rabbit in the moon, and they'll give you everything." She believed it, too. "But not until the tea is drunk. Otherwise they will grow bored with you and never give you the gift. This game is won with squeezed thighs and pretty conversation."

So many *cai* believed these lies and fantasies.

I performed the ceremonies well but carefully avoided perfection. A few *peng-zu* delighted in my grace, praised me, called me 'wife' instead of '*cai*.' Grabbed at me with their greedy hands, tearing my vermilion silks away.

But none was ever overwhelmingly enchanted. I made them grunt but never made one call out my name.

Most of the *cai* are uneducated: simple country girls, they are convinced that their 'husbands'—their owners— are magical beings.

But I know the real story of Peng Zu. He was a legendary *Shen Xian*, a methuselah who survived for eight centuries. The many emperors envied him, sent bribes, but he shared no secrets with them. He took a long-lived woman named Lady Cai as a lover, taught her the secrets of immortality: sex magic, and tonics of reindeer horn and mica dust.

They claim this fairy tale monster who never existed as their ancestor and Lady Cai as ours, just as they say Peng Zu claimed the Yellow Emperor as his. A lineage of liars. But I know that they are not immortal.

I *know*. Because I have seen them die.

With every forced march, it grew harder to understand the soldiers' words. Their translators began failing to make sense to us, as if language were slowly slipping from us.

On the last march, down the high mountain, one tried to speak to me through his translator machine.

"Nya ho," he said. It took me a moment to realize he was greeting me, his accent was so strange. He fiddled with the machine.

"What's your name?" he asked through it.

I looked at his face like I would an empty bowl.

He spoke slowly: "Is there an endless *cai* among you?"

We locked eyes, and I realized he meant *immortal*. "Why?"

He glanced around, checking perhaps for an angry superior. Then, leaning close to me, he said: "I *know*. The *peng-zu* virus... that it's a sex disease. I want to wash my prick in an immortal woman's..."

"What? Those monsters have..." I caught myself too late. "Our husbands enjoy us often. If it were a sex disease, every *cai* would be immortal. Do I look like it to you?"

"How old were you?" he whispered. "When you were captured?"

"Fifteen. They called it 'liberated' back then."

He squinted. "What year was that?"

I thought it over and told him a year a few years after the real one.

If he thought me recently captured, maybe he'd go away.

He was awed, instead, and spoke as he would to an old woman. "That was over a century ago," he whispered, his face suddenly pale as the machine softly translated.

I looked away.

"I'll see you again," he said, touching my arm.

Halfway down the mountain we reached some trucks, waiting at a rest stop. We were sorted, it seemed randomly, and sent into different trucks. I ended up in a group with only one *cai* I knew, although I couldn't remember from where. Neither of us spoke, as the others were unchained and herded in behind us. I saw the soldier who'd talked to me, unlocking their neck-bonds. He stood watching me as the truck's door slammed shut, leaving us in darkness.

"Upgrades," the *cai* whose face I knew whispered to me. Her breath was hot and strangely sweet, like mine.

"What?"

"Upgrades. You haven't noticed? We're stronger now."

I closed my eyes, flexed my muscles. I couldn't tell, except that my legs didn't ache.

"That was a Taishan complex we were at. The *peng-zu* there are the head researchers. They're always upgrading the bug, testing it on us, and then sending us out to spread it to the others. That's why we've all been split up, sent apart."

Another crazy wives' tale? Was that what I was, after all these years? Not just a slave, but a container for a disease? But why the newly -captured girls?

"Bug... *disease*, you mean? But I'm not sick..."

"You're over a hundred years old, and your tits still haven't come in," she hissed. "You don't *feel* sick, but you're infected."

"What's your name?" I asked.

She was quiet as if thinking. The weak, still-human girls around us sobbed and whispered, a few coughing and sniffling. Poor things.

"I can't remember," she finally answered.

I nodded. "Neither can I."

Sleep took forever to swallow me down, like an enormous snake swallowing a broken-necked child.

When my body slammed down against something soft, I woke.

It was another body. Bones cracked beneath me. Shrieks filled the dark, as I was thrown sideways and then down, and suddenly the bodies were crashing down against me.

My bones did not break.

The darkness was spinning and, inside it, the screams and bodies of terrified girls and women tangled and writhed within the truck.

Something exploded outside.

The truck was rolling downhill, sideways. I couldn't stabilize myself, so I relaxed, let my body follow the movements. The other girls fought too hard, resisted gravity's pull, stiffened themselves against it. That was why their bones were cracking. While they hollered in pain, I hummed one of my mother's night-songs quietly to myself.

Another voice joined in with me. The *cai* whose face I knew. As we hummed the melody, the truck's spin seemed to slow, and with a final clattering of teeth and limbs, crashed to a stop.

The smell of blood and piss filled the inside of the truck, and the moaning quickly reached a crescendo. I was in the middle of a pile of jarred bodies, ribs and legs snapped into terrible angles. I kept breathing slowly and began to dig through them toward the exit.

Someone ripped the door open, and the noise of battle crashed in. Explosions, bombs screaming their way down toward us. Guns stuttered all around, the flashes of their muzzles lighting my way out of the jumbled mess of bodies.

A dozen soldiers piloted springing, bouncing jeeps all around us. In the dark they looked a little like frogs with salt dropped onto their backs, leaping around frantically. Their pilots were blasting terrible-looking cannons at some enemy up above. Everyone was staring uphill at the invisible attackers.

Everyone but him. He grabbed my hand and dragged me out of the mess of whimpering, broken girls.

"Come with me," he yelled.

I turned, straining against the glare of the explosions to search the truck's inner darkness, and I saw her eyes—only her eyes—focused on mine. She didn't move.

I shivered. The soldier assumed I was frightened and forcefully led me away from the battle, off behind some rocks.

"I want to be immortal," he said, reaching for the zipper of his pants.

I looked at his face. *You're all the same*, I thought to myself.

"Can you give me that?"

"Let me go..." I said, and turned to leave. The sudden wave of dizziness that washed over me was startling: somewhere along the way, I'd forgotten how to think of leaving. I felt like I was dream-walking, still really trapped in the *peng-zu's* strange, closed world, even out here. My legs locked for a moment, locked completely still.

That was all he needed. He clubbed me on the head, and I collapsed—not unconscious, just shocked by the pain. He dragged me off quickly into the shadows, and then rolled me over and began struggling with my clothing. Robes are not difficult to yank open, but by then I was fighting back, ignoring the pain blooming in my skull as I clawed at his face.

"Stop it," he hollered, and slapped me. "Don't you want to be free?"

I was walking away, I thought then, gouging at one of his eyes. *How can you bargain with me for what was already mine?*

Then he had a pistol in his hand. I stared at it, wondered whether it could kill me, whether he knew if it could.

But that didn't matter. She had followed us. I saw her creeping up behind him and tensed. While he struggled with the belt on my robe, she pounced, digging her fingers into his throat from behind.

"Die, bastard!" she screamed. They both fell on top of me, and he raised the pistol behind him in a single lunge.

I grabbed for it too late. The noise of the shot stunned me. She went slack, hands suddenly limp, and he shoved her corpse off, down to the muddy ground. I could smell her blood all over me, all over him.

With her body still shuddering, her head blown open, he said, "I didn't want to do that. I don't want to hurt you." Her face twitched— one eye open, the other fluttering. Spilled out of her skull, covered in foamy blood, were jittering threads of shattered crystal.

I leaned closer. Light flickered through the crystalline fibers. A garden of tiny buds sprouted from them, flowered into wriggling crystalline threads as I watched. Her shattered brain was trying to heal itself. It didn't know yet that her body was dying.

Is that what's inside my head, too?, I asked myself.

"All I want is immortality," he said, his hand on my shoulder, holding me down. "You can give that to me, or I can take it."

He rolled off me suddenly, barely dodging her hand as it lunged at him. With a curse, he shot five more bullets into her head and chest, and then turned the gun on me. I wondered how many shots he had left.

"You'll let me go?" I asked, as he stood.

"I promise. Over here, let's go." He pointed into a deep ditch nearby. "Take off your clothes." He wasn't speaking to me like an old woman anymore.

One last time, I thought to myself as I yanked my robe open, knowing then that he would be immortal after this.

Knowing I would someday hunt him down. And I will, someday.

The distant city lights flickered. I saw instead the terrifying flickering within her broken crystal brain.

I had wandered, lonely and dazed, ever since. But not toward the city. Where?

Part of me had known. As a girl, I'd studied the way birds know where to go, when the seasons turn. Cranes and storks, they have no maps and no names for the places they abandon, breed in, and return from, but they know the places just the same. They are called, just the same.

That was the instinct I felt. Like a crane being called softly, insistently northward.

I fought it, at first, so hard my hands shook and I spat blood onto the ground. The city lights filled me with fear. *But I could hide there*, I told myself. My stomach squeezed tightly at the thought, and my throat closed off until I turned my eyes from the city to the mountain in the distance.

Taishan. I was being called back to Mount Tai.

No, I thought to myself, desperate in a way I'd never been before. *I could hide on a farm, sleep in the millet fields, pay a farmer by washing his prick inside me, or kill him. Nobody would ever find me.* I felt my legs shaking, and my bowels released suddenly as I fell to the ground.

I turned my mind's eye back to Taishan, and suddenly I could breathe again.

Later—how much, who knows?—within my scarlet chamber in the Taishan complex, I curled up in mind-wrenching pain.

Since my return, my belly had slowly expanded. I had hidden it as best I could. It was all wrong. Vomiting, craving sour oranges and plain rice, a soft kick inside the belly. Those were the correct signs. Not this brutal, sharp-edged scraping. Something within me, hard and vicious, was quickening.

It was supposed to be impossible. No *peng-zu* wife had ever borne a child. That night, some shadow within me rejoiced, finally to have its own possession, something actually *mine*. This part of me seemed not to notice my terror and agony, not over its bitter, gleeful revenge on my husbands.

I hissed a curse for the nameless—now probably immortal—soldier who'd fathered the thing. Just then, the door to my chamber opened.

It was the oldest *peng-zu* in Taishan, with a lustful look in his eyes. He wasn't always that way. Sometimes he only came seeking a game of *weiqi*, or some tea and a long nap beside me. But that night, the old monster had come looking for a wife.

"I don't think..." I began, and then I winced and leaned forward as a shock of pain exploded inside me.

"Are you pretending?" he asked. "You can't get sick of sex. You're programmed that way." He knew that I knew how it worked, infection and all. He even described himself in the same way, programmed.

"It's not that... there's something wrong."

"Let me see," he said, not at all seriously, and pushed me onto my back. I complied, unable to make myself say no or explain. Pulling apart the hems of my robe, he ran his hand over my body, cupping one breast and squeezing it softly before slipping his other hand between my thighs. I went slick in moments, just as I was programmed to do. Then he touched me inside.

I felt a sharp jolt of pain, as something inside me grasped his fingers and held, tight. He tried to pull his hand away from me, but he couldn't move it at all. When he realized this, he looked at me in horror. "What are you? What have you done?"

"Please," I said, because I knew if he left the room, he would tell the others. I'd heard of what they did with disobedient *cai*.

Another jolt of agony exploded within my abdomen, and his body suddenly went tense from terrific pain. "What have you done?" he roared, and tried to tear his hand back away from me. But the grip held firm, and he ended up on the floor with me standing above him. I gasped, wondering what could have done this to him, what I was carrying inside me.

"Please," I begged, but he began to scream as loudly as he could and pounded his free hand against the wall.

I couldn't breathe or think clearly. I did the first thing that came to mind, grabbing the oil-lamp-stand beside the bed and slamming it into the back of his head as hard as I could.

After the first strike he collapsed, but I kept pounding at him until his skull split open and the crystal threads spilled out, jittering into a mess of blood and brains. Panic gushed up within me, the same drowning panic I'd felt when I thought of fleeing the *peng-zu* world forever. Terror forced me to slow down, but it did not master me.

When I calmed for a moment, his hand dropped down to the ground with a thud, fingers bruised black and crushed flat. Staring into the still-flickering, trembling bloody filaments of braincrystal at my feet, I realized that nothing could stop me as long as I could swallow the pain. I could be like a giant snake, too, and swallow the stricken crane of my instincts.

My mind choking, I fled the palace into the night.

The other *cai* were horrified when, a few days later, I returned at dawn. I told them, all these wives of the monsters, about the abandoned truck I'd found not far away full of guns and bombs and dead soldiers, and told them what I wanted to do.

"Come with me," I begged.

"Are you insane? Leave, now," hissed the thinnest *cai*, who'd never liked me. "They'll kill us all. After the murder..."

"I want to," I explained, bristling at the word murder. "I can't go unless I destroy this place. I'm bound here. It's some kind of..." They wouldn't understand the notion of programming. "A... a spell," I said.

"We can't leave either," whined a younger *cai*. "You know that. The pain... it's too much." She shook her head.

"You can. If I can do it, you can."

"No," several of them said at once, and backed away from me. I worried that they might call the *peng-zu*. They didn't.

"Please," I repeated over and over again, weeping. "I'll carry you. Anything. I have to destroy this place." A sharp-edged squirm tore at my insides, and I knelt down in pain. "I'm going to burn it to the ground."

They all stood there staring at me. Most of them frightened, but a few looked relieved to know it might soon end. A few of them even smiled.

When I left, to return to my truck, I went alone. But not one of them tried to stop me.

Why haven't the soldiers come?

Surely they've seen the smoke by now, pouring skyward. Perhaps their programming, like mine, went silent after the palace was burned to cinders. Or have they fled, terrified that whatever burned down Taishan complex–the center of *peng-zu* society—will come for them next?

I can't be bothered to kill them. Standing outside the ruins, I have stared for hours into the smoking mess. The sweet stink of burning flesh turned my stomach as I waited for their piled corpses to finish burning, but now it is done. They are as charred as possible—a fire that would turn them to ash and cinder was too much to ask for.

First, the wives. Rummaging through the charred mound of bodies, I dig out each of the skulls. With a hammer, I smash each one open. The blood is baked around their crystalline brains, and I have to completely shatter the skull to free it. Still quivering and glinting—still *thinking*— their crystal brains wriggle free and, as they do, I hammer them to tiny, mindless fragments. The tiny shards are still budding new filaments, glittering, but they cannot house a whole mind. This is the best mercy I can show them, to make them finally free.

Then I turn to the *peng-zu*'s shot, stabbed, bodies, now burned as well. So many tried to flee. And failed. With their skulls, I am far more careful. If they break free and connect to other crystal brains, perhaps they will build or steal themselves new bodies and live again.

I handle each skull like a fragile egg, wrap it in a thick square of plastic cut from the tarpaulins left on the truck. That will do until I can embed them in iron and bury them. Minds whole, they can flicker alone, forever, in darkness.

That tug: I feel it again. Smoke still thick in the air, human grease and ash caked on my hands and face, I turn northward... to Beijing. I can see the ruined city, the red gate, and the *peng-zu* palace beyond it, in my mind. I touch my bulging belly, wonder, "How can I go there like this?"

I begin to sing my mother's song, for strength.

Dark Planet

Lavie Tidhar

One: Weirdies and Bombies

The Weirdy was directly ahead of Chamberlain, partially obscured by the thick foliage of the jungle, but *there*. Chamberlain's gun was in his hand but it was hard to take aim. The Weirdy was moving. It looked like a localized maelstrom of air, a cone of turbulence tapering onto the ground where it stirred the rotting leaves into new configurations. The only organic part of the Weirdy was at the top where air gave way to a face like a dragonfly, at least if the insect had been gene-spliced with a tiger. Worse, the head remained still while the body-storm continued to rotate. Chamberlain's gun was a Vacuum 300 and, theoretically, it could take out one of the Weirdies, *no* problem. Theoretically.

Chamberlain took a careful step forward and brought the gun up...

The maelstrom stopped moving. Dark multi-faceted eyes seemed to look directly at him and for a moment he thought—it *knows* I'm here.

He pressed the trigger.

The blast tore through the foliage, bursting veins in the living trees' trunks, creating a localized implosion that threatened to suck Chamberlain into it. He'd fallen down as soon as he'd fired, minimizing the amount of exposed body, but still it tugged at him, trying to drag him into the temporary vacuum. He shut his eyes and his fingers dug into the mud.

When the blast had abated, Chamberlain opened his eyes and stared forward. Total devastation. Where before there had been a thick, almost impenetrable jungle, there was now a clearing, and the ground was covered in bleeding, fresh kindling; the only remains of the living trees.

There was no sign of the Weirdy. A blue-black insect as thick as an eye-patch buzzed over Chamberlain's head and settled on his outstretched fingers. He stared at it for a long moment. The insect's feelers moved as if in a greeting. Then some knowledge forced its way back into Chamberlain's mind and the fear was back, a thousand times worse, and he had to bite down on his lip, drawing blood, trying to stop himself from moving, to be perfectly and absolutely *still*.

The insect was a Bombie.

It seemed to stare at him. Chamberlain stared back at the Bombie, trying not to blink. Silently, he counted planets, based on their distance from the sun: Monkey, Jaguar, Wolf, Fly, Elephant, Dog, Firefly. There was a song by Li Tsheng you learned, like a children's song, like a nursery rhyme, (although it didn't rhyme), when you came here:

> Firefly is dead and cold
> Monkey burns, Jaguar sleeps
> Wolf and Dog circle
> Elephant is home
> —Don't send me to Fly.

The Bombie buzzed at him. How did he get into this mess? It was Colonel Piet, old Colonel Piet with his yellow teeth and close-cropped grey hair who sent him like this, to his death. So calmly, too. The order came in the night. Chamberlain, Mastorakis and Shen, report to Command immediately. When they came, Colonel Piet saluted them and then showed them a map of the nearby territory. "Having some problems around this area," he said, circling one bit of jungle that looked exactly like any other bit of jungle. "We need some people to go in and take a look, thought of you. Got good records. If you could just pop in there and look around, see what you can find, why the Weirdies seem so bothered about this particular area. Think that would be all right?"

"Sir."

"Sir."

"Sir."

"Good." The colonel gestured at the projected map. "Kill any Weirdies you find, of course. And come back, do you hear? We need at least one of you alive."

"Sir."

"Sir."

"Sir."

"Dismissed."

Mastorakis got it not five hours out of base: a living tree engulfed him in its branches and by the time they got to him, the tree was pulsating with blood, its branches shaking, and Mastorakis's emaciated corpse was lying on the ground. They had torched the tree, but that didn't help Mastorakis.

Shen was with him up to and including the region of penetration. A Gorp got him. Chamberlain shuddered. He didn't want to think about the Gorp.

The shudder seemed to have alarmed the Bombie. Chamberlain froze. The Bombie stopped (it was now positioned half-way up his arm) and began to vibrate. The vibrations went up Chamberlain's arm. Please please please don't.

The vibrations grew more frantic. Please please pl—

"Bombie makes baby," a voice close to his ear said. He almost jumped. The voice was pleasant, soft, a little childish. "Makes many baby. You no like?"

Trying not to move his lips, the words escaping like a hiss of air through closed teeth: "Don't want to die."

"What is die? You think."

Somehow he understood the speaker. The voice made him picture a young girl standing there, which was insane. There were no young girls on Fly. But he did what the voice told him. He thought of death.

Pain, and the absence of pain... and the thing that is, that was, Chamberlain spread out over a large area, no heart to beat blood into the brain, neurons no longer firing, the I/We group-mind that is the human brain dispersing like mist—

The voice said, "Die—strange. You wait."

On his arm the Bombie was ready to explode. Its wings juddered and its feelers moved frantically in an ecstatic display. It had grown larger, inflated, until it was the size of a hand-grenade.

He whispered: "Can't... wait. No time."

"You no like? Bombie funny."

Funny?

Something leaned over him. He tried not to see it. It was nothing human. It was like two transparent arms made of glass, or air, passing over him, through him, and delicately cupping the Bombie. He saw it as a glass globe encircling the insect, right there on his arm.

The Bombie exploded. Chamberlain screamed.

"You silly," the voice said in his ear.

The Bombie exploded inside its cage. A cage, Chamberlain thought. He tried to ignore the spreading wetness in his combat suit. The Bombie exploded into a thousand tiny fragments, sharp black slivers that shot away from it as it disintegrated, ready to cut, maim, and embed themselves in any and all available surfaces, but instead—

They'd frozen in a perfect moment of explosion, within the boundary of an invisible globe. The globe rested on Chamberlain's arm. He stared at it. "Better now?" the childish voice said. "Pretty Bombie."

Chamberlain rolled on his back, bringing the gun up in one smooth motion, pointing it at the—

Weirdie.

A maelstrom of wind, a face above it like a whiskered cat, eyes bright and twinkling. His finger tightened on the trigger—

"Release Bombie?" the voice said. It came from the Weirdie, although the lips in that face did not move. And Chamberlain froze with his finger on the trigger. The threat in the words was self-evident, with or without the childish voice.

He relaxed his finger, slowly, and equally slowly he stowed away the gun. Above him the Weirdie was holding the Bombie. It looked like a grotesque aquarium, like something you got in the restaurants back on Elephant, only with a living bomb inside.

"You... Chamberlain? Pretty name. Pretty face. Me—"

Instead of words, an image, shoved into his brain like fingers into soft dough. Images, confused, incoherent. Weirdies, in formation. An area of jungle like all the others and yet somehow he knew it was the one he was in, the one he had been sent to, although it looked strange, somehow, as if the jungle were overlaid on top of something else, like two versions of the same thing getting mixed up. The area of penetration, he thought.

"Penetration," the Weirdy voice said. More images. This Weirdy, with a companion, travelling through the forest. The companion-

Weirdy disappearing in a blaze of—Chamberlain closed his eyes. The Weirdy had been killed with a vacuum gun. His.

"Mission, take look," the Weirdy said. "Mission—learn. After fix. No problem. Now I learn you. Yes?"

"No," Chamberlain said.

"Now I learn you," the Weirdy said. "No problem."

And again, it was like fingers digging into his skull, but this time it was worse, and he screamed. The maelstrom of wind picked him up and tendrils of air stroked him, touched him... "Please!" he said.

"No problem," the Weirdy said. "Must relax."

Tendrils of air studied him, caressed him, from his ears down to his neck, to his chest and back, to his buttocks and—

"No, you don't understand," he said.

"Is true," the Weirdy said. "Not understand. Must learn. You now. No problem."

"Stop saying that!"

Then a tentacle of air entered him and he screamed, and his mind was filled with images of the war, and back, back, back to:

Two: Brainstorm

He is at home and there is a solar-system swirling above his head made of soft colourful foam, all six planets in rotation. Daddy stands above him. "Monkey," Chamberlain says. "Monkey!"

"And this one, little Shambi?" Daddy says.

"Monkey!"

"Jaguar," Daddy says. "And this one?"

"Monkey?"

"Firefly. And this one is Wolf, and this one is Dog—see how they always circle close to each other, but never quite meet?—and this is home, this is—"

"Elephant!" Shambi says, and Daddy smiles and lifts him from the crib and gives him a hug. "You are a smart boy, Shambilan."

(somewhere far away—No, don't call me that! I'm Chamberlain now, and Shambilan is long gone, along with the house, the crib and that old useless toy—

—Where is other one?

—What?

—Where other one?

—There is no other one.

—No! Must look again!

And dissolve)

"Monkey!" Little Shambilan says.

"And this one?"

"Monkey!"

There is another planet on a string, but it is small and ugly, and father sees it and he frowns and he says, "That's not supposed to be there. Hold on," and he goes and he comes back and he has scissors and he cuts the wire and everything is pretty again. And Shambilan thinks of a word he had heard somewhere but doesn't know where, and he shouts, "Fly!"

"What did you say?"

"Monkey?"

"You should not talk of that place. It is evil."

(—What is evil?

—This is.

—No, this memory only. No evil. What is evil?

—Fly, Chamberlain says. Fly is evil.

And fade)

"What is evil, Daddy?"

Daddy is looking at him as if looking at something alien and strange. "Get away from my son," he says.

"Daddy?"

But his father still looks at him as if he has never seen him before, and there is a hard, scary look in his eyes. "There is no such place as Fly," he says. "Get away from him. Now."

And the scene disappears and it is later, years later, and—

(—Man no like new friend?

—Is this real?

—What is real?

And Chamberlain groans, and the wind probes deep inside him—

And dissipate)

—and he is lying in the grass under the stars with Rashmi and they both have their shirts off and her skin is soft and dark and his heart is beating loudly in his chest and she says, "One day I'm going to go to the stars."

"Why? Nothing there," he says, and his fingers trace a line under her arm and she giggles. "Don't you wonder what it's like, up there?"

"Rocks," he says, with the certainty of a boy. "Why go anywhere? Our ancestors came here because it was the best place to be."

"Do you really believe it?"

"The Party says—"

"I'm not asking you what the Party says. I'm asking what *you* believe."

"If they call me I'll go," he says, changing tack, his fingers trying to work their way below her navel, but she turns and blocks him. "Go where?"

"Into the service. You could come with me. Then we'll see what it's really like out there, on Firefly and Monkey, Jaguar and Wolf and Dog, maybe even further, back where people come from, I forget what it's called."

"Mars," Rashmi says. He shrugs. "Whatever." She smiles and turns toward him for a kiss—

(—Where is one?

—Oh, come on!

—You are distressed? Young boy likes young girl?

—Just... can we go back? Just for a moment?

—But where is other? Where is one?

—I—

And disperse)

"Rashmi? What is it?"

But she is backing away from him now, and her eyes are round with fear.

"What did I say?" He doesn't understand. "We could go to all of them," he says again, trying somehow to get her back. "You'll like Fly. It's beautiful. When the living trees are in bloom and the Gorp are hunting through the woods, and you can hear the music of the Skaar-et-lam when true night falls—"

"Get away from me! Get away!"

(—But I don't understand! This never happened. I don't know what Skaar-et-lam is—

—Very beautiful. Must experience. Now more.

—No more.

—Must.

—Kill me.

—I do not understand kill.

—Dying?

—Ah, yes, picture-story you tell. No, no dying.

And—)

The Party Congress, and he is a young man, standing in the auditorium with all the other cadets. The Chairman speaks, an elderly man in a plain blue shirt. "Prosperity is our watchword," the Chairman says. "Under the Party's leadership the six worlds are at peace. The world we have made for ourselves is a world of *good*."

Cheers.

"Unity!"

Cheers.

"The path of enlightenment is glorious before us—"

(—Not understand.

But Chamberlain does not even remember a party conference, does not remember the auditorium, does not remember the speech, and he says—What are you looking for?

—One! One plus one plus one plus one plus one plus one plus *one*!

—Ah, Chamberlain says. Mathematics. Right.

—Where is one?

And—)

He stands up in the audience and everyone turns to look and their eyes are hard and uncomprehending. He shouts, "What about the seventh planet?" and there is an uproar, and somebody screams, and the soldiers turn and the guns are pointing at him and the speaker roars— "There is no seventh planet!" and the guns—

(and fade. And back. And—)

Three: Soldier Plus One

The Weirdy hovered above him. "One dark," it said. Its body swirled in an excited turbulence. "One missing. Like puzzle, in memory of you, one time. You make puzzle with Daddy, and piece is missing. You cry."

"I did not *cry*," Chamberlain said indignantly. He pulled himself up. The Weirdy did not stop him. Chamberlain glared at the Weirdy. The trapped, exploding Bombie was still frozen by their side in its bubble of—of what?

"What did you do to it?" Chamberlain asked.

"Bombie? Make it sleep, only. Sleep small. You look?"

He looked, and looked away.

"Come," the Weirdy said. "You, me, go now. Take Bombie."

"Go where?"

"Home," the Weirdy said. "Source. Must change thing that is wrong. Fault of us, you. Never mind. All same."

"I should kill you," Chamberlain said. He stood up. His hand was on the butt of the Vacuum 300.

"Kill, not kill, all same," the Weirdy said.

"Whatever," Chamberlain said, resigned.

He followed the Weirdy. The Weirdy carried the frozen Bombie. What was he supposed to do? The alien could have killed him. It chose to keep him alive. Did that make him, technically, a prisoner of war? He'd never heard of anyone being captured by the Weirdies. And he still had his gun, so technically...

He thought about it. If he threw down his gun, would *that* make him a prisoner of war? They couldn't blame him then, could they? I mean, didn't he have to obey some kind of convention then? He said, "Do you want my gun?"

The Weirdy turned to him, the cat's eyes inscrutable. "You keep wind-toy. Gorp coming. Gorp no like you. Smell wrong."

Gorp.

"Where?" he said. Panic made him raise his voice. "Where Gorp?"

"You must quiet. Gorp coming. Many Gorp. Like you no like you."

What the hell did that mean?

They walked through the jungle. Chamberlain felt the ground shake under his feet. They passed through the trees, and suddenly they were out of them and into open space.

Chamberlain stared. He had thought this was all jungle, yet below him a vast open plane spread out in all directions, and in the distance he saw the outline of mountains, their peaks covered in snow, and a great, distant waterfall whose water rose again into the sky as it hit the ground, creating a haze of mist. Below, on the plane, were the Gorp.

"What is this place?" he said.

"Source," the Weirdy said. "Fly inside Fly. You say—amber?"

"Amber?"

"Fly in amber. Fly in Fly in amber."

"I have no idea what you just said."

The Weirdy seemed to shrug. "Matter no matter," it said. Chamberlain sighed.

Below, the Gorp thundered past them.

"Why are they—" he said, and stopped, thinking back on the Weirdy's words. "Like me not like me?"

"Not Fly. Come from—not source. Like you. Now belong Fly. Like you. But different."

"Not from Fly?" He stared at the Gorp. He had never seen so many. They ran past, appearing not to sense him, which suited Chamberlain fine. "Belong Fly, like me? How? I don't belong here!" Was that a wisp of panic in his voice? He stared at the Gorp and prayed they would keep on not noticing him.

"Belong Fly long time. No matter. Fix source first time. See after."

"What's the—where's the—what source? How do you fix it?"

"You come. Wait first time. Gorp go. Gorp fight you, fight me. Like fight."

They were *aliens*? That is, *other* aliens? Where did they come from? When? He said, "And the Bombies? Also from not here?"

"Bombies?" The Weirdy sounded surprised. "Nice toy. Nice Bombie. Like play-play. All same wind-toy."

Wind-toy? He meant his gun, Chamberlain realised. So the Weirdy thought the gun was a *toy*? He said, "Gun no toy. Gun kill."

"Kill, all same play-play," the Weirdy said. "You no die. Like Bombie."

Chamberlain gave up. They watched the Gorp in silence.

When the last Gorp had passed, Chamberlain sighed with relief and the Weirdy, without speaking, began to flow down the hill to the plane. Chamberlain followed him.

They walked in silence. It was a strange place. It should not have been there, he thought. There should be only jungle, living trees, darkness, mud, not—this.

There were tracks in the dust, and as they walked Chamberlain's perspective seemed to shift uncontrollably, as if a great lens were pinpointed at him and he stared through it at the plane and saw —

The tracks — made by the Gorp? By others? — seemed magnified, lines and circles running and criss-crossing each other, forming —

Somehow they began to make sense. They were like a writing, if someone could write on an entire world. Not random, but carrying a meaning, like an ancient magic spell, and he could almost understand it...

"Source," the Weirdy said, and it sounded sad. "You understand?"

Understanding was hovering on the edge of his mind. It was there in the lines in the dirt, in the great rising mountains which shouldn't have been there, in the plane itself. The old song came back to him then.

Firefly is dead and cold
Monkey burns, Jaguar sleeps
Wolf and Dog circle
Elephant is home.

"No!" the Weirdy said. It stopped and faced Chamberlain. Its cat's eyes were wide and unblinking. Its whirlwind body sent dust flying in the air. Chamberlain blinked back tears. "One, you see? You understand!"

"One is missing?" he found himself whispering the words.

"Must fix!"

Was there another line to the song? There were six worlds, and he counted them, ranked based on their distance from the sun: Monkey, Jaguar, Wolf, Elephant, Dog, Firefly. Six.

"No! Mistake! Never-mind, no fault. Must fix all same."

"I wish you'd stop saying that."

But the plane grew around him and he could see the world emanating from it, from that single point, growing outwards, and the script upon the world was like a curse, a seal, a —

"What did you do?" he whispered. And then he thought — *was it us?*

"All same," the Weirdy said.

All same. And stop. And the world shrank around him, the lens lifted.

"Source," the Weirdy said.

"Here?"

It was just another patch of dust, nothing to distinguish it. Nothing around them for miles. Something lying in the dirt, a metal cylinder half a meter across. He looked at it. Ours? he thought. Theirs?

"Never mind," the Weirdy said. "You fix, now."

"Me?"

The Weirdy released the frozen Bombie sphere. "Wait," Chamberlain said, "What are you—"

The Weirdy threw the Bombie high in the air. The bubble rose, rose, rose and then—

"Shit!" Chamberlain yelled. He looked up—

The transparent bubble disappeared. The Bombie explosion, as if there had been no interruption, expanded outwards from its nucleus.

"Shit!" Chamberlain said again, and—

Four: Elephant and Fly

He was Shambalin, and then he was Chamberlain, and he was sent to Fly with all the others. He said goodbye to his parents. His mother cried. His father shook his hand, awkwardly. He wore his cadet uniform. There were many others like him. The Deputy Chairman of the Party gave a speech.

(—What happened?

No answer in words, but the scene disappeared, and was replaced—)

He was on the ship coming to land. They were playing cards. Shen and Mastorakis were still alive. Shen said, "I wonder what's happening back home?" Mastorakis said, "Same old." A screen came alive then, a news-feed from home, the Chairman speaking. "Peace must be achieved at all costs."

"Hear, hear," someone said.

"Our boys on Fly are sacrificing themselves daily to protect our rights, our livelihoods, our very *humanity* against the monsters."

"I don't want to be a sacrifice," Chamberlain said.

(—Sacrifice, a voice said. Yes. Sacrifice.

—No!

—Doesn't matter.

—It does to me!

Fade again, and—)

He was on Fly, walking through the jungle with his platoon, and the Weirdies where coming out of nowhere, and he fired at them, but always there were more Weirdies, more bloody trees, more exploding insects. Only when you found Gorp did you get a real fight; the Gorp were the worst, blood-thirsty and cunning and huge—

He was at the base, relaxing after the fight. They'd lost three people that day, including Shen.

He was in the jungle when the Gorp attacked. He remembered dying, now.

(—what?

—Play-play. You, me, Gorp, play. Now tired—)

He was at the base when Colonel Piet ordered him and Mastorakis on a scouting mission.

He was in the jungle when Mastorakis was killed by a living tree and a Weirdy, coming out of nowhere, stole over Chamberlain and the wind ripped him apart—

He was at the base when they brought Colonel Piet's body back from the jungle and he thought, so they got you at last, you bastard.

He was at the base when Mastorakis came in carrying Shen's body, Colonel Piet watching dispassionately from the side.

He was at the base when the Gorp attacked, screams, Shen dying beside him, Mastorakis, Piet and he was—

He was in the jungle—

(—Please. Stop!—)

He was in the base—

Mastorakis—

He was in the base and the voice of the Chairman of the Party on the news-feed said, "We have peace."

He was in the jungle and a Bombie was resting on his arm and he tried not to move and counted the planets based on distance from the sun. Monkey, Jaguar, Wolf, Fly, Elephant, Dog, Firefly. Monkey, Jaguar, Wolf—

(—Fly!

—Fly. Fly and... Elephant.)

Fly. Fly. Fly. Fly. It was there. It had always been there.

And so had he.

(—How long? he said.

—Don't know. Don't count time. Long time?

—How long?

—Many solar circles. Many many. Full up.

—And all this time—

—Play-play. Tired now.

But—)

He was on a plane and above his head a Bombie exploded, shards raining down, and he knew there was no escape. "Have I been here before?" he said.

"No. First time. Last time. Fly now."

The Bombie shards hit him, and he died.

Five: Shambalin

He was lying on the grass under the stars with Rashmi and they both had their shirts off and her skin was soft and dark and his heart was beating loudly in his chest.

Rashmi said, "One day I'm going to go to the stars."

"Can I come with you?" he said, and his fingers traced a line under her arm and she giggled. "If you like. Where shall we go?"

"We could go anywhere. See what it's really like out there, on Firefly and Monkey, Jaguar and Wolf and Dog, maybe even further, back where people come from, I forget what it's called."

"Mars," Rashmi said. He shrugged. "Whatever."

"We can go to Fly," she said, and Shambalin said, "They say the forests of the living trees are beautiful."

"I want to see a Weirdy!"

"They're strange. Hard to talk to."

"How do *you* know?" she said, and punched him on the arm and he rolled over her and smiled into her face. "I saw this programme."

"I never want to see a Gorp though!"

"No," he said. "No Gorp."

He rolled on his back. Rashmi put her arms around him and nestled her head in the crook of his neck. He stared up at the stars, and said, softly, "Sometimes, when true night falls, and the living trees are quiet, if you stand still, you can hear the music of the Skaar-et-lam."

"What does it sound like?"

He thought about it, looking up at the stars. "Like dying," he said. "And then being reborn."

"Where did you hear that?" she said, and he said, "I don't know. It just came to me."

He turned his head and looked into her face and she smiled. He kissed her.

The Puma

Theodora Goss

M r. Prendick, there's a lady here to see you."

I must have jumped, because I remember my knee banging into the desk. In the years since I had moved to this obscure corner of England, where even the trains did not come and I could walk over the hills for hours without seeing a human face, I had received only one visitor, the local vicar. There must have been something in my speech, perhaps even in my face, that agitated him, because he would not stay for dinner, and he left without urging me to attend services in the small stone church where he preached, in the valley below. I was sorry to see him leave. He had seemed like a reasonable man, although his inquisitive brown eyes and pinched face, a probable indication of early poverty, reminded me of a lemur. In all that time, I had never been threatened with a visit by anything that could remotely be described as a lady.

"A what?" I wondered what Mrs. Pertwee meant by a lady, exactly. Perhaps one of the female parishioners who lived in the village that surrounded the stone church, with its post office, pub, and collection of six or seven houses, coming to solicit for some missionary society to help our savage brethren.

"A lady, Mr. Prendick. She—" Mrs. Pertwee hesitated. "She calls herself Mrs. Prendick."

I tripped over the chair. The next day, Mrs. Pertwee had to wash the spot where my fountain pen had sputtered on the carpet with strong soap.

She was waiting for me in the parlor, a sanctuary that Mrs. Pertwee only entered to do whatever housekeepers customarily do to horsehair sofas and china ornaments. I had not used the room since renting the cottage, and had seen no need to alter it.

She was heavily veiled.

"Edward," she said. "How nice to see you again."

We are divided beings. One half of me had known that it could not logically be she. The other half had known that no one else in the wide world could claim to be my wife. That other half had been right. I could not mistake her voice, almost too deep for a woman, with a resonance to it, as though she were speaking from the depth of her throat. Like a viol.

"You look better than when I last saw you, on the island."

"Catherine."

"So I have a name now. Did you forget it when you wrote this?" She held up a copy of my book. The book I should never have written, that my alienist had urged me to write. "Did you forget that we all had names? What a terrible liar you are, Edward."

"Let me see your face," I said. The veil was disconcerting. I needed to know, for certain, that she really was speaking to me, that this was not some sort of hallucination.

She laughed, like an ordinary woman, and lifted her veil.

When I had last seen her, her face had been seamed with scars, the remnants of Moreau's work. Now, her face was perfectly smooth. The high cheekbones were still there, the nose aquiline, the best I think that Moreau ever created. The eyes yellow and brown together, like Baltic amber. The tops of her ears were hidden by her hair. Were they still pointed? She noticed me looking, laughed again, and pulled her hair back. They looked completely human. I am a scientist, and no judge of female beauty. But she was the most beautiful woman I have ever seen.

"How did you..."

"Walk with me, Edward." She indicated the French doors, which opened onto the garden. Her gestures were unnaturally graceful. "Let's reminisce, like old friends. Eventually, I'll have a favor to ask of you. But first, I'll tell you what I've been doing with myself for the last few years. Since, that is, you left me to die on the island."

"I didn't leave you to die."

"Didn't you?"

I followed her into the garden. It was an ordinary autumn day, the sky grey above us, with clouds blowing across it, and a herd of sheep like clouds in the valley below. I could see a dog driving them, first from one side of the herd and then the other. Somewhere, there was a man, and it was at his whistle that the dog ran to and fro. What dogs had done, and men had done, and sheep had done, for a hundred years. A quintessentially English scene.

"To what fate, exactly, did you intend to leave me?"

Her voice took me back to another scene, an entirely different scene. The southern sunlight on Moreau, lying in the mud, flies crawling over his shirt where the linen was stained red.

"The Puma," said Montgomery. "We have to find her."

"How did she do this?" I felt sick, mostly I think with shock. I had never, somehow, imagined that Moreau could die. Certainly not like this.

He pointed to Moreau's head. "She struck him. Look, the back of his skull is smashed in. Probably with her own fetters. She must have torn them out of the wall. Damn."

As a word, it seemed completely inadequate.

We followed her trail easily enough. She was heading, not toward the village of the Beast Men, but toward the sea. I wondered for a moment if she might try to drown herself, as I had tried to drown myself, my first few days on the island. But Beast Men did not do such things. They killed others, not themselves. It took a man to do that.

"There she is." Montgomery gestured with his gun.

She stood, up to her hips in the water. She looked at us, then shook herself, flinging spray from her wet hair. She walked toward us. So might Aphrodite have walked when she rose from the sea. But this was an Aphrodite with skin like gold rather than ivory, and the eyes of a beast. Everywhere, her body was covered with fresh scars.

"My God," said Montgomery. "So that's what he's been hiding from me."

"Hiding?"

"For a month, he wouldn't let me into the laboratory. He said the process was working at last. And look at her. She's his masterpiece. Poor bastard."

"I killed the one with the whip," she said. Her voice reverberated, like waves in a cavern beneath the sea. "Will you kill me for what I have done?"

"We will not kill you," said Montgomery. "It was not right to kill him, but we will not punish you for it."

"Have you gone mad?" I whispered to Montgomery. I aimed, but Montgomery caught hold of my arm.

"Can't you see what he did to her?" he whispered. "The man was a brute."

"It was right to kill him, and it gave me pleasure," she said. She walked out of the sea, like a statue of burnished gold.

With that unprepossessing statement began our time with the Puma Woman.

Her scars faded, but they remained visible all over her face and body. She looked like a south sea islander, marked with cicatrices.

Montgomery took her to live with us, in the enclosure. He gave her his bedroom and slept in mine. We cleaned out the laboratory, releasing whatever still had its own form, killing the results of Moreau's experiments. We had food, guns, and M'Ling, Montgomery's favorite Beast Man, to guard us at night. We planned to wait until the next supply ship came, and then—what? I assumed that we would leave the island, leave Moreau's abominations to their own fate. But what about her? Montgomery seemed to have become particularly attached to her. She walked around the enclosure in one of his shirts, tucked into a pair of his trousers tied at the waist with rope. She looked like a gypsy boy.

She walked so quietly that I never knew, until she spoke, that she was beside me. When I launched one of the boats to go fishing, she would suddenly appear, help me push off, and leap into the boat. Montgomery would stare at us from the shore, with one hand on his gun belt. I didn't want her with me, but what was I supposed to do, push her into the water? She would sit, silent, and stare at me with her golden brown eyes—a woman, and not a woman. No woman could have sat so still.

It was Montgomery who named her Catherine. "Catherine, get it?" he said. "Cat-in-here. There's a cat in here!" He had been drinking. He watched her cross the enclosure, so lightly, so silently, that she seemed to walk on her toes. I did not like the way he looked at her. Perhaps he had initially been disgusted by the Beast Men, as I had been when I landed on the island, but he had long ago grown accustomed to them. They seemed to him human, and natural. I suspect that if you had set him down in the middle of London, he would have exclaimed at the deformity of the men and women who passed. She was Moreau's finest creation. Montgomery had always had his favorites among the Beast Men: M'Ling, Septimus, Adolphus. What did he think of her?

It was he who taught her to shoot, to read the books in Moreau's collection. As she learned, he answered all of her questions, first about the island, then about the world from which we had been isolated, and finally about Moreau's research. If we had been rescued then, I think he would have taken her with him. I imagined her scarred face, her long brown limbs, in an English drawing room. But it seemed to me, sometimes, that she had a preference for my company. And sometimes at night I would imagine her as I had first seen her, rising from the sea like Aphrodite, fresh from her kill.

Once, sitting in the boat, she said to me, "Prendick, how large is your country?"

"Much larger than this island, but smaller than some countries."

"Like India?"

"Yes, like India. Damn Montgomery. What has he been telling you?"

"That your English queen is the Empress of India. How could a country as small as yours conquer a country as large as India?"

"We had guns."

"Ah, yes, guns." She looked at her own complacently. "So, like on this island, it was a matter of guns and whips."

"No!" I tossed a fish with bright orange scales into the basket. "It was a matter of civilization."

"I see," she said. "You taught them to walk upright and wear clothes and worship the English queen. I would like to see this English queen of yours. She must have a long whip."

What were the Beast Men doing all this time? With the control that Moreau had exercised over them gone, they reverted to their natural behaviors. The predators formed a pack, with Nero, the Hyena-Swine, at its head. They moved to the other side of the island. The others stayed in the village, with Gladstone, the Sayer of the Law, to organize what vestiges of government they retained and Adolphus, the Dog

Man, to organize their defense. Septimus, the jabbering Ape Man who had been the first Beast Man I had met in my initial flight from Moreau, attempted to create a new religion for them, with various Big Thinks and Little Thinks, but the others would have none of it. Montgomery thought that we should give them guns, but I refused. His sympathy for them angered me. Let them all perish, I thought, and let the earth be cleansed of Moreau's work.

So we went on for several months. It was, I later realized, a period of calm between the killing of Moreau and what came after.

She walked through the garden, stopping once to touch a lily with her gloved hands. "Your native English flowers," she said, "have many admirers. But have you seen anything more beautiful than this? The original bulb was brought generations ago from the slopes of the Himalayas. It flourishes in your English soil."

"Where did you learn botany?" I asked her.

She did not answer, but walked ahead of me, over the fields, up the hill, so quickly that I had difficulty keeping up with her. At the top of the hill, we looked down on the valley, with its English village sleeping under the grey sky.

"Would you like to hear what happened after you abandoned me on the island?"

I nodded. I looked at her again, sidelong. What had she done, to become what she was? She had a way of moving her hands when she spoke that was charming, almost Italian, although no woman could have had her fluidity of movement. Her grace was inhuman.

"I lived in the cave we had shared. I kept track of the time, as you had taught me. I had a gun, but no bullets, and anyway there were only a few of his creatures left on the island. You think that I cannot say his name, but I can—Moreau, the Beast Master. It was burned into my brain, remember? Doubtless it will be the last word I say before I die. But that will not be for a long while yet.

"You wrote that the Beast Men reverted to their animal state. What a liar you are, my husband! You know that would have been an anatomical impossibility. But you do not want your English public to know that after Montgomery's death, after the supplies were gone, you feasted on men. Oh, they had the snouts of pigs, or they jabbered like apes, but they cried out as men before you shot them. Do you remember when you shot and ate Adolphus, your Dog Man, whom you had hunted with, and who had curled up at your feet during the night?

I looked down at the valley. She was bringing them all back, the memories. My hands were shaking. I lifted them to my mouth, as though they could help with the wave of nausea that threatened to engulf me.

"They were animals."

"So too, if your friend Professor Huxley is right, are you an animal. As am I. You are startled. Why? Because I mentioned Huxley? I have done more things than you can imagine, since I left the island. I too have taken a class with Professor Huxley, whom you described so often. Your descriptions of his examinations served me well. He thought, of course, that the questions I asked him after his lectures were theoretical. He was delighted, he told me, to find such a scientific mind in a young lady. He did not know that I had been created by a biologist. I cut my teeth, as you might say, on the biological sciences. Or had my teeth cut on them."

During our time together on the island, after the death of Montgomery, I taught her about the origin and history of life on earth. We looked at geological formations, examined and cataloged what we found in the tidal pools, or the birds that roosted on the island. There were no species native to the island higher than a sea-turtle that laid its eggs there, but we studied the anatomy of the Beast Men we shot, discussing their peculiarities. I explained to her what Moreau had joined together, how pig had been joined to dog, or wolf had been joined to bear. I even, eloquently as I thought then, showed her what Moreau must have intended, where the beast became the man.

"You feasted on them too."

"They were my natural prey. If I had still been the animal Montgomery bought in a market in Argentina, I would have hunted them without thought, without scruple. But I'm getting ahead of myself. For months, I was alone. I reverted, not in appearance but in behavior. I hunted at night, ripped open my prey, ate it raw. After I thought all of Moreau's creations were gone, I lived on what I could find in the tidal pools—fish when I could catch them, clams that I smashed open on the stones. I dug for turtle eggs. I was half starved when the *Scorpion* came. There was nothing left on the island but some rabbits and a Pig Man that had somehow managed to escape me, and rats that I could not catch in my weakened state. They would have devoured me eventually.

"It was searching for the remains of the *Ipecacuanha*. The captain took particular care of me. He thought I was an Englishwoman who had been captured by pirates, and brutally treated. I have to thank you, Edward, for teaching me to speak so correctly! I did not realize, when I imitated your accent, that I was learning to sound like a lady. Montgomery's cruder accent would not have suited me so well. I told the captain that I had lost my memory. He took me to Tasmania, where the Governor treated me kindly, and a collection was taken up for me. Imagine all those Englishmen and women, donating money so that I could return home, to England! It was a great deal of money, enough for my voyage to England and a surgeon, a very good surgeon, to complete what Moreau had left undone.

"After the surgery, I had no more money, and money is necessary in this civilized world of yours. But I found that men will pay money for the company of a beautiful woman. And I am beautiful, am I not, Edward? I should be grateful to the Beast Master. I was his masterpiece."

She smiled, and I did not like it. Her canines were still longer than they should have been. Sometimes, when we lay together, she had bitten me. I wanted to believe she had done so by accident, but had she?

"And so I began to study. In this England of yours, a woman cannot attend universities, but she can attend scientific lectures. She can read at the British Museum. And if she is beautiful, she can ask as many questions as she wishes, and important men are flattered by her interest. I would venture, Edward, that I am now more knowledgeable about biology than you are. I intend to put that knowledge to use. But I need your help. I have come here," her hand swept to indicate the hills around us, the birds that were flying above, the clouds floating against the grey sky, "with the most vulgar of motives. I require money. You see, I have a particular project in mind. The surgeon who repaired me, who erased the scars that Moreau had left, is a Russian émigré, a Jew driven out of his country by religious persecution. How fond your species is of persecutions! For two years I have worked with him, learning everything he could teach me. I am now, he has been generous enough to say, even more skilled than he is. Your women who are agitating for the right to vote believe that they should have professions other than marriage. I too wish to have a profession. I propose to follow in my father's footsteps and become a vivisector."

I stared at her. Gazing over the hills, with the wind whipping her skirts back and tossing her veil, she looked like the figurehead on the prow of a ship. But where was she headed? Moreau's work had brought us once to disaster. Was she now truly planning to continue what he had begun?

After his death, the more peaceable Beast Men had developed the habit of coming to the enclosure to trade what they grew in their gardens for our flour and salt. Twice a week they came, crowding into the enclosure, like an English market crossed with a menagerie, or a Renaissance painting of some level of Dante's Inferno.

Montgomery should have noticed that Nero and the Wolf-Bear Tiberius had entered the enclosure. M'Ling should have been guarding the gate, but his attention was elsewhere. The Beast Men had begun adopting our vices, for which Montgomery was in no small measure to blame. He had taught them the use of tobacco, which he traded for food, and to pass the time he had whittled a pair of dice, with which they gambled for onions, turtle eggs, whatever the Beast Men had brought to trade. That morning, M'Ling was gambling with the Beast Men.

"Why does she carry a whip?" I heard the shout and went to the window. I usually avoided these market days. I still found it disconcerting to be in the company of so many of Moreau's creations.

Montgomery stood by the door of the storeroom, which held our barrels of tobacco, flour, biscuits, salted meat. Next to him stood Catherine, dressed as he was, with a gun in her holster and a whip tucked into her belt. All around stood the Beast Men with the goods that they had brought, and in the back, close to the gate, stood the Hyena-Swine.

"She is one of us, one of the made. Why does she carry a gun? Why does she carry a whip? Let her join her own people."

The Beast Men stood, staring, and I could see the inquisitive look in their eyes.

"Why does she not come to us?" said Catullus, the Satyr. "We have few females. Why does she not come to live in our huts, and work in our gardens, like the other females?"

"Yes," said the Ape Man. "Let her live with us, with us, with us!

She can be my mate."

Then others spoke and said that she could be their mate as well.

I could see Montgómery looking puzzled. He had been up late drinking, the night before, and was still nursing a hangover. He could not understand this rebellion among the usually peaceable Beast Men. From where he stood, he could not see the Hyena-Swine.

I could see Catherine's hand on her gun.

The Beast Men began arguing among themselves, each claiming her. Moreau had never made enough Beast Women, and they were constantly trying to lure the ones they had away from each other. One pushed another. Soon there would be a fight.

I stepped through the doorway, into the enclosure.

"The Master, who has gone to live among the stars, and watches you from above, has intended her for another purpose. She will not be any of your mates. She will be without a mate, but will bear a child that will perpetuate your race. That is the purpose for which he has created her. She will be the mother of a new race of men. Bow to her, who is dedicated to such a high purpose!"

They stared at me.

"Bow!" I said, raising my gun. I could see the Hyena-Swine slinking through the gate.

One by one, reluctantly, they inclined their heads.

"Hail to the holy mother," said the Ape Man. He had always been sillier than the rest.

"Well then," I said. "You may continue to trade. There will be no punishment today, despite your disobedience."

That night, Montgomery lit the bonfire. He lit it every night. If there was a ship sailing within sight of the island, we did not want it to miss us. Sometimes the Beast Men came and danced by the light of the bonfire. "A regular corroboree," Montgomery called it.

"Catherine," he called, after the fire was lit. I could see him standing in the enclosure, with the full moon behind him, larger than it ever is in England. "Come to the dance. There's a regular crowd of them tonight."

"Not tonight," she answered. "Tonight I wish to speak with Edward."

"Damn Edward. Come on, Catherine." I realized that he had already started drinking, or perhaps had never stopped.

I did not hear her answer, but he shouted, "All right then, damn you!" And then I heard the gate crash shut.

"He's gone," she said a moment later, standing in my doorway.

"What did you want to speak to me about?"

She came closer. She had a smell about her, not unpleasant but particularly, I thought, feline.

"Do you think he had a purpose for me?"

"Who?"

"Moreau. You can see that I'm made—differently from the others. My hands—he must have taken particular care."

He hands were on my shoulders. I could feel her claws through my shirt.

"Am I not well made, Edward?"

I looked down into her eyes, dark in the darkness. I don't know what possessed me. "You are—divinely made."

Where my shirt was open, she licked my chest, then my neck. She was almost as tall as I was. I could not help remembering Moreau's neck, torn open.

He had done his work well. Standing on an English hillside, watching her with her veil blown back by the wind, I shuddered at the memory of her brown thighs, with a down on them softer than the hair of any woman.

She smiled at me, and despite my sweater and mackintosh, I felt cold.

We were lying together in a tangle of sheets when we heard the shot.

"Get your gun," she said.

We ran out, me in my trousers, she in Montgomery's shirt. As we passed the storeroom, she disappeared suddenly, then reappeared with an ammunition belt over her shoulder.

On the beach, around the bonfire, Beast Men were dancing. There was a throb in the air, and after a moment I realized that it was a drum. Someone—it looked like the Sayer of the Law— was keeping time while the Beast Men turned and leaped and shook their hands in the air, and shouted each in his own way—some like the grunting of a pig, some like the barking of a dog, one caterwauling. I will never forget that sight, watching from the shadowed dunes while the Beast Men capered together and the Puma Woman stood, with her gun in her hand, the ammunition belt slung over her shoulder, at my side.

"The fire is larger tonight," she said. "What are they burning?"

I looked again, more carefully. "The boats!" They had not been large enough to carry us away from the island, but they had at least been tangible signs that escape was possible.

Without thinking, I ran among them. "Damn you to hell! Damn you all to hell! What beast among you—"

One of the Beast Men turned toward me. I started back with a cry. He was wearing a mask that made him look like a gorilla. But the eyes behind it were Montgomery's. The other Beast Men stopped, stumbling into one another in confusion.

"What the hell—"

"I'm the—the Gorilla Man. See?" He began to caper about, with the stooping gate, the hanging arms, of a gorilla.

The other Beast Men laughed. I could see the firelight on their teeth.

"Drunk! You're all drunk! It's disgusting—"

"Come on, old stick-in-the-mud Prendick. Old hypocrite Prendick. Having your fun with the Cat. I deserve some fun too, don't you think?"

"Come on, Montgomery," I said. I tried to grab him, but he swung at me, punching me in the mouth. He could have hit harder had he not lost his balance, but I tasted blood. And then I saw a gleaming pair of eyes, and then another, staring at me. The Wolf-Bear was there, as was the Hyena-Swine, and with the instinctive reaction of a predator, the Hyena-Swine leaped at me.

I heard a crack. The Hyena-Swine fell at my feet. Then another crack, and another, and more Beast Men fell. They began screaming, running toward the darkness of the jungle. I thought I would be deafened by the cacophony or crushed as they ran. But the last of them vanished into the jungle, and suddenly there was silence. I was still standing, alone. At my feet lay the body of the Hyena-Swine. Beyond him lay M'Ling, a Wolf Woman, one of the Pig Men, and the Gorilla Man, Montgomery.

"You killed him," I said.

"He became one of them," she said, out of the darkness.

I did not answer. Silently, I turned, intending to walk back to the enclosure. It was a mass of flames. I heard a scream that I though might come from one of the Beast Men, until I realized that I was the one screaming. For the second time that night, I began to run.

We saved nothing. There was nothing left to save. We had lost our supplies, and worse, we had lost the rest of our bullets. After the ones that Catherine had taken ran out, our guns would be useless.

"One of us must have overturned the lamp," she said. She was, as always, perfectly calm. The only evidence I had seen of her anger had been Moreau's throat, or what was left of it.

What could I say to her? If I had overturned the lamp, it had been by accident. But she, so agile—could she have done it deliberately? I hated her then, more than I had hated Moreau. If I thought I could have, I would have killed her. But I did not want to die Moreau's death, to be buried, or worse, on that island of beasts that looked like men.

When I remember it now, I realize that I must have overturned the lamp. Montgomery had burned the boats to revenge himself upon me, but she had no use for revenge. Her motives were always simple, logical. What she wanted, she obtained directly, not with human indirection. Although she looked and laughed at me like an English lady, she still thought with the mind of a beast.

And so began the longer part of our stay on the island. Montgomery's body we burned, but the other bodies... She was a predator, and slowly, unwillingly, I fell in with her ways. We hunted together, and with practice my vision became keener, although never, of course, equal to hers. I insisted on cooking our food, although she laughed at me. I would not watch her when she ate it fresh from the kill. We drank from the stream, sucking the water up. Our clothes grew ragged and hung on our brown hides. I lay with her in the cave we called our home, hating her, hating what I had become, but unable to leave her. Even now, I remember her touch, the rasp of her tongue on my skin, the gold of her eyes as she stared down at me and said, "What are you thinking, Ape Man?"

"Don't call me that!"

She would laugh and push her nose against me like a cat that wants to be stroked, and make a sound in her throat that was neither a purr nor a growl.

One day, I was walking along the beach, scavenging what I could, crabs, clams, seaweed. We were using our bullets judiciously, but they were beginning to run out. Soon we would be reduced to hunting like beasts. I would become like her. I saw something floating toward me. A sail! But the boat reeled, like a drunken sailor. It was the boat I have described in my book, with the captain and the first mate of the *Ipecacuanha* sitting aboard, dead. This might be my only chance to escape the island. If I died on the ocean, at least I died as a man.

I stepped into the boat. I was certain, then, that I would never see her again.

"Perhaps," she said, "you would like to know in what way you can help me."

A light rain had begun. Her veil caught drops of moisture, like a spider's web.

I turned away. I did not want to know, and yet I could not stop listening. As a scientist, and a man, I wanted to know what she intended.

"I would have liked to bear children myself. But I cannot. You and I proved that, did we not, Edward? Would you have liked that, to have had children with me? What would they have been like, I wonder? Moreau took away my ability to breed with my kind, and could not give me the ability to breed with yours. Even Dr. Radzinsky was not able to give me that, although he tried. Somewhere, there is an incompatibility that goes beyond the anatomical. Perhaps someday your scientists will find it, and then we will be able to create a true race of Beast Men. But I am impatient. I want my children to flourish and populate the earth. Surely a natural desire, according to Mr. Darwin.

"Here, in England, I will create a clinic, to revive and perfect Moreau's research. But my clinic will be no House of Pain. We will incorporate all the technological advances of the last decade—and the educational advances, since my clinic will also be a school. Think, Edward! My children will be educated along the latest scientific lines. Educated to be the inheritors of a new age."

"What makes you think that I would finance such a—such a mad scheme? Is it not enough that Moreau did it once? Why would you wish to create such abominations yourself?"

"Not abominations. Look at me, Edward. Am I an abomination?"

I did not know how to answer.

"You will finance my mad scheme, as you call it, for three reasons. First, because you are a gentleman, and a gentleman cares about his reputation. If you do not provide me with the financing I require, I will inform your English press. There are two laws, Edward, that all civilized men obey: not to lie with their mothers or sisters or daughters, and not to eat the flesh of other men. You have broken the second of those laws."

"Why should I care what the public thinks of me?"

"Because there will be inquiries. And because nothing will be proven, people will think the worst. You will become notorious. Wherever you go, people will follow you, to interview you, to take photographs. Imagine the newspapers! 'What Mr. Prendick the cannibal had for breakfast. How it compares with human flesh.' But second, you are a scientist. What I am proposing is an experiment. I will bring pumas from the Americas, young ones, less than two years old. Fine, healthy specimens. I will operate on them in stages, changing them gradually. Allowing them, at each stage, to become accustomed to their new forms. Educating them. There will be no pain. There will be no deformity. My children will be as beautiful as I am."

I grasped at straws. "Your plan is impossible. You will never be able to build a clinic like that in England. Where would you hide? There is no part of the countryside that is uninhabited, no place obscure enough that your work won't be observed. You will be found out."

She laughed. "I do not propose to put my clinic in the countryside. No, my clinic will be in the heart of England, in London itself."

"But surely the police—"

"There are parts of London where the police never go. Parts where the inhabitants speak a babble of language, and everything you want to purchase is to be had, from a girl fresh from the English countryside to a pipe of opium that will give you distinctly un-English dreams. I have become familiar with them over the last few years. Do not worry about the practicalities. Those I have thought of already."

"And third—I did tell you there are three reasons—you are a follower of Mr. Darwin. Consider, Edward." She turned again to look at the valley below. "The operation of natural selection is necessary for evolution. Without selective pressure, a species stagnates, perhaps even degenerates, reverting to atavistic forms. How long has it been since selective pressure operated on the human species? You have killed all your predators. How many men are killed by wolves or bears, in Europe? You care for your poor, your sick, your idiots, your mad, who give birth to more of their kind, filling your cities Your intelligent classes, who spend so much of their energy in their work, do not breed. This is not new to you, I know. You have read it in Nordau, Lombroso. Your very strength and compassion as a species will be your undoing. You will grow weaker by the year, the decade, the century. Eventually, like the dodo, you will become extinct. That is the fate of mankind. Unless... "

"Unless what?"

"You once again introduce a predator. That is what I'm offering you, Edward. Selective predation. A species that I create, to feed off the weakest among you, to make humanity strong."

She was mad, I thought. And I think so still. But there is a kind of reason in madness. Moreau had it, and as she claimed, she was Moreau's daughter. He too had the directness, the simplicity, of a beast.

I have not seen her since that day on the hillside. The money I send her is deposited into a bank account, and where it goes from there, I do not know. Do I believe that the creatures she creates will strengthen rather than weaken mankind? I do not know, but she has never lied to me. It takes a man to do that.

There was a fourth reason that she did not mention. Perhaps it was kindness on her part not to mention it. But I do not think that, in all her interactions with men, she has learned kindness. Surely she must have known. Sometimes at night I still think of her, her fingers twining in my hair, her legs tangled in mine, her lips close, so close, to my throat. I do not think I loved her. But it was a madness that resembled love, and perhaps I still am mad, because I have not refused her. She must have known, because as she stood in the doorway, ready to depart, as respectable as any English lady, she stepped close to me and licked my neck. I felt the rasp of her tongue.

"Goodbye, Edward," she said. "When I am ready, not before, I will invite you to my clinic, and you can see the first of our children. Yours and mine."

Yesterday, in the post, I received her invitation. Will I go? I have not decided. But I am a scientist, cursed with curiosity. I would like to see what she creates and whether she is, indeed, a worthy successor to Moreau.

Editor's Note:

I hesitate to publish this manuscript, left to me by my late uncle, Edward Prendick, because credulous members of the public may connect it with the series of brutal murders that is currently taxing the ingenuity of Scotland Yard. However, Professor Huxley, my uncle's former teacher, has asked me to publish it as an addendum to my uncle's manuscript of his time on the island. I believe the conversation it records was a hallucination. It must be remembered that my uncle's health was severely affected by the shipwreck that left him the sole inhabitant of an island in the South Seas, and that at the time of his death, he was attended by an alienist. I am satisfied that the cause of his death was natural. Heart failure can strike a comparatively young man, and even if we give no credence to the fantastical occurrences that he claimed to have witnessed, my uncle must have suffered a great deal. It is true that upon the execution of his will, his fortune was found to be significantly diminished. However, there are a number of possible explanations for the state of his affairs, and we should not draw conclusions before the investigation into his death is complete. I hope the public will do justice to the memory of my uncle, who, although disturbed in mind, was a man of intellectual promise before the shipwreck that embittered him toward mankind. And I hope the public will dismiss the ridiculous fancies of Fleet Street, and assist our police in catching the perpetrator of the Limehouse Murders.

—*Charles Prendick*

THE MIND OF A PIG

EKATERINA SEDIA

A first shock of Joel's life came when he saw a mirror for the first time. That elaborate affair of glass and wood was delivered to decorate Cassie's room, and Joel approached it to investigate. He had not given much thought to his appearance, but assumed without ever considering that he looked like the people around him. He was conscious of some slight differences between himself and others, such as he walked on four legs, and did not speak. Still, he did not expect his reflection to be quite so grotesque.

He twitched his snout, discomfited, and the creature in the mirror did the same. A real snout with a flat fleshy circle surrounding his nostrils. Joel surveyed slack ears, nothing at all like Cassie's, the small eyes hiding in the folds of fat, a long corpulent body supported by four stubby hoofed legs, and a comma of a tail. Joel had seen enough picture books to recognize the image. A pig.

He turned his back to the mirror and trotted away, his cloven hooves clacking on the hardwood floors of his home. He moved his legs carefully, afraid that an abrupt movement would shatter his heart, already aching as if from a blow.

Joel pushed a door open with his forehead and lay in the straw bed of his pen. The pen took up most of the open porch of a great, old house, and Joel had a view of flowerbeds, bursting forth with blue of irises and red and black of tulips, and a vast green lawn. He needed to think.

His discovery, as unsettling as it was, explained much. He now knew why Cassie and her father talked about him as if he were not there, and why newspapers were often snatched from under his nose. Most importantly, he realized why Cassie never acknowledged small signs of affection he offered. At least, it wasn't about his personality. It was about him being a pig.

His ears pricked up, and he raised his snout to inhale the smell of gas and hot metal. Cassie's Dad came home. Normally, Joel was not very interested in the old man—he seemed more of an aged barnacle appended to Cassie's loveliness than a being in his own right. This time, Joel watched him.

Cassie's Dad heaved his old body up the steps with the help of his cane, and spoke addressing a young man with a tape recorder in hand, who followed close behind. "I hope the tour of the farm assuaged some of your and your readers' concerns. As you could see, it's a perfectly scientific and humane operation."

"Yes." The young man stopped and cocked his head. "But did you have any issues with patients being squeamish about their transplants? About these organs being grown in pigs?"

The old man rasped a laugh. "You have to understand that people who need a transplant do not have the luxury of being squeamish. And think of the alternatives—would you rather receive a liver extracted from a human corpse?"

The young man made a small non-committal sound and looked away.

"You're too young to remember it, but back in the day..." Cassie's Dad looked over the flowerbeds, his fingers tapping on the railing of the porch. "There was a lot of controversy over human cloning—human rights activists feared that people will be cloned only to harvest their organs. That never happened, of course—it is much easier to grow human organs in pigs, and there's a whole lot fewer ethical questions. Animal Righters, of course, made a fuss, but they always do. Most of them don't even know what they believe in."

"Why pigs?"

"They are similar to us." The old man smiled, and snapped his fingers at Joel. "Joel, come here, boy."

Joel trotted up, obedient, hoping that his dark unease did not reflect on his face.

"Joel, here," the old man said, "is a miracle pig. He has a human brain—he's the only one of his kind. A real innovation. Hope your paper will enjoy this little factoid."

The young man rubbed his face. "A brain? Forgive me, Dr. Kernicke, but a brain transplant reeks of a bad joke. Why would you need a brain?"

Cassie's Dad rolled his eyes, and petted Joel's sagging head. "Not a whole one. But you know that people suffer injuries, or—God forbid!—tumors. Wouldn't it be nice to have a replacement frontal lobe in case you lost one?"

The young man nodded. "I suppose. But what about personality?"

Cassie's Dad shook his head, impatient. "What personality? He's a pig. He's just keeping this brain warm, in a manner of speaking. It's a blank slate. A person who receives Joel's frontal lobe will eventually develop connections between his brain and the transplant, and gradually claim it as his own, regaining function as the time goes by. Brain tissue is just tissue until a human mind shapes it into something grander."

The young man turned off his tape recorder. "Doctor," he said in a hushed voice, and gave Joel a sideways look. "How do you know that this pig is not sentient?"

"Because pigs did not evolve with this brain!" Cassie's Dad struck the boards of the porch with his cane for emphasis. "It's like sewing albatross' wings on a pigeon—it won't make him a better flyer, and chances are that he won't fly at all. Every animal is made by evolution, and all parts should fit together to function. Joel's DNA says that he's a pig, and thus he will remain a pig forever, whether we furnish him with a different brain or not. He has no other human equipment, such as neurotransmitters and sensory system, and thus he cannot make use of the brain. Interview is over."

The young man ran down the steps, traipsed across the lawn, and disappeared behind the bend of the driveway. A part of Joel wanted to run after the man, to seek his help, while the rest of his soul reeled, as if an abyss had opened in front of his hooves. Betrayed by the very people who took care of him and pretended to love him—surely, Joseph did not feel worse after being sold to Egypt! If Joel could speak, he would've called anathema upon the old man's aging, balding head. If he could cry, bloody tears would have stained his face. Joel did the only thing he could do. He ran.

The gravel of the driveway exploded from under his hooves in small, angry fountains, and the greenery of the hedge melted into a green smudge. He careened around the turn, just in time to see the young man's car exhale a pungent cloud of exhaust and disappear behind the gate.

Joel's heart pumped harder than ever as he kept running. The metal bars of the gate came into motion, sliding, silent, smell of grease and black metal radiating from them. Through the opening, Joel could see a grey snake of the road, he could hear honking of the cars, he could smell an unfamiliar world that he had previously seen through the gate but never entered.

Until now. Joel's face thrust into the street, into the warm shimmering air filled with asphalt fumes, just as the gate slid into his flank. He could feel the pain of bruised flesh, followed with a jolt the likes of which he had never felt. Every muscle twitched with the searing shock that radiated from the metal grid of the gate. Then, it ceased. Joel planted his front hooves in the pallid grass that separated the gates from the sidewalk, and pulled. The pain renewed—another jolt, then another pause. Joel thought that he could smell burnt hair, but it seemed too inconsequential in the face of the necessity to free himself. He pulled and strained, until the next shock set his flank afire, radiating across his back and down every nerve. Joel looked outside, at the traffic that flowed by, oblivious to a pig stuck in the gates. The next shock exploded in his eyes, in a shower of white stars, and Joel saw no more.

Joel woke up in hell. Before he even opened his eyes, he realized that he was paralyzed. He sent his muscles a signal to move, to close his mouth, but they would not obey. His throat and tongue felt dry as felt, and he could not swallow. His ears hurt.

Joel opened his eyes. The white light sliced across his retinas like a knife, and he squeezed his eyelids shut. Cautiously peering into the whiteness through his sparse eyelashes, Joel discerned the shapes of people around him. They were dressed in white, and blended with the white walls, the instruments in their hands the same color as the chrome fixtures. The chrome fixtures that held his mouth open, thrust into his throat far enough to scratch it and make him want to gag. Steel shafts penetrated his ears, holding his head immobile.

This is it, Joel thought. *They've found someone who wants my brain—*

wants me. He swiveled his eyes around, half-expecting to see the perpetrator. He imagined him reaching greedily for Joel, an unholy gleam in his eyes.

Cassie's Dad came into Joel's field of vision, moving his face closer. "You gave us quite a scare, Joel," he said. "What were you doing, getting stuck in the gate? Did you want to get out?"

Joel would've nodded if the mechanical gear did not prevent him.

"Silly boy," the old man cawed. "You got quite an electric shock, you did. Now, you just relax, and we'll make sure that you did not damage anything."

Despite his discomfort, Joel breathed easier. It wasn't the time, then. If he was lucky, the time would never come. With all his heart he hoped that the old man would find something wrong. Some imperfection that would let Joel live.

The old man gave a signal, and his helpers, white-gowned people with their faces hidden behind white cloths, wheeled Joel's table into a large, humming tunnel. Joel closed his eyes, and in his mind repeated the words he heard Cassie whisper before going to sleep. "Please Lord, have mercy on us all." He thought a bit, and added, "Especially Joel."

Lord did not listen—perhaps, because Joel was a pig, and not a young girl with curly hair and eyes like blackberries. After an eternity of loud humming and beams of light that shot at him from different angles, Cassie's Dad wheeled Joel out of the tunnel, and patted his snout. "Good as new. Good boy."

Joel wept silently as the masked people unstrapped him and freed his mouth from the ravages of steel. He was too wrapped up in his misery to look around as Cassie's Dad nudged him outside of the low stone building into the yard covered in asphalt. The old man opened the door of his car, and Joel climbed onto a back seat. He looked out of the window, but nothing shook him out of the stupor—neither the flowering cherry trees, nor people milling about, nor the low wooden pens. He watched a row of pigs' faces pressed against the bars. He guessed that they housed human livers, hearts and kidneys. *But not minds,* Joel thought bitterly. That cross was his to bear.

Since that day, Joel thought of ways to escape. He circled the perimeter of the yard surrounded by thin wires. But the wires gave him the same jolt as the gates. He tried to root under the fence, and made good progress, but was discovered. The old man moved Joel's bed into the shed, where he could be locked. His only solace was Cassie, who visited him occasionally. The old man tagged along on such visits, short and awkward as they were.

"What's got into him?" the old man said, looking at Joel with consternation. He stood in the doorway, the afternoon sun creating a halo around his misshapen, hunched silhouette.

Cassie crouched down and patted Joel's head. "Perhaps he knows." She looked up at her father, her eyes rounded with emphasis.

"Nonsense," the old man said.

Joel's heart leapt with hope. He grunted and rubbed against Cassie's knees, almost knocking her over.

"Dad," she said.

The old man sighed. "There's nothing I can do," he said. "It's not just *my* project. Perhaps it was a bad idea to keep him as a pet—I should've known that you'd get attached."

Cassie stood. "What do you mean? Did you find someone?" The old man nodded. "Ever since it's been in the papers, we've been flooded with mail and phone calls. The Congress got involved, and the FDA is pushing for clinical trials. I think we found a recipient."

"Who?"

"A young man," Cassie's Dad said. "He was in a car accident some years back, suffered a loss of a large portion of the right hemisphere. Think of it, Cassie—Joel will help someone to live a normal life. Think how you would feel if you were half a person."

Cassie heaved a sigh, and thrust her hands deep into her jeans pockets. "I guess. I would hate to lose Joel though."

The old man smiled. "You don't have to lose him, dear. He'll retain most of his brain—more than enough for a pet."

Joel could not sleep all night. Cassie was an ally. If only he could send her a sign, let her know somehow that he was just like her, that he could think and understand everything... A sudden thought struck him. He almost laughed in disbelief—it was so simple. Why didn't he think of it before? He picked up a twig with his mouth, and started drawing letters in the dust. Letters that he remembered since Cassie and he were both carefree and young, when she learned the symbols on the bright painted cubes. Joel was there, and he had learned too.

It was a hard going—the letters came out shaky and clumsy, and he had to start over a few times. He wanted them to be perfect, so that no one would doubt his abilities. He labored all night, often stopping to rest. By the morning, the inscription was ready. Large, blocky letters stood out clearly against the grey dirt. "Cassie," he wrote, "I love you." She would come in the morning and see that he had both a heart and a mind.

When the morning came, Joel circled around the cramped pen—a far cry from the luxury of the old house, where he could roam free and see Cassie whenever he wanted to. He even moved all the straw into the corner, so that nothing obscured his letter.

He heard footsteps outside, and his heart almost stopped, and then raced, once he realized that there were several people there. All of them came in, wearing green coats, loud and laughing. Their heavy shoes trampled his message back into dust, and their hands grabbed Joel. He fought back, crying out for help, until a needle jabbed his flank.

The afternoon sun flooded the porch, and Joel closed his eyes. It was a nice day, although his aching skull told him that it might rain later. Cassie shifted in her chair, and tickled Joel's chin with her bare toes. He grunted and stretched his neck. He almost dozed off when he heard crunching of the gravel of the driveway. Someone was coming.

He opened his eyes. Cassie looked too, shielding her eyes from the glare, and put down her book. Joel glanced at the squiggly lines, and then at Cassie. For the life of him, he could not understand why she spent all day staring at the black worms that crawled on the white pages.

"Excuse me." The visitor walked halfway up the steps that led to the porch and stopped, as if uncertain. "I was told that this is Dr. Kernicke's house."

Cassie nodded. "He's at the Institute. It's down the road, by the farm."

"I know," the visitor said. "I just wanted to talk in a more informal manner." His eyes met Joel's, and he whistled. "Say, is that the pig that..." He swallowed a few times but did not continue.

Cassie looked puzzled for a moment, but then smiled. "Oh yes, this is Joel, the wonder-pig."

Joel lifted his head at the mentioning of his name. The rest of the words escaped him somehow, no matter how hard he listened.

"Joel," the visitor repeated. "I'm Phil Marshall."

"Oh yes." Cassie looked at the visitor with awe. "You're the recipient."

The word evoked a vague displeasure in Joel, but the day was too nice to get agitated over anything. He grunted and rolled to his side, trying to capture as many rays as he could before the sunset.

"And you're Cassie," Phil said.

"How did you know?"

Phil frowned, shook his head, and shrugged. "I don't know. Probably heard it somewhere."

"Probably," Cassie agreed. "Father will be home soon. You want to see the garden meanwhile?"

Joel watched the two people walk down the steps and stroll across the green lawn. He tried to focus his thoughts, but they just stumbled about, unruly, chasing each other's tails. There was something about that man, something about the way he looked at Joel that seemed familiar. The words 'blank slate' floated into his mind and dissipated, leaving no impression or understanding. Joel yawned. All the thinking made him tired, and he closed his eyes, savoring the warmth and the sun. No need to worry about things one could not change. And truly, Joel had no reason to complain. He was treated well, and he had anything a pig could desire. And it was getting even better—every day, he found that he had fewer things to worry about, that the concerns of yesterday made no sense today, and often left no memory. He had forgotten the smell of blood, and the searing pain, and the sickening sound of the tissue tearing like fabric. Soon, he would be truly happy.

Hindsight, in Neon

Jamie Todd Rubin

1

The last science fiction writer sits in an all-night diner beneath the sizzling haze of a neon "Live Nudes" sign. His agent, a vaporous figure of a man, sits across from him sipping at coffee, blurred by the rising steam.

"It was sixty-nine years ago," the last SF writer says, poking at his clam chowder, "that *Dying Inside* first appeared; one of the true classics, a first rate effort and so forth."

The agent mutters something incomprehensible under his breath and continues to suck at the coffee.

"*I* am dying inside," says the last SF writer.

The agent has heard this all before. "You haven't written anything worth publishing in thirty years," he says.

"I am losing my power," the last SF writer says. He wears a faded periwinkle suit, as deformed as a crumbled manuscript page. From an inside pocket he pulls a yellowed paperback and thumbs though the pages. "David Selig—now there's a character with whom I can sympathize. There is a danger in knowing too much."

"There is a danger giving in too easily," the agent says, in disinterested tones.

The last SF writer sets the book down on the table. "It's out of my hands now," he says.

"It's not really your fault," the agent says, this time with a hint of sympathy. "You have to have *readers*. You have to have people who can make sense of the letters and words on the page, who can be moved by the drama and imagery."

"No one remembers," the last SF writer says, sadly.

"*You* remember," the agent says.

But the last SF writer is shaking his head, staring into the cold clam chowder, beneath the hot anachronistic neon light. "Too late," he mutters, "It's all gone."

2

The last SF writer sits in the all-night diner, fiddling with a flaking copy of an ancient science fiction magazine. The pages have been annotated in microscopic print. As a weary waitress refills his coffee cup, he says to her, "They don't make life like they used to."

"Preachin' to the choir, sweetheart." the waitress says, and with leaden steps disappears somewhere behind the counter.

"She has no idea what you're talking about," the agent says from behind a pair of thin-framed eyeglasses perched precariously on the bridge of his bulbous nose.

The last SF writer waves the magazine in the air, creating a minor blizzard of decayed pulp all about the table top. "It was seventy-eight years ago when this story first appeared. It was true then, and it's true now."

"Ironic, isn't it," the agent says dryly without looking up from the contract he's been reading.

"You know why I come here every night?"

"Because it's just around the corner from your apartment," the agent says.

The last SF writer ignores him. "Because they still have menus that you can *read* and because flesh-and-blood waitresses still serve the food. Not like those new diners, with the voice-recognition ordering systems, computerized chefs, robotic servers..."

"Yes," says the agent, finally looking up from his papers, "but those places have something that this place does not."

"Such as?"

"Patrons."

"I can sympathize," the last SF writer says. "It is a different world now. It has evolved beyond me. Beyond this—" he shakes more flakes of paper off the ancient magazine. He glances toward the waitress standing behind the counter at the far end of the diner staring catatonically at the door. "She could be Linda Nielsen," he says.

"And you could be Jim Mayo," the agent says.

"And it would all end the same, regardless."

Staring at his papers, the agent says, "They don't make life like they used to."

3

The last SF writer sits in the all-night diner with ancient newspaper clippings spread out across his table. From an inner coat pocket, he pulls out a ball-point pen and adds to the notes he has scribbled on the napkin before him. It takes him quite some time, and before he is through, he has filled both sides of its surface with tiny print.

The waitress stops by the table with more coffee and the last SF writer says to her, "Would you be a doll and bring me some more napkins? Thank you, dear." She smiles at him vacuously and walks off.

Then he says to his agent, "We were too smart for our own good. That was our downfall. Ahead of our time would be an understatement. We were ahead of *any* time. Listen to this—" he glances down at his napkin, "—'The Rocket Man', published ninety years ago; 'The Skylark of Space', one hundred and thirteen years ago; 'Requiem', one hundred and one years ago. The list goes on and on.

"Do you know when human beings last set foot on the moon?" He does not wait for an answer. "Over sixty-eight years ago! I was virtually a newborn then. No sir, we have outsmarted ourselves. We were the leaders. We were there before the rest of them in every single case: the moon, the solar system, the galaxy, the universe. We had the *vision* to see what they could not see. We inspired the last great generation, I tell you. Ask any one of those twelve dead astronauts who actually stood on the moon—*stood on the moon!*—ask any one of them what inspired them to do something so incredibly outrageous and they will undoubtedly point to some aspect of science fiction.

"And where are we today? We have solved the problem of literacy by eliminating it: 'Books' (if you can call them that) are sensory interactive, require no knowledge of letters, and no imagination on the part of the reader. Automobiles drive themselves—oftentimes without any passengers. Food preparation does not require human participation. Dogs can be walked by autonomous leashes. Hair can be colored by genetic pills. They have taken the ideas that we gave to them, and used them to solve every *trivial* problem they could think of."

This thought has been recurring to the last SF writer with increasing frequency. He wipes sweat from his forehead allowing several large drops to fall into his napkin, smearing the blue ink in several places.

"We are no closer to the moon," he says, scribbling madly as he speaks, "no closer to cold fusion, or curing cancer or a dozen other diseases. We have become preoccupied with a world-girdling network of electronic interaction and narcissism. The universe outside does not exist. It cannot affect us and we cannot affect it."

Finally, he breaks down and says what he is really thinking: "It is hard to watch a species on its way to extinction." He thinks the ambiguity of this is profound, for while by "species" he means "science fiction writer," he could just as easily be referring to the human race.

It is at this point he realizes that he has been alone in the diner the entire time. His agent is not there, and he has been talking aloud to an invisible audience. Perhaps he has not even been talking. Perhaps it has all been in his head.

4

The last SF writer sits in the all-night diner and stares at the neon "Live Nudes" sign just outside the window. It is a mark of the deterioration in this part of town that the nude dancers are, in fact, live. In most places the dancers are computer-generated simulacrums, virtually indistinguishable from the real thing—until you try and touch them.

His agent sits across from him, sipping at his coffee and reading a newspaper, but newspapers are rare, except in museums, and in fact, the agent himself seems rarified, fading in and out, at times appearing solid, and at other times like those ghostly holographic dancers.

"When was the last time you actually *sold* a story of mine?" the last SF writer asks.

"When was the last time you *wrote* a story for me to sell.?"

"I am no longer able to write. I've lost that power. It has withered away out of disgust."

"There is no longer a market."

"We are a dying breed."

"*You* are a dying breed."

The last SF writer scratches at his chin and stares into his soup bowl. "This is how Hwoogh felt."

The agent flickers out for a moment and then reconstitutes himself. He shrugs his shoulders and says, "Survival of the fittest. Nothing personal, you understand."

The last SF writer nods sadly. "The day is done."

"How long?"

"One hundred and two years."

5

The last SF writer sits in the all-night diner. He is not well. The mild aches now make him restless. The cough, which started as a tickle in his throat, has grown into some kind of infection in his lungs. He avoids looking at himself in the mirror.

"We never really made it beyond Apollo," he says to his agent. "Do you realize that it has been sixty-nine years since human beings have set foot on the moon? Since Barry Malzberg's *Beyond Apollo* was first published?" In his mind, both were the same.

"I always thought that a most depressing book," the agent says, sipping his coffee.

"A most *insightful* book," the last SF writer says, and then is overcome by a siege of coughing. When he recovers, wiping bits of green sputum from the table with a greasy napkin, he says, "I can sympathize with Harry Evans. The conditions were intolerable."

"The conditions *are* intolerable," the agent says. Then he changes the subject. "Have you heard that scientists at M.I.T. think they've built a time machine that will actually work?"

"I don't listen to tabloids," the last SF writer says.

"It was the headline of all the major news organizations this morning."

"I no longer pay any attention to the news."

With a hint of emotion, the agent says, "With a time machine, you could go back in time an change things—you know, so that events turn out differently."

"And what would I change?" the last SF writer asks.

"Well... maybe what gets written, how it is received and so forth."

"Too late, it's already been done, seventy-six years ago in a story called 'The Longest Science Fiction Story Ever Told.'"

"Ah, but that was a *story*. I am talking about *life*, altering our reality, *making a difference*."

The last SF writer hawks spits something unpleasant into his napkin. He says, "It will never work."

"Why not?"

"There has never been a successful science fiction story involving time travel, that didn't end ironically, or dramatically. Call it a writer's intuition, but I'd wager that even if their so-called time machine worked, altering the past would not achieve the desired goals. It would only make things far worse."

"How could you possibly know that?" the agent asks.

"I am not the first to know it, just the last. Harry Evans knew it. The reasoning is clear: the conditions were intolerable. A time machine? Ha! That will never work out."

6

The last SF writer sits in the all-night diner, or perhaps he is asleep on his bed in the tiny, one-room studio he maintains around the corner from a diner which he has never actually visited. It is August 15, 2041 and as he nibbles at his toast and soup, or perhaps just rolls over in bed to face away from the calendar, he realizes that he is probably the only person on Earth who knows that one hundred years ago today, "Nightfall" first made its appearance on the magazine racks.

"The greatest science fiction story ever written was more prescient than anyone could have possibly known," he says to his agent—to the empty room. "We humans used to be fascinated by the stars. They roused the spirit of our ancestors and some of the mystery that surrounded them seemed to evaporate over the centuries."

"You are not making sense," the agent says; or so the last SF writer thinks to himself. "This is why you stopped writing; this is why you haven't written a story in thirty years."

"Some of that fascination," the last SF writer continues, "inspired a couple of generations of writers, and during that brief interval, they shined like a golden sun.

"Now, we are afraid of the stars. We do not understand them; cannot understand them. No—worse—we have *forgotten* them. We focused on trivialities, a quest for the ultimate in leisure when we should have been inspired to focus on industry and the quest for knowledge. That is what those men and women inspired in others. Somewhere along the way, though, something went terribly wrong."

He casts about the restaurant as though looking for an answer, catches the eye of the waitress and holds up his empty cup of coffee. She quickly refills the cup, and the last SF writer reaches toward the small nightstand next to his bed to take a sip of water from the glass there, but manages only to knock the glass to the floor with a crash. He does not have the strength to get out of bed and clean it up.

"Perhaps it is a cycle," the agent says.

"Yes, a cycle. And maybe someday, it will start itself up all over again from scratch. That would be nice to believe, would it not? All of the old stories, retold exactly as they were told then, but to sound brand new. Like the library of Babel..." his voice trails off.

The agent (who is now a discorporate whisper in the mind of the last SF writer) says, "The question remains: will they get it right?"

The last SF writer does not know the answer to this. He can *hope*, but he does not know. He will not know. He says nothing for a long time, laying very still in the dark, empty room around the corner from the "Live Nudes" sign, his breath coming at irregular intervals. He thinks only of the great stories, and does not think of the future. He thinks of the stars, which others cannot see and which he cannot see, but which he *knows* are there, slowing winking out one by one.

WAITING FOR JAKIE

BARBARA KRASNOFF

I like the blue pills best. I have others, of course—the purple ones, and the green and yellow ones. The tiny white ones? Those are just for blood pressure, and all they really do, in my opinion, is give a living to the drug companies. Not that I have anything against drug companies, God forbid; after all, they not only allow me to face each day, but gave my son Benjamin a decent living for many years until the AIDS got him, poor boy.

Anyway, the blue pills are the ones I take when I'm feeling nervous or depressed, which is most of the time, actually. I tell the doctors this, and they try to put me on other medications, more long term, they call it, but a week goes by and I'm feeling like taking a steak knife to my wrists, so I throw away the new ones and go back to the ones that at least keep me operating on, as Samuel used to say, all six cylinders.

And sometimes, if I've taken just a little bit more than I'm supposed to—not much, only a few more milligrams, nothing, an extra pill or more, who would begrudge it?—then, if I squint my eyes a little and let the living room furniture blur a bit, then sometimes, if I'm lucky, I can see Jakie. Not very clear, I admit, and usually only a little, but it's him. It's him.

And I miss him so much. Our time together was short, so short, but it was like a lifetime together. It should have been a lifetime together.

Usually he's sitting in the big stuffed chair where Samuel used to sit, with his long legs stretched out in front, and a book or a newspaper in his large hands. I love it when I can see Jakie. I could just sit and look at him forever. He's tall, and thin, and his hair is still thick and brown. And his eyes—oy, his eyes. Those eyes are what I used to dream about after he left—large and dark and ironic. Like my father's. Which is why I first trusted him, that day when he and the other Americans came walking into the camp.

But enough of me.

He doesn't always read, Jakie. Sometimes he leans his chin on his hand and stares off to the side, his head nodding slightly, up and down. He's listening to music, I think, maybe one of the Italian operas he was so fond of. Once, one of the girls found an old scratched recording of Rigoletto in a bombed-out house somewhere, and I traded her a full meal for it and gave it to Jakie, and he found an old wind-up victrola and brought it to his quarters. As soon as the music started, *E Donna Mobile*, all the other soldiers started snorting through their noses like horses, as though Jakie listening to opera was the funniest thing they'd seen.

But I saw how the record helped him go away from the war, and I knew that this was the mark of a truly civilized man. I know—I grew up in a beautiful, rich home outside of Berlin, and we attended concerts, and went on holiday in Switzerland. When we went to the theatre, men and women in lovely clothing would nod respectfully at my parents and my uncle and smile at me, and I would feel so special. Jakie may have been born in America, but he too was special.

I don't think he sees me, Jakie, when he sits in Samuel's chair. If I thought that, I'd die. Me with my bloated body and thin hair and God! I used to be so beautiful.

Even right after the camp, when I looked like a scarecrow, my hair still short and dry and no meat on my bones, Jakie used to tease me and tell me that I looked like Veronica Lake. And I'd laugh at him and say no, I'm too skinny. And finally he came to the barracks one day, where we were waiting to find out what would happen and where we should go, and he told me to get two girl friends, we were "going out on the town."

And he got me a beautiful dress, and a nice pair of shoes—I never asked where he got them. And, would you believe it, lipstick—and three of us girls got together, and brushed our hair until it hurt, and scrubbed, and colored our lips and a little on our cheeks. We went to a local cafe where Jakie and two other boys whose names I don't remember, we sat and the Americans gave the proprietor, a German pig who stared at us as though he wondered why we weren't still in the camp where we belonged, they gave him money and told him they wanted wine and sausages, and we all drank, and ate, and tried to understand each other, and one of the Americans said something that made Jakie slap him on the head, and they all laughed, and when I asked Jakie in Yiddish what the boy said, he wouldn't say.

I was alone, and my family was dead, and we were diseased Jewish whores from the camps, but we ate, and drank, and pretended we were regular girls out on dates with three boys who would try to steal a kiss and then deliver us back to our parents. Oh, god. I was so happy that evening.

And when I went back with Jakie, and kissed him, and wanted to give him of my own free will what I had been forced to give up for the last three years, he kissed me gently as if I was a bride, and told me that we had the rest of our lives and that I deserved more than a forest behind the barracks.

I let him take me back. The two other girls told me I was an idiot. And they were right.

Because in the morning, Jakie and the lovely boy soldiers were gone. And although he had promised to write, I never heard from him again. (Years later, Samuel said he could probably find my soldier—I had told him some of it, but not all—but I told him no. It was too late. I was married, and older, and didn't want to know.)

Eventually, I found a job as a secretary to one of the Red Cross officials. And one day Samuel walked in, quiet and clean and polite, in a beautiful suit that made him look like a banker or a movie star, although he wasn't really tall enough. I thought then, what was a Jew doing in a suit like that, with so much meat on him? I thought, a collaborator, a bastard who sold Jewish lives in trade for his own. Later, I found out he had escaped and worked for the OSS, the American spies. And what did he do during the war? He never told me.

But he looked so like the boys I used to see at the skiing lodges where we spent our school holidays that my breath caught in my throat. And it was the same for Samuel—he told me later that when he first saw me, for one moment he was walking into the office of his father's *shul* where, he said, his friend's pretty sister used to help with the paperwork. So we found each other in a mist of dreams of the dead.

That is why I don't like admitting that it is Jakie I see, and not Samuel. After all, Samuel was my dear husband for nearly fifty years, and it was his chair, and he was the one who took care of me and tried to help me. When we were living in Berlin, and when I found out I was pregnant and told Samuel that I would kill the baby and myself before I would let it be born in that damned country, didn't he tell his bosses that he had to leave Europe, and bring me to America? And when one day I started crying and couldn't stop, didn't he take me to that doctor who gave me those pills and said they'd help me? And if they didn't help me the way he'd planned, if I needed to take more of them over the years, was it his fault? He meant it for the best.

And now Samuel is dead. My poor Benjamin, the only child we had, our hope for the future, is dead. And Jakie, if he is still alive, is probably married to some smart American woman with smart American children. And he is probably fat, and balding, and has forgotten all about me.

But I don't care.

I can still see my Jakie in my living room, thin and dark and laughing like when he took me to dinner. But he is still misty, still like a dream. So I limp to the bathroom, and find my pills, all the different colors and shapes, and take them back to the living room with a glass of water. I take two more pills and wait for a few minutes, and then I squint my eyes and concentrate like I used to concentrate over my French lessons as a girl. And suddenly, I don't have to pretend any more—Jackie is here, sharp and clear and looking at me with that saucy American grin on his face. I take two more pills and stand, and so does he, and I take his hand and lead him back to the cafe.

And we are sitting at the table again, and I can hear the chatter of the other two couples. My stomach is full, and I am wearing a nice dress and real shoes, and I take Jakie's hand, and he takes one of the wine bottles off the table, and we stand and walk into the forest while his friends laugh and cheer and call out things in English that would probably have made my mother faint. But I don't care—when we are far enough away, I kiss Jakie hard on the lips. He tells me that we have the rest of our lives, but I know better this time. I will have this moment, this lovely moment.

After, Jakie strokes my hair, and touches my lips, and says he loves me, and will find out how he can get permission to marry me and take me to America. But now, he says, he's hungry, and he goes off to find some food, and I sit in the pine needles and straighten my clothes, and take out the comb he gave me to fix my hair. There is still some wine in the bottle, and I raise it to the strange God who killed so many but let me live, and drink it down.

And then, out of the corner of my eye, I see an old woman who is standing a little ways off. She is a terrible old woman; her hair is white and thinning, her figure is thick and flabby underneath the cotton dress; she wears slippers on her nasty bare feet and only a single gold ring on her wrinkled hands. She smiles at me. "Now you are happy," she says.

Happy? Stupid old woman—how can I be happy? I am thin and used up. My family is dead, my childhood is gone, and I have spent three years screwing Nazi soldiers so that I can live.

The old woman starts to cry. "I thought this was the right time," she sobs, and I can't stand it, so I stand and walk into the forest. It is an old, beautiful forest, full of moss and thick trees. They remind me of the tall firs near our home, and the hours I spent as a girl playing there, and dreaming about my future. In the woods next to my uncle's house. Before.

My uncle's large home with the red shutters and large wooden door, and the fat cat who would not stay in the house no matter how often we tried to shut her in, and Peter the butler who frightened me because he was so tall and stern, but who would let me sit in the kitchen and watch the servants prepare dinner. This morning my father and my uncle were quieter than usual after the meal, and I knew it was because of the letter my uncle had received that morning, and that it had something to do with the political situation. They talked together until my mother came over, and touched my father on the shoulder. He smiled at her, and then we played cards because it was raining outside.

The rain stops, and although my mother tells me to put on my galoshes, it's still wet outside, I run outside and stand in the grass. It is lovely; in the sunlight, the wet grass is as bright a green as I have ever seen in my life.

There is a noise, and I look down the wide drive, and there are men in uniforms approaching, the sun bouncing off their belt buckles and buttons. I'm wearing my favorite dress, the one that my uncle just bought me for my thirteenth birthday party, and I'm so glad that I'm wearing it now because there is a handsome soldier behind the four men who is dressed differently than the others. His uniform is dirty and creased and he needs a shave, but he has lovely brown hair and nice eyes.

The adults have come out too, despite the wet. My mother says my name, low and with a tremor in her voice that is so strange I turn and look at her. Her face has gone still and she is standing so stiffly that for a moment she doesn't look like my mother. She is motioning me to come back to the house in quick, angry, waves of her hand, as though she is afraid somebody will see her.

My father and my uncle are closer, though. They have walked down the wide front drive, and have now stopped, waiting. My father stands a little behind my uncle, his pipe in his mouth. His hands are clasped behind his back. My uncle, shorter and stouter, is shaking his head just a little, the way he does when I come to him with some complaint about my mother, his hands pushed deep into his pockets.

Just beyond them is a strange woman standing on the grass, wearing a flowered dress that is a too big on her. She is very thin and has funny short hair and she is smiling at me. Nobody else seems to notice her — maybe because they are all looking at the soldiers.

"Now you are happy," she says, and that sounds strange at first. But then I realize that the sun is shining, and I am with my family, and looking forward to my birthday, and only worried about my algebra homework and whether I'll ever grow breasts.

"She can't be happy. Jakie isn't here," and it isn't the young woman talking, but an old woman who looks a bit like the beggar in town who sells eggs by the road. She is very ugly, but then she smiles at me too, so to be polite I smile back.

My mother calls my name louder but instead I run to my uncle and take him by the arm. Before I can ask, he says quietly, not looking at me, "Darling, go to your mama. Now, please."

The child pauses, not knowing what to do. She looks back at the soldiers and squints at something — and there, down the driveway, as insubstantial as hope, is a tall young man with dark hair and eyes, and suddenly it's hard to breathe. "Jakie!" we scream. "Save me!" But he is not alone—he is holding the hand of a stranger, a woman with knowing American eyes, and he is not looking at us.

We two, the camp whore and the crazy old woman, remember running to our mother's side, watching as the world suddenly changed, but we know that this time she will not go. We watch as the young girl in her first grownup dress stands and holds her uncle's arm, her hands only trembling a little. She is young enough to be brave; to believe, to the bottom of her soul, that nothing really bad can happen.

The old woman is sniffling again—doesn't she ever stop?—and her nose is all red. "I thought he would save me from this," the old woman moans. "From the memories. I thought he would save me."

I stroke her hair, and remember the lipstick, and the cafe, and Jakie's kind eyes. "I know," I tell her. "I know. But we will have to do it ourselves."

She nods, and wipes her eyes. "You are right," she says. "Of course. It's all up to us."

My uncle has stepped forward, and one of the clean German soldiers, an officer I think, takes a gun from his pocket and points it at him just like the gangsters in the American movies. I know I should run back, but I won't leave my uncle. "You fucking Jew," the officer says, calm as if he were just saying hello, "You fucking rich Jew, you think you own the world?"

My uncle pushes me away. "Back to the house," he says, his teeth clenched, every word distinct. "Now! Do you hear?"

The soldiers are scaring me, so I look at the two women. They are crying about something, but then they hold their arms out to me. "Come, sweetheart," says the old lady. "It's a beautiful morning. Forget the handsome American soldier. He will not save you. Come to us— come and show us your lovely new dress."

I walk toward them, passing in front of my uncle. There is a loud sharp sound from far away, and it all stops.

Clockwork, Patchwork and Ravens

Peter M. Ball

Jackson said she'd been hanging with the Corvidae before he found her, that she was one of those girls that bounced between gangers named Jackdaw6 or Raven8. They'd pumped her full of genemorphs laced with avian DNA, hoping she'd be lucky and avoid the bad reaction. It had already affected her teeth, turning the molars into rotting shards. Her lips were growing hard, thickening into dark cartilage, and I could see the shadow of her organs beneath the bleached skin stretched across her ribcage. Jackson said he found her wandering in the alley behind the crow boy's nest, trying to staunch the fluid seeping from her fresh-plucked eye-socket. He brought her home, patched her up, and turned her over to me for safe-keeping while he went downstairs to work. I stood over her and watched her, letting the hours tick by, and eventually I kissed her.

My kiss didn't wake her, though she stirred a little at my touch. Downside is not a place where fairytales happen, and no-one would mistake me for a handsome prince. It was a clumsy kiss, as you'd expect, but a kiss. A kiss!

When she did not wake I stood, resuming my vigil. I could feel myself blushing, my right cheek warm. I turned my other cheek toward her, hiding behind the copper mask.

Even now, looking back, I'm still not sure why I did it. It's not as if she was a pretty thing, with her bruises and her missing eye, but there was still some remnant of beauty beneath the blue stitches of Jackson's repair. She was a creature of the Downside streets, all feral promise and rough allure. I didn't love her—that would be unseemly for a half-man like me—but I envied her, desperately, for the blue stitching that held her together and the heart that still beat in her chest. I wished, for just a moment, that Jackson had done the same for me. I could feel the steady flick of that pulse when our lips touched. It was alive; faint, but eager to exist. My own heart ticked on, steady and regular, the soft tick-tock marking a regular beat as it pulped blood through those veins I still possessed.

Jackson wanted to be a hero, I knew that without asking. When I was little, just after he took me in, Jackson used to tell me stories about heroes, about knights and princes and ducks that turned into swans. I would listen to his stories, curled up in bed, crying as the pain of a new graft wracked my chest and shoulder. I had to ignore the sound of the gangs and the crowds that filled the Downside streets, the occasional brawl or gunshot cutting through the din. Jackson would fill my head with heroes, with worlds where heroes still existed. I never believed in his stories, but I always believed in Jackson. It was easier, cleaner, but it was just as dangerous in the end.

The girl slept for three days, sedated and monitored. I spent my nights watching her fight against the painkillers, twisting against the thin sheets in Jackson's cot. I was afraid to move, afraid the grinding cogs in my arms would disturb her bad dreams. I dreamt of kissing her again, dreamt of her waking up and looking on my copper mask and grafted limbs without the inevitable shudder. It was not to be. She woke in the dim light of the third morning, jettisoned from her nightmares with a gurgling scream. She cast about the room with her good eye, looking for something familiar, but all she got was me, and the mangled nubbin of flesh that had been her tongue started making strangled sounds that could have been words. I knelt beside her, putting my good hand on hers, making sure there was contact between her flesh and mine.

"It's okay," I said. "You're safe here."

She struggled and I held her down, the steady tick-tock of my heart frightening her more than the cold grip of my hand. She had a coppery, nervous scent and I saw blood stains on her bandages. Her good eye stared at my face as I leaned in to check the stitches. She waited, trembling and sluggish, still woozy from the barbiturates. I pulled back and limped away. She was scared of me, so scared her fear emerged through the painkiller haze, and I couldn't calm her down.

"You've pulled your stitches," I told her. I couldn't make my voice sound soothing, no matter how hard I tried. "You're bleeding. Wait here, I'll go get Jackson." And I ran, fleeing the bedroom, as she let loose an angry gurgle that should have been a scream.

There was comfort in the clutter of Jackson's workshop downstairs; the overburdened workbenches piled high with bits of clockwork and old tech and equipment we scavenged from the burnt-out hospital on the river. I followed the sound of Jackson's snoring through the cramped maze of junk and spare parts, found him in the overstuffed chair he left by the boiler, soaking up warmth as he slept. He looked old, even for Jackson, the wrinkled features like the grooves of a thumbprint, the wisps of hair hanging limp around his face. I leant over and shook him, letting the metal fingers close over his shoulder. "Jackson," I said. "Jackson, the girl's awake."

He slept, stubbornly, until I placed a cold right hand against his bare forehead. Jackson had built me that arm from scratch, and the one I'd worn before it, and the one before that. Its touch woke him faster than any jostling or loud noise ever could. "Randal?" he said, blinking. His eyes were never good, especially in the dark. I lifted the notebook off his lap and helped him to his feet, setting his journal on a nearby bench while he straightened himself up.

"It's morning, Jackson," I told him. The left side of my mouth twisted into a wry smile. "She's awake and she's pulled some stitches. I think I might have frightened her."

"She'll calm down," he said. "And pulling the stitches won't harm her anymore than she's been harmed." Jackson rubbed his eyes with one hand and smiled his forlorn smile. "How is she?"

"Struggling to speak." I clenched my fist, metal straining against metal. "They took her tongue, Jackson. The crow boys, they cut it right out." It was a mistake to mention the tongue. Jackson nodded, eyes growing distant, and I knew that I'd lost him, that his mind had the association it needed to turn toward to his beloved work. Jackson picked up his notebook, finger tracing the anatomical sketches and blueprints. He was making plans, figuring out a way to replace what was lost. I touched his arm again.

"We should run," I said. "We can. She's awake now. We should run before they come for her."

Jackson looked up and shook his head. "It would kill her," he said. "To move her now, so soon, so soon after..." He shook his head again and sighed. "We need a week. Maybe two. Enough time for her to heal. Then we can leave. Then we can run." His eyes dropped to the notebook as he said it, the blue-and-black plans and the detailed annotations. There was a thump upstairs as she fell out of bed. A loud moan of pain filtering down through the floorboards. I thought of the mangled face, the blue stitching and the scars. Beaten by the Corvidae, Jackson had said. We both knew what would happen when they realised the girl had lived.

"They'll find us before then," I told him.

"I know." My heart beat, tick-tock, tick-tock, as I watched Jackson blink back tears. His face set, trying to hold back a shiver of fear. The Corvidae were bad news; both of us knew that. He put his hand on my shoulder, fingers wrapping across the scars. "But I'm going to take care of her," Jackson said. "She didn't deserve this, Randal."

No-one ever does. Jackson didn't look at me, just tore a page from his notebook and held it out. It was a list of parts, carefully annotated, written in Jackson's sloppy script. I ran down the list, noting the unfamiliar names. They were small parts, tiny. Expensive, too, with our finances.

"I'll take care of her stitches," Jackson said, limping toward the stairs. "It will be okay, Randal. We'll get away before you know it."

I double-checked the locks as I left, nervous about leaving him alone. Most of the time, shopping for Jackson takes effort rather than money. This time he was working small, and that meant parts with names I didn't recognise. Technology; state of the art; the kind with names that read like a secret code. Finding those parts meant someone with black-market contacts. It meant shopping fast and getting off the streets before someone noticed what I was doing. It meant Jackie Pelican.

I went down to the river and found him sitting near the harbour tunnel, hawking cheap tech to Cityside tourists heading home after a day in their favourite kink-house. There was an art to the way Jackie worked, pretending to thumb a ride and then hustling the drivers with cheap promises and stolen tech the moment the car stopped. Pelican always said that anyone stupid enough to stop for a Downsider wearing six jackets as he thumbed a ride was going to be an easy mark for his patter, and it turned out he was right more often than not.

He was cutting a deal when I found him, a lump of layered coats and furs pushing data-chips through the window of a Cityside Lexus. I hung back, out of sight. The Pelican didn't need me interrupting his business, and I knew better than to get in his way. It took him five, maybe six minutes to close the deal. Money changed hands and the Lexus sped off, threading into the tunnel that linked the Downside grime with the towers and gleaming lights of the city. The Pelican stood by the side of the road, shuffling through his bills, then nodded and slipped the cash into the pockets of his second jacket. I lumbered across the concrete, coming up behind him. Pelican heard me coming, recognised the tick and the steady thump of my limp. "Randal," he said, making a wide turn, his small face beaming among the layered jacket collars. I clapped Pelican on the shoulder and the gears in my arm groaned. He feigned a shudder at the noise. "Clockwork was a bad fad, Randy. When are you going to let me fix you up with something a little less retro?"

"I don't have money for your upgrades, Pelican. You know that."

"You could work it off, Randal," Pelican said. "You're a good kid, talented, and you're wasted in Jackson's workshop. I'm sure I could find a job for you."

"I like the workshop," I said. "It's homey."

Pelican rolled his eyes and laughed, the thick layers of coats wobbling, his throat swelling up as his humour boomed out. "Fine," he said. "If you can't be lured away from the aging reprobate, why don't you tell me what the Pelican can do for you? I assume Jackson's sent you on another shopping trip?"

I held out the list and pointed at the items I needed, letting the Pelican study them through the cracked lens of his glasses. He puffed his cheeks out as he read, fleshy jowls ballooning as he chewed on the air. "That's a strange list, Randal. What's Jackson up to?"

"I don't know, but if I had to guess..."

"Yeah?"

I shook my head and shrugged. "If I had to guess, I'd say he's building someone a tongue."

The Pelican's eyes went narrow and his teeth clicked together. He breathed in, hissing. "A tongue for whom?"

He was standing straight now, drawing up to his full height, bulging jowls starting to quiver. I stumbled backwards, putting weight on the bad leg. Jackie didn't move to help me, he just settled back into the seat he kept near his hitching spot. "I don't know," I said. "Some girl he found."

The Pelican whistled through his yellowing teeth. "Jackson and his strays," he said. "Fuck." He closed his eyes and quivered. I knelt down next to him, waited for him to explain, watching the watery eyes that refused to meet mine. I put the clockwork arm on his shoulder, let him feel its weight.

"What do you know, Jackie Pelican?"

The Pelican let out a soft snort, glancing to either side. "Nothing, kid," he said. "I know nothing. Just be careful, okay?"

He smiled at me, cheeks rosy, and named me a price. I paid it and collected the parts, lugged them home, worrying.

Jackson had the girl awake by the time I made it back, the steady patter of his speech broken by the stilted syllables of a synthesizer linked to a touch pad. I listened to the dead, cold voice as it answered questions, carrying on her half of the conversation. It was raspy, empty. There were better programs available, but Jackson preferred the retro feel of passive inflections and static. I put the supplies down on the nearest workbench and locked the door, double checking all three deadbolts before stepping back. The alleyway outside was empty, dark even during the day, but talking to Pelican had left me feeling anxious and worried about what was coming. I'd stumbled down three or four different alleyways on my way home, backtracking and cutting through side-streets. I wondered how long it would be before I was actually being followed; sooner or later the news that the girl had survived would filter its way to the Corvidae and they'd come looking for her. I contemplated pulling a workbench in front of the door, damn the mess that moving one would make.

"Randal?" Jackson's voice floated down the stairwell. "Randal, is that you?" There was fear in his voice, but he disguised it well.

"It's me." I limped to the stairwell and waved.

"Randal," Jackson said, "Come up and meet our guest." I shook my head and Jackson frowned at me, his thick eyebrows drawing together. I pointed to the lopsided mask, the arm that had frightened her earlier, and Jackson snorted

"Randal," he said, and I lowered my head. I started climbing up the stairs, my right foot thumping on the wood. Jackson smiled and took my arm as I reached the top, leading me into the room. The girl was still limp, still caught in the numb painkiller haze, she shuddered when she saw my face. Jackson led me over and sat on the corner of the cot. "This is Randal," he said, keeping his voice calm and low. "You'd call him my assistant, I guess. He took care of you during the evenings."

"Hi," I said. I gave her a lopsided grin. "You look like you're healing well."

She was pale now, paler than when I'd left the workshop, and there were bloodstains on her bandages. Jackson had been drugging her, prepping her for more surgery, re-working the lines of blue stitches that held her battered body together. There were sutures on her cheeks that hadn't been there when I left. The girl scratched her hand across the touchpad, letting the computer beside the cot translate the movements into speech. *Thank. You. Randal. My. Name. Is. Rose.*

There was something lucid beneath the drug haze, something aware of where she'd found herself. She studied my face with her good eye, following the lines of steel and scarred skin, suddenly focused on what those scars could mean. "It's an old job," I said. "And I'm too cantankerous a patient for Jackson to replace things or make them pretty. Don't worry; he'll make sure you're still beautiful when he's done."

She smiled at me then, a terrible expression on her broken face, and winced as the smile tugged at the sutures. Jackson slipped a hypodermic into her neck, easing opiates into her bloodstream. I stepped back, giving him room, watching as she went under.

"Sleep now, Miss Rose," Jackson said. "We'll have you up and talking soon." She shook her head, fingers fumbling for the pad, but the drugs hit and she faded. Her hand went limp again.

Jackson stood up and ran his fingers through the pale wisps of his hair, looking pensive as she studied the ruin of her face. "She isn't going to be pretty, Randal. You shouldn't have lied to her."

I turned around and walked toward the stairs.

"She'll be pretty enough," I said. "You'll rebuild her and she'll be pretty enough."

We both knew he planned to install the tongue before we ran away.

We argued after that, Jackson and I. Argued about running, about rescuing the girl, about trying to install a new tongue while we both knew the Corvidae were coming to find us. Jackson won, as always; he's a smart man, and he has arguments aplenty when he needs them.

"We shall stay," he said. "Who would find us, if they looked for her? Who would even consider looking for a girl in a place like this?"

"Pelican knows," I told him. "He knew the moment I asked for the parts. He *knows*, Jackson, and they'll know to ask him. They're looking, Jackson. They're going to come."

Jackson shook his head, his eyes sad. "We are safe enough, Randall. She'll heal before they find us, and there is always the tunnel if she does not. Pelican knows many things, but he does not know about that." He settled down behind his workbench, sitting in the battered hardwood chair with its back stiff and straight like a throne. Jackson, king of clockwork, master of the world he surveyed. I didn't share his faith in the tunnel. We could get out if we used it, yes, but we still had to run. And the tunnel has been here longer than I have, longer than Jackson and his towering piles of junk. He always told me it was a service entrance, built in the days when the workshop was home to grander creations than ours. It wasn't a secret then, and it was barely a secret now.

That night I took a lantern and walked down the dark length of the tunnel. We had used it as a graveyard, a crypt for the gutted husks of grandfather clocks we'd salvaged for parts. The slow tick-tock of my heart echoed against the stones, mocking the dead clock-faces.

"Safe enough," I told myself, and the words echoed off the walls. It took hours to clear a path, to make sure the tunnel was ready if we needed it. I checked the locks and the keys at the far end, just to be sure. I ambled down the narrow corridor. It would be a short sprint, if running was needed, but I'm not built for speed and Jackson was old. My faith in his plan waned as I contemplated the possibilities.

They found us the day after Jackson installed Rose's new tongue.

Jackson and Rose were asleep when it happened. He, lost in a quiet slump beside the cot, she, twisting and turning through another night of medicated slumber. I stood by the doorway, my heart a metronome beat beneath the steady rhythm of Jackson's snoring, and I heard the muffled thump in the workshop downstairs. I thought it might have been an invention, or a pile of Jackson's parts collapsing in the night. Such things weren't unheard of in a workshop such as ours. It wasn't until the second thump, and then the third, that I realized what it was: someone kicking, hammering, trying to batter down our door. I heard the wood give way, the locks bending inwards, the soft crunch of someone walking across the workshop floor.

We had an intruder, and that wasn't a pleasant thought.

I heard the glass face of Jackson's second-favourite clock shattering beneath a heavy fist, and I allowed myself a few seconds to consider the merits of cowardice. It was tempting; I am ill-equipped for stealth, what with my steel-shod limp and the endless tick-tock tick-tock eliminating the possibility of approaching unannounced. Investigation meant a confrontation, facing the intruder down, and I was coward enough that the thought gave me pause.

I picked up Jackson's poker, a cast-iron antique he'd acquired at an auction. I'd scoffed at him when he bought it, claiming it was useless, but it felt comforting to have a weapon in hand. The poker felt solid, weighted for a quick swing should I need to bludgeon a potential thief, and I held it before me as I limped down the stairs and switched on the workshop lights.

There was a Corvidae in the workshop, languid and ready for my approach. He was an angry snarl of a boy, just like the rest of them, black-feather hair, fingers like raptor talons, eyes as smooth and dark as marbles. He stank of carrion, thick and overripe. I raised the poker, holding it like a sword, ready to cave in the boy's skull with its iron head. The Corvidae sneered. "Ya bully dreaming, Tick-Tock. Me-and-I pluck your vitreous; squish-squish, sweet'n'juicy, yum-yum-ha." He cawed then, cackling. He had a crow's laugh, a harsh croak. "Where da patch?"

I charged him, swinging the poker, a futile gesture fuelled by anger and fear. He moved fast, a dash of shadow against the sulphurous yellow light. It didn't take long, no more than three ticks of my heart, and it was over. I saw him move, felt the poker rip free of my hand, then he crashed backwards with his hollow weight bearing me to the floor. I looked up into a wicked grin, grubby talons hovering over my eyes.

"Where da patch?" he croaked. He kept his voice low, all secret whispers. I shook my head. "Gone," I said. "Jackson's gone. He isn't here."

His talons wove an eager pattern in the air as a narrow, black tongue licked pointed Corvidae teeth. "Where da girl den, Tick-Tock? You hide our pretty-pretty, our little birdy-bird? We want her back, Tick-Tock. Gotta finish what we started."

"She's not hiding." My treacherous voice quavered, just a little, giving away my fear. "She's not here, she ran away."

The Corvidae gave me a harlequin's smile, leaning forwards to run his long tongue across the tender flesh of my good eye. "Tell da patch I came, Tick-Tock. Tell him Rook3 wants 'is dolly back, no matter what." And I nodded, stiff-necked, my eye following the pointed claw dancing a hair's breadth from my pupil. Rook3 laughed, drunk on my fear. He floated to his feet in a flurry of limbs, dancing and spinning his way to the gaping maw of our broken doorway. "Me-and-I be seeing you, Tick-Tock," he said, and then he was gone, nothing more than a caw of laughter on the wind.

I lay on the floor for a long time.

Jackson had shown me his blueprints for my arm and chest, the detailed plans and notes he'd compiled explaining how and why they work. I know that there are three-hundred and fifty-seven cogs and gears in my arm alone. I lay on the ground and listened to my heart, the steady tick-tock that never felt the surge of adrenaline, never sped up when danger loomed. When I flexed my fingers, pondering their movement, I knew that another hundred and twenty cogs came to life. I tried to console myself with this knowledge, telling myself that clocks are works of precision and delicacy, that they do not lend themselves to strength, or violence.

It didn't help.

Jackson unlocked the bedroom door; his feet padded down the stairs. My good arm trembled. Jackson stood next to me, staring at the broken door. "They came," he said.

"Just one." I stood up, busying myself clearing a bench, moving the junk onto the surrounding piles. When I was done I tipped it on its side, pushing it against the doorframe to replace the door. I leant my weight against it, holding it secure. "He's fast and he's angry. I'm sure he'll collect the rest of them."

Jackson clucked his tongue and forced me to sit, fussing with my arm. He checked mechanisms and servos, double-checking to be sure. He always worried when I fell, always wanted to make sure that I hadn't damaged the intricate parts of his creation. "They want her back, Jackson," I told him. "They want us to hand her over, or they'll kill us both. Kill us and eat our eyes."

Jackson bowed his head and kept his attention on the arm. His face pinched, locked into a frown of concentration. "It doesn't matter," he said. "We'll keep her safe, somehow."

"We need to run. Tonight."

Jackson shook his head, closed the casing on my arm. "If they found us, it's too late. They're expecting us to run and she still needs rest, another day or two at least. We need to stay, keep them out somehow. Give her time to heal, then use the tunnel to sneak away."

I looked at the upright bench, thinner and weaker than our stout wooden door. "How?"

"Somehow," Jackson said. He rapped my arm with a sharp knuckle, the soft echo filling the room. "We haven't got a choice here, Randal. We must do the best we can."

I went back to Pelican the next morning. I bought the best security system our money could afford. "Lethal or non-lethal," Pelican asked me.

"Whichever you've got," I told him. "As long as I can walk away with it today and have it installed by nightfall." He gave me a queer look and a price, and I gave him the money. It took the better part of a day to get the workshop straightened out and the new locks installed, repairing the door and barricading the windows with steel bars and old workbenches I bolted into place. I spent the afternoon installing Pelican's toys: taser banks and motion detectors; thick Kevlar sheets that sat over the doorjamb, securing it against gunfire and battering shoulders; voltage packs that would pass a charge through anything metal that was tampered with on the exterior of the workshop, leaving a claw blackened and the man behind it stunned. Jackson was upstairs while I toiled below; he checked his work on Rose's prosthetic tongue.

I finished the security job after sunset, just in time for the first Corvidae's croaky laughter to echo at the end of our alleyway. Jackson came down as I was making dinner, flinching at the distant laughter outside. "Done," he said, wiping his hands on a rag. His blue, worn overalls stained with patches of rust. "She can talk."

"Can she eat?" I ladled soup into a bowl and pushed it toward him, then filled a second when Jackson nodded. I started limping toward the stairs, bowl on a plastic tray.

"She's probably sleeping," Jackson said. "And she'll be groggy, even if she's not. Make sure she doesn't choke, Randal—she'll need some practice before she's used to swallowing with the prosthetic."

The whole gang arrived while I was climbing the stairs, loud caws and laughter shrill in the alleyway. I ignored them and kept climbing, opened the door to Rose's room. She wasn't sleeping, but her eyes were glassy from Jackson's painkillers. She was insulated by the drugs, able to look into my face without flinching. She seemed numb to the point where even the noise outside was absent. I sat down next to her and she smiled at me, wincing. "Randal," she said. Her new tongue stumbled around the name, blunting the n, but I could recognise the word through the awkwardness. "Your name is Randal."

"I brought you food," I said. "Something soft. Soup. Jackson wants you to practice swallowing."

"I can hear birds," she said. Her face turned toward the window, toward the aftermath of sunset lingering behind the skyline. The song of the Corvidae filled the air.

"Nothing to worry about." I tried to look her in the eye. "You should eat."

I held a spoon before her face, the soup steaming and thick. I watched the patchwork plastic and Kevlar move when she opened her mouth, the faint flicker at the base of her throat as Jackson's prosthetic worked with the torn scraps of her real tongue. Jackson was right—it was ugly work, but Rose remained beautiful. I fed her a spoon at a time, using my good hand to guide the spoon. The crow calls grew louder, cutting through the groggy haze. She stopped eating and turned to the window, shuddering.

"It's them." She said. "They... hated me. They told me to leave. Why are they here?"

"No one likes to lose," I said.

She blinked back tears, remembering. "Why am I here? Why aren't I dead?"

I thought of Jackson, sitting downstairs, working his way through a bowl of soup. "Jackson likes old stories," I told her, and she frowned. "Fairytales and stuff. You needed help and he helped you." I clenched my fist, listening to the gears creak. "He does that, sometimes."

The painkillers kicked in, responding to her stress. She drifted off, unable to fight Jackson's drugs, and I went downstairs to listen to the bird calls. Jackson was by the stove again, hidden in the corner of the workshop. He cradled a half-full bowl of soup in his lap. The Corvidae were right outside now. I turned the lights off, one by one, relying on the shadows to give us some cover.

"She's scared," I said, settling into the stool next to him.

"She's a smart girl," Jackson answered. He lowered his head and stared into the murkiness of the soup, wispy hair falling in front of his face. Something thumped hard against the front door and the charge went off, filling the air with ozone. We listened to something young and birdlike squeal in pain, then the sound of a limping body retreating into the distance. "We should have closed-circuit," Jackson said. "I don't like hearing them without seeing what they're up to." The second thump was more solid, prepared for the shock that followed. The sound echoed across the workshop as the taser's hiss cut through the darkness.

"Pelican didn't have any cameras," I said. "It'd take at least a week to get some in."

Jackson slept in his chair, fitful, flinching with every measured assault against our doorway. I stayed awake, keeping vigil, the poker gripped in the clockwork hand. My slow hand, the hated hand, but it was strong enough to shatter bone if I could land a solid blow. Jackson used to tell me stories about a broken boy who was put back together by kindly elves with a talent for magic and clockwork. He would tell me the boy's arm was magical, that his heart was a wonder in a world where hearts rarely beat, where all too often hearts were lost for no reason. Love was a powerful thing in Jackson's stories. It could conquer armies and rewrite time. It could make the broken whole again.

I passed the time by counting the thumps of Corvidae against the door, the rattle-rattle-buzz of claws against the window bars, the electrified charge sending bodies reeling back with scorched hands and strangled cries. They paced themselves, syncopated the assaults, used the silence as a weapon to keep us on edge. I counted the thumps, one after the other; one bird, two birds, three birds burned. Four birds, five birds, six birds harmed. Occasionally I stood by the doorway, listening to the quiet scuffle of clawed boots against the concrete. Sometimes they were swift and raucous, using the echoes of the alley to their advantage. They filled the air with birdcalls, making it impossible to be sure of their numbers. Other times they were silent, murmurs in the darkness. I figured there were twenty three of them out there, including those who'd been shocked by the taser bank on the door, birds shocked by enough voltage to leave them twitching and stunned until morning. Sometimes I pressed my weight against the door, keeping it steady against the assault.

Around 2 a.m. it all went quiet. I listened to the steps of someone loping up to the doorway, leaning in without touching it. "We know you're in there, Tick-Tock," Rook3 whispered. "Me-and-I hear your heart; tick-tick-tick."

"No-one here but us chickens," I told him, voice cracking. I picked a spot by the door, raising the poker high, just in case. "Bars on the windows and steel plates on the doors. Go bother someone else, little bird."

Rook3 knocked, three sharp raps that echoed on the steel. The air filled with a whiff of ozone and Rook3 screamed, then cawed and cackled as his screams turned to laughter. "Nothing save you from me-and-I, Tick-Tock," he said. "You come out, sun or no-sun, and Rook3 be waiting."

There was no more knocking after that, no more electrical discharge or rattled windows to break the silence. Later, as the sun rose, I peeked through a crack on a second-floor window and watched the Corvidae perched on the fire-escape next door, waiting and watching like an army of twisted shadows. I woke Jackson and pointed. "We're locked in,"

I said. "It appears they're laying siege."

Cops are an expensive proposition in Downside, but Jackson tried calling them anyway. His first attempt got him a busy signal, the second just the hazy buzz of a scrambler attached to the line. The third call was answered by Rook3's croaking laughter. "Nobody going to help you, Patch. You goin' to die if you don't give me-and-I back da girl." Jackson hung up. His knuckles were pale and his hands trembled, but he drew himself straight as he glared at the door. Defiant, angry, but that wouldn't last. I could see the fear there, lurking behind his eyes.

"We should go," I told him. "Use the tunnel, get out while we can." Jackson didn't answer. He went back to his chair and rocked, his face pinched so tight I could barely see his eyes beneath the press of wrinkles. Small, gentle Jackson, determined to do what was right. "So many of them," he said. "I wasn't expecting there to be so many."

I left him there, huddled against the darkness, and checked on Rose myself.

"I couldn't sleep," Rose told me, fighting against the painkillers. "All the noise, it was like being back there. Like living with them." She was still weak, barely able to lift her head off the pillow, but there was life in her cheeks. She winced with every s she used, a sting of pain from the sutures as the tongue touched her teeth. It gave her voice an old lilt, at odds with the face full of bruises and patchwork stitches. So many grafts, so many repairs.

"No one slept," I said. "Don't worry, they can't hurt you here. We've locked the place up tight, and we've held off worse than this."

Rose pursed her lips and frowned at me, the patchwork tongue bulging against her cheeks. It was a little too large for her mouth, the mechanism heavy against her jaw. She would never look right with her mouth closed, but at least she could speak.

"How..." She shook her head, trying to dislodge the question, but her hand reached out anyway. The dark nails and fingers withered into claws, hovering over the steel, preparing to stroke it. I pulled away, the cogs grinding.

"Jackson found me when I was a kid," I said. "Beaten, cut up, almost dead. He put me back together, the same as you. Replaced the parts as I grew older so I didn't get lopsided." I raised the arm and looked at it, flexed my fingers and took her withered claw in mine. "He's a good man. Foolish, really, and stubborn, but a good man nonetheless."

Outside there was a loud caw, the fizzing snap of a rock thrown against the windows. Rose flinched. "You never... there are other options," she said. "You could get it replaced."

I shook my head. "Jackson calls it his finest work," I told her. "The arm, the heart, the knee. Replacing them would break his heart."

I stood there until Rose gave in to the painkillers, drifting off into sleep with a frown across her face. I held her hand, studied her scars, wondered how far she could make it. Jackson was wrong; we could move her if we had too. Slowly, using a gurney, with enough drugs to keep her sedated and free of pain. We could run if we had to, but we might not get away. The tunnel could get us out, but they would have someone watching. Just in case we had allies, on the off chance someone heard the noise and could be bothered to investigate. If we were spotted as we left, if they saw us sneaking out...

I went downstairs. Jackson was huddled in his chair, shaking. "They won't stop," Jackson said. "They'll never leave us alone, Randal. They just won't stop."

"Then we run," I told him, and I laid out the plan. Jackson listened, eyes flat, and nodded when I reached the end. I sent him upstairs to get things ready. When I was alone in the workshop I let myself shake, skin crawling against the prosthetics. I tightened my grip on the poker, steel grinding against steel. My heart tick-tocked, slow and steady, heedless of my fear.

The Corvidae left us alone during the day, disappearing into the shadows or lingering in knots of two or three, hanging on the fire escapes like birds on a wire. I spent the afternoon taking practice swings with the poker, trying to get comfortable with its leverage and its weight. Violence is easy to practice: swing, parry, thrust; make use of my longer reach. Don't let them get close enough to use speed against me, try to take them down before they rip me apart with their claws. Jackson watched me, lips drawn, trying not to state the obvious.

"You'll need food," he said. "Sooner or later, you'll run out of food."

"I won't run out of food," I said. "And you'll need it more than I do." I smiled at him, awkward and lopsided. Jackson hugged me and patted my arm.

"It'll be dark soon," I said. "You should get ready."

"Sit," Jackson said, and he waited until I did. He told me a story. "It's easier," he said, in the silence at the end. The shadows inside the workshop were growing longer and darker. "In the stories, it's always easier."

"We should get her ready to move," I said. "You'll need help with the gurney, for the first part at least.

This time the bird calls started right on sunset, a whole murder of Corvidae starting their mockery at once. I sent Jackson upstairs with two bowls of soup and a pair of spoons, keeping up appearances in case their spies had an angle to see into the house. He pretended he was weary, stomping as he climbed the stairs. He snuck back down quietly, taking each stair with a graceful limp. The wood didn't squeak beneath him, and perhaps the ruse was pointless at this late hour; the plan would work or it wouldn't, whether we maintained the ruse or not. He nodded at me, eyes shining. We turned out the lights.

"Tick-Tock," Rook3 said, calling through the door. "Hey, Tick-Tock? We-and-I getting bored. We be cracking your cage tonight." I heard the regular chk-chk-chk of the taser discharge, the sharp squeal of nails against the metal bars over the window. "Insulated, Tick-Tock," Rook3 taunted. "Me-and-I saw your little friend, saw the fat little Pelican. Got me what I need to break down your little toys." He knocked on the door again; rap-rap-rap. This time it wasn't followed by a scream.

I heard the door to the tunnel slide shut, the quiet click of a lock settling in place. "Me-and-I eat your eyes tonight, Tick-Tock. Eat your eyes and taste the sweet-meat upstairs, after we gut da patch. He shouldn'a saved her, Tick-Tock." Chk-chk-chk as the taser spluttered, useless, against the claws sliding over the door. Nails on the metal, sharp squeal like a knife to the gut. The sound drew goosebumps from what flesh I still possessed.

I readied the poker and stood next to the door; if I was lucky I could brain one as he came through, crack his head open like a stale egg and be done with it before the others swarmed. Maybe I could frighten the rest of the pack off, make them think we were dangerous, better equipped than they'd suspected. They struggled with the windows and kicked at the doors, insulated against the taser discharge but still struggling to break down the barricade. It would take time, but not a lot. I waited. I waited, and the minutes ticked by. I thought about Jackson and his stories, about Rose and her mangled tongue, the patchwork scars that will cover her body when the stitches are pulled out and she's finally healed for good. Jackson was right, she wouldn't be beautiful, but I was right too. I knew it.

Jackson is in the tunnel now, waiting for his chance to run. I wish that I were with him. I wish that I had kissed Rose, just one more time. I wish so many things.

I can hear the Corvidae outside now, a murder of thugs and runaways, hungry for a fight. They're almost in. It's time. I think about Jackson, about his stories. Outside the Corvidae gather, jangling the windows and kicking the door. Four-and-twenty skinny boys, their flesh twisted by drugs and designer mutagens, black claws ready to rend and tear until I'm nothing but blood and parts. I can hear something hissing, see sparks underneath the doorjamb. I hold my breath, waiting for the inevitable. My heart tick-tocks, measuring out the silence. I repeat the same phrase like a mantra, reminding myself why I'm staying: *Downside isn't a place where fairytales happen.* I hope I'm wrong. I know I'm right.

The front door slides sideways, hinges and locks worn down by the careful application of a blow torch. The first of the Corvidae comes in, a smaller bird with a nervous tick, his caw humming in the back of his throat. "Tick-Tock," Rook3 croons, calling through the open doorway. "We coming to get you Tick-Tock." The smaller bird hasn't noticed me lurking in the darkness; the clockwork arm steady, the poker raised and ready to strike.

I can buy some time. They're going to need it. Jackson isn't fast, and he certainly can't fight, and the gurney will slow him down even if they don't spot him the moment he breaks cover. Downside is not a place where fairytales happen, but maybe just this once we can sneak one by.

The Corvidae scout takes a few steps into the room, hunched over and eager. He sniffs the air, cocks his head to one side. He can hear my heart ticking, low and ominous in the darkness.

"Go," I whisper, "Please Jackson, get away," and I swing the poker down. It bites into the feathered scalp of Rook3's scout, sends him sprawling to the floor in a pile of blood and skewed limbs. My heart beats steadily, no adrenaline can speed it up. Steadily like a clock, dependable and slow. Jackson isn't fast, but he's always been faster than me. I can hear Rook3's keening, the murder of black figures joining his angry scream. They surge, a dark cloud of anger. I think I can hear my pulse, roaring in my ears. I raise the poker. I wait for them. This is not a place for chivalry, but I can pretend I'm a champion. I can stand against the tide, for a few moments at least. I can buy time for Jackson and Rose. I can. She is not a princess, but she deserves this chance. My kiss did not wake her, but she can still be saved. She deserves this. She does. I hope I'm right.

My pulse rattles in my ears as they swarm in, swarm over me, clawing, slashing; Tick-tock. Tick-tock. Tick-tock. Tick-

Hideki and the Gnomes

Mark Lee Pearson

There were twelve moons in the night sky: one from this dimension, the others reflections of the eleven dimensions. One switched off like a computer monitor. On the blank screen, Hideki watched the Space Shuttle, *Confronter*, hurtling to Earth, out of control.

There were eleven moons in the night sky: one from this universe, the others from ten parallel universes. One turned off like a television, digital blocks deconstructing a digital world. There was a high pitched screeching. Hideki ran into the garden to witness a Boeing 747 crash into the garden next door. According to the *Ten O'clock News*, planes were falling out of the sky worldwide, for no apparent reason.

There were ten moons in the night sky: one orbiting this world, the others orbiting nine parallel worlds. One faded slowly into the black analog tube. Hideki stood by the fishpond and called up to his mother's bedroom window. She was in bed watching the *Ten O'clock News*. The screen showed a picture of a man in a shopping center, reeling on the ground, holding his throat in pain as if he'd swallowed his entire set of false teeth.

There were nine moons in the night sky: one from this time, the others from other times. One cut the radio signals, killing the static and the background radiation. Hideki ran into the house and up the stairs to his mother's room. He yelled at her, "We have to go, now! There are only eight moons left." She didn't see the significance, so he dragged her out of bed.

There were eight moons in the night sky: one made of rock, the seven others made from each of the sins. One expired like a lighthouse in a blackout. Magnetic fields moved, and migrating birds lost their way. Hideki dragged his mother, kicking and screaming, down the stairs. He bound her from head to toe with a twenty meter LAN wire.

There were seven moons in the night sky: one made of rock, and six made of cheese. One was swallowed up by the dark night sky. Birds hit the windows. Hideki pulled down the shutters and then went through his father's desk, looking for the gun.

There were six moons in the sky: one for each of the bullets Hideki loaded into the gun chambers.

There were five moons in the sky: four signifying death, and one signifying nothing. Hideki's mother lay sprawled on the tatami with a hole in her head.

There were four moons in the sky: one real, and the others symbolizing the Holy Trinity. Hideki stuffed his mother's body into the refrigerator, nailed the door closed and then cleaned the tatami mat.

There were three moons in the sky: one true, one false, one neither true nor false. Hideki pulled the plug, sending asteroids hurtling toward Earth. He led the gnomes at the garden pond to a revolution.

There were two moons in the sky: one for reason, one for folly. Hideki had the switch now. He had to make a choice for his people. Men and women ran for cover as mushrooms pushed their way up through the lawns, signaling dawn.

There was one moon in the sky; Hideki and the gnomes worshipped it, but they were unsure whether it was the right one.

BIOGRAPHIES

JAMES WALTON LANGOLF is a full time mother and part time college student from Mesa, Arizona. She believes that crazy from the heat is a valid defense for just about anything.

Previously published in *Surreal Magazine* and the erotic anthology *Love at First Sting*, her literary influences include Tom Piccirilli, Joe Lansdale, Ken Bruen and many, many more.

KATHERINE SPARROW is a social worker and social science fiction writer who lives in Santa Cruz. She's been published in *Apex Digest*, *Escape Pod*, Nightshade Press, and a few others. She attended the Clarion West Workshop in 2005, and is currently working on a young adult novel about mental illness and superpowers. When not writing she can be found taking urban hikes and dreaming about apocalyptic punk rock bands.

ANDREW C. PORTER was born in Kentucky but now calls Nashville home. He has written one novel which is currently unpublished. His work often explores the emergent forms of awareness brought about by new technologies, although he has an abiding love of H.P. Lovecraft. "In the Seams" is a story borne of the latter's influence. You can contact Andrew at silverstairs@gmail.com.

GEORGE MANN is the author of *The Affinity Bridge*, *The Osiris Ritual* and *Ghosts of Manhattan*, as well as numerous short stories, novellas and an original *Doctor Who* audiobook. He has edited a number of anthologies including *The Solaris Book of New Science Fiction*, *The Solaris Book of New Fantasy* and a retrospective collection of Sexton Blake stories, *Sexton Blake, Detective*. He lives near Grantham, UK, with his wife, son and daughter.

MARY ROBINETTE KOWAL is the 2008 recipient of the Campbell Award for Best New Writer. Her short fiction has appeared in *Strange Horizons*, *Cosmos* and *Asimov's*. Mary, a professional puppeteer and voice actor, lives in NYC with her husband Rob and eight manual typewriters.

She has performed for LazyTown (CBS), the Center for Puppetry Arts, Jim Henson Pictures and founded Other Hand Productions. Her design work has garnered two UNIMA-USA Citations of Excellence, the highest award an American puppeteer can achieve.

Steven Francis Murphy is a reluctant resident of Kansas City, Missouri. A veteran of Operation Desert Storm, he took advantage of his Army College Fund to pay most of his way through a Bachelor of Arts in History. He topped that endeavor by going into debt for his Master of Arts in European History with a specialization in Gender Studies at the University of Missouri-Kansas City. These days he is freed from his cage in an undisclosed location for the purpose of teaching history; and ever so often, he gets to write science fiction. The nominal compensation is fifty-five gallon drums of black tea.

Nathan Rosen is the founder and editor of MicroHorror.com. He lives in a crumbling old Victorian in Baltimore with his wife Jenesta Matthews and three spoiled cats. A mild-mannered paralegal by day, by night he can be found singing and carousing with Pirates for Sail as the dread pirate Black Dog Nate.

Lavie Tidhar is the author of the Apex Publications' book *Hebrew-Punk*, a collection of dark fantasy stories centered around three mystical Jewish characters.

Lavie grew up on a kibbutz in Israel, lived in Israel and South Africa, traveled widely in Africa and Asia, and lived in London for a number of years. Currently, he is living on the island nation of Vanuatu where he spends the days farming and the nights writing.

In 2003, Lavie won the Clarke-Bradbury Prize (awarded by the European Space Agency). He has edited the *Michael Marshall Smith: The Annotated Bibliography* (PS Publishing, 2004) and the anthology *A Dick and Jane Primer for Adults* (The British Fantasy Society, 2006), and is the author of the novella *An Occupation of Angels* (Pendragon Press, 2005). His stories have appeared in *Apex Digest*, *Sci Fiction*, *Chizine*, *Clarkesworld*, *Postscripts*, *Nemonymous*, *Infinity Plus*, *Aeon*, *Book of Dark Wisdom*, *Fortean Bureau*, and many others.

Visit him on the web at www.lavietidhar.co.uk.

Jason Heller has been writing sporadically since his epic poem about alligators appeared in *Humpty Dumpty's Magazine* when he was eight. His words and comics have popped up in dozens of zines and alt-weeklies over the years, and he's currently the Denver editor of *The Onion A.V. Club*. He also plays in a punk band called The Fire Drills;

they do the worst Cheap Trick cover you've ever heard. "Behold: Skowt!" is his first published short story, but more stuff is forthcoming in *Kaleidotrope* and *Expanded Horizons*. He's also launching a punk-skewed SF zine titled *New Dawn Fades*.

Find him at www.puzzledpanther.blogspot.com

William T. Vandemark can be found wandering the back roads of America in a pickup powered by vegetable oil. He chases storms, photographs weather vanes, and buries mason jars. A lock of Houdini's hair, a fragment of Poe's headstone, and a pair of Jackson Pollock's shoe strings were recently laid to rest one foot below grade at a crossroads in Indiana.

When not wandering, William T. Vandemark hangs out in Maine, in Texas, or in Oregon, depending on season and inclination. His permanent e-residence can be found at www.williamtvandemark.com.

"A Splash of Color" was written at Odyssey, The Fantasy Writing Workshop, directed by the amazing Jeanne Cavelos and was Vandermark's first sale!

Geoffrey W. Cole graduated from Simon Fraser University's Writers Studio in 2007, and since then his work has appeared in *The Ubyssey*, where he won the annual science fiction rant, *emerge 2007*, and is forthcoming in *Clarkesworld Magazine*. Geoff has degrees in biology and engineering, and lives with his wonderful fiancé in Vancouver, British Columbia.

You can visit Geoff at www.geoffreywcole.com.

Jason Fischer is based in Adelaide, South Australia. He is a graduate of the 2007 Clarion South workshop, and a recent finalist in the Writers of the Future contest. He has a story in Jack Dann's new anthology *Dreaming Again*, and stories in *Andromeda Spaceways Inflight Magazine* and *Aurealis Magazine*. Jason likes zombies and post-apocalyptic settings, and when he's not writing he wishes he was. He can be found lurking online at http://jasonfischer.livejournal.com/, and is a contributing member of the Daily Cabal.

Jennifer Pelland is a Waltham, MA based writer of dark science fiction and fantasy. Her work has been nominated for the Nebula and Gaylactic Spectrum awards. In 2008, her first collection of stories, *Unwelcome Bodies*, was published by Apex Book Company.

Visit her blog at jenniferpelland.livejournal.com.

Joy Marchand holds a B.A. in Classical Studies from the University of the Pacific. She lives in Salem, Massachusetts, where she takes photos of odd signage, churchyards and the occasional roadside shrine. Joy's poems and short stories have been featured in *Bare Bone, Writers of the Future Volume XX,* the *Elastic Book of Numbers, Modern Magic, Time for Bedlam, Polyphony 5, Interfictions, Talebones, Apex Digest,* and *Interzone,* among others. Joy has also worked as an editor for *Shimmer,* a small magazine packed with quality short fiction and stunning artwork. She is currently at work on a road novel set on Route 66.

Visit her website at http://www.joymarchand.com.

Jason Palmer's published and upcoming fiction ranges from dark fantasy to high science fiction to science horror. Look for more from him in the pages of *Murky Depths, Spacesuits and Sixguns,* and the *Terrible Beauty/Fearful Symmetry* anthology from Dark Hart Press.

Ruth Nestvold's short fiction has appeared in numerous markets, including *Asimov's, F&SF, Realms of Fantasy, Baen's Universe, Strange Horizons,* and several Year's Best anthologies. Her novella "Looking Through Lace" made the short list for the Tiptree award and was nominated for the Sturgeon award. In 2007, the Italian translation won the "Premio Italia" award for best international work.

Ruth maintains a web page at www.ruthnestvold.com.

Gord Sellar is a Canadian living in South Korea, where he lectures at a University in the suburbs of Seoul. Since attending Clarion West in 2006, his work has appeared in various venues including *Asimov's SF, Interzone, Fantasy,* and *Flurb.* His story "Lester Young and the Jupiter's Moons' Blues" appears in *The Year's Best Science Fiction, Twenty-Sixth Annual Collection* edited by Gardner Dozois.

Gord's website can be found at http://gordsellar.com.

Theodora Goss lives in Boston, where she is completing a PhD in English literature, with her husband and daughter, in an apartment filled with books and cats. Her short story collection, *In the Forest of Forgetting,* was published by Prime Books in 2006. Her short stories and poems have been reprinted in *Year's Best Fantasy, The Year's Best Fantasy and Horror,* and *The Year's Best Science Fiction and Fantasy for Teens.* Visit her website at www.theodoragoss.com, and find out more about her short story collection at www.forestofforgetting.com.

Ekaterina Sedia resides in the Pinelands of New Jersey. Her critically acclaimed novels, *The Secret History of Moscow* and *The Alchemy of Stone* were published by Prime Books. Her next one, *The House of Discarded Dreams*, is coming out in 2010. Her short stories have sold to *Analog*, *Baen's Universe*, *Dark Wisdom*, and *Clarkesworld*, as well as *Japanese Dreams* and *Magic in the Mirrorstone* anthologies. Visit her at www.ekaterinasedia.com.

Jamie Todd Rubin has been reading science fiction since he first picked up Madeleine L'Engle's *A Wrinkle In Time* back in the fourth grade. He is a big fan of the Golden Age of science fiction. His influences include Isaac Asimov, Barry Malzberg, Alfred Bester, Cyril Kornbluth, and Harlan Ellison.

Jamie lives in Arlington, Virginia where he works as a software developer. His fiction has previously appeared in *InterGalactic Medicine Show*. His website is www.jamierubin.net.

Barbara Krasnoff's short fiction has appeared in a wide variety of publications. Magazines: *Space and Time, Electric Velocipede, Doorways, Sybil's Garage, Behind the Wainscot, Escape Velocity, Weird Tales, Descant, Lady Churchill's Rosebud Wristlet, Amazing Stories*. Anthologies: *Clockwork Phoenix 2, Things Aren't What They Seem, Such A Pretty Face: Tales of Power & Abundance, Memories and Visions: Women's Fantasy & Science Fiction*. She lives in Brooklyn, NY and earns her keep as a technology writer and editor; her web site is www.brooklynwriter.com.

Peter M. Ball is a writer from Brisbane, Australia, whose work has appeared in *Fantasy Magazine* and the *Dreaming Again* anthology. He attended the Clarion South workshop in 2007 and he's currently trying to break the habit of being a perpetual post-grad student. He can found online at www.petermball.com.

Mark Lee Pearson's fiction has appeared in *Space and Time, The Book of Tentacles, Monkeybicycle, Alienskin, Strange,Weird, and Wonderful, Liars' League, Twisted Tongue*, Susurrus Press, and Eternal Press. He lives and works in Japan, teaching English by day and writing tall tales at night. Visit his blog at markleepearson.blogspot.com

Jason B. Sizemore is best known as the Editor-in-Chief of Apex Publications. A small press begun in 2005 with the first issue of *Apex Science Fiction and Horror Digest*, Apex Publishing now puts out approximately twelve books per year from award-winning authors and both established and new voices in the speculative fiction genre.

As a quarterly print magazine, *Apex Digest* earned critical acclaim and positive reviews over the course of three years and twelve issues. With the move to digital in 2008, *Apex Magazine* was able to raise its author pay rates to SFWA professional level, allowing it to be declared a SFWA qualifying market in July 2009. By then, the magazine was only one small part of the Apex Publishing oeuvre. The book division of Apex allowed Sizemore to feature longer collections from rising stars within the genre such as Black Quill Award winner and Bram Stoker Award nominee Fran Friel, reader favorite Lavie Tidhar, and multiple Hugo Award nominee Michael A. Burstein. A series of novellas and anthologies from Apex have also earned critical and fan acclaim, including a recent *Publisher's Weekly* starred review for Gene O'Neill's *Taste of the Tenderloin*. Earlier this year, Sizemore began a search for Apex's first novel project; the company now has a zombie dark comedy scheduled for release in December 2009.

Vitaly S. Alexius is a Russian-born digital artist currently working as a freelance illustrator/photographer. His work has adorned posters, CDs, book, comic covers, and more. Stop by svitart.n-tek.ca to see more of Vitaly's work.

Acknowledgments

Jason would like to thank the following people for all the hard work and dedication that make such a thing as *Descended From Darkness* and *Apex Magazine* possible: Deb Taber, Sarah Brandel, Jennifer Brozek, Chris Einhaus, Mari Adkins, and Maggie Jamison.

Justin Stewart has been the singular constant with Apex from the start. Without his outstanding design work, we'd just be another boring fish in the sea.

I'd like to make a call out to the following supporters of Apex: Kathryn Viswanathan, Robert Fleck, Brandy Betz, Sara Larson, Jamie Rubin, Lydia Ondrusek, Mike Dominic, Brenton Tomlinson, Inga Gorslar, Nicholas Demarino, Aliette de Bodard, Michele Lee, Dennis Johnson, Jeffrey Spock, Andrea Boyd, Stacy Johnson, Dwayne Taylor, Sandra Niehaus, and Laura Petersen. Thank you.

And we extend a special thanks to Monica Valentenilli, Maurice Broaddus, Alethea Kontis, Mary Robinette Kowal, James Stitzel, Deena Warner, and Geoffrey Girard.